I0668039

Fire on Iron

ANDREW FOX

This is a work of fiction. All events portrayed in this book are fictitious, and any resemblance to real events is purely coincidental. Portrayals of historic figures are fictionalized. Any resemblance of other characters to real persons is purely coincidental. All rights reserved, including the right to re-produce this book or portions thereof in any form. Brief portions of this book may be reproduced for reviews or other forms of allowable public use.

MonstraCity Press
Manassas, Virginia

www.monstracitypress.com

Copyright © 2013 Andrew Fox

All rights reserved.

ISBN: 0989802701
ISBN-13: 978-0989802703

DEDICATION

For Dara my Captain of Logistics

And for George Alec Effinger and Mark McCandless,
who liked this one

PROLOGUE:

The Captured Blockade Runner

Ship Island, Mississippi, February 26, 1862

Captain Zachery Douglas hated Ship Island. He hated the inescapable dampness of Fort Massachusetts, the half-finished fortress which served as his headquarters. He hated the pervasive mold which invaded the garrison's rations like a conquering army. He hated the snakes and alligators that slithered out of the mosquito-infested swamp which formed the island's long, narrow heart. Most of all, he ha-ted the quiet.

In the three months since the Federals had occupied the island, not a single event with the tiniest military significance had occurred anywhere near. The garrison spent its endless days battling nothing more than boredom.

Yet today, something was different. Captain Douglas stood away from his desk and strode to the open window overlooking the empty waters. Something unsettling was blowing in from the Gulf of Mexico. He couldn't quite put his finger on it.

He made a futile sweep of the empty horizon and scowled. He turned to his sergeant of Marines, a gangly young man sitting at a desk at the room's opposite corner. "Johnson, can you please explain to me why I've been planted on this mosquito-hive of a mud pile in the middle of God-forsaken nowhere, hundreds of miles away from the fight?"

Johnson gathered his patience before replying. This particular exchange had become a tiresome game. "Sir," he said, "Ship Island is the linchpin of the entire blockade of the Gulf Coast. If we weren't here—if you weren't here, sir—the rebels could run their contraband goods in and out of Mobile and New Orleans just as pretty as they please."

"Oh? And isn't that just what they've been doing? How many blockade runners have we captured since I've taken command? Fifty? A hundred?"

Johnson quietly sighed. "None, sir."

"That's right, none! Not a damned one!"

"Sir, we've only recently been assigned enough ships to make the blockade more than a piece of paper—"

"And what does that tell you, Johnson?" Douglas's face had turned livid. "What does that tell you about the top brass's opinion of me? It makes my blood boil, Johnson. I should be at Hampton Roads, commanding the *Monitor*; I'd show them how to finish off that rebel ironclad. Or at least Flag Officer Foote should have requested me as one of his gunboat captains—that's right, my old friend, Andy Foote! I should be on the Cumberland and Tennessee Rivers, blasting the rebel forts to smithereens, making a name for myself! But where am I?" He swung his arms wide with withering contempt. "Here! This pathetic little spit of sand—I tell you, Johnson, for a young, talented officer like myself, it's nothing more than an open grave..."

Fingers shaking with emotion, Douglas struck a match to light his cigar. Staring into the tiny flame, wavering in the warm, humid spring breeze, he suddenly felt—dizzy. He smelled the stink of decaying flesh. He was staring out of other eyes...eyes accustomed to the dark; and all around was water, the hated water, kept away from him by only a thin, wooden shell—

He yelped as the match burned down to his fingers. He didn't have time to question this strange infringement on his senses, though, for Johnson had clasped his shoulder and was pointing towards the horizon. "There, sir! Look! Two sets of masts! Our boys have caught themselves a prize!"

One set of masts belonged to the Union sloop-of-war *Powhatan.* The other belonged to her prize, a freighter the warship had taken under tow. Cheers erupted on the island's docks as the two vessels hove into view. A crowd of enlisted men gathered at the water's edge.

"I suppose we'd better get down there, Johnson. Round up a boarding party of your Marines."

The sergeant delivered his snappiest salute. "Yes, sir!"

At the docks, sailors placed bets on what types of contraband the blockade runner would have in her holds. "I'll give you ten-to-one odds she'll be loaded with them British Enfield rifles!"

"Really? Five-to-two she's filled to the gunwales with bolts of silk for New Orleans Carnival gowns!"

The Federal sloop-of-war, her captive in tow, steamed slowly into the harbor. Most of the bluejackets waiting to greet her remembered her as a sparkling vessel, the white stripe delineating her gunports freshly painted, her brasswork gleaming. Months of ceaseless patrolling at the mouth of the Mississippi, however, had taken their toll. The Gulf waves and ever-present humidity had begun to strip the paint from her flanks, and the older dockhands muttered among themselves as they contemplated the tens of thousands of barnacles they would have to scrape from her bottom. Compared to her prize, however, the *Powhatan* gleamed.

The bluejacket who had bet on the Enfield rifles spat in disgust. "She's a real pig, that one," he said to his companion. "If'n I were you, I'd cancel that bet about her having silk aboard. Where the devil do you suppose she's been?"

His companion never got a chance to reply, for Captain Douglas stepped onto the dock, followed by Johnson and a small contingent of Marines. They waited while the *Powhatan* and her prize anchored and a gangway was extended from the warship to the pier. Lieutenant Eriksson, the *Powhatan*'s captain, descended the gangway, followed by a disheveled man chained in double-irons, and two burly guards.

3

Lieutenant Eriksson and Captain Douglas exchanged salutes. "This man is Captain Rodney O'Dowell," Eriksson said, pointing to his prisoner, "owner of that vessel there. Her papers say she is the *City of Tuscaloosa*, but they say little else. And O'Dowell here will tell us even less."

"Have you determined what she's carrying?" Douglas asked, staring up at the forlorn vessel's torn sails.

"No, sir. Her holds are very securely locked. We could have forced them open at sea, but I judged it more prudent to wait until we returned to base, on the chance there might be armed men hiding below."

The prisoner laughed. "There are no armed men in my holds. Though what men there were probably wished they had been armed."

Douglas turned to the five Marines standing behind him. "Let's board her, gentlemen, and see what this fool is hiding."

Stepping onto the deck of the captured sloop, he regretted his decision almost immediately. The scarred wood was caked with dried animal dung and mud. Strange funguses, the color of an ill man's phlegm, sprouted from the deck. Douglas considered his boots, fine new pieces of leatherwork. Perhaps he should ask Eriksson to lead this distasteful expedition? But no, the entire garrison was watching him; he could not back away from the task. So he carefully stepped around the piles of dung and the unnerving fungi and led his Marines to the forward hold.

"Johnson, strike that lock off."

The Marine sergeant smashed the lock repeatedly with his rifle butt, until the rusted mechanism fell to the slippery deck. Two of the Marines struggled to open the heavy doors over the hold. What they uncovered hardly seemed worth the sweat.

"What the devil—?" Douglas peered closely into the dark hold. "It's...dirt. Just dirt. These fools must've filled half their hold with soil. Whatever for?"

Stunted trees grew in small clusters near the middle of the hold, bearing heavy, sallow fruit. Had the crew been circumnavigating the globe, and so needed a renewable food supply? But the fruit of these trees hardly looked appetizing.

They turned toward the aft hold. Douglas's nose twitched as it recoiled from a strong odor. The door above the aft hold, a hatchway only four feet square, was much smaller than the ones above the forward hold. Its lock, too, quickly gave way to the sergeant's rifle. Johnson flung the hatchway open, then ran to the side of the ship to retch. The stench, overpowering, rose from the hold like a deathly vapor.

Captain Douglas felt dizzy again. He was intensely grateful that he did not have a weak stomach. The hold was black as pitch. "Bring us up a lantern," he called to Lieutenant Eriksson. Eriksson brought one of the *Powhatan*'s lamps.

Johnson, looking acutely embarrassed, took the lamp from Eriksson's hand. "Sir, if you would permit me..." he sheepishly asked. "I would like to be the first to descend."

"Of course, Johnson. By all means."

The steps were steep, and slippery. The first things they saw were the cages. Some of the animals had not survived the journey. Those still breathing were crouched in filthy hay, seemingly too weak and hungry to move. Food and water buckets lay overturned outside the cages. Douglas recalled the traveling menageries that had swept through Maine when he had been a boy, displaying creatures too fantastical to be imagined. These animals were equally fantastic. He had never seen their like before.

The largest cage was empty.

"Sir!" Johnson cried. "Over here—"

The four Negroes were dead. Not merely dead—dismembered. And their limbs had been...gnawed upon.

There was a sound of nails scraping wood. In a dark corner of the hold, something snorted. Johnson dropped his lantern. Before he could bring his rifle to his shoulder, the thing had disemboweled him.

Just before the light died, Captain Douglas saw the glimmer of bloody tusks. And eyes of unearthly fire.

CHAPTER ONE

A Commander Who Lost His Ship

*Central Train Station and the Cairo Navy Yard,
Cairo, Illinois, April 1862*

The train lurched to a stop, wheezing clouds of steam. Lieutenant Commander August Micholson, USN, stared out his window with eyes the color of beaten iron. Flecks of cold rain fell through the open window and spattered his face, cratered with childhood smallpox scars.

It had rained or sleeted almost the entire journey from Washington. Thirty-two years old, he felt like a tired, defeated old man. Although his hair retained the flamboyant redness of its youth, he imagined it gray, the color of the old, filthy snow his train had rolled through at stations across Ohio and Indiana. He pulled his dark blue wool overcoat closed. The coat, extending four inches below his knees, double breasted with two parallel columns of eight gold buttons, enfolded him like a blanket. He touched those buttons, embossed with anchors, and the doubled bars and twin gold stars at the cuffs, dreading the day his final surviving joy, the extended family provided by the U.S. Navy, would be denied him. That day could come frightfully soon. During his sixteen years of naval service, he had fought only one battle, less than three months ago. The battle that had killed one hundred and eleven of his men and sent his ship, the steam frigate *Northport*, to the bottom of Hampton Roads.

His train car was filled with fresh naval recruits for the Union's Western Flotilla, young men barely half his age, green enough to still be entranced by the romance and

7

excitement of war. Slowed by the minor but chronic fever which had dogged him ever since his ascent from the sinking *Northport*, Micholson gathered his bags from the bin above his seat and headed for the exit. His boyish traveling companions, still dressed in the homespun overalls and raw leather shoes of civilian life, eager for their first glimpse of the naval station and the gunboats they would man, jostled his gaunt form as they surged off the train.

This is the last time they'll be treating an officer this way, he thought, but his irritation did not last long. They were too much like he and Paul had been at their age, arriving in Norfolk from Mississippi's rural hinterlands, desperate to obtain berths aboard one of the Navy's great ships.

Two teenaged boys, hungry for adventure and glory. Had it been Paul's idea to enlist, or his? He couldn't remember. They'd been like twin brothers, completing each other's thoughts and sentences. *Yes, exactly like a twin,* he thought. *A replacement twin.* His real twin brother, Nicholas, had perished of the same smallpox outbreak which had nearly taken Micholson's life at the age of five. His parents had recounted for him many times how long he had mourned his brother, even losing the power of speech for half a year after Nicholas had been laid into the earth.

Meeting Paul at the age of thirteen had revived his spirit from eight years of numbness and loneliness, oxygen for a dying flame. Micholson tried to remember his dead friend's boyish, handsome face. The Mexican War had been on. Paul had brought each fresh newspaper to Micholson's house, eager to share the U.S. Navy's latest exploits. Only August had obtained his father's permission before making the journey to enlist; Paul secretly absconded. The train trip to Norfolk was exotic and exciting. But no excitement the sixteen year old August Micholson had ever known could compare to the exhilaration he felt when he saw his first tall ship. Staring at her long, graceful black hull, her towering masts adorned with a blaze of flags and canvas, he knew with liberating certainty that he'd found the axis around which his life would forever revolve.

Paul's and August's dreams of glory had ended fifteen years and nine months after their first glimpse of that tall ship, entombed between the shattered oak ribs of a steam frigate on the cold, muddy bottom of Hampton Roads. If God's justice had been swifter, Micholson, the USS *Northport*'s commanding officer, would have shared that tomb. But God, or Fate, had seen fit to preserve him that terrible morning, had given strength to his limbs as he'd kicked his way free of the *Northport*'s entangling shrouds and swam mindlessly towards the surface, possessed of an animal's blind passion for survival.

And now he was here. Why had the Navy Department ordered him halfway across the continent instead of immediately drumming him out of the service? *Men who lose their ships are rarely given a new command,* he thought. *Why have I been singled out for "special service?" Is this some euphemism for a court-martial? No—had they wished to subject me to court-martial, they would have done so back at Fortress Monroe on Hampton Roads.*

He stepped onto the wooden platform, slick with rain, and suddenly realized he had no idea where to go. He had never been in Cairo before. He cinched his overcoat around his waist with his belt, noticing he pulled it two notches more tightly than he had just a few months earlier. The last of the recruits hurried off the dripping platform, leaving it almost deserted. A lone porter leaned against one of the platform's square pillars, taking long drags on a stubby cigarette, shielding its weak fire from the wind.

Micholson hoisted his heavy kit bag to his shoulder and approached him. "Good afternoon. I'm Lieutenant Commander August Micholson. I've been ordered to the Cairo Naval Station. Do you know of anyone who is supposed to meet me here?"

"Commander Micholson, eh?" Under the man's hard gaze, Micholson briefly re-experienced the youthful chagrin he had felt whenever anyone stared too long at his smallpox scars. "Yeah, there was someone askin' after you. A nigra."

"A Negro?"

"An old darkie, yeah. Sprightly ol' fella. He was askin' after your train just this mornin'. Ain't seen him since then."

Micholson frowned. Unless Flag Officer Foote had sent a porter to fetch him, Micholson knew of only one Negro who had reason to search him out. And he had given that man strict instructions to stay at Elizabeth's side at her and August's apartment in Baltimore. "How far is it to the naval station?"

"Not very. Maybe half a mile. Follow the road out front of here to your right, and you'll come to a bluff pretty quick. You can't miss your naval station then."

"Thank you."

"Want me to call you a carriage?"

"No. I'd rather walk."

The porter's face brightened as he noticed something behind Micholson. "Say," he said, "here comes that darkie now. He's wavin' for you."

Micholson turned. The man climbing to the platform was definitely Nehemiah, his man servant and, until the start of the war, Micholson's family property. He experienced conflicting emotions upon seeing him. His anger that Nehemiah had disregarded his instructions conflicted with his undeniable gratitude that his oldest friend, his childhood tutor, the man who had done more than any other to nurse him through the corrosive grief he'd experienced after his brother's death, had arrived to support him in the darkest crisis he'd endured since Nicholas's burial.

As the black man approached, Micholson took care to preserve a stern face. Any show of emotion now would tear asunder the correct relationship between the two men; and once the flow of emotions started, he couldn't be sure it wouldn't crack him into a thousand pieces, ten fragments for each man who had died under his command.

Nehemiah spoke first. "Mister August, I'm sorry I wasn't here when you came in. The train got here ten minutes
earlier than the schedule man said it would." He carried a basket; the aromas of freshly baked bread and smoked sausage made Micholson's mouth water. He hadn't realized how famished he'd been. "Thought you'd be hungry after your journey."

"Nehemiah," Micholson said, resisting an impulse to throw his arms around his servant's neck, "you shouldn't be here. I gave you very clear, very firm instructions to stay with Elizabeth. She is carrying—" His voice caught before he could say the words, *a child.* Other words, searing hot, flashed through his brain...

Not mine.

"She is great with," he managed to continue, "with *child.* She needs you."

Nehemiah shook his head. "She don't need me, Mister August. She's not in Baltimore anymore. She got her brother to fetch her back to her father's place. They's all in Petersburg together now."

"You should have gone with her. If I can't be there to watch over her, to protect her, then I need you to be there in my stead—" He began crumbling under the weight of his kit bag. Fever and hunger had weakened him more than he'd admitted to himself. Nehemiah helped him set the heavy satchel down on the platform. "I'm *your* man, Mister August. Not hers. She didn't want me along. And when I got word as to what'd happened to you and your ship in Hampton Roads—"

"That," Micholson gasped, holding onto his servant's strong shoulder, "doesn't matter. You had your instructions."

"Almost a year ago, you made me a free man," Nehemiah said. The Negro suddenly seemed far younger than his sixty-plus years; if not for his wreath of white hair and the cracked lines surrounding his eyes, he could pass for a man in his thirties. "I earn wages now. I spent them wages on a train ticket to come out here. You's my employer, you got a right to fire me for disobeying, and I got a right to go to work for somebody else. But I got my own mind now, and that mind told me you need me. So am I fired, or no?"

Such assertiveness surprised Micholson. After years of witnessing Nehemiah follow Micholson's father's instructions without question, for the man to display a will of his own seemed against nature. But he reminded himself that emancipating Nehemiah had been more than a mere legal formality; he'd returned to the man a dignity and autonomy which Nehemiah hadn't known since his childhood in Africa. If Nehemiah wanted to help him now, he was proving himself, not a servant, but a friend.

"No," Micholson said, "you're not fired."

"Maybe I should be," Nehemiah said. His face turned grim. "Maybe I should be caned within an inch of my life."

"Good Lord, man, *why?*"

"For what I told you the day before your battle. It was evil judgment, a wickedness on my part. I threw your mind into a twister storm, just when you most needed your wits. I can't help but thinkin'...maybe I helped kill them hundred sailors of yours, same as the *Virginia's* guns did."

Micholson squeezed his eyes tightly shut. "No," he said. "Don't put that upon yourself. You couldn't have seen the future. And...and I needed to know. I needed to know what you told me. Let's not speak about it just now."

"All right," Nehemiah said. He handed Micholson the basket. "How about you eat something? You look ready to pitch over."

Micholson broke himself off a hunk of warm brown bread. The humble loaf tasted as good as any meal he'd ever eaten. He offered part of the loaf to Nehemiah, but his companion shook his head and shouldered the kit bag. They descended the steps to the muddy dirt road and began walking in the direction the porter had indicated. A light rain returned, making their footing even more treacherous.

Turning the wool collar of his pea coat against the rain, Micholson reached the top of a low rise overlooking the river. He assumed he would be able to see the navy yard in its entirety. What met his tired grey eyes was like no naval establishment he had ever seen. "Navy yard" was clearly a misnomer. "Yard" implied land, and the Navy appeared to own not one square foot of soil here. All of its facilities— repair derricks, dormitories, dry docks and machine shops—were afloat, mounted on a mélange of wharf-boats, steamers, flat-boats, and rafts, connected to each other with a spider's web of rickety plank bridges. It looked as though the Lord had abandoned his eons-old promise to Noah and had released the flood again, dooming mankind to a precarious, water-logged existence.

Nehemiah must have been imagining the same apocalyptic scenario. "Mister August, them things down there by them docks, are they the roofs of barns swept away by some flood?"

Micholson shook his head. "Not barn roofs, no." His voice cracked slightly when he spoke his next word. "Ironclads."

Focusing on the long, low black objects, each about one hundred and eighty feet long and sixty feet across the beam, Micholson counted the fat, round muzzles which pierced their sloping sides. Each of those cannons could hurl up to a hundred pounds of high-explosives or iron at a velocity sufficient to smash seasoned oak several feet thick...or render a man a corpse so misshapen that not even its own brother could recognize it. These "barn roofs," now silhouetted by the setting orange sun, were the reason for the floating navy yard's existence: the ironclad gunboats of the Western Flotilla. Staring down at their dark, menacing shapes, so terribly familiar to him even though he had never before seen the flotilla or any of its vessels, he suppressed a shiver. One of the gunboats down there was his new command. The *James B. Eads*.

"Sir, are you Lieutenant Commander Micholson?"

Micholson turned to see a young cadet, face and ears turned bright red by the bitter weather, standing rigidly at attention. His pea coat was at least two sizes too large. Micholson smiled, picturing himself sixteen years ago. "Yes, I'm the man you're looking for, Cadet...?"

"Cadet Sumner, sir. I'm sorry I missed you at the station. Flag Officer Foote is very anxious to meet with you, sir."

Micholson was just as anxious to meet with Foote. What had the Flag Officer meant in his letter by "special service"? "Then take me to him directly."

"Yes, sir!"

He followed Sumner down a narrow cobblestone lane to the water's edge. While descending, he was able to take a closer look at the ironclads. Workmen swarmed over several, even at this late hour, hammering fresh planks into place or replacing battered auxiliary boats. One ironclad in particular was a sad specimen. One of her twin smoke stacks had pitched forward onto her pilot house. Her casemate had been pierced in several places, revealing a fire-blackened interior, and her roof was a shambles.

"Cadet, what happened to the ironclads? I thought..." Memories of the battle at Hampton Roads assaulted him, images of shot from his ship's most powerful cannon bouncing off the greased sides of the Southern marauder and exploding harmlessly in the air. "I thought no power on earth could do this to them."

"These boats are the toughest this Mississippi's ever seen, sir," the cadet stammered, anxious that this new officer should have a good opinion of the fleet. "But they aren't invincible. That iron armor you've heard talk about only protects the fronts of their casemates and along the sides where the engines are. The rest is plain wood, just like any other boat. And sometimes freak accidents happen.

Like what happened to poor *Esser* in the fight at Fort Henry." He pointed to a vessel at the far end of the anchorage, covered with more than her fair share of dockhands. "She took a cannonball through one of her gun ports, and it smashed into her boilers. Half her crew was scalded to death, including her captain."

What is the better death, Micholson asked himself—to drown, pinned beneath smashed timbers, or to have the life scorched from you by high-pressure steam? "And that ship there," he asked quietly. "The one with the toppled smoke stack? What happened to her?"

Micholson watched the cadet swell with pride. "That's the *St. Louis*, sir. She was Flag Officer Foote's command at Fort Donelson, so she led the boats in under the fort's guns. Got a little too close, maybe, but did she ever give them a fight! And next to her is the *Carondolet*, the hero of the fleet. She hung on the longest in front of Fort Donelson, even though she took the worst pounding. But not all that damage kept her from being the first to run past the guns of Island Number Ten, just a couple of weeks ago. She's a great ship, sir. A couple more days and they'll have her patched up again, good as new."

They reached the edge of the water. "Where is the vessel mentioned in my orders? The *James B. Eads*?"

"That's the *Eads*, sir." Sumner pointed out a low, black bulk lying alongside the *Esser* at the edge of the anchorage, conspicuous by the freshness of her paint and the absence of any visible damage. "She's brand-new. They're just finishing fitting her out now. You're lucky to be getting such a new command, sir."

"Yes, Mr. Sumner. More lucky than you know." He paused to take a long look at his new command. She was uglier than any ship he had ever set foot upon. Compared to the grace of the *Constitution* or the *Northport*, with their long, straight decks, towering masts, and majestic swells of canvas, the *Eads* was a toad. With no masts save signaling poles, thick smoke stacks set side by side atop a coffin-like casemate, and double humps at her stern that covered her twin paddle wheels, the *Eads* lay upon the water like a hunchbacked scow. Yet he knew this toad could demolish either of those obsolescent swans inside a half hour.

What right had he, after all that had happened, to take command of one of the Union's newest and most powerful men-of-war? And what right did Flag Officer Foote have to offer it to him?

Micholson did his best to banish such despairing, defeatist thoughts. Foote was one of the most highly regarded senior officers in the Union Navy. He wouldn't be offering Michelson command of such an important vessel without firm rationale.

Nehemiah, silent since the cadet's arrival, seemed to sense his companion's internal struggles. He placed his hand lightly on his employer's shoulder.

"Take us to Flag Officer Foote, Mr. Sumner," Micholson said. "And let us discover our fate."

CHAPTER TWO

The Master of Adderwood

Adderwood Plantation, north of Yazoo City, Mississippi,
April 12, 1862

Joseph Babbage stood atop his levee, the earthen bulwark
his grandfather had built to protect his lands from the
depredations of the Yazoo River. He watched for the
steamers carrying his precious cargo. The wind blew cold
this gray morning, carrying the promise of rain. He angrily
tightened his greatcoat, the fingers of his one good arm
fumbling with ivory buttons. The ships were more than a
week overdue.

As a boy he had loved standing on this mound of earth,
which formed the river border of Adderwood Plantation, to
watch the steamboats and keelboats ply their courses. Now,
however, he took little pleasure in staring at the wind-
distended waters and the horizon. As a precaution against
disaster, he had hired two freighters, despite the doubling of
his expense. There were so many hazards that could upend
his plans—the Federal blockade, the trans-Atlantic voyage
itself, and who knew how many unknown perils within the
interior of mysterious, mystical Africa...

He cast a furtive glance at the elderly slave who sat so
calmly a few feet distant. As a child, he had adored Old
Daniel and his magic tricks. *I wish the old wizard would
snap his fingers and make the ships appear this instant,* he
thought.

A smudge of black smoke dirtied the southern horizon.
Babbage's face immediately brightened. "There!" he cried.
"Do you see it? Finally, one of our ships approaches!"

"Be patient. That is not the watercraft we wait for." The ancient slave's voice was as dark as the distant, curling smoke. Old Daniel sat impassively on the windswept levee, dressed only in threadbare trousers and a thin, muslin shirt. His large eyes, islands within a mass of black, wrinkled flesh, did not shift toward the coming vessel.

"But how—?" Babbage stifled his impulse to demand how Daniel could be so certain of the ship's identity without even seeing it. He would receive no satisfactory answer, only eventual proof that the elderly slave, as always, was correct. Yet hope died unwillingly within the plantation owner's heart. "The timing of it is right, Daniel. I say we'll be celebrating before this morning is done."

Old Daniel made no response. The only reply came from the lumber mill upstream. The still air was split by the shriek of giant buzz-saws. Babbage had grown to manhood nurtured by the quiet aural landscape of his home, the gentle songs of cicadas and river birds, the oddly soothing work songs of the slaves. Yet once the Confederate Navy Department had made its decision to build a hidden boat yard on the western shore of the Yazoo, the beloved silence of his Adderwood became a thing of the past.

The sharp reports of six inch bolts being battered into green wood echoed off the levee. He desperately clamped his left hand over his left ear. His right arm, the withered one, remained trapped in its sleeve, unable to shield his other ear from the agonizing noise. "Great God in heaven! They begin their infernal torture earlier each morning! I wish the river would swallow the whole foul lot of them!"

"They will soon be gone, master," Daniel said. "But it will not be the river which swallows them up. You will have a hand in stilling their noise."

Babbage barely heard the cryptic remark. A spasm of pain shot through the nerve endings connecting the base of his skull and his right arm, the withered one, deformed at birth. He massaged it with the strong fingers of his left hand, trying to return it to its usual near-numbness. The arm had been aching these last few weeks, giving him such pain as he had not felt since young childhood. Then, neither his mother nor his physicians could end the agonies that would not let him sleep, his hallucinatory terrors that the shriveled limb so hated him, it was trying to wrench itself free from his torso...The nightmares and pains could be ended by only one man, who drove them away with his salves and his chanted murmurings. Old Daniel. The house slave purchased by his grandfather.

Daniel could rid me of this pain, Babbage thought. He could cure me in a moment. But he crushed the notion as he would a dung beetle. I am a grown man now, a colonel in the Confederate Army, the sole master of Adderwood Plantation—not a mewling child of five years, running to the arms of an ancient Negro whenever my nose itches. I can only ask so much of the old man. Ask too much, and I will be his slave, not he mine.

Why had the agonizing pain returned now, after twenty-seven years? It must be the boat yard, hidden in the bayou across the river. The industrial cacophony invaded the vulnerable regions of his skull at all hours of the day. It was pushing him to the edge of his sanity.

"Those fools and their ironclad rams," he growled. "Pouring their energies and fortunes into them, praying to the ugly hulls like heathens before idols. Trusting in floating iron to provide them victory. Idiots!" Babbage had traveled in the North, years before, when his mother had sent him away from Adderwood to be educated. He had seen the great factories, the iron works, the humming and tireless industry of the place. *Whatever vessels these frantic efforts on the banks of the Yazoo can produce*, he thought, *the North can match them ten to one. It is a race we can never win.*

Seeking to distract himself from his pain, he watched the black clouds from the approaching vessel's smoke stack climb higher into the sky. They seemed to take on the shape of a woman in a ball gown. Babbage frowned. He had heard the whisperings, vile gossip in Vicksburg and Yazoo City, that he would be the last master of Adderwood. He had stopped attending town dances years ago. The women had stared at his withered arm, even when it was hidden in a silk sleeve, and delicately recoiled. They then left him to stand by their tables, a hard smile frozen on his lips, while they were escorted to the dance floor by more ordinary men. The gossips were wrong, however. He would have an heir, even if he had to purchase a wife from the Republic of Mexico.

But how their tongues rattled on, those shrews...about how Babbage had grown up without a father, how the boy had practically been raised by an elderly slave at Adderwood. Yet they had never seen the respect, the fear that Old Daniel commanded from the other slaves. As a boy, Babbage had been fascinated by the mysterious authority Daniel exercised over the other Negroes. It certainly had nothing to do with the old man's physical stature. Daniel had always been stooped and frail, his tall forehead a mass of wrinkles, his arms nearly as thin and puny as Babbage's own right limb. Oddly, such was the way Babbage's mother had remembered Old Daniel from her girlhood, forty years earlier. As a boy he had asked Charles, a junior house slave, why the other slaves seemed so afraid of Daniel. Charles took him carefully aside, to the library where they would be alone, then explained to him that Daniel was of a different nation than the rest of Adderwood's Negroes, a village-state that had stood for centuries on an island in the middle of a great river. But that was all he would say.

A second buzz-saw went to work in the boat yard, adding its dismal shriek to the cacophony. A fresh storm surge of pain hit Babbage. He fought back a tide of nausea; his normally steady legs trembled beneath him.

"Let me help you, master." Old Daniel's voice burbled like black molasses. "Come away from here. I can make the pain go away."

"No! I will remain here to greet the ship—"

"Do not be foolish. I have already told you that is not the vessel we wait for. Let me help you."

"Keep your distance, Daniel!" Babbage stumbled a few yards from the elderly slave, then half-sat, half-collapsed onto the damp earth. "I'll—I'll manage this myself!" He tried to massage his right arm and shoulder, wincing as the pressure made the spasms worse. "You know," he said, talking quickly, "as a little boy, I pitied you. You were always alone. An old man without any friends of your own kind. I was the only person in all Adderwood willing to spend time with you, listening to your tales and watching your magic tricks. But by the time I was a young man, I didn't pity you any longer. You had no friends because you didn't *need* them. I—I learned much from that."

The oncoming vessel rounded the final bend that hid it from Adderwood. It was a stern-wheeled river freighter, its sun-bleached decks burdened with sheets of heavy iron. It slowly passed the two figures waiting on the levee and continued upriver to the boat yard.

Old Daniel knelt beside Babbage. "Now will you come inside, Master Joseph? The ship from Africa will not reach us today."

Disappointment slapped Babbage like the chill hand of a disdainful woman. He found he could tolerate his pain no longer. "Yes, yes, I'll come inside. Just let me rest here a moment." Old Daniel began to gently squeeze the jerking muscles of his master's stunted right arm. The plantation owner sighed with the beginnings of relief. "Tell me about the power, Daniel. I want to hear about it."

"It will be a great power. All men will fear it."

"It will be the greatest power on the continent?"

"Yes. Greater than armies of men."

The brutal blows of hammers beating iron plates echoed from the levee. "Greater than fleets of ironclads?"

"Yes. Far greater than any war boats."

"And it will all be mine? Mine alone?"

21

The ancient slave gradually increased the pressure he applied to the muscles of the withered arm. The pain drained from Babbage like pus from a lanced wound.

"The power will be yours alone, master," Old Daniel said.

CHAPTER THREE

The Flag Officer's Plan

Aboard the Maria Denning, *Cairo, Illinois,*
April 12, 1862

Cadet Sumner led Lieutenant Commander Micholson and Nehemiah to the gangplank which ascended to the deck of the *Maria Denning*, the Cairo Navy Yard's receiving boat. Flag Officer Foote maintained his headquarters in a stateroom at the rear of the vessel.

Micholson paused before following Sumner up the gangplank. He turned to Nehemiah. "I'll need to discuss my orders with the flag officer alone. Will you wait for me down here? You can shelter from the rain there, beneath that empty repair shed."

The black man nodded. "Yes, Mister August. I'll be waiting there when you're done."

"I have no assurance that you'll be able to accompany me on my assignment. The flag officer may feel that your presence would be...inappropriate." Now that his old friend was here, Micholson was loath to leave him behind. "If I can arrange such, would you accept an assignment as a coal stoker? Such positions require no special training, only a strong back and arms. It's hard and dirty work, but vital to the operation of any modern war boat. It is the only position I can think of which might offer you immediate and unquestioned entry."

Nehemiah nodded his gray-crowned head once more. "I didn't come all this way to be left behind. I'll do whatever needs be done. This is my war, too."

Micholson felt a lump grow in his throat. He wondered whether he deserved such loyalty. "Good man," he said. "I hope I'll return to you by nightfall."

Micholson followed Sumner aboard the *Maria Denning.* The vessel must have served as a passenger steamer in her past life, for her corridors were lined with polished walnut paneling and lanterns of burnished brass. The cadet knocked on the door of the flag officer's stateroom. A gravelly, tired voice answered. "Yes? Who is it? If that's you again, Chesterfield, you can take your hard tack and salt pork back to the galley. I've told you, I'm not hungry!"

"It's Cadet Sumner, sir! I've brought Lieutenant Commander Micholson, as you requested, sir!"

"Well, that's a different matter entirely. Bring him in!"

The stateroom was surprisingly spacious. Its starboard wall was covered with a huge map of the Mississippi River basin. Known Confederate strong-holds were marked with red flags pinned to the map. The largest of these flags was placed at Vicksburg, Mississippi; one only slightly less prominent was pinned at Fort Pillow, Tennessee. A long gauntlet of red flags followed the serpentine path of the Mississippi from Fort Pillow to the Gulf of Mexico, nearly a thousand river miles away.

The flag officer was a man of advanced middle age, his beard streaked with yellowish grey. The shoulders of his dress uniform jacket were freighted with the gold epaulets and medals and ribbons which denoted his lofty rank. His eyes had sunken so far back into his skull that they almost disappeared in the shadows cast by their sockets. Should he ever allow them to close, Micholson reflected, he looked likely to sleep a hundred years.

Micholson saluted as sharply as he could manage. "Lieutenant Commander August Micholson reporting for duty, sir."

Foote remained seated and returned the salute. "Forgive me for not standing to greet you, Lieutenant. I stand when I must, but all other times I remain rooted to this chair, by doctor's orders. No matter how high a rank you achieve, your doctor is always your commanding officer." For the first time, Micholson noticed the flag officer's right leg, swathed in bandages from knee to arch and supported on a small ottoman beneath his desk. The toes protruded from the bandages, swollen and purple. Some had begun to turn black. Micholson's eyes widened. "A souvenir of my cruise to Fort Donelson," Foote said. "I made the tactical error of bringing the gunboats in too close. In too much of a hurry to get the whole brutish business done with, I suppose. The rebels' guns were mounted high on a bluff, and their shells pierced our unarmored roofs like knives through biscuits. As our casemate clearly wasn't up to the job, I decided to stop a few pieces of hot iron myself. Did a fine job of it, wouldn't you say?"

"I hadn't heard you were wounded, sir," Micholson said.

"Yes, well, I'm not the sort to go parading my wounds to the newspaper men. I'm not planning on running for President, like some of the damn generals are." He turned his sickly glare on Cadet Sumner. "Cadet! Go make yourself useful somewhere! I need to speak with Lieutenant Micholson in private."

"Yes, sir!"

The flag officer watched the cadet scurry from the room. "Sumner will make a good officer someday. He loves this fleet. Almost as much as I do." Foote frowned. "This damn rebellion has taken a horrible toll of the young. And not merely by bullet or cannonball. I received word just this past week that I lost a young cousin, stationed at Ship Island in the Gulf. Kenneth Johnson, a sergeant of the Marines."

"The rebels have attacked Ship Island?" Micholson asked, surprised.

"Not directly, no. It was the strangest damn thing I've heard since the war began. One of our blockaders, the *Powhatan*, captured a freighter heading for the mouth of the

Mississippi. This foul mystery ship was loaded with nothing but dirt and cages full of wild animals. Kenneth was investigating the hold when one of the creatures—a huge boar, I believe it was—tore into him before the other Marines were able to kill it. He bled to death. Senseless. Absolutely senseless."

The faces of his own dead shipmates hovered in Micholson's mind. "You have my sympathy, sir. I know what it is to suffer...a loss of such magnitude."

"Yes. Thank you, Lieutenant. But I haven't summoned you across half a continent to tell you my sorrows."

Micholson's attention was captured by a model of the famous old frigate *Constitution*, on display atop a pedestal behind the flag officer's desk. "You trained aboard the *Constitution*, didn't you?" Foote asked.

"Yes, sir, I did."

"I did some service in her myself, as a younger man. And what wonderful things we learned aboard her. Spreading the canvas! Working the great guns! How amazing it is, that a single shell from the largest gun aboard your new command, the *James B. Eads*, carries more destructive power than an entire broadside from the old *Constitution*. Still, she remains a beautiful ship, the *Constitution*. A thing of grace. Much like your old command, the *Northport*."

Micholson winced. He hoped his reaction had been minuscule enough for the flag officer to overlook, but he could tell the wily old commander was not one to miss such telling expressions. "The *Northport*..." His voice caught in his throat. "Yes. She was a beautiful ship. I miss her."

The flag officer maintained his stare, his sunken eyes as unwavering as two grey musket balls. "Yes. I'm sure that you do. You lost—how many was it? One hundred and eleven men? Even more than went down with the poor *Cumberland*. That's a heavy cross for a young officer to bear. Your executive officer went down with her, didn't he? Ensign...Legarde. Is that right?"

Micholson steadied himself against the oak desk in front of him. "Yes. Ensign Paul Legarde. He was up for a promotion when the *Virginia* attacked. This week...he would have been given his own ship." His throat seemed filled with fast drying mud. "He had been my best friend. Since we were boys together."

Until he betrayed me in the sharpest way known. Until, enraged to an extent I couldn't have imagined, I dashed my ship and my men to pieces against the iron sides of the rebel monster.

"I know all that," Foote said. "You both joined the service together, at the age of sixteen. Rather unusual for a pair of lads from the interior of Mississippi."

Micholson had known the fate of the *Northport* would be discussed; it was inevitable. But why had Foote brought up Paul Legarde? Was this some kind of a test? "Sir. I must be honest with you. Your invitation of me to interview for a command in your fleet makes little sense to me. I was expecting a court martial, not an offer of a new ship."

The flag officer's eyebrows arched. "Is that so? I assure you, Lieutenant, this is no surreptitious inquiry into your conduct. But tell me—if you could relive that afternoon in Hampton Roads, would you repeat your actions? Would you still confront the *Virginia*?"

How many times had he replayed the action in his mind? A hundred times? A thousand? He could almost smell the acrid stench of funnel fumes again, blowing north ahead of the advancing Confederate flotilla. The tall masts of the *Cumberland, Congress,* and *St. Lawrence,* his squadron mates, stood ominously motionless a mile to starboard. Old-style sailing frigates, they were doomed by an absence of wind to be sitting targets that day. The *Minnesota* and the *Roanoke,* powerful warships with auxiliary steam engines, were closer; like the *Northport,* they were not subject to the vagaries of the wind. Yet they were every bit as helpless as their sailing brethren, for, in their haste to come to the *Northport*'s aid, they had grounded their prows deeply in the unforgiving mud of the shoals. And less than a hundred yards in front of Micholson steamed the *Virginia*, Confederate colossus, bristling with deadly cannon, her black, sloping, iron-plated sides shimmering with a slippery layer of grease which made cannonballs bounce harmlessly into the sky.

If Micholson had been in his right mind, not seething with fury and grief, would he have given the same orders he gave? Would he have impetuously directed that the *Northport* confront the *Virginia* on her own, riding his fragile vessel like a maddened Ahab towards this invincible sea beast, counting on the power of the *Northport*'s mightiest gun to save the helpless squadron from its wrath...?

"Would I still confront the *Virginia*? I...I don't know. Yet I can't see what else I could have done. My squadron mates were sitting targets, trapped by mud or the lack of wind. Perhaps I shouldn't have closed with the ironclad...but no, I could see that long-range gunfire was having no effect on her greased armor—I had to close the range and see if fire from my eleven inch pivot gun could pierce her casemate." In the dank coldness of the cabin, his nervous sweat felt like ice ripping through the pores of his armpits. Why wouldn't the old man invite him to sit down? "Sir, tell me. What would you have done?"

"What would I have done?" At last the flag officer's eyes showed some signs of warmth, of empathy and, perhaps, pity. "Lieutenant, I'd like to think I would have done precisely what you did. Not to say that your actions weren't foolhardy. Once you saw that your pivot gun was unable to penetrate the ironclad's armor, you still had time to retreat, to withdraw near where the *Roanoke* and the *Minnesota* were stranded. You three could have concentrated your firepower then, perhaps to better effect. Yet I second-guess your decisions from the safety and distance of this chair. Yes, you acted foolhardily, and recklessly, but also in the best traditions of the U.S. Navy. And that is why you are being offered a fresh command, rather than facing a court martial."

Micholson felt himself redden. The last thing he had expected to hear was praise. Any praise belonged to the gallant dead, he felt; not to him.

"Now," Foote continued, "let us discuss the rather special nature of your assignment. You may sit, Lieutenant. This will take a while."

Micholson sank gratefully onto one of the two chairs facing the flag officer's desk. "Thank you, sir. The sealed orders I received specified only that I was to take command of the *Eads* and render special service with her. Beyond this, I know nothing."

"Such secrecy was called for, as you'll soon understand. Very few men are aware of the nature of your mission. Only I, General Grant, and the captains of the ironclads *Cairo* and *Mound City* are cognizant of the entire plan." The flag officer turned to the map mounted on the wall to his right, displaying the entire lower Mississippi River basin. He pointed to a tiny dot in the northern waters of the Gulf of Mexico. "Rear Admiral Farragut is stationed here, at Ship Island, with a fleet of deep water wooden warships, awaiting the time—I'm not privy to the precise information—when he will enter the river and attempt to run past Forts St. Philip and Jackson to capture New Orleans. The rebels have at New Orleans several insignificant wooden gunboats, and the *Manassas*, a small, slow ironclad ram mounting only one gun. But they've been at work on two much more powerful ironclads—the *Mississippi* and the *Louisiana*. We know the *Mississippi* is months from completion; she hasn't received her guns or armor yet. But the *Louisiana* may be ready to give Farragut a fight."

Micholson's eyes widened as he counted the red flags, each representing a Confederate stronghold, between Cairo and New Orleans. "So my mission is to steam south to assist Admiral Farragut?"

"In a manner of speaking, yes. But not in the obvious way." Foote pointed to a spot higher on the map. "Your objective lies here, far to the north of New Orleans; somewhere along the Yazoo River, above the fortress city of Vicksburg. Our intelligence has indicated that the *Mississippi* and *Louisiana* are merely the known elements of a tremendous rebel building program. We have reports that they are now building between four and six ironclad rams at a hidden shipyard along the Yazoo River, somewhere north of Yazoo City, possibly as far north as the mouth of the Tallahatchie River."

A fleet of eight Virginia*s?* This was a nightmare beyond reckoning. "Sir, how is this possible? The rebels have extremely limited industrial capacity. The construction of so many rams would require six or seven first-class foundries running day and night, and there are no more than three such facilities in the entire Confederacy. Might this be mere propaganda, an attempt to divert your and General Grant's resources to dead ends?"

"I wish it were only that. Our task would be much easier. But our spies have already suggested an answer to your question. Apparently the British have been assisting our industrious countrymen-in-rebellion."

"The British? What have they to gain from such traffic? Should this be true, and should it become generally known, it would mean war between our two countries. And all the cotton in the South cannot be worth war to the English."

Foote nodded. "Cotton alone would not be worth their while, I agree. But territory would. Apparently Queen Victoria and her ministers have grown alarmed by Napoleon the Third's machinations in Mexico. Our sources indicate that, in exchange for Britain's provision of cannon, iron plating, and marine engines, secreted through our blockage on swift English freighters, the British have been promised part of the California Territory at the successful conclusion of the rebellion. A counterbalance to a potential French puppet state in Mexico."

"The British must be mad to take on such a bargain! How can they dream that the Confederacy could ever wrest away the western territories from the Union? The rebels have made a fine deal for themselves, receiving hard goods for such bombast!"

"The British are not lacking a calculating imagination, Lieutenant. Think what a fleet of rebel ironclads would mean. Think what such a fleet could do to Farragut's wooden ships at New Orleans. You have seen such deviltry before, close at hand, and that was the work of just one rebel ram. A fleet of ironclads in rebel hands, combined with their existing fortresses along the Mississippi, would render unthinkable our grand strategy of splitting the Confederacy in two by capturing the river. That alone could lengthen this damned war by years. And it is not beyond possibility that the rebels could force a brutal peace upon us, by sending their ironclads north to St. Louis, Cincinnati, and Pittsburgh...River towns, all."

Women on their way to market, children playing in schoolyards, all blissfully unaware of the coming rain of explosive shells..."But the Western Flotilla is here at Cairo," Micholson countered. "You have ten ironclads in all. Even if the rebels can complete six Yazoo rams, plus the *Mississippi* and *Louisiana*, surely—"

The flag officer wearily raised his hand to cut Micholson off. "My boy, I'm afraid you greatly overestimate the powers of our gunboats. They were designed to conquer river forts, support the Army in its advances, nothing more. They weren't built for ship-to-ship combat. Calling them 'ironclads' overstates their potency. They are armored on the fronts of their casemates and alongside their engines only. Their builder, Captain Eads—for whom your new vessel is named, by the way—was instructed that the gunboats would always engage the enemy fortresses head-on. Arrayed against true ironclad opponents, our gunboats would be at a severe disadvantage. A rebel ram need only get alongside or to the rear of one of our boats, and she could drill shells through the wooden parts of our casemate at her leisure. Or she could drive her iron prow into our wooden side."

So this is what he was to take command of, then? A frail hermaphrodite, half-ironclad and half-timberclad, not trusted by her admiral to face a floating opponent in even combat? For the briefest of instants, he considered declining the offer of command. But he quickly banished this thought. He was an officer of the U.S. Navy, and he would accept, without protest, whichever cards were dealt him. "I take it, then, that my mission will be to find these rams before they have reached completion. I am to slay the serpents in their nest, before they have emerged from their eggs?"

"You are correct. That is the mission I am entrusting to you and the crew of the *Eads*."

If ever there could be a mission of redemption, this is what I am being gifted with. A cleansing wave of fresh determination brought with it the confidence, once second nature, which he'd been lacking since his immersion in the frigid Chesapeake. Yet he cautioned himself not to become drunk with returning potency. His eyes traced on the map the path his ship would have to follow, dotted with angry red flags.

He cleared his throat. "Considering the dangers, sir—the batteries at Fort Pillow and Fort Randolph, the obstructions and weapons the rebels will have undoubtedly placed along the Yazoo—wouldn't it be prudent to send more of the fleet than just the *Eads*? I have seen what well-placed batteries are capable of doing to the gunboats. Were this a journey of a single night, I could imagine a lone ship making the dash successfully under cover of darkness, like the *Carondolet*'s recent triumph running past the guns of Island Number Ten. But there are hundreds of miles of river to travel, and the rebels will be more than ready—"

"Oh, they'll know you're coming, all right. But it won't matter. They'll think you're coming to assist them, not hinder them."

"I don't understand, sir."

"Espionage." Foote smiled. "Lieutenant, what General Grant and I have planned for you is the most elaborate ruse yet attempted in this war. But it has become late, my friend! Let us continue in the morning. You've just completed an exhausting journey, and you look as though you could use a solid night's sleep."

"But sir, I'm very anxious to hear—"

"No, Lieutenant. With this mission, as with most, the devil is in the details, and I refuse to trouble you with them tonight. But there is one further thing I wish to bring to your attention this evening. Given the extraordinary nature of this duty, I wish your acceptance of this assignment to be voluntary. Too much is at stake for the commander of the *Eads* to lead his vessel on a mission he feels overmatched by. Say but a few words, either tonight or tomorrow morning, and I will commence to finding another captain for the *Eads* from my current roster. Your esteem in my eyes will not be diminished by refusal. You will still be given command of one of the ironclad gunboats, and your service record will carry no mention of such assignment ever being offered to you."

Refuse a chance to redeem himself? The gods of war would not offer him such a gift more than once. "Sir, in my sixteen years of naval service, I have never refused an assignment. And I shall not begin doing so now."

"Good. That is what I was hoping to hear."

Micholson thought of Nehemiah, still waiting outside in the cold and wet. "I have but one favor to ask. An exceptionally loyal manservant has followed me here from Baltimore. He has been with my family since before I was born, and he pleads with me that I permit him to remain at my side. He is a Negro, formally a slave, whom I made a freeman almost a year ago. He is willing to do any sort of

33

work available for strong but unskilled hands. Can a place be found for him aboard the *Eads*?"

Foote pulled at his beard, and his eyes narrowed with contemplation. "A Negro, you say? And a freeman? Tell me, Lieutenant, would this man of yours be willing to act as though he is still your personal property?"

"I believe Nehemiah would do anything in his power to help ensure the success of my mission. However, may I ask why such subterfuge would be necessary?"

"Let us save that for the morning. Suffice to say that, should your man be capable of a bit of play-acting, it would add all the more verisimilitude to the scenario General Grant and I have in mind. Now go get your rest. Sumner will show you to your cabin. Good night, Lieutenant. And welcome to the Western Flotilla."

They exchanged salutes. Micholson set his hand on the doorknob. Yet he could not turn it. Not without asking. "Sir, why did you select me for this mission? You have nine current gunboat commanders to choose from, all of whom have served with great valor. Each of them has infinitely more knowledge of the gunboats than I do. Why look half-way across the country to me?"

"General Grant asked me exactly the same question. Your childhood spent near the shores of the Yazoo River was a factor, of course. But when faced with a decision such as this, I often rely on those subjective aspects I know of a man, the intangibles. What fire in his belly does one man have that will keep him swimming against the icy current, when another man, equally as fit, will falter and drown? Lieutenant Micholson, you are the weapon I want to unleash on that hidden Confederate building yard. I believe there is no living officer in the U.S. Navy with a fiercer or more justified hatred of rebel ironclad rams than you."

Micholson left the room. An unsheathed sword, wreathed in fire...that is how Foote thought of him. As he closed the heavy oak door behind him, he saw the older man finally surrender to exhaustion and rest his head heavily on his desk.

Fire in the belly, Micholson reflected. *Surely that's what keeps Andrew Foote going, leading his gunboats inexorably down the Mississippi, even as his wounds slowly kill him.*

CHAPTER FOUR

The Ancient African's Bitter Smile

Adderwood Plantation, Mississippi,
April 12, 1862

M'Lundowi sat in his crooked, self-made chair on the wide veranda of the great house, that part of the porch which faced the green levee and the brown river. His task this late afternoon was to polish Master Joseph's large collection of shoes. His hard, dark hands, made even darker by the polish's residues, traced intricate patterns across the leather. He had polished Master Joseph's father's shoes, and his grandfather's shoes years before. He considered this task a small gift of his servitude, for it aided greatly in his meditation. And now he had so much to meditate on.

It was coming. The earth from his homeland. One vessel had been diverted, he knew, into the hands of the men from the North. He had felt it pull closer, from the far end of the sea, and then recede and disappear. But the second vessel had entered the mouth of the great river, where it would be safe. Though it was several days' travel distant yet, he could smell the tang of the rich, black humus hidden in its damp hold. He could already feel its tendrils of strength brush his spirit, suffusing him with energies he could barely recall, the like of which he had not felt for sixty years.

The time of his vengeance was drawing near. In order for it to have its sweetest taste, he would need to remember all, every humiliation and torture piled upon his sacred person, every stratagem he'd been forced to employ in order to survive this long. He sensed visions seeping into his hairless skull, and he surrendered to them.

* * *

A vision of home.

Bulrushes swayed in a flower-scented wind. A silver fish leaped into the air, then reentered its liquid kingdom with a slap that echoed off the wide banks of the river. The island, a green jewel, shone as beautiful and solitary as the morning star. Lundowa, the island-nation. Inviolate for centuries, self-sufficient in all ways. Feared and envied by her neighbors, yet secure in the hands of her wielders of the spirits, great and honored protectors whose arcane skills were passed in whispers from father to elder son.

M'Lundowi, eldest of his brothers, scion of the Twenty-Third Generation, reveled in his honors. He boasted the steadfast fealty of five noble brothers; beautiful and fertile wives, selected from the island's oldest families; a fortress-palace in which to raise his sons; and great annual feasts held to praise his name. All this, and more, was his in return for holding the rival nations of Gwaal and Habanna at bay beyond the river...a task not at all difficult when the fire spirits were cooperative. And M'Lundowi ensured, through constant exercise of his ancient skills, that they would always remain thus.

Throughout his years of standing watch, he had never found it necessary to actually unleash the spirits upon his foes. Ancestral memories were very much alive along both banks of the great river; fear proved a stronger bulwark for Lundowa than a thousand shields. Behind its wall of terror, the island-nation rested content and complacent. Yet even the strongest bulwark needed shoring up over time. Decades of peace could make the most stalwart men of war into seekers of advantage and sensuality. To his everlasting subsequent shame, M'Lundowi allowed himself to be seduced by a search for even greater personal power, more potent sources of knowledge and influence over the spirits than any of his predecessors had ever uncovered. He justified these activities as being for the greater good of Lundowa, but in his blind pride he ignored his brothers' warnings that he was neglecting a man of the spirits' most basic responsibilities.

"Eldest Brother, Shield of Our People, when did you last offer sacrifices to the rain and the river spirits?" his younger brother, third-born N'Mehayah, had asked. "You hide your face from your people, spend endless weeks in private retreat. Meanwhile, the offerings urns fill with dust. If you are too busy to attend to the gods of the crops and the fish, teach me, Eldest Brother, and I will happily shoulder those tasks."

M'Lundowi heard more challenge than support in those words. "Do not think to overreach yourself, third-born one," he answered. "I traffic in forces far beyond your meager understanding. Go back to sharpening the spears of your toy warriors and leave me to my work."

Both Lundowa and her renowned protector were unprepared for the drought when it came. Within a month, the river fell to less than one third its normal flow, and its sunbaked banks became littered with dead and stinking fish. Even M'Lundowi's sacred grove was not immune to the sun's depredations. The delicate plants withered in the heat; their precious fruits, vital to the all-important rituals, became as dry and cracked as the feet of old men.

M'Lundowi, confronted with the angry council of his brothers, refused to coat his body with ashes in penance to the spirits. He could not and would not admit error. Instead, he announced he would undertake a solitary quest to find new seeds for the island's sacred grove.

For weeks he wandered the forests bordering the river, then the savannahs that stretched beyond them, collecting those plants and seeds that his special vision allowed him to recognize, taking care never to come in contact with another human being. His trail took the shape of a great circle. When he again approached the banks of the familiar river, he saw plumes of black smoke rising from the distant island.

M'Lundowi's first reaction was anger. *Can they be so unsure of my powers that they light bonfires to guide my footsteps home?*

Wading across the dismal mud flats to his home, he saw how terribly mistaken his assumption had been. The plumes of smoke did not rise from beacons. He had expected his brothers would be present at the shore to welcome him. And indeed they were. But only their heads, set upon stakes ten feet high.

Dazed, hoping beyond hope that this was merely a vision, a premonition of a disaster which could still be averted, M'Lundowi stumbled through his smoking, silent village. He searched for his wives, his sons. The only people he found were the bodies of ten warriors strewn across the central square, their torsos marked with small, round wounds, gory holes which had been gouged by no weapon known to him.

He sat amidst the corpses of his warriors and waited for death to take him, as it had all his countrymen. Death did not. The Gwaalese, returned to see if the fires had spared anything of value, did. Recognizing him by his ritual scars, the invaders pointed their strange polished sticks at him. It was then that he heard the terrible crack for the first time— louder than the tallest tree's death-fall—and felt himself flung backwards by an invisible blow. He knew then, as blood streamed down his side, that there were other magicks in the world beside his own.

A vision of the endless waters of Hell, seen from the belly of a wooden crocodile.

The fierce new magic failed to kill him. Seeing how he stubbornly clung to life, the Gwaalese took him down the shrunken river to the camp of their new allies, white creatures who traded death sticks for flesh. These creatures removed the iron ball from his side and bound his wound. They then placed him in chains of heavy iron, linked him to a row of Lundowan commoners who had formerly been beneath his notice, and Habanan filth beneath even his contempt, and forced him to march.

The march lasted five agonizing days. M'Lundowi quickly learned not to allow his wounded body to succumb to exhaustion; such surrenders earned him a fusillade of blows and kicks. His terrible journey came to a pause at the edge of a body of water such as M'Lundowi had never before witnessed, a river with only one shore. He was permitted to briefly rest in a fortress of stone. Then he and his fellow captives were cast into the belly of a creaking wooden crocodile with four wings of fluttering cloth.

How bitter was this punishment the gods had chosen for him! The crocodile's dark belly stank of death and things worse than death, of ignored corpses dishonored by the attentions of rats. The pale creatures, men-shaped demons the sickly color of grubs, showed no appreciation for M'Lundowi's exalted status. He was pressed on all sides by the putrid bodies of the suffering and dying, his once sacred personage defiled innumerable times by their sweat and swelling pools of their excrement. Worse, his own body, once so dignified, betrayed him again and again, until he knew he smelled as rank as the hated Habanans alongside him.

Worst of all, however, was the presence of his women, the once perfumed and cosseted voluptuaries who had filled his nights with pleasure. They were chained on the far side of the crocodile's belly, and before light was banished, they had seen he was down in the pit with them. For what felt like an eternity, M'Lundowi was forced to endure their curses and accusations, their howls that he had failed them and their children.

Then, when M'Lundowi thought the gods could humiliate him no further, the crocodile's motions came to an abrupt halt. The grub-colored men opened the creature's belly to the outside air. Sunlight streamed in, blinding him. A breeze brought strange scents of a new land, a new world. A world of cruelties, loneliness, and despair.

But a world he would come to know well. A world he would strive to master. For his vengeance demanded no less.

A vision of sweating glass.

Windows shed tears of morning dew. Adderwood Manor's gilded mirrors sobbed through patinas of fine dust. The mansion's mistress gasped with the pain of the final moments of childbirth, the violence of her breath making surrounding candle flames flicker.

M'Lundowi had tended to the Mistress Anna Babbage all through her pregnancy. Now he waited outside her bedroom door for the moment when the child would be brought to him. Throughout the oppressive Mississippi summer, he had eased Mistress Anna's burden of pregnancy with herbal beverages he had prepared, lightly narcotic in their effect. Due to his ministrations, she was only dimly aware that the time had come for her son to be born.

M'Lundowi noted the child's birth cries with grim satisfaction. When the door opened and the midwife handed him the boy to be swaddled, he knew precisely how to touch it, there in the concealing dark. So simple it had been; barely a touch, the pain of it masked by the newborn's expected wailing.

In the years to come, he would note with hidden satisfaction the child Joseph's abnormal sensitivity to noise, and the way in which his right arm failed to keep pace with the rest of him, growing more visibly stunted with each passing season. The boy's mother tried to love him, yet each season she withdrew further into a personal fog, becoming increasingly more dependent upon her servant's soothing beverages, until she was little more than a child herself, dreamily lost amid the folds of her bed.

The boy's father tried to love him, but he was ashamed of his son's deformity. So he distanced himself with business ventures and travels. Until that day when he was lost to his son forever, stolen away by the dumb, uncomprehending terror of horses.

A vision of horses.

Startled eyes, brute terror, slashing hooves. It was so easy, so simple. The business did not require even the most basic of conjurings. Only patience, cunning, and the stupidity of beasts.

When Master Joseph was five years old, the senior Master Babbage had taken to making weekly visits to Yazoo City, in order to build up a new trading venture. He had commissioned the building of an elaborate carriage, pulled by a team of four horses, so that he might arrive in town each week in a properly elegant style. It did not take long for M'Lundowi to discern the pattern of Master Babbage's comings and goings. He departed Monday mornings with the sunrise and returned Wednesday evenings at dusk, his team of horses filthy with mud, their eyes tired and wild in the fading light. That winter, the plantation's main well had gone dry, and M'Lundowi was told to direct the digging of a fresh well. He located it on a slight rise, close to the horse path which led to the river road. Digging the well through the hard earth was arduous work, and M'Lundowi directed that a shelter be built over the hole, to shade the diggers from the sun. It was an innocent enough exercise, he knew. No blame would ever be laid up-on his head.

The shelter, a simple thing of sticks and canvas, was erected on a Monday afternoon, while Master Babbage was in town. The sunset was a brilliant vermillion the following Wednesday evening. The horses, shocked by the change in their pathway, reared as violently as if gunpowder had exploded beneath their hooves. Master Babbage never again set living foot in the great house of Adderwood.

After the fatal "accident," a series of uncles and cousins undertook the upkeep of Adderwood until the plantation's heir reached the age of majority. Yet most of these were more interested in raising profitable crops of cotton than raising the lonely, awkward boy. Joseph gained no friends apart from Old Daniel; his pride would not allow him to accept overtures of friendship from the only available source, an equally lonely boy who hailed from a ramshackle neighboring farm. His formal education was left to a series of tutors, imported from the North or from England. His nurturance, dark and hidden as the growth of a fungus within a rotting log, was left to the one person who valued it, the ancient slave who claimed it as partial payment for the sons that had been taken from him.

And so was M'Lundowi's arrogation of his master's child made complete.

A vision of fellow conjurers of the spirits.

Smiles on creased, red faces. Hands that had known intimate secrets of the earth. Houses of animal skins, encasing rich smells of fecund women and cooking fish. During M'Lundowi's first decade in this dismal land of Mississippi, they had still been here, the Original Ones, living in the forests outside the plantation. He had watched them with keen interest when they approached the great house with their furs and tanned skins, seeking to trade with the white people. The aura of one of the visitors had caused M'Lundowi to recognize him as a fellow man of the spirits.

How magnificent that first escape felt, stretching forth atrophied mystical muscles to cloud the vision of his white overlords...M'Lundowi fled to the camp of the Original Ones, the Choctaw. They had known other escaped Africans, several of whom had been initiated into the tribe, and so he was made welcome in the house of their man of the spirits. He stayed for several days in this oasis, drinking in the hospitality of the great man, establishing a learning relationship which would last a span of four years.

M'Lundowi never stayed with the Choctaw for more than three days at a time, nor did he visit them more often than once per cycle of the moon. Always he returned to Adderwood, to resume his servile duties in the great house. This behavior greatly puzzled his benefactors. But much as he wished to sever his servitude, his will for vengeance was far stronger. He learned quickly that the spirit powers of this strange America were not the same as those of his homeland. Given enough time, he could likely master the invisible forces of this new world. But to do so would take at least two lifetimes, due to his handicap of birth across the sea, and thus his lack of an organic connection with this soil, these spirits. Although extraordinarily patient, he had not sufficient patience for that.

Stealing his white master's life and son was only a beginning, a faint foretaste of his coming banquet of vengeance. For not only this family had wronged and humiliated him; the entire race of white men, all the pale grubs who befouled this continent, had committed unanswered crimes against him and his people. If he could not command the unseen powers of this land in a timely enough fashion, he would scheme to somehow bring the invisible forces of his own land to him, here in his place of captivity. He would plan and scheme within the walls of the great white mansion itself. And his prime tool would be the child Joseph, the future master of Adderwood.

When the Choctaw were forced from their lands, beginning their exile in the west, their spirit-whisperer offered to take M'Lundowi with them. The African reluctantly bid them farewell.

A vision of goats, of the jealous, grasping Death spirit.

M'Lundowi felt it once again, the cold numbness of the approaching touch of the dark, grasping shadow. It had been too many years since his last sacrifice, and so powerful a spirit, so hungry an entity, if not bribed with the proper rituals, would surely take its rightful and ultimate ownership of his flesh. One could only cheat Death for so long before payment came due.

Master Joseph was a young, sickly boy when M'Lundowi had sensed the accumulated years creeping up on him again. One evening, during a winter storm of unusual violence, the gods of the tempest had provided the aging African with the means of eluding his relentless pursuer once more. Master Joseph's pet animal, a young she-goat, was killed in the storm, its neck broken by a large chunk of hail. This was a kind of beast well familiar to M'Lundowi—an animal of his homeland, fecund with the seeds of magic.

Since his forced parting from the Choctaw, he had endeavored to expand upon the knowledge they had imparted upon him. In those years, Master Joseph was inseparable from him. The moody child with the withered arm, shunned by his peers, spent many long, damp afternoons seated on the rough floor of "Old Daniel's" cabin, listening to the old man's fantastical tales. M'Lundowi filled his young charge's head with magic, thrilling him with simple conjurings and illusions, whispering to him of the power that could be his if only he would take it, take it...So it was only natural that the boy should bring his dead pet to the cabin of the gray-headed slave, demanding in a shrill, trembling voice that the animal be brought back to life.

A gleam in his clouded eye, M'Lundowi eagerly complied. Using herbs the Choctaw had gifted him with, intoning words he had brought with him from Lundowa, the man of the spirits imparted stolen animation to the dead she-goat. Joseph was delighted. He capered about the cabin with his pet, singing nursery rhymes. The goat moved jerkily on stiff legs, its head tilted at an unnatural angle, its eyes the color of oysters.

The boy begged M'Lundowi to perform the same trick for his father, buried two months earlier at the top of a hill overlooking Adderwood. The ancient African laughed at the lad's naively grotesque demand, and then told the boy the straightforward truth. His father had been in the cold earth too long for such weak magicks to have any effect. He convinced the boy to leave the goat with him that night, telling him it could not live outside the enchanted walls of his cabin.

Alone, he slit the undead creature's throat, catching its cold blood in an urn. He lifted the urn to his lips, tasting the bitter dead salts, and the creature's stolen life flowed into his own veins. Not enough life-force to return the vigor of youth to his limbs, but enough to brush aside the grasping hands of the Death spirit for a few years more. He buried the twice-dead goat between the roots of the oak tree which shaded his shack, telling Joseph the next morning that the animal had escaped from the enchanted cabin and expired.

* * *

M'Lundowi watched Master Joseph pacing the high levee. *He is my creature, more so even than the goat which fueled my years with its undead blood. How impatient he is, waiting for the power he assumes will be his to command.*

He applied a fresh coat of polish to a pair of riding boots, then paused for a moment to appreciate a cool river breeze that swept the veranda with the coming setting of the sun. *Such breezes can only make the ship arrive faster. It grows nearer with every circle of my rag.* An unfamiliar impulse possessed his face, drawing the muscles of his cheeks and jaw into long-forgotten contractions. For the first time in five decades, the ancient African smiled.

CHAPTER FIVE

Boiling Over on the Boiler Deck

Cairo, Illinois, April 12–13, 1862

Cyril Oates had heard the news that evening at the officers' mess table of August Micholson's arrival in Cairo. He didn't like it. He didn't like it at all.

The *Eads*'s stocky chief engineer angrily paced alongside the gunboat's seven boilers, nestled together in the ironclad's deepest hold. The seven "iron cigars" were packed tightly into the close space, like serpents nesting in the bottom of a log, slithering restlessly against one another to share the residual heat that remained after a day's sunning. Oates, however, needed to share heat with no one; he generated plenty of it on his own.

He was making adjustments to a pressure valve when a stranger slowly descended the steps to the engine room, a man wearing the stripes of a lieutenant commander. The stranger was accompanied by James Rutherford, the *Eads*'s executive officer.

"Captain Micholson, you must be tired," Rutherford said. "We could continue our tour in the morning—"

"I'm fine, Mr. Rutherford." The newcomer stepped onto the boiler deck. "I don't think I could get to sleep without at least a short walk around the gunboat."

So this is the infamous August Micholson, Oates thought. *The scuttlebutt passed around the mess table was correct. The glory-grubbing bastard has arrived.*

Rutherford approached the engineer, who openly gawked at his new commanding officer. "Sir, this is Chief

47

Engineer Cyril Oates. Mr. Oates, this is Lieutenant Commander August Micholson, our new captain."

Micholson extended his hand to Oates. "Engineer Oates, Mr. Rutherford has told me good things about you. I see you maintain a very clean engine room."

Oates reluctantly shook Micholson's hand, not bothering to wipe the engine grease from his thick fingers before doing so. The new commander had a strong grip, at least; much more forceful than Rutherford's, which Oates had always considered embarrassingly weak. "You needn't ever worry about the state of this engine room," he said gruffly. "My men all know their jobs. I've served aboard enough steamboats to know my life depends on the condition of my equipment."

Micholson glanced around the engine room. "Flag Officer Foote tells me this is the fastest of the ironclads. Do the engines require any extra care?"

Even with this unwelcome interloper, the chief engineer could not pass up an opportunity to boast of his boat. "The Flag Officer is correct. The *Cairo* is second fastest, and we beat her by a good two knots. As for your question, no, our engines are no more temperamental than those aboard the *Essex* were; less so, in fact, since they're newer."

"Good. Very good. I will be asking much from your engines over the next few weeks."

"The *Northport* was also a fast ship, I understand."

Micholson raised an eyebrow. His smile faded somewhat as he detected a hint of a challenge. "Yes. She was."

"Captain," Rutherford interjected, glancing quickly between the two men, "perhaps we should continue with your tour. If you'd like to speak with some of the other officers—"

"That can wait, Mr. Rutherford." Micholson turned back to the engineer. "Did you know anyone aboard the *Northport*, Mr. Oates?"

"I did. Do you remember Calvin Brierly?"

"Of course. He was my chief engineer for nearly four years. A fine sailor. And a brave man."

"I knew Calvin Brierly." Oates made no effort to disguise the bitterness in his voice. "And others, as well, when they were still alive. I had friends aboard the *Northport.*"

"As did I, Mr. Oates." Micholson's eyes locked with Oates's for a full ten seconds before the engineer turned abruptly away. "As did I."

"Captain Micholson," Rutherford interjected, flustered and embarrassed, "we really must move on. I'm sure that Mr. Broadhurst, your gunnery captain, is anxious to meet you. And Dr. Travis, our ship's surgeon."

"Of course, Mr. Rutherford. I will follow your lead." He turned back to Oates, who had resumed working on the stubborn pressure valve. "Good evening, Mr. Oates."

Oates, who was raising a clatter with his tools, pretended not to hear. Unlike his boilers, the chief engineer did not come equipped with a pressure release valve.

Oates rose hours before the sun. He loved few things, but the quiet of a still-dark morning was one of them. Beneath the yellow, wavering glow of a lantern held high within his thick-fleshed fist, he inspected his boilers, the first of many such inspections he would carry out through the new day.

His trained eyes scanned the conical iron surfaces for signs of wear: dents, cracks, pits, rust...even the tiniest of fissures, barely visible to the unaided eye, could allow the steam to escape, making the pressure plummet like a waterfowl shot through the guts, stilling the great paddlewheels and abandoning the gunboat to the uncertain mercies of the current. A single bent rivet could mean the difference between a boiler that would stand like the Mount of Olympus, a titan of reliability throughout an honorable work life of thirty years, and one that would burst like an overstretched balloon at the first surge of high pressure.

These boilers were new, so fresh from the foundry that the brass plates which ascribed their parentage to the Cincinnati Ironworks still gleamed. The boilers on his last vessel, the ill-fated *Essex*, had been old; like the hips of a fat, arthritic dowager, they'd been girdled with jury-rigged support hoops. Yet, three hundred yards below Fort Henry on the Tennessee River, it hadn't been the boilers' age that had doomed thirty-two sailors. It had been a well-aimed Confederate cannonball, eighty-one pounds of hot iron, which had pierced the casemate and gundeck, then smashed into the middle boiler, releasing the scalding breath of the demon caged inside.

Not even the newest boilers on the Mississippi were proof against eighty-one pounds of plunging iron. He had applied for transfer to the *Eads* because he knew of the modifications worked into her design before launching—the wider beam and two additional boilers, the double paddlewheel for greater maneuverability, and, most importantly, the added armor. Yet even the *Eads* lacked an armored deck above her boilers.

Since his assignment to the gunboat two weeks earlier, Oates had been applying his considerable energies towards remedying that defect. He walked to the rear of the boiler deck, where he had been stockpiling whatever lumber he could connive out of the Cairo naval stores clerk. There were also upwards of two dozen bales of cotton, confiscated by the gunboat USS *Lexington* during her raid up the Tennessee River. He intended to construct a protective barrier around the boilers—enough of one, anyway, to hopefully deflect incoming shells back up through the gundeck, away from the machinery. Grunting, he lifted one end of a cotton bale and began pulling his awkward burden closer to the iron cigars.

"Chief Oates? Could you use a hand down there, sir?"

Surprised, Oates dropped the bale. It was merely Jack Bainbridge, youngest of the powder boys at age fourteen. What was he doing up at four-thirty in the morning, peering into the engine room from a hatch in the gundeck?

"Mr. Bainbridge? What are you doing out of your hammock at this ungodly hour?"

"I couldn't sleep, sir," Jack whispered. "It's those fogs. They creep inside your blanket, then your great coat, your skin, and finally into your bones. I think my blood is frozen."

Oates smiled. He found himself welcoming Jack's company; the enthusiastic lad was popular with most members of the crew. "Why don't you come down on deck? It's warmer down here."

"Thank you, sir!" The boy shimmied down the rope ladder with the grace of a squirrel.

"Where do you hang your hammock that it's so bitterly cold? Out on the hurricane deck, between the funnels?" Oates was amused, watching his companion place his hands first against one boiler, then another, searching for the one which retained the most heat.

"No, sir. I sleep with the rest of the powder boys, in the aft gundeck, between the two cannons there. The wind is always creeping in through the gunports, even with the shutters closed."

"Where are you from, Mr. Bainbridge?"

"Florida, sir. Saint Augustine."

Another one of our Unionist Southerners, Oates mused, understanding now why he hadn't been able to place the boy's accent. He came from Boston, himself. A New Englander didn't get many opportunities to meet a Floridian. "Why don't you speak to Mr. Rutherford about transferring your hammock somewhere away from the gunports? He's a reasonable man."

"Thank you, sir. It's just that—well, to be honest, I've tried all the other open hammock berths, and it's impossible to get away from the draft anywhere, on any of the gundecks. I hope you don't mind, sir, but I've been coming down here most nights this week, catching a few hours of good shut-eye next to the boilers. They're the warmest things on the boat, apart from the biscuit oven. And I'm afraid if I crawl in there, I'll end up as breakfast!"

"Yes. Our men will eat just about anything, so long as it's browned enough." Oates suddenly wished Jack hadn't mentioned the subject of breakfast. It would be nearly two hours until the crew were piped to the mess table. "Mr. Praeger never mentioned stumbling across you at first light. Where have you been squirreling yourself away?"

The boy shifted uneasily. "Actually, sir—and I hope this causes no trouble for Mr. Praeger—he *did* come across me, but he said it didn't bother him none if I stretched out on the floor for a few hours."

Kaleb Praeger was the Engineer's Mate, assigned to the *Eads* when she had first been commissioned, so his arrival aboard predated Oates' by several weeks. Oates made a mental note to remind Mr. Praeger that he was no longer the senior engineering officer aboard. "Ah, don't worry yourself about it. You may continue to come down here for the duration of these fogs, so long as you don't mention it to any of your deck mates. I'd rather not be running a twenty-bed hotel between my boilers."

"Thank you, sir! That's very kind of you, sir!" He pumped Oates' thick hand vigorously.

"However, I'm afraid sleeping down here for the remainder of this morning is out of the question. I'm plotting out some urgent work, and you would be in my way."

The boy's eyes fell upon the building supplies stacked at the rear of the deck. "Is that what all those planks and bales of cotton are for?"

"Yes. I've been planning to erect a barricade—a shield, if you will—around the engines and boilers."

"Really? I wouldn't have thought it necessary, what with the strength of our iron."

Another believer in the myth of the invincible gunboats. Oates recalled the screams of the *Essex*'s men as the steam had hit them...he had never imagined human vocal cords could release such sounds. "It is very necessary, Mr. Bainbridge. Trust me."

"Of course I trust you, sir! If you say we need a barricade, than we should have ten of them! May I have the honor of assisting you?"

"I would not deny you that," Oates said. "Such labors always leave me short of breath, I'm afraid—"

Jack bounded across the deck and had his arms around the nearest bale in less time than it took a rabbit to disappear down its hole. "Just tell me where you want it, sir!"

"Don't try to lift it by yourself, boy! You'll wrench your arms out of their sockets! *Slide* it, don't lift it, wait for me to push from the other end—"

But Jack had already moved the bale fifteen feet with a series of vigorous jerks, meeting Oates halfway. "Don't worry about me, sir! I used to help my father at the docks all the time, when I was just half the size I am now."

In less than ten minutes, Jack had moved all the bales into position. Ah, the vigor of youth! Oates mused. With a few more years and a little extra meat on him, the boy will be a regular Hercules.

"This is a right wonderful barricade you have planned," Jack said, barely breathing hard as he shouldered the last bale into place. "Have you had a chance to tell the new captain about it? I'm sure he'll be very pleased."

Oates's smile faded. "Our new captain is not yet aware of this project. I trust he will have sense enough to respect my prerogatives as Chief Engineer to run my own department as I see fit." He watched the boy pull his perspiration-soaked undershirt away from his skin. "I suspect the coldness of the morning is no longer a nuisance for you," he said, handing Jack one of the towels the firemen used to keep sweat out of their eyes.

"Indeed not," Jack replied, burying his face in the towel. "Ten minutes of good exercise is better than an hour's worth of snuggling up to your boilers." He sat on a bale across from the one where Oates had settled himself. "Actually, sir, I'm glad I got this chance to show you what I can do. A lot of the men on board, they take one look at me—I know I'm not fully grown yet—and, well, they figure all I'm good for is carrying bags of powder to the guns. If they'd just let me, I could carry the powder *and* the shell. Not that that's what I really want to be doing..." The boy's voice, so strong with conviction, now wavered with an adolescent quivering. "Actually, sir, I would be most pleased if you would permit me to become one of your firemen."

Oates raised a bushy eyebrow. The job of fireman, shoveling coal into the gunboat's furnaces, was one of the dirtiest, most exhausting, and least pleasant tasks aboard. "Shoveling coal is no lark. It's filthy, hot work. There's good reason my firemen are called 'the black gang,' you know."

"I know that, sir. I have...personal reasons for wanting the job."

Oates did not like the sound of this. Was the boy unnerved by the prospect of imminent engagement with the enemy? If so, he would do better at the guns than at the furnace; on the gundeck, the enthusiasm of the gunners would likely sweep him along, whereas down on the boiler deck, he and his fellows would be helpless to strike back at the enemy. "I need more than that. I won't get into a tussle with the gunnery captain about 'stealing' you just due to some secret whim of yours. If this is about your fear of the gundeck—"

"I have no fear of the gundeck, sir! I joined the Navy to fight. I know the hazards. It's just that...I wish to honor a commandment of my father's."

"Your father commanded you to shovel coal?"

"No, sir. My father, he commanded me—" Jack's face twisted into a white mask of sorrow. Oates suddenly regretted pushing the boy for his secret. "He...he always told me to face up to whatever frightened me. Never to turn my back on anything horrible, lest I become a coward." Jack regained his equilibrium. "I have been an orphan these past three years, Mr. Oates. My family's house burned to the ground one night. I was the only one the rescuers were able to pull to safety. I'll never forget the heat, the screams...So, you see, Mr. Oates, it is very important to me to stand at the doors of your furnace, with a shovel in my hands. So that I may learn to become the master of the fire, and never allow it again to master me."

How his thoughts echo my own! To be sure, Oates could always use a relief fireman. Extended steaming always exhausted his men, and he would end up pulling temporary replacements from the gun crews anyway. The boy might actually be safer below the boilers than above them on the gundeck. Aboard the *Essex* , steam had risen from the punctured boiler like gas from a volcano, and the only men who had escaped scalding had been the engineers and firemen on the bottom deck. "I will speak with the captain of the guns. Tell me his name...?"

"Mr. Lawrence Broadhurst. He comes from the *St. Louis.*"

"I'll speak with Mr. Broadhurst. I'm sure we can come to some accommodation. In the meantime, you have my permission to visit the boiler deck in your spare hours. I'll see to it that my men familiarize you with your new duties."

"Thank you, sir! That's very generous of you. I promise, I'll be nothing but a credit to you and the whole boiler deck. Perhaps if I watch you well enough, someday I may be an engineer myself!"

A protégé? The more Oates turned the thought over in his head, the more appealing it became. "Yes, well, there's more to it than just watching. There's plenty of book learning, proper schooling...but I may consent to show you a thing or two. Meantime, get yourself some sleep! The sun will be with us soon, and it would not surprise me if we steam off on our first mission this day or on the morrow."

Jack bundled his overshirt into a pillow and gathered his greatcoat for a blanket. "Do you know where we're heading to, sir?"

"No. I won't know until we officers have our first meeting with this new captain of ours." He suppressed a scowl; no sense in teaching a fine young lad contempt for superior officers, even for a scoundrel such as August Micholson.

"I'm sure it will be very exciting, wherever we go. Good morning, sir. And thank you again."

"Good morning, Mr. Bainbridge. Keep my boilers company. Together, we will see about making you master of the fire."

CHAPTER SIX

The Ritual of the Claw

Adderwood Plantation, Mississippi,
April 14, 1862

The black freighter docked at the Adderwood levee at sunrise. The day and hour of its arrival precisely matched predictions made by M'Lundowi.

He and Babbage were present to greet the vessel. They stood atop the levee and watched four of Adderwood's slaves catch mooring ropes thrown from the freighter's deck. Babbage, his face aglow with pride and anticipation, waved heartily to the ship's captain and crew. His shriveled right arm jumped with quivers of excitement within its tightly tailored sleeve.

"Ho, captain!" Babbage cried. "I'm pleased to see you've had better luck than the City of Tuscaloosa did. Welcome back to the heart of the Confederacy!"

The captain, a leathery, full-bearded man who looked older than his forty years, flicked the spent butt of a cigarette into the Yazoo River. "Save your welcomes for the queer beasties we'll be unloading, sir. As for my luck, the best luck I'll ever have is to unload this chunk of filthy Africa from my hold and collect that fortune you've promised."

"Have no fear, sir! Your full payment awaits you within an iron safe in my home."

"Good. I intend to buy a right fancy house in New Orleans, start my own trading company, and let younger, more foolish men take my risks for me."

M'Lundowi stood near Babbage atop the grass-covered levee. In honor of this day, he had cast aside his usual

57

ANDREW FOX

frayed, patched, colorless garments in favor of brightly colored robes reminiscent of the priestly robes of Lundowa. Babbage had ordered that several sets of such robes be made by Adderwood's seamstresses, under M'Lundowi's guidance. The ancient African's unyielding gaze was fixed on the gangplank which had been lowered to meet the Adderwood pier. After a few moments, a tall, reedy black man, bent like a palm in the aftermath of a storm, descended the gangplank with the aid of a walking stick. His wiry hair was streaked with wide swathes of gray. An ignorant eye might judge him to be nearly as old as M'Lundowi himself.

M'Lundowi held forth his hand to the returned traveler. The tall man reverently grasped the outstretched hand and knelt as crisply as his aged joints would allow. M'Lundowi smiled. "Alaltho. My heart sings to see you safely returned, my cherished young one, you who are like an adopted grandson."

"Being returned to you, my Guide and Guardian, Shield of Our People, the vigor of youth fills me." They spoke the long-unspoken language of Lundowa, rich with nuance, piety, and ceremonial flourishes. Alaltho stood. "Morning and evening I thank the whole pantheon of spirits that you remembered me and thought me worthy of serving you again. During my long servitude in Alabama, I never allowed memories of your exalted deeds to fade."

"How was it to see our home again?"

Alaltho's face grew clouded. "The island rests in the river like a dreamer caught in a trance. The men of Habanna and the cursed Gwaalese never cross the river to our home. They say it is a haunted place, filled with the ghosts of hundreds of demons. The walls of your palace remain standing, but your great halls fill with dust. I wept to see our home so fallen and forsaken."

"It shall be avenged, beginning this day." He followed Alaltho's gaze to the deck of the ship. "Your son fares well?"

"He does. He will join us shortly."

"Good. How were you treated on the voyage?"

Alaltho scowled. "With contempt. Even far from this place of servitude, the pale ones believe the lowliest among them may grind the princes of our nation beneath their heels. Initially, we were berthed in the place where they stored their salted meats and casks of water. On the return trip, we were forced to sleep amidst the beasts we had captured. Although, given a choice, I would prefer the intimacy of such creatures to that of our supposed masters."

M'Lundowi watched the freighter's crew enjoy their tobacco while, all around them, Adderwood's slaves labored to unload the ship's holds. "Such contempt will soon receive its due recompense."

"How, my Guide? These knaves will soon rejoin the sea birds, worlds away from here."

"It will be done. Watch and listen." M'Lundowi walked to where Babbage anxiously paced. A group of eight slaves struggled to carry a cage imprisoning a three hundred pound boar up the levee steps. The tusked creature snorted and bellowed its displeasure, butting the bars of its cage fiercely. "Master Joseph. Pardon my intrusion. What are the plans of the men with the great boat?"

Babbage's eyes unwillingly left the impressive beast. "You're curious about the sailors, hmmn? Most of these ruffians will want to throw away their wages on liquor and women, I imagine. Why?" Babbage's face suddenly clouded with concern. "Why, Daniel? Will we be needing them again? Do you mean to tell me they didn't bring back quantities adequate to your purposes?"

M'Lundowi held up a hand to quiet him. "No, Master Joseph. Our commands were followed. What this boat has brought us is plentiful and good. We can begin our rituals. But once the ceremony is begun, the spirits may tell me they need something more. Perhaps not from Africa. Perhaps from this land. What is the port-town which is nearest to here?"

"That would be Yazoo City, thirty miles downriver from Adderwood."

"There is wine there for the boat men, and the women they desire?"

"Certainly. Yazoo City is a sewer of vile lusts. Are you asking me to have them remain there? It will cost me considerably."

M'Lundowi lightly touched Babbage's right arm. "Ah, but Master, have you not already spent a considerable fortune? What are a few coins more? It will only be for several days, I assure you."

Babbage counted the heads of the crewmen on deck, calculating the likely payments required, and frowned. "Very well. I'll make arrangements. They'll remain at Yazoo City a week."

"You are wise and prudent, Master Joseph. A week is all we will require."

The ancient African returned to Alaltho's side. "It is done," he said quietly. "The insult to you and your son will be burned from this world, for Yazoo City will be the first of the white men's cities to know the touch of the *Mikithi.*"

The freighter was not completely unloaded until the day's shadows had grown long. The caged animals, sheaves of herbs and grasses, trees in their heavy clay pots, and baskets full of rich, black earth, hundreds of baskets, were gathered in a clearing behind Adderwood's main house. Field slaves emptied the baskets of earth until a wide, low mound of African soil covered the Mississippi loam. The slaves hastily erected screens prefabricated of canvas and wood around the clearing, fearfully averting their faces so as not to gaze at the assembled flora and fauna an instant longer than necessary.

Babbage, with M'Lundowi at his side, observed these final preparations. "I say, Daniel, are those canvas screens truly necessary?"

"Yes. No outside eyes must observe what will be done."

"Those 'outside eyes' wouldn't include *mine*, would they? After all the money and time I've sunk into this project, I have every intention of seeing what you do and how you do it."

M'Lundowi's words, though spoken softly, carried the weight of iron. "No, Master. Understand me, please. I do not mean to disrespect you. But the presence of a white man at the ritual—the presence of any outlander—would ruin it, turning all our work to ashes."

Babbage's voice quivered with a petulant echo of the spoiled, lonely child he had once been. "But you can't expect me to simply stay in the house with my eyes shut. I've put too much into this, Daniel. I *deserve* to see this ceremony."

"Be patient, Master. My methods are unimportant. Great power I promised you. You will have it, when I am done. It will be *in* you."

"Dig deeper," M'Lundowi commanded. "The earth brought from our homeland must be thoroughly mixed with the alien soul beneath our feet. Or the spirits will ignore our requests, for they will not feel comfortable in this foreign land."

Eight men sank shovels deep into black soil enriched by thousands of years of Yazoo River floods. Three of the men were aged more than seventy years; they had been boys when the men of Gwaal had thrust them into the white men's ships. The other five were younger, less stooped with age and the privations of servitude. They were the sons of the old men, born in America, who had grown to adulthood knowing Lundowa only from whispered myths and songs choked with grief.

Now the old men sang joyously and freely as they sweated with their work, filling the darkening air with the words and rhythms of lost Lundowa. The old men's sons sang with them as best they could. All were dressed in the colorful robes Adderwood's seamstresses had made under M'Lundowi's guidance. The men's songs were punctuated by the angry, vicious snarls of a pair of caged panthers. And the snorting of a giant boar, a beast whose bone-white tusks and red eyes glimmered in the fading light.

M'Lundowi examined the mound of mingled earth with satisfaction. "Now you must take the plants and cut them, bleed them so their sap runs freely over this soil."

One of the younger men, whose Lundowan name was Kapatho, approached M'Lundowi. "My Guide," he said in English, "it gets very dark. Should I light the torches now?"

The ancient African recoiled as if slapped. He glared at Kapatho's father, fury boiling from his face. "The white man's tongue! He dares speak the white man's tongue here! What manner of teaching did you provide your son, Rawatha?"

Rawatha's deeply lined face crumpled with shame. "I—I am sorry, my Guide. I taught him the best I could. It—it has not been easy, in this land, to teach the young. Kapatho understands our mother tongue very well, but the speaking of it—he has always found this difficult. He is ashamed of this shortcoming, and so speaks the alien tongue he knows best. Please forgive him, and his miserable, failed father—"

M'Lundowi grabbed a loose clod of Adderwood earth and hurled it at Rawatha's bowed head. The damp missile struck the old man on his cheek. "Out!" M'Lundowi shrieked. "I cast you both *out!* Go be with your precious worm men! Speak their filthy tongue with them! You do not deserve your freedom! You will never be more than slaves!"

The two outcasts silently turned toward the flap in one of the screens. Alakko, who was Alaltho's son, watched them depart, his handsome face heavy with pity and sorrow. Kapatho had been his close kinsman and friend. "My Guide," he said to M'Lundowi, "is this wise? Are we not already few in number? We cannot afford to toss aside willing hands—"

"*Silence!*" The ancient African turned the full weight of his terrible, dark gaze on Alakko. "Utter another word, foolish child, and you will join those I have banished."

The next set of labors was carried out within a haze of uncomfortable quiet. The remaining men lit torches at the four corners of the enclosure and carried potted trees to the earth mound, cutting deep wounds in their branches so that thick drops of sap fell upon the mingled soil.

M'Lundowi signaled for all activity to cease. "Stand away from this mound," he said. He gestured for Alaltho to go to the cage that imprisoned the giant boar. "The time of testing has come. I stand before you as one who is become Lundowa this night. I am the receptacle of her strength, her knowledge, her ancient alliance with spirits and gods alike. Should I fail now, should I fall, all that we have struggled for will be ashes. Our knowledge will have no more meaning than the scratchings fools leave in dust. And you will taste nothing but ashes and dust for the rest of your lives.

"Alaltho, boy who has become gray-haired man in the years since we were stolen from our home, you who were destined to have been my trusted minister—have you made for me my claw?"

"Yes, my Guide and Guardian." Alaltho reached into the cage where the bristled beast glowered and unbound from one of the cage's bars a short spear made of dark, dense wood. "Your claw was carved from the wood of the *tubikaal* tree. Its length is that of the span from your shoulder to your fingertips, as our fathers' fathers' fathers instructed."

Alaltho placed the spear in M'Lundowi's outstretched hands. The ancient African gauged the sharpness of its point between his thumb and forefinger and nodded with satisfaction. Then he held the claw aloft for all to see. "It is good," he said. He removed his robe and his sandals. "As the beast which is so honored by the spirits is naked of garments, so am I naked of garments." His frail, ebony form glistened with a sweat half spawned of bodily terror

63

and half of spiritual exultation. "All is in readiness. All is in balance. The beast has its two tusks, and four hooves, and hundreds of sharp bristles. I have my one claw, and my soul-strength, and the eyes of all of you upon me."

He turned to Alaltho. "Release the house of the spirits."

Alaltho unlatched the cage's door, flung it open, then quickly retreated. The great boar warily emerged from its prison. It sniffed the night air, then scratched the soil with its sharp hoof, as if testing the worthiness of the ground.

M'Lundowi, twenty paces distant, waved his claw above his head and uttered a series of short, sharp cries. *I am your antagonist, the champion of men. Pay me your full attention!* The boar turned its massive skull, nearly as heavy as M'Lundowi's whole body, toward the ancient African. Its red eyes flickered with what seemed to be recognition. It again pawed the earth, tensing for its initial charge.

The boar hurled itself into furious motion. M'Lundowi quickly backed away, climbing the uneven slope of the earth mound. *Honored creature, do you think I would grant you such advantage as to stay on flat ground?* The boar's run ended at the mound. Snorting with anger and frustration, it began to climb the low heap, hampered by its short legs and compact hooves, which sank into the soft soil.

Man and beast glared at each other upon the mound's crest, a plateau barely six paces wide. M'Lundowi feinted with his claw, jabbing it towards the boar in a series of sharp, stylized motions. "Come for me, my death-brother," he said. "I will retreat no more."

The boar grunted contemptuously. It lowered its great head, scraping the earth with curved tusks. Every muscle in its blunt, three hundred pound form tensed. Then it charged.

M'Lundowi braced himself, spiritually and physically. The entire mound shook with the beast's coming. When it was close enough for him to feel its rancid breath, he quickly sidestepped and with the same fluid motion thrust his claw between the boar's thundering legs.

The collision smashed the claw from his fists and hurled him to the ground. But his stratagem had served its purpose. The boar lost its footing and rolled off the mound in a cloud of distended dirt, bellowing its fury. It landed heavily and lay on its side, momentarily stunned.

M'Lundowi pulled himself to his feet and retrieved his claw. The boar's vulnerable underside gleamed in the torchlight. *Victory is mine, my death-mate!* He hoisted the short spear above his head, then leapt off the mound's crest, aiming for the beast's blazing heart.

Yet the mound was treacherous for boar and man alike. M'Lundowi's right foot landed in a rut created by the creature's descent, savagely wrenching his ankle. The claw's point tore into the beast's gut, a painful wound, but far from a fatal one. As the boar bellowed in feral agony and struggled to right itself, M'Lundowi found he lacked the leverage to retrieve his weapon.

The boar regained its footing. M'Lundowi desperately tried to stand on his injured ankle, its torn ligaments flooding his mind with red. The boar sensed its tormentor's weakness. It tried to shake the barb from its underbelly, but the claw remained stubbornly lodged between two of its ribs. Dragging the spear along the ground, it pursued the slowly retreating M'Lundowi. Even a moderate trot was sufficient to catch the crippled chieftain. It knocked him to the dust with a vicious swipe of its massive head. Then it began to gore him.

The other men looked on in incredulous horror. "My Guide! We will save you!"

"No!" M'Lundowi screamed. Blood streamed into his mouth, choking him with its taste of salt. "Stay away, fools!" The men retreated. M'Lundowi's senses tightened, as if he were in the grip of a vision. At the very edge of his collapsing consciousness, he saw his claw, still protruding from the boar's grayish-white underside. With a strength born more of will than of body, he kicked at the wooden shaft.

65

The impact jarred the claw against the boar's ribs, ripping the wound wider. The beast roared with renewed torment and backed away from its mangled foe.

M'Lundowi crawled toward the part of the enclosure where the potted trees stood. Behind him, the boar advanced warily. Blood flowed down its tusks from scraps of steaming flesh that remained skewered on the tips. M'Lundowi held both hands over the slimy cavity where the taut flesh of his belly had once been. He was almost beneath the branches of the *gumbakka* trees now. Their sturdy, sheltering trunks were close, so close...

The ground shook. He closed his eyes tightly. *Either death or victory now!* He felt three ribs shatter as the boar's skull bludgeoned him and carried his helpless body through the air. Then a fresh avalanche of pain inundated his senses as he and the boar smashed into the center of the grove.

The trees, precariously balanced in slender pots, toppled as if in the grip of an earthquake. M'Lundowi's ears were battered by a cacophony of cracking wood, smashing pottery, and, most satisfying, the furious, pained bellows of a trapped beast. He and the boar lay entangled and immobile, its foul breath gusting against his bleeding face. Several minutes passed before he could force his broken body to move. He thanked the spirits for his smallness of form. Unlike the boar, which was held fast in the grip of dead wood, he could painfully, slowly wiggle free.

After two agonized minutes, M'Lundowi knelt at the boar's side. It breathed in ragged gasps, as did he. One red eye gazed at him with resignation. M'Lundowi felt his life draining away. He groped for the claw. It had broken in two. With the dregs of his strength, he pulled the remaining piece free.

"I apologize, glorious creature, that I no longer have the strength to do this any other way." The stars above began to spin in his sight. He plunged the claw's point into the beast's eye.

The boar's death cry was like no other sound that M'Lundowi had ever heard. It echoed in his mind as he listened to the quick footfalls of the men running to his side. Many hands lifted him from the tangle of bloody branches.

"My Guide, your wounds are severe." A quiver of dread ran through Alaltho's voice. "We must tend to you before the ceremony can continue."

"Do not be—an idiot, Alaltho!" Voicing those words was as tremendous a trial as wrenching the claw free had been. "Continue! The ceremony...must be completed! Or my great triumph is wasted. I must eat of the beast."

Alaltho nodded. "It must be as he says," he told the others. "Remove the boar's heart, brain, and tongue. Extract the one undamaged eye. Make these palatable with the spices I have brought. He must eat these things before the blood in them grows cold, or he will surely die."

The men removed long knives from their robes and quickly and crudely butchered the beast's carcass. Alaltho prepared a gory stew. Then, fingers dripping with the boar's cooling blood, he fed the raw stew to M'Lundowi.

When the bowl was emptied, Alaltho stood and joined the circle which had formed around M'Lundowi. Beneath the flickering light of the torches and the newly-risen stars, the ancient African underwent a subtle metamorphosis. Healthy color gradually returned to his face and limbs. He stirred, then rose slowly to his feet, accepting the help of none. His lifeblood continued to course from deep wounds in his abdomen and chest, yet this had no effect upon his newly surging vitality.

He held the broken fragment of claw aloft. "I have proved myself worthy." The voice which issued from his lips was deeper and stronger than it ever had been. "The might of many gods beats within my breast. We will continue with the ceremony." He gestured toward the cages which held the remaining animals. "You will build a fire at the edge of the earth mound. Those beasts you will sacrifice within the flames—all, except for the two great cats."

Alakko, who had earlier protested the banishment of Rawatha and Kapatho, observed the twin panthers with increasing unease. "And what is to be the fate of the cats, my Guide? Will it be necessary for you to conquer these as you did the boar?"

"The spirits of fire run strong in these ones," M'Lundowi said, "but it is not my place to contend with them." He inserted his hand between the bars of their cage and allowed each of them to taste the blood which had dried on his fingers. "A great sacrifice is needed for the spirits to rend the veils between their place of waiting and this alien land; a far greater sacrifice than we can now provide here. Here, we only prepare the way. To fully emerge in this alien land, the spirits of fire require the blood of hundreds of mortals born in this land. Especially sweet to them are sacrifices which occur by the offerings' own hands. And the cats?" He rubbed behind the ears of one of the panthers; the beast purred heavily, and every man in the circle felt the vibrations of that sound ripple against his skin. "These great ones are the spreaders of chaos, the hunters of the sacrificed. Their sacred claws will shred the veils which separate this world from other worlds, welcoming to this foul America the living infernos which are the *Mikithi*."

At the voicing of the name of the spirits of fire and vengeance, a name whispered only among the highest of priests, an audible gasp arose among the circle of watchers. Only Alaltho kept his composure. As the men of Lundowa began to realize what they were party to, their hearts quickened with dread anticipation. But one heart swelled with a biting sense of betrayal and horror—Alakko's.

He whirled toward Alaltho. "My father! How is this? You told me we would seek the spirits' aid in gaining our freedom. You spoke only of beseeching the spirits to influence the minds of men, to show our enslavers their folly. Never did you say one word about the—" he half choked before he could utter the name; "—the *Mikithi!*"

Alaltho shuddered with growing alarm as he recalled the fate of his friend Rawatha. "My son, control yourself!" he pleaded. "I am sorry—it was not permitted for me to speak of it until this time." Seeking to shield Alakko by drawing the others into sharing his son's indiscretion, he shouted a challenge at them. "You! Would any of you have willingly taken part in our sacred task had you known beforehand that it involved the *Mikithi?*" His questioning was met with silence. "But now we are all committed to this. We stand at the cusp of victory. Circumstances such as ours call for awful measures, terrible deeds. So, my son, you will control your emotions and be true to your heritage."

Alakko's face remained defiant. "No, father! This is a desecration of our heritage! Our history tells us the fire spirits were unleashed only once, to force the Gwaalese to surrender Lundowa to our ancestors." He pointed sharply at M'Lundowi. "What he plans isn't freedom! Nor justice! It is an abomination!"

Alaltho's face drained of blood. "My son, if you value your life and your father's honor, be silent!"

Alakko ignored him. He tried to capture the eyes of each of the remaining servitors. "Who here recognizes the horror of what you are doing? Will you taint your souls forever?" None would look at him. "Very well. I will no longer take part in this." He flung his ceremonial knife to the ground. "I go to join Kapatho and Rawatha."

"No, you will not," M'Lundowi said. His voice held an eerie, iron confidence, far more unsettling than his earlier outbursts of wrath. "Restrain him," he told the servitors. "Do not allow him to escape, or you will share his fate."

Four of the men surrounded Alakko and held him. Alaltho, stricken with dread and grief, fell to his knees. "Have mercy, my Guide and Guardian! He is foolish and willful, but he is my only living son—"

Alaltho's plea ended in a shower of blood. M'Lundowi plunged the remnant of his claw into Alakko's heart. "Now he has joined his dead siblings," the man of the spirits said.

"Alaltho, in gratitude for your years of noble service, I will do you the honor of permitting your son's body to join those of the slain beasts in the flames."

The men allowed Alakko's corpse to slump to the ground. Alaltho's sobs rent the night air. He plunged his face into the distended earth and tore the fabric of his robes.

The men gathered wood to build the sacrificial pyre. The wind grew in intensity. M'Lundowi returned to the panthers' cages. He reached into one of the cages and grasped a piece of dried dung, which he crumbled between his fingers. Then he cast the black powder into the air: a portion to the south, a portion to the north, a portion to the east. But not to the west, where lay the silent barrier of the Yazoo River.

He unbolted the doors of both cages. The great black cats emerged into the damp Mississippi night, rubbing roughly against M'Lundowi's thin legs before silently disappearing through flaps in the canvas screens.

"Go, my choosers of the sacrificed," the ancient African whispered, watching them stealthily vanish. "Go speedily, and hasten my day of vengeance."

CHAPTER SEVEN

The Squall Before the Storm

*Aboard the USS James B. Eads, en route to
Plum Point Bend on the Mississippi River,
April 16, 1862*

I have their attention, August Micholson thought as he looked into the faces of his officers, gathered around the conference table for his debriefing. *Whether I will have their loyalty...that is another question entirely.*

"And so we will accomplish our objective through stealth," he continued. "For purposes of security, I could not deliver this debriefing until after we had embarked. All members of the crew were hand-picked from a pool of border state volunteers—men from Maryland, Kentucky, lower Missouri, and the western part of Virginia. There are some Unionist Mississippians aboard, myself among them. The necessary uniforms have been acquired from captured Confederate depots or specially made in accordance with the most recent C.S.N. uniform regulations. We will proceed to the section of river above Memphis and Fort Pillow, where we will take over from the *Louisville* the duty of guarding the mortar boat which has been bombarding the fortress. Three evenings hence, it will appear to the rebels ashore that they have succeeded in damaging the *Eads* with one of their submerged torpedoes. We will make it look to them that we have driven her aground before she could fully sink and that we then abandoned her in the dark, to seek reinforcements and a salvage crew. In the morning, we will return. Not as ourselves, however. We will return as a local company of Confederate soldiers and sailors, who will appear to successfully repair the hole in the *Eads*'s side and commandeer her for the rebel cause."

An appreciative whistle split the heavy silence of the room. It came from Valery Delaup, the chief pilot, the only man in the room to have taken the liberty of propping his expensively shod feet on the conference table. Delaup's lips relaxed into an insouciant grin as he fondly stroked his well-groomed beard. "That's quite a plan, eh? I wouldn't have thought ol' Andy Foote had it in him. We pull this one off, they'll write an opera 'bout us for sure."

"This is absurd!" Hosiah Pierce sputtered, slamming his fist on the table and glaring evilly at Delaup. "Simply absurd! My men will never countenance putting on the uniform of the enemy. And I can almost promise you, should anyone attempt to pull down Old Glory and raise the rebel flag at our sternpost, there will be rebellion on board this gunboat!"

Despite the rising color in his cheeks, Micholson coolly stared the quartermaster down. "I will have no talk of mutiny at this table, Mr. Pierce. You may not have yet mustered proper respect for me as your commanding officer, but I know that Flag Officer Foote has your full loyalty. And this plan is his, his and General Grant's. As for whether or not your men will don the Confederate uniforms stored aboard this vessel, it is your duty to convince them of the necessity of doing so. Any officer who fails in this will be tossed into the brig and summarily demoted."

Pierce then simmered in silence, scratching his pocked nose and saying not another word during the entire briefing. Cyril Oates, the heavyset engineer, spoke next. "What I don't understand is, why was the decision made to send the *Eads* by herself? If destroying these rebel ironclads is so important, why not send the entire Flotilla? Surely ten gunboats—even eight, discounting the *Essex* and *St. Louis* with their damages—stand a much better chance of successfully completing this mission than one."

"I have already explained this, Mr. Oates," Micholson sighed, feeling fatigue creep up on him again. "Stealth is of absolute necessity—"

Rutherford attempted to come to his assistance. "The basic problem with your suggestion, Mr. Oates, is, well, should the entire Flotilla be seen steaming south toward Vicksburg, the rebels would fill the Yazoo with so many floating torpedoes, I daresay, a small boy could walk from one bank to another, using them as stepping stones. One boat, however, properly disguised, would not excite the rebels to such defensive measures."

"There's just one more problem with this little raiding party, though, the way I see it," Delaup said. He removed his feet from the table and straightened in his chair. "Them rebels aren't as stupid as our high command may think they are. How can we be *sure* our friends downriver will swallow this tall tale we're concocting? We'll meet some bad nastiness at Fort Pillow if they don't."

Micholson allowed himself a faint smile. The tone of the pilot's question indicated that, even if he could not yet be counted an ally, at least he was no enemy. "I agree with you, Mr. Delaup," he said. "False costumes and banners, by themselves, will not ensure our safe passage. However, the flag officer has made arrangements to make our masquerade more convincing. To observers on shore, it will appear that we battled our way past the gunboats *Mound City* and *Cairo*, using the *Eads*'s superior speed to escape downriver."

"Will this 'battle' involve live ammunition?"

"Some, yes, to ensure verisimilitude. Even a battle between friends is not without risk. The three boats will fire mostly unfused shells, however. The engagement will take place at dusk, when poor lighting conditions will aid its realism."

"So the officers and gunners aboard the *Mound City* and the *Cairo* are as aware of our tom-foolery as we are?"

"Of course. Otherwise, we'd be fighting a true engagement."

"Right. But it don't sit well with me, that nearly four hundred men and officers are in the know about this. It only takes one set of loose lips for word to travel south."

"I'm very aware of that, Mr. Delaup. It is an unfortunate but necessary risk."

"This is all fine and good, I suppose," Oates said, craning his neck to see the expressions of the other men sitting around the conference table. "But how will we coal? The *Eads* eats coal faster than an elephant sucks down hay. Do we intend to dock at rebel ports along the rivers and attempt to buy fuel? Won't every additional contact with the enemy put our ruse more and more in jeopardy?"

Micholson silently thanked Andrew Foote for his careful planning. "The flag officer has made adequate arrangements for us. Following our run past the *Mound City* and *Cairo*, we will 'capture' the *Molly Downings*, a Federal river freighter carrying coal and iron plating officially intended for the mortar scows bombarding Fort Pillow. The coal we will appropriate for our own use. The iron plating we will offer to the builders of the Confederate rams at their dockyard hidden somewhere on the Yazoo. It will be our ticket of entry into that most likely very well-defended installation."

"And our exit?" Dr. John Travis spoke for the first time. Micholson turned his attention to the gunboat's thin, balding, bespectacled surgeon. "Please pardon me, captain. I have no desire to be unduly pessimistic. But the welfare of the men aboard this vessel is my primary concern. What is Commodore Foote's opinion of our chances of returning home?"

Micholson struggled for the right words to answer the physician, whose piercing blue eyes were a silent rebuke to any man who would place the crew in unnecessary jeopardy. Once they opened fire on that boatyard, the thin shield of their masquerade would be instantly stripped away.

Then they would have to rely on the protection of their real shield: railroad iron three inches thick.

"An...excellent question, Dr. Travis. Once we have destroyed the boatyard and whatever vessels are docked there, we will be dependent upon our own qualities as a fighting vessel and crew to return north. This is why the *Eads* was chosen. She is better protected than her sisters, and the fastest of them by two or three knots. The Western Flotilla will stand by to cover our run past Fort Pillow, dividing the fortress's fire among eight to ten gunboats."

"You did not answer the doctor's question, sir!" Oates thundered.

"I thought I had, Mr. Oates," Micholson replied as coolly as he could manage. "To which question do you refer?"

"Does Andy Foote consider this to be a suicide mission?"

Rutherford turned white. "Mister—Mr. Oates, you are *gravely* out of line—"

"No," Micholson said. "Let him speak. Say your piece, Mr. Oates."

Oates stared around the table, clearly seeking support in the eyes of the other officers. "We will be trapped two hundred nautical miles behind the enemy's lines. You mean to say we will not receive any assistance from the Western Flotilla until we are at Fort Pillow? By then, we shall need no such assistance, for we will be sitting on the bottom of the Yazoo or the Mississippi. Does the flag officer mean to make sacrificial lambs of us? Is that why he chose *you*, of all the officers available to lead us?"

It's coming to a head, Micholson thought. *Let's get it all out in the open, before the cancer grows worse.* "I cannot say that I like the implications of that last remark, Mr. Oates. Would you care to explain yourself?"

Perhaps Oates had been expecting a murmur of agreement and support from his fellow officers. When this failed to materialize, air leaked rapidly from his bluster and bravado. "There...there have been rumors," he stuttered. "Among the crew. Once word reached the decks that you were to command the *Eads*, the story of the loss of the *Northport* spread like wildfire. Some of the men had read about the engagement in *Harper's Weekly*. The paper printed highly impressionistic drawings of the bloodshed which occurred on the *Northport*."

"I don't care about the doodlings of some sketch artist eager to earn his bread through sensationalism. What is the nature of these rumors you speak of?"

"That you are...unbalanced, sir. That you are a modern Captain Ahab, ready to throw away the lives of your men to avenge yourself on a great white whale made of rebel iron."

He'd expected something like this. But to hear it put so plainly, and for the entire retinue of officers to hear, caused a pounding in the base of his skull. For an instant, he wished he held Ahab's harpoon in his hand, so he could skewer Oates like a pig on a spit.

"And the rest of you?" he asked the others. "Have you encountered these vile rumors among your own men, as well?"

More than a few heads nodded.

"As officers of this vessel," he snapped at them, "it is your responsibility to quell such corrosive rumors as soon as they came to your attention. Would you not agree? Failure to do so constitutes *gross* negligence of duty. Any man who spreads lies about his commander, and any officer who allows such lies to be spread, shall be drummed off this gunboat in disgrace. Do I make myself perfectly clear?"

The officers met his rebuke with silence.

Rutherford nervously cleared his throat. "Sir, if I might proffer a suggestion, sir. I think...I would deign to suggest that you speak directly to the crew. None of us can defend you better than you yourself can. Make yourself known to them, explain the mission in your own words. Dispel these negative rumors by instilling the men with confidence and zeal. Ardor for the task ahead, that's what's most needed now, I must say!"

Micholson took a deep breath and willed his anger to melt. *Swallow your pride, man.* The course Rutherford suggested offered him perhaps his only chance to stave off disaster. "You provide wise counsel, Mr. Rutherford." He took care to meet the gazes of each of the officers sitting around the table, even that of Oates. "Gentlemen, you have done me and the whole complement of the *Eads* a service by bringing this matter to my attention. Regarding some of the men having misgivings about my assignment as their commander...that is not overly surprising, given my re-cent...experiences. But these misgivings must not deteriorate into mistrust, or our mission is doomed even before we reach our initial objective. I will speak with the crew once we reach our station at Plum Point Bend, north of Fort Pillow, prior to the execution of our hoped-for deception of the enemy."

A familiar knock made Micholson look up from the letter he had been writing, scribbling out, and rewriting for the past hour.

"Come," he said, having no need to ask who it was.

Nehemiah entered the cabin. "I hope I'm not intrudin', Mister August."

"You know you aren't," Micholson said. The mere presence of his lifelong companion allowed some of the accumulated tension to drain from his shoulders and back. "I don't think it is possible for you to intrude upon me, Nehemiah. You have a near-magical ability to know when your presence is most wanted. Comes from having raised me, I suppose."

"I suppose," Nehemiah said. Micholson gestured for him to sit on the edge of the cot. "I had a notion you might be in need of some company. Are you writin' to Missus Elizabeth again?"

Micholson frowned down at the paper on his desk. "What a senseless exercise," he sighed. "Not only would a letter most likely never reach her in Petersburg, but the contents change like the wind, with every shift in my mood. One moment I am casting her and her future bastard child away, and the next, I am begging for a reconciliation and a renewal of our love and vows."

"What you're really tryin' to do, I imagine, is distract yourself from one trial by focusin' on another. How did your meetin' with the officers go?"

Micholson couldn't help but faintly smile. His old friend had pinned him as neatly as a lepidopterist would secure a butterfly to a corkboard. But the smile didn't last long. "Ahh, *that*. I don't...I'm not sure that I'm up to this task, Nehemiah. Being captain of the *Eads*. Which would be bad enough if the consequences would sit on my shoulders alone. But any failure on my part will terribly affect the lives and well-being of a hundred and eighty-seven men, more than served on the *Northport*. The men have grave misgivings about me. And why shouldn't they? I would, were I standing in their boots. Could Flag Officer Foote have made a dreadful mistake in selecting me?"

"Do you trust him?"

"I trust him like I would have my own father."

"Then you must trust his judgment, as well. He must've seen qualities in you that you don't let yourself see, Mister August."

"I pray that you are correct."

"Now, how many times have you known me to be *wrong?*"

Micholson smiled again. "Still, I can't help but wish that Paul could be here, even given the...rupture between us. How is it possible, to so detest a man and his actions, yet love him and yearn for him at the same time? One cannot make bricks to build a pyramid without both mud and straw. He was the straw to my mud. We were always thrice more effective as a team than either of us alone could be. I cannot help but think—and the thought makes me suffer the agonies of the damned—if Paul and I could have stood indivisible on the command deck of the *Northport* the morning the *Virginia* attacked, together we would have conjured a way to beat the rebel."

Nehemiah slowly shook his gray head. "You don't need him, Mister August. You never did. I never approved of that lad as your friend, you know."

"I know. Many, many were the times you attempted to discourage me from pursuing him as a companion. But I proved stubborn as a young bull."

"I understood that stubbornness, Mister August, surely I did. That's why I never complained about Paul and his ways to your parents. You were trying to fill a void in your soul. A bottomless hole that opened up when your brother Nicholas died of the pox, and you managed to survive him. And I knew there weren't many boys your own age within ten miles of our farm for you to befriend. The only worse choice you could've made than Paul Legarde would have been that crippled boy from Adderwood—"

"Joseph Babbage? The one with the withered arm?"

"Yes, him. Thankfully, his pride prevented him from accepting friendship with a neighbor from such humble circumstances as you. That, and...and..."

"And what? Nehemiah, suddenly you don't look well."

"Ahh, it's nothin'. Just an old, evil memory. Bad as gettin' involved with that Joseph Babbage and his...minder would've been for you, I can't help but feel terribly sorry for that boy. I could never tell if he'd been born bad, or if he'd been *made* that way. You're fortunate, Mister August, to have only loving memories of your brother, few an' dim as those memories are. I could never begrudge you your efforts to replace Nicholas, even with so faulty a vessel as Paul Legarde."

"You never told me *why* you disapproved of Paul. Although recent events have proved you had justification."

"That Legarde boy...he reminded me a little too much of another man, a man I knew well. A kinsman."

Micholson raised an eyebrow. "In all our years together, you've never spoken of your family. Is this family you had in Africa, or a family you founded in the years before my father purchased you?"

Nehemiah did not reply. *Never spoken of your family,* Micholson thought, *and it appears you never will.* After a moment, the servant continued the conversation as though Micholson had never voiced his question. "From the first I listened to that Legarde boy boast and brag to you, I knew he cloaked a weak regard for himself with false conceit."

"He was outgoing, boisterous, that was all. Given my shyness, I admired him for that."

"He was jealous of you. Of your intelligence and good sense. That's why he always tried to drown out your voice with his. How do you think he must've felt when, having joined the Navy together with him, at the same lowly rank, you were continuously promoted over his head?"

Micholson frowned. "You're wrong. He always expressed pride in my accomplishments. I told you, we were a team. He was my right arm, and I was his legs."

"Even now, you defend him! Then tell me, if you truly were so close to've been like parts of the same body, how could he have betrayed you so cruelly?"

Micholson turned away. "He and Elizabeth...they were always fond of each other, from the very day the three of us first met. Many times, I expected that, faced with a choice, she would marry Paul, not me."

"But she chose *you*. She exchanged vows with *you*, not him. A true friend, whatever the power of his 'fondness' for the wife of his friend, would have found the strength to respect those vows, not defile them."

"Elizabeth...came to hate the Navy. You spoke of jealousy before. If that emotion played any role in this affair, it was my wife's jealousy of the demands my profession makes of me. Particularly during those distressful months of her hard pregnancy with our little David, she hated the fact that I was away, showing the flag on the far side of the world. Matters only grew worse when I took command of the *Northport*. I think...I think she fell into Paul's arms as a way of striking back at me, of warning me our union was in dire peril."

"If she sought a replacement mate, she surely chose poorly. She would've faced the same hardships with Legarde as she did with you. He offered no advantage. They both set out to hurt you. They both made that choice, and so they must bear responsibility for all the consequences that come of that choice. *All* the consequences, Mister August, captain of the *James B. Eads.*"

"What do you mean?"

"I mean you need to stop blamin' yourself for Legarde's death."

"I was his captain—"

"Yes, you were his captain, and captain of a hundred and fifty other sailors, besides. But a captain does not control Fate. A captain cannot even control the winds which fill his sails. The day of the iron ship's attack, you were not the God of Abraham the Patriarch. You were not even a spirit of the waters or a spirit of the fires. You were a man, only a man. You told me Flag Officer Foote accepted as valid your reasoning' for your actions that day. Why do you yourself not accept this?"

Micholson could provide no answer.

"You said to me that you doubt your ability to be captain of this gunboat. I say that all which holds you back from being leader of these men is the guilt you *insist* on carryin'. Let it go! Drop it from your shoulders! You did not kill Paul Legarde! You did not slay a hundred of your own men in your quest to kill the man who stole knowledge of your wife! Guilt...guilt is harsher than lye, Mister August. I *know* guilt. It eats one from the inside, startin' from the liver and the holders of bile, then workin' its way to the outer organs like a host of maggots.

"When you next speak to the men, show them the August Micholson who *I* know! Show them a brave man, a wise man, a compassionate man. Show them a man unhobbled by guilt. The rivers we will follow will lead us to a great evil. An evil beyond any posed by a fleet of iron ships. The men and their captain must act as the fingers of one hand. Show them the August Micholson *I* know, and all will go well for you. This I can promise you."

"How? Are you a conjurer? Can you mystically cleanse men's minds of libels they have read in *Harper's Weekly*?"

Nehemiah merely smiled. He stood and walked to the desk. Then he leaned down and kissed Micholson's forehead. "You are stronger than you know, son of my heart. Meditate on what I have told you, and your lips will find the words you need to say."

CHAPTER EIGHT

Slow Evil

Adderwood Plantation, Mississippi, April 17, 1862

Nothing!

Babbage felt he would scream. All the months of planning, the tens of thousands of dollars spent...He tried not to think of it, knowing it would only make the pounding in his head and the ache in his shriveled arm worse, but still the waste—the *humiliation!*—tormented him.

And now, to make matters on this dreadful day even worse, his insufferable cousin, that preening popinjay who commanded the ironclad squadron taking form on the Yazoo's opposite shore, had insisted that he visit him at that hellhole of a boatyard. Unable to decline the invitation of so senior an officer, Babbage had been forced to arrange to be ferried across the river. He clutched the cutter's gunwale with such vicious strength he was amazed it did not shatter into splinters.

Three days—! He had endured three whole days of staring at those damnable canvas screens as though he were nothing more than a servant on his own plantation. Three whole days of agonizing, gnawing curiosity. Oh, but there had been no lack of hints as to what darkness transpired behind the screens. For three days and three even worse nights his ears had been assaulted by the hideous cries of misshapen beasts prodded into a bonfire. His eyes and nose had been savaged by the fires' unending, nauseating smokes.

And what had three excruciating days and nights of this mumbo-jumbo produced? *Nothing!* Where was the power

83

he'd been promised? The only change Babbage had seen was a decidedly negative one—the newfound willingness of many of his slaves to flee Adderwood. He had found it necessary to strip his workforce of many of its white overseers, sending them into the woods to search for the runaways. If only Daniel would explain! Babbage respected the old man; he would listen to any and all explanations. But the withered old witch doctor refused to pay his master any heed.

The western shore did not seem to be any closer than it did a moment ago. "Damn it, man, can't you row any faster? The faster we reach shore, the faster I see my cousin and get whatever infernal balderdash he has in mind over and done with!"

"I be rowing as best I can, master." Sweat poured down Thomas's face, despite the cool spring air. "There's a bad wind whippin' up. The current's gone fierce—"

"Damn your excuses! Put your back into it, or I'll pitch you overboard and take the oars myself!"

At last they reached the far shore. The entrance to the inlet which held the boatyard was hidden to all but the most observant eye. In its natural state about seventy feet wide, the cut was now obscured by a long barge, which had been covered with earth and vines and willow trees, making it seem an extension of the muddy banks which surrounded it. Babbage had often watched from his levee the soldiers open this camouflaged trapdoor; a system of steam winches, chains, and pulleys swung the barge inward on a hinge, allowing supply vessels to enter or exit the inlet. Were this contrivance the product of any man's cleverness but his cousin's, he would allow himself to admire it.

He waved at the tops of the transplanted trees. "Ho! You at the winch up there! We have business with Commander Stoddard! Let our boat pass."

A voice, its owner hidden by the unnatural trees, called back to him. "I ain't gonna pull this here thing open for no rowboat. Have your darkie pull the boat across the top o' the barge."

Babbage felt blood rush to his head. "We have very important business with your commander! Open this device at once!"

"You come up here and make me, you one-armed goon!"

"Damn your eyes! The *insolence—*"

"Master." Thomas tugged on his good arm. "Master, I'll do like he says, or I thinks we may never get in there."

Thomas, despite the limitations of his feeble brain, was right, Babbage told himself. Cousin Louis could very well be standing behind the trees, watching the little scene, waiting for the plantation owner to rant and make a jack-assed fool of himself. He would not give his cousin the pleasure. He gestured for Thomas to drag the boat across the barge, and be quick about it.

"Very well," he shouted at the trees. "I'll have my man move my boat. But be assured, I'll be speaking with your commander about this incident." There was no response from the treetops, other than a low chuckle.

The far side of the barge overlooked an impressive vista. What had once been a marshy bayou, clogged with cypress trees, had been transformed into a sizable harbor. Its deep-water status was ensured by a high, semi-circular levee, which held in the green waters like a bowl. The boatyard stretched along the inner rim of the harbor. Babbage counted five vessels under construction, three already afloat and two still in dry dock. He directed Thomas to steer for the vessel furthest to the left, the one closest to completion, which Babbage assumed would be his cousin's flagboat. It was a slab-sided, menacing man-of-war, its armored gunbox rising fifteen feet from a low deck. Several puffs of black smoke rose from its smokestack, indicating its engines were already in working order. What looked to be the arm of a giant mantis poked into the vessel. As they rowed closer, Babbage could see this was a huge derrick which slowly lowered black cannons through the ironclad's open roof. *How delighted my cousin must be,* he thought; *he feels his manhood grow with each new cannon.*

He directed Thomas to tie the boat to the pier next to the ironclad. The commander of a nearby squadron of soldiers eyed the pair warily, but they were not accosted as they climbed onto the ironclad's low deck and stepped through an open gunport. They found Commander Stoddard inside the casemate, directing the placement of the heavy cannons onto their carriages.

"Cousin Joseph!" he said. "How wonderful to see you! I'm so pleased you received my invitation." Louis Stoddard was everything Babbage was not: tall, handsome, and confident to a fault. The brass buttons on his gray naval uniform shone as brightly as his cunning eyes. His double breasted overcoat, with its jaunty cape, fit his torso as if it were specially tailored (as it most likely had been). "Welcome aboard the CSS *Arkansas*! She will be the flagboat of the squadron, a name to be feared throughout the North. What do you think of these cannon, eh?" He patted one of the long, black weapons on its breach. "Beauties, aren't they? Armstrong hundred-pounder rifles, straight from the foundry in England. Breach-loaders! These'll put those antiquated smoothbores aboard Foote's coal scows to shame, you'll see. They won't have the rivers all to themselves anymore."

"How wonderful for you, cousin," Babbage replied, quietly.

"So how are things across the river at old Adderwood? I hear you've been having the devil's own time with runaways, lately. Could you use an assist from some of my men? Running down a few stray darkies would be good exercise."

Thomas shivered. Babbage frowned. "No, thank you, cousin. We have matters in hand. Now, please tell me why you sent for me. I hope I haven't rowed across the Yazoo merely to hear you cackle about my runaway slaves."

Stoddard's eyes widened in mock surprise. "Cousin! You wound me! Why the poisonous tongue? Am I not the only family you have left in this world?" He stepped forward to embrace the smaller man, but Babbage flinched away. "Very well. I see that words are not enough to prove my sincere affection. Little cousin, I am about to offer you a privilege that few men in the Confederacy will ever know, but most will jealously covet. Step over here with me." Babbage followed Stoddard to an open gunport. The commander pointed through the aperture to another vessel, moored about fifty yards away, in as nearly a completed condition as the *Arkansas* herself. "That, Joseph, is the *Vicksburg*. She should have all her equipment and armor in place within a week or so. She is somewhat smaller than my *Arkansas*, and will carry six guns, rather than ten, but she is still a very formidable ironclad. She is yours, if you want her. I have the power to make you her captain."

Babbage was momentarily speechless. This was not what he had expected at all. "Why—why would you offer me one of your ironclads? I know nothing about ships, or the Navy—"

"Tut, tut, there's nothing to it. It's much easier than running a plantation. Three weeks under my tutelage and I'll have you running her like you were born to the water. Nowadays, in any case, it's the engineers and gunners who do the hard work. The captain is mostly window-dressing."

"But Louis, I already have a commission. I'm a colonel in the Army—"

"Of course you are. But where is your regiment? Why haven't you raised a body of men? Personally, cousin, I don't think you're cut out for the Army." Babbage winced as Stoddard lolled his tongue around the syllable *arm*. "You sit in that grand old house of yours all day and mope. What kind of an existence is that, especially in such days as these? A new nation is being born, cousin! A new nation!" Babbage looked unconvinced. "Really, I must get you out of that house. Tell me, in all honesty—don't you like her?"

he asked, pointing again through the gunport. "If you don't care for the name *Vicksburg*, call her whatever you wish. Name her the CSS *Adderwood*, if you like."

Babbage stared out at the nearly completed ironclad. She was shaping up to be a handsome vessel, with balanced proportions and a nicely sloped casemate; prettier than the *Arkansas*. His gambit with Old Daniel was seemingly a fiasco. He wanted to make a difference in this war, wanted a piece of that glory, before the war was over and all the glory gone.

"If I were to become her captain, would she be truly mine?"

Stoddard draped his arm around his cousin's hunched shoulders. "Of course. You would be her captain, her master."

"So I would have full independence of action? I could take her on any mission I choose?"

Stoddard frowned. "Let's not get ahead of ourselves, Joseph. Your vessel would be part of my squadron, so of course you would be under my command—"

Babbage stiffened. His cousin's arm felt like a lead weight. *Of course*, he thought. *How like him. Imagine the indignities he could pile on me as my commanding officer...He invites me into Hell's foyer, and like the fool I am, I nearly leaped through the door!*

"Damn you and your foul ironclads!" he said, wiggling free of Stoddard's arm. "You would dearly love it, wouldn't you, having me on your leash, always under your thumb? Don't you think I recognized how you directed that idiot sentry at the barge to humiliate me?"

"Joseph, what are you babbling about? Get yourself under control, man—"

"Stay away from me, Louis! I'm my *own* man, you hear me? The master of Adderwood! And you, with your shining uniform and fleet of ironclads—you're *nothing! I'll* be the man to win this war. What I have planned...it is so far beyond the grasp of your puny mind...you and your rams will matter as little as a boy in a bathtub, playing with his toy boats..."

All traces of a smile had fled from Stoddard's face. "Get off my ship, you lunatic. Before I have you pitched overboard."

"Daniel! Daniel!! Where are you, old man? Show yourself, damn you!"

Babbage was so furious he could barely breathe. The old man had not been out in the field with his pile of earth and his bonfires. Could he have run off, too? No; somehow Babbage could faintly sense his presence. He was somewhere in the main house. Babbage stormed from room to elaborately furnished room, his shriveled arm flailing with a life of its own, scattering the servants, who superstitiously feared its touch. *Where can the old charlatan be hiding?* Had he dared to desecrate the rooms of the third floor? The Mother Babbage's suite of rooms (*blessed be her memory*)?

He had. M'Lundowi was not hiding. He sat in plain sight, legs crossed, in the middle of Mother Babbage's four-poster bed. Covering his lap was the severed head of a gigantic boar. The quilts on which his mother and grandmother had lavished hundreds of hours were now caked with gore. The old man tightly clutched the skull's great tusks, his fingers convulsing in time with an internal rhythm. His unblinking eyes had turned entirely back into his head.

Babbage howled like a rabid dog. *He* dares *defile Mother's blessed bed—?* He leaped at the old man, ready to tear out his throat with his one good hand.

M'Lundowi's throat was like an iron pipe. Half of Babbage's fury evaporated with the unnatural sensation of unyielding, stone flesh. He franticly searched for a weapon, any weapon to force this abomination from his mother's bed. *What? Where?* His horse whip was down in the stables. His guns were in a locked cabinet at the lodge, a quarter mile distant. Then he remembered. His father's cane. It was mounted on the wall in the next bedroom.

He swung the heavy wooden cane viciously at the old man's back. "Get *out!*" The cane rebounded as if struck against a marble pillar. "How dare—how *dare* you defile my mother's bed!" He swung again, this time at M'Lundowi's unmoving head. "You lowly piece of *filth!*" The cane rebounded more sharply than before, sending violent shocks up Babbage's arm and shoulder. "I spent half my fortune fetching your damned dirt from Africa—I believed your promises—you lied to me, damn you!"

Babbage slumped onto the edge of the bed. The old man's head had not turned so much as an inch in his direction. "Speak to me! Tell me why nothing has happened. I'll listen. I've always listened to you, you know that. Just tell me how much longer I have to wait before the power is mine."

Still there was no answer. "Where is the power? Don't ignore me, Daniel. I'm warning you. Speak to me, damn you!" He swung his father's cane a final time, a furious but futile blow to the old man's face.

The solid oak staff shattered into splinters. At last the sightless white orbs turned slowly in his direction. And Joseph Babbage experienced an emotion he had hoped never to remember, one locked tightly away since the death of his father: the lonely terror of a little boy abandoned.

* * *

On the outskirts of Satartia, Mississippi, a town of three hundred souls on the shore of the Yazoo, a great cat prowled. Liquid fire raced through its powerful black limbs.

Aboard the excursion steamer *Germania*, docked alongside Satartia's single pier, Camilla Schoenberg, all alone on the moonlit decks, was not feeling at all herself. She caressed the tin face of a clockwork child, lovingly fashioned by her husband's hands. Its glass eyes stared into space. Why should she complain of childlessness, her spouse often asked, when he could make her such children as these?

She sat in one of the leather smoking chairs lining the walls of the dining cabin and listened to the quiet that prevailed aboard her husband's empty excursion steamer. Normally the deck's rocking, caused tonight by strong gusts which had blown in from the north, would be a comfort to her. But not this evening. Not this strange evening, when a cool, humid Yazoo River dusk had been infiltrated by warm, dry winds. Desert winds.

What was it? What was wrong with her? She ran her fingertips up and down her smooth white arms, young arms that had only known an old man's caresses. Her limbs burned with a strange fever. At home, in her kitchen, she had placed a medical thermometer beneath her tongue. It had read one hundred and two degrees. She should be in bed, allowing Johann to care for her; she should be trembling beneath layers of heavy blankets, waiting for the doctor to arrive. Yet she trembled not. Her sole sensation was a disturbing restlessness, like she was a dry leaf shaking at the end of a withered twig; a leaf waiting for a sudden hot gust to send her flittering towards freedoms unimagined.

Why had she crept out of her house and come here, to this dark, empty riverboat? She stared at the clusters of clockwork figures which stood motionless around the dining hall, bathed in the moonlight streaming through grand crystal windows. Had she come for their company? The *oompah-pah* band, dressed in *lederhosen* and vests of green velvet, hovered over their brass instruments, ready to pantomime the making of music. The dancers, tin arms raised above their heads, waited to begin their curious folk dances. Clockwork waiters stood with silver trays, endlessly patient, ready to serve the crowded tables of paying guests who would double, then quadruple Johann's fortune, someday when the war would be over and the gentry could devote themselves to pleasure once more.

Camilla knew what they all waited for. *Steam.* Steam was their lifeblood, their breath. Their soul. She could fire up the boilers on the lower deck. She knew how; she had watched Johann enough times. But the steamboat's coal bunkers were empty. The local Navy commander had confiscated every spare lump, just as the local army commander had stripped Satartia bare of able-bodied young men. Camilla was one of the few young women of the village to still have a husband at home; he had been too old to march off to battle.

She disembarked from the *Germania.* The warm, dry winds whipped the light cotton fabric of her summer house dress around her bare ankles. Somewhere in the back of her mind, a shrill voice scolded her for having left her home in such a state of undress, like some half-tamed Negress. She ignored the voice. In normal times, the streets of Satartia would be filled with men at this hour: men heading home from their shops, men returning from the woods with game, men stumbling from tavern to tavern. But now the lantern-lit streets were empty, save for the occasional whimpering dog. Camilla, not quite herself, was quite alone.

No, not alone. A door shut quietly. Mary Bellerophon descended from her porch, an open parasol in her small hand. A gust quickly rent the fragile device inside-out, and she offered the broken sunshade to the wind. It skittered through the streets of Satartia, like a skeletal ghost fleeing its own shadow. Mary was the oldest daughter of a proper, moneyed family. She had always looked down upon Camilla, daughter of poor farmers, an uneducated girl who traded her youthful voluptuousness for an elderly immigrant's wealth. Camilla walked slowly, languorously, toward the other young woman. All her slights, all her haughty scorn, none of that mattered now. They pulsed with the same heat.

A low, dark figure emerged from behind a parked carriage. It approached the women with the smooth speed of black mercury. The great cat wound its way sinuously around Camilla's skirts, caressing her hips with the sides of its fierce face, growling with barely contained hunger. Camilla trembled slightly as the guttural thrumming, intensely tactile, quivered her spine. The sensation was delicious. She and Mary fondled the cat's ears. They ran their hands along its warm, supple coat, sensing the raging heat just beneath its skin.

The trio walked together down the narrow main street of Satartia, the panther rubbing against their slowly moving legs. Doors opened as they passed. Other women joined them.

They stopped beneath a large swaying lantern, hanging precariously from a post in front of the Baptist church. Camilla watched the flickering flames. They danced with such joy, such abandon. She stared into the flames, and the flames stared into her, and she knew then what they all must do.

CHAPTER NINE

The Federals' Opening Gambit

*Plum Point Bend on the Mississippi River,
north of Memphis, Tennessee, April 18–19, 1862*

It all begins tonight, this very hour, this moment.

Micholson walked onto the gundeck. One hundred and twenty sailors, the two-thirds of the crew who were to accompany him on the night march along the Missouri shore, had gathered with packs and rifles between the massive black cannons to hear their orders. Staring into their varied faces, some creased with decades of hard living, others barely sprouting a first growth of beard, Micholson recalled the last time he had addressed such a body of men, on the gundeck of the *Northport,* the morning of March 8, 1862. The morning the *Virginia* had emerged from the Elizabeth River. That morning, the faces staring up at him had been trusting, friendly, eager for the coming battle; Micholson had cultivated a warm relationship with the men of the *Northport.* These faces were harder to read. Some were puckered with barely concealed contempt. Others were marked with uneasy expectancy. Many appeared stoic, their features hard and unmoving.

"Men, we are called upon to perform an extraordinary duty this evening. We are told to temporarily lay aside our accustomed roles as seamen of the United States Navy, to take on the raiment of the enemy, and to raise the enemy's flag above our own vessel, all this so as to confound that enemy. I understand that to sail under the rebel flag, to wear a Confederate uniform, even for purpose of deception, is repulsive to many of you. I ask you, not merely as your commanding officer, but as a fellow citizen of these United States, to willingly and cheerfully make this sacrifice. Should we succeed in our mission, as I believe we have an excellent chance of doing, we will destroy a great portion of the rebels' offensive and defensive power on the Mississippi. We will protect women and children from terror and death in such places as Cincinnati, St. Louis, and Pittsburgh. We will shorten this terrible war between brothers—by how much, I cannot say. But its end will be hastened by our valiant actions these next few days.

"As for me, I ask for your forbearance and patience. Do not rush to judge me by stories you have read in the newspapers or rumors you may have heard. I am a stranger to all of you. Allow me the same fairness you would any stranger in your midst. I know that many of you would have preferred a captain from the existing pool of gunboat commanders, fine officers who proved their bravery at Forts Henry and Donelson. I also know that all of you have the utmost respect and affection for Flag Officer Foote. This distinguished and courageous gentleman, utilizing his best judgment, selected me to lead you. Know this: I understand the anguish this war causes each of you, because I share that anguish. Like most of you, I am a Southerner by birth, and I am torn between loyalties to my family, my State, and my Nation. Like all of you, I heeded the call of Nation and Navy, but not without personal sacrifice. So, like all of you, I have not merely the duty, but the unyielding desire, the invincible conviction to bring this awful conflict to its swiftest and most just resolution. And men, we are greatly blessed by God Almighty to have been given such a role in ending this war."

He looked out at the sea of faces. Had his words achieved any impact? Some of the younger men appeared newly heartened, inspired, perhaps, because they desperately wanted and needed to be inspired. *They need to believe in their commander,* he thought. *The alternative is far too terrifying.* At least a few of the old tars seemed to have progressed from outright hostility to a wary, wait-and-see stance.

"In closing, let me assure you that at no time will I order any man who serves aboard this gunboat to confront any risks or dangers which I would not personally take upon myself. I will lead you on this evening's march. I will stand exposed upon the hurricane deck, wearing rebel raiment as my only shield, when we pass beneath the guns of Fort Pillow. I will utilize every art of subterfuge, at whatever cost to my personal honor, to uncover the location of the Confederate boatyard, and I will guide this vessel and its valiant crew through gauntlets of torpedoes and shore batteries, if necessary, to come to grips with the rebel ironclads now a' building. I will trust in God and His Providence to grant us victory, and I will trust in my crew to serve as the instruments of that victory, as I pray you will trust in me.

"Now, with the arrival of twilight, we play our opening gambit. Load up your gear, men. Then brace yourselves firmly, for, thanks to the ingenuity of your gunnery captain and the excellent skills of our pilot, we will soon put on a memorable show for the men of Tennessee."

Inside the gunboat's pilothouse, Micholson gave the order for the submerged device to be detonated.

The underwater explosion hurled a geyser twenty feet into the dusk air and showered the *Eads*'s upperworks with wooden shards. The sound, although muffled by five feet of muddy river water, reverberated from the eastern tree line, a quarter mile distant. Sailors who failed to heed warnings to secure themselves were hurled to the deck by the shock.

"That was an excellent 'torpedo' explosion you arranged, Mr. Broadhurst," Micholson said. He scanned the distant Tennessee shore with his retractable spyglass for signs of Confederate observers. "I thought the addition of the 'hull shards' was an especially fine touch. The flying wood may not have been noticed by our friends in Tennessee, but the submerged wooden wall your bomb demolished undoubtedly helped protect our own hull."

"Thank you, sir," the captain of the guns replied. "This wasn't a situation mentioned in our tactics manuals, so I had to be creative." Lawrence Broadhurst and Valery Delaup, the head pilot, shared the tight confines of the armored pilothouse with their commander. The octagon-shaped space seemed especially crowded with Broadhurst, a naval Paul Bunyan, present. Micholson had quickly begun to like the affable giant.

"I think this mission will demand much original thinking from all of us," Micholson said. "Mr. Delaup, take us in toward the Missouri shore, at the best speed our boilers will muster. Sound those alarm bells while you're at it. Let's make this look like we've been shot through the heart."

Delaup spun the wheel to the right. "Fire up those boilers, Oates! Top speed!" he barked through the speaking tube. His insouciant grin showed he enjoyed being in a position to shout curt orders at the chief engineer. "I'll give us a little waggle heading in to shore, *m'sieur.* Make it look like we're takin' on water like we're a big bucket!"

The alarm bells clanged across the rippling waters. A trio of powerful men struggled in the chain locker to retract the anchor from the muddy river bottom. Then the gunboat shuddered as her great wheels began turning, slowly pushing her massive bulk toward the tall reeds of the Missouri shore. The gunboat's speed gradually increased as deep black smoke belched from her twin stacks. Thirty yards from the marshy shore, Delaup called for engine power to be cut to one quarter. The gunboat's forward momentum carried her through banks of high cattails, until her broad prow forcefully embedded itself in the thick mud.

"Good work, Mr. Delaup. Go gather your things for the march. I'll see you below." Micholson waited until Delaup had climbed down the ladder to the gundeck, then stepped onto the top rung himself. He reached out to shake

Broadhurst's giant hand. "Thank you again, Mr. Broadhurst. I know that underwater work of yours couldn't have been pleasant at this time of year, even with a diving suit on. Take good care of the *Eads* while I'm gone."

Broadhurst flashed a confident smile. "Mr. Rutherford and I will have things well in hand. Good luck, sir."

Delaup handed Micholson a heavy burlap pack and helped his commander strap it on. Inside were the grey uniform and personal effects of a Confederate naval commander. A gunnery crew pulled the eight-inch smoothbore cannon and the two forty-two pounder rifles away from the three forward gunports so the departing men could exit through them onto the narrow outer deck. Other sailors lowered planks from the tip of the bow to the mud flats. Even with these aids, Micholson ruefully noted, they would have to wade through a good stretch of mud and water before reaching solid ground.

Signaling for the men to follow him, he stepped out onto the outer deck. His breath turned to mist in the fading glimmers of dusk. A river swim would do his fever no good, but such were the hardships of war. He led his men into the marsh, holding his twin Colt pistols above his head. He felt his boots sink deeply into the thick mud. The cold water, quickened by the melting snows of Illinois and Iowa, soaked his uniform to his waist. Shivering, he looked forward to the brisk march. Some of the men, perhaps hoping their voices would reach the Tennessee shore, took up a spirited rendition of "John Brown's Body."

On dry ground, the men formed two columns, one behind Micholson, the other behind Delaup. The moon had yet to rise, so their footing was treacherous. The columns were forced to snake around endless spectral willow trees and live oaks. They roughly paralleled the river, marching north, and hoped watching eyes on the eastern shore would assume they were seeking assistance for their stricken ironclad.

"That was a fine and dandy speech you gave back there, *m'sieur*," Delaup said. "You spoke words that needed to be said. It has helped, trust me."

"I'm glad you think so. It'll be a while before I can accurately gauge the reactions of this crew." A sliver of moon rose above the Tennessee tree line. "How are you bearing up under this damp cold? I imagine it must be a considerable change from what you're used to, down in Louisiana."

"Yes, there are few nights like this in *ma belle Louisianne*, even fewer in *Nouveau Orleáns*, where I used to hang my hat. But as a boy, I spent many a frosty season in Provence, visiting cousins and such. And as captain of my own steamboat, I traversed the whole Mississippi, from Minnesota to the Head of Passes—any time of year, too, so long as there weren't no ice on the river. How about you, captain? Mississippi tain't in the Arctic regions, neither, last time I checked."

Micholson smiled. "No, but the open Atlantic can get plenty cold in January. I'll be fine."

They came upon a wagon path, and the march became much easier. It was a clear night, with many familiar constellations visible. The stars made Micholson think of old voyages, old ships, friends and family long unseen. "Mr. Delaup, do you have family in New Orleans?"

"Not much to speak of, really. My father and my uncle."

"No wife?"

Delaup chuckled. "No wife, no. Lady friends, yes. Many who would like to claim me as husband, would they ever get me and a priest in the same room."

"Do you worry about your father and uncle, down there in New Orleans?"

Delaup was quiet for a few seconds. "I can't say I pay it much mind, no."

Micholson debated whether to tell him what he knew. Would it only cause the pilot needless mental anguish? Finally, he decided Delaup had a right to know. "Farragut is at Ship Island with nearly twenty men-o'-war, waiting for the right time to force his way past the river forts. Assuming he makes it past the forts, he may be forced to bombard New Orleans, if the city won't surrender. When this mission is over, I wouldn't begrudge you some leave time, if you want to try to make it down there and retrieve your relations, or at least warn them."

"Thank you, captain. That's generous of you, but it's not needed. My father and my uncle, they are both smart men. They knew what might be ahead when they supported this rebellion. They saw profit in it. So whatever comes, it comes."

Micholson declined to probe further. He thought of Elizabeth in Petersburg, and McClellan's army at Fortress Monroe, waiting to march up the Virginia Peninsula towards Richmond. But he quickly pushed the thought from his mind. Instead, he concentrated on the chances of fooling the gunners at Fort Pillow, just a few river miles south. Would they believe the evidence of their eyes—the Stars and Bars flying from the *Eads*'s flagstaff?

For now, his priority was finding a secluded space where he and his men could change uniforms. They needed to move away from the wagon path. Micholson pointed to a thick grove of trees standing on the slope of the bluff above them. "How does that spot look to you, Mr. Delaup?"

"Looks fine, *m'sieur.* I haven't seen a fire or any movement on the other shore for quite a while now."

The men climbed the rise to the sheltering grove of oaks. Micholson slipped his pack from his shoulders and opened it. He stared at the grey frock coat and overcoat, the lettering on their brass buttons barely readable by the faint moonlight: C.S.N. Apart from their color, these coats were cut from the same pattern as his own—the traditional Navy coats, worn at least as far back as the War of 1812. The only noticeable difference in pattern was the designation of rank: two gold stripes at the shoulder and the cuff for a commander. He had never worn any uniform but the blue uniform of the United States Navy. Indeed, he had sacrificed nearly all that was personal and dear in his life for that privilege. Now his duty commanded him to take up his foe's colors, even as duty had called on him a year ago—yes, it had already been a year since the firing on Sumter!—to remain with the color blue.

Micholson pulled the new coats on. A bit long in the sleeves, but the shoulders fit well. Best of all, they were dry and warm. Micholson pulled off his wet boots. A fresh, crisp set of wool trousers would feel wonderful, fresh socks even better. The gray cap, emblazoned with oak clusters, anchor, and twin stars, sat uneasily on his head.

Delaup was already newly dressed, parading around like a French king adoring his reflection in the Hall of Mirrors at Versailles. "I am rather handsome in this new uniform, wouldn't you say, captain?"

"I think you are taking far too much pleasure in this transformation, Mr. Delaup." Micholson watched the other men putting on the alien uniforms, some with obvious disdain. "Doesn't your old uniform mean anything to you?"

Delaup sat himself down next to Micholson. "Ah, captain, that is the difference between us. For you, the blue uniform, she is a wife, a great love. For me, she is merely a servant girl, a means to an end. I would cheerfully wear any uniform that allows me to pilot a good boat up and down this river. You Federals looked as though you'd have the better river Navy, so I happily signed up. My only patriotism is to the flowing nation of Ohio, Missouri, Mississippi, and Yazoo!"

"I wouldn't trumpet those sentiments too loudly. Some of the men may begin to wonder whose side you're on."

"Oh, not these men, captain. These are *ma frères*. They shoot the men who would shoot me, and I steer the boat away from snags that would sink and drown us. A fine exchange, no? Indeed, if there must be war, this is my kind of war. Why march up the hill straight into the enemy's guns? Far better to put on his uniform and pretend you are his fine and good compatriot, then sneak around when he isn't looking and give him a big—"

A muzzle flash pierced the darkness, followed by the echoing sound of a discharge. Micholson felt the air above his head distend; an iron ball buried itself in the tree trunk no more than a foot above his scalp. Another shot rang out, followed by the agonized cry of one of the young gunnery mates in Delaup's division. Rebel yells sounded from the forest around them.

Micholson grabbed his twin Colts from his bag. "Return fire, men! Aim at their muzzle flashes!" The near-miss had come from up high. He heard a rustling of branches. He aimed his pistol where he thought the sound came from and fired. Then he quickly rolled to another position before the sniper could target his flash.

Delaup crawled over to him. "Damnation! I thought there weren't no rebel units in this area—"

"There aren't," Micholson whispered. "At least not to our best knowledge. These men are most likely irregulars. Local militia."

"Maybe so. But they're shootin' as good as the real thing!"

Shots continued to thunk into tree trunks or thud into the earth. A sailor screamed as a ball tore into his shoulder. Return fire was confused and hesitant. Micholson could see from the enemy's muzzle flashes that he and his men were at least partially surrounded.

"Delaup," he whispered. "Organize your division into a firing line. Have them aim due west, away from the river. Half should fire at the trees, the other half straight ahead. After their first volley, have them pivot ninety degrees to the north and repeat. I'll do the same with my division, only starting to the east and pivoting south. Prime your men to fire when mine do."

"I'll do that. We'll clean them out, yessir!" Delaup crawled off toward his men, moving as fast as a scalded sidewinder.

Micholson reached a small group of sailors cowering at the base of a giant oak. Three of the five were still partially undressed. He recognized one of them.

"Johnson!" he whispered. "Where is your rifle?"

The sailor frantically pawed at the ground. "Here, sir! Under my old coat."

"Good. Load quickly and aim at the trees in the direction of the river. Fire on my command, then pivot ninety degrees to the right, reload, and fire again at the tree line when I command it. You others, do the same. Keep your heads down, or you'll lose them."

He crawled from group to group, repeating his instructions. When he located petty officers, he ordered them to fan out and repeat the plan. Creeping on his belly, he prayed that the bullets which occasionally creased the air around his ears would have the good sense to keep their distance—he had an appointment to keep on the Yazoo. At last the frantic whispering around him ceased, and he guessed all the men now knew what to do. He gave the order.

"Fire!"

The guns of his division barked out in jagged unison, followed quickly by the massed rifles of Delaup's men, exploding in the opposite direction. It was a good sound, a back-stiffening sound. Micholson could tell from the agonized shrieks in the high branches and dull thuds of bodies hitting the earth that at least some of their blind bullets had found their marks. The volley had given his men back their confidence. He could hear them rapidly reloading, their panic banished by the sounds of their own massed rifles.

"Turn!" he ordered. A hundred and twenty bodies shifted in the sandy soil. "Fire!" Again the rifles spoke, this time in greater unison than before. The sound seemed to split the sky open. Micholson heard more cries of mortally wounded men, then the sounds of survivors leaping from the branches and fleeing deeper into the woods. The cheers of the victorious sailors followed them like pursuing furies. *We cannot allow them to escape,* Micholson realized. *Having seen what they have, even a single one of them can destroy any chances.* Reluctantly, he shouted his next two orders: "Fix bayonets! General pursuit!"

His men bounded into the dark woods, chasing any sound. The wounded militiamen were quickly caught and put to a sharp and bloody end. Others, unscathed, and knowing the lay of the land far better than their pursuers, began to outdistance the charging sailors. The woods echoed with ragged rifle shots fired on the run. Those militiamen not caught by a blind bullet gradually disappeared into the dark forest. A handful of dogged sailors continued the chase until they were exhausted. Within twenty minutes, a majority of the men had returned to the clearing where they had been switching uniforms.

Delaup, panting heavily, approached Micholson. "What now, captain? A handful of them rascals got clean away."

"How many wounded do we have?"

"Brier caught a ball in the shoulder, Richardson one in the leg. A couple of others got creased."

"How are they?"

"Brier's the worst off, but he'll make it. Hampton, the surgeon's mate, is patching him up. All the men can walk, I think."

*An unlucky start for the mission...*Micholson quickly pushed the notion from his mind. "Are all the men accounted for?" He peered around the clearing. Some of the sailors had fought in half-Federal, half-Confederate clothing; they were now searching desperately for their knapsacks and a pair of grey trousers that fit.

"According to my count, we've still got a few stragglers in the woods."

"While we're waiting, let's bury what dead we can find."

"Captain? You think we have time for that?"

"There is always time to honor the dead, who were created in the image of our Lord."

"I beg to disagree, *m'sieur.* We got to get back to the boat, hurry up with our 'repairs,' and shove off as soon as we can."

"Mr. Delaup, I fully understand the need for haste. But if we are required by our stragglers to remain a few moments in any case, I refuse to leave those dead out there unburied. I left too many corpses untended in the sunken hulk of the *Northport.*"

The men used their trenching tools to dig a wide, shallow grave. Then they again fanned out into the woods, searching for their opponents a second time. Within fifteen minutes, they dragged back twenty-six bodies and placed them in the pit. Few of the dead wore uniforms of any kind; several were old enough to be fathers of the men who had killed them.

"We done left our preacher back at the boat," Delaup said. "You want to say a few words over them, captain?"

Micholson nodded. One of the men had fashioned a crude cross from a pair of discarded carbines and some rope. The captain plunged it into the shallow mound. "May we soon be reunited as brotherly neighbors in one nation. May the wounds we inflict on each other quickly be forgotten. May God have mercy on their souls. And on ours." He turned away from the dead to face the living. "Let's get back to the *Eads,* men."

By the time the party, slowed by the need to assist the wounded sailors, rounded the last long bend of the river, the moon had begun setting behind the western tree line. Its final, silvery rays revealed the *Eads's* twin smokestacks, rising like a pair of shorn trees from a humpbacked island.

Rutherford, now wearing a grey uniform and British-made cutlass, awaited them on the gundeck. "Welcome back, captain. We expected you several hours ago. Did you run into difficulties? We heard, just barely, sounds of widespread gunfire from upriver—"

"Have the surgeon come forward immediately. There are several wounded men right behind me."

Rutherford sent a gunner's mate aft to fetch the gunboat's surgeon. "How did this happen, sir? Our scouts indicated there weren't supposed to be any rebel troops for miles—"

"These were auxiliaries. Only about a third of our number, but they ambushed us. We managed to kill most of them, after our initial surprise, but at least ten escaped."

Rutherford's eyes widened. "But that could mean..."

"It means our time here is extremely limited. Send three men in the steam launch two miles upstream. Direct them to return immediately—*immediately*—upon sighting any movement of troops in our direction. Have the rest of the men get to work 'patching up' the gunboat. We may not have the luxury of waiting for our scheduled rendezvous with the *Cairo* and the *Mound City*."

"I'll see to it immediately, sir!"

Micholson signaled for Delaup. "Mr. Delaup, come with me. I have an unpleasant errand to attend to, and I need your assistance."

They climbed a ladder to the open hurricane deck, then walked aft to Micholson's cabin, just past the great hump of the paddle-wheel housing. Inside, Micholson went to his chest of drawers and lifted a bundle of white, red, and blue cloth from the bottom drawer. Delaup followed him outside to the flagstaff. Old Glory fluttered fitfully in the cold, damp breeze. The sky above the eastern tree line was just beginning to lighten from a starry onyx to a dull grey. Micholson stared at the flag above him, the emblem of all he had sworn to serve and protect. With hands that felt wooden, he lowered the *Eads*'s ensign.

"That, I believe, was one of the hardest things I've ever done," he said. Delaup grasped the far corners of the flag, and together they folded it into tight triangular sections. "I couldn't order anyone else to do it..."

"At least it wasn't lowered in surrender, *m'sieur*."

"Yes."

"We'll raise it again, *m'sieur*, after those rebel ironclads are on the bottom of the Yazoo. Do you need me for, uh, the other?"

Micholson shook his head. After Delaup departed for the pilothouse, the captain removed the squared bundle of cloth from his coat. He unfurled it, fastened it to the stays, then raised the Stars and Bars.

The morning brought fog. Dense fog that covered the river like a milky shroud. The sounds of hammering rose ethereally through the white blanket.

Micholson opened one of the armored shutters of the pilothouse and peered out over the river. He might as well have peered out the window of a submerged diving bell. He let the shutter fall shut with a clang. "Mr. Delaup, how well do you know this stretch of river?"

"'Bout as well as I know my way around a woman."

"Will you be able to pilot us through this fog?"

"Normally, I wouldn't advise it. I know which way the river goes, but in this soup, I won't be able to spot any snags—floating trees and such that could rip out our bottom. But if the cannonballs start flying and there's one might have my name on it, I'll pilot this boat across the River Styx with my eyes plucked out and half a mind."

"Good. You've instructed Mr. Oates to raise steam?"

"Over a half hour ago. Give him a little more time, and we'll be ready to make a dash downriver, if it comes to that."

Rutherford's head appeared through the hatchway, his eyes wide with alarm. "Captain, the men on the picket boat launched their signal rocket. There must be troops heading our way!"

Micholson grabbed the voice pipe which led to the engine room. "Mr. Oates! We have a probable emergency! Throw everything you have on the fire—soak rags in oil, if you have to. Can we have steam up within five minutes?"

A distant voice, distorted by echoes, crackled from the voice pipe. "Five minutes? Hell and damnation! We'll do the best we can..."

Micholson unbolted the small door that led to the hurricane deck. "Mr. Delaup, stand by the wheel. Be ready to back us off this mud bank, on my order." He kicked the tiny iron door open and crawled through onto the exposed deck. The fog, weblike, clung to everything. He ran aft to the rear edge of the casemate, the direction his scouts would be returning from.

He crouched by the flag post, straining his ears for any sound. Which would he hear first—the sounds of their tiny steam engine, or a volley of rebel cannon? The most prudent course would be to cast off immediately. But that would mean abandoning the steam launch and the three men aboard her. They might be picked up by one of the other gunboats—or they might be picked off by enemy sharpshooters...

He heard it. A rhythmic, approaching thrumming. Were they yet in shouting range? "Hail the launch! This is Captain Micholson! What have you to report?"

The responding voice was barely discernible above the sounds of the *Eads*'s awakening engines. "...large body...troops...mile upriver...*Mound City...Cairo*...coming full speed..."

The other ironclads? They weren't supposed to make contact until mid-day. Unless they had seen the approaching rebel troops—

The still morning was shattered by distant thunder. Three enormous cannons spoke, their great voices reverberating downriver. Those were no rebel fieldpieces. That thunder issued from the heavy guns of a Union ironclad.

"No!" Micholson cried, waiting for the shells to pierce the mist. "The damned fools!"

Firing blindly into the fog, their friends could prove deadlier than enemies!

CHAPTER TEN

The Battle of the Tortoises and the Turtle-Hare

*Plum Point Bend on the Mississippi River,
north of Memphis, Tennessee,
April 19, 1862*

The shells arced invisibly through the fog with the ominous roar of swiftly approaching locomotives. Micholson realized how terribly exposed he was at the edge of the casemate. The first salvo overshot the gunboat, raising three tremendous splashes a hundred yards downriver. Even before the first shells landed, he heard the thunder of a second salvo, fired from the bow battery of the other approaching ironclad. *What can they be thinking? That we are already free of the mud bank, fleeing downriver at top speed? If one of those plunging shots were somehow to strike our boilers—*

The first cannonball pierced the fog. It struck the armored side of the casemate with the force of Thor's hammer, sending a tremendous jolt through the entire vessel. Then it rebounded high into the air, landing in the trees with a hissing crash. Micholson rolled on his back, stunned senseless by the impact.

The other two shells…where are they?

Twin geysers erupted around the steam launch, now only fifty yards from the *Eads.* The impact of the shell splashes ejected the small boat from the water, flipping it over in midair. Micholson shook himself from his stupor.

*The men…*Two heads emerged from the water close to the

capsized launch. Sputtering and spitting, they grasped the sides of the boat, then looked frantically around for their companion.

"Bainbridge! Where's Bainbridge?"

"Oh, God! I don't know—"

A muffled scream emerged from the water thirty feet from the swamped launch. Flailing arms broke the dark surface. Micholson briefly saw the terrified face of the young sailor. "There he is!" he shouted to the men at the launch. "Swim over to him, he's drowning—"

The older, bearded man glanced quickly at his companion, then replied in a voice choked with agony: "But sir, neither of us can swim neither!"

There was no boat-hook long enough to pull the boy in with. Just one slim chance—Micholson took three running steps and dove off the edge of the casemate. The river, fifteen feet below, hit him like a sheet of ice. His body screamed. He swam in what he thought was the boy's direction, but it could be any direction...up, down, north, south, they had no meaning.

He broke the surface. The black bulk of the *Eads* was behind him, the launch several boats' lengths to his left. He couldn't see the boy anywhere. Ten feet to his right, the surface rippled with bubbles. He took a deep breath and dove. The weak sunlight only penetrated two feet into the silty waters. As the pressure pounded in his ears, he grasped as widely as he could, praying for the touch of another hand. *Blind man's bluff.* Nothing. Again he broke the surface, gulped a chest full of air, and dove. This time he felt something—weeds? No. Hair. He grabbed the boy's jacket and struggled for the surface.

The current had assisted him, bringing him half the distance back to the gunboat. The overturned launch had drifted close to the ironclad's low main deck, where a group of sailors stood ready to assist the men in the water. He thanked the river for both boons, for he doubted he could swim very far while keeping the unconscious sailor's head above the surface. The intense cold made it hard for him to move, even to breathe. His heavy boots pulled at his legs with the force of sucking quicksand. Screaming mental orders at his near-deaf muscles, he blessed his mother, who had taught him to swim in the Yazoo before he could even walk. At last powerful hands grasped his shoulders. He and his young charge were pulled onto the slender shelf of deck at the gunboat's stern.

He hoisted himself unsteadily to his feet. "Take...good care of that boy," he said, reassured by the sight of the lad weakly vomiting a goodly portion of the Mississippi.

"Sir? Do you need any help?"

It was a petty officer, a captain of the guns whose name Micholson regretfully couldn't remember. "No, I'll be fine. Just get inside and ready the men at the guns. Half-charges—remind them, half-charges only!"

"Yes, sir!"

He turned to the ladder leading to the hurricane deck and the pilothouse. Instantly, he regretted not accepting the petty officer's offer of assistance. His legs felt like globs of India rubber, but he had to reach the pilothouse immediately—slow and lumbering though they might be, the two pursuing ironclads would be on top of them at any moment. Numbly, he pulled himself up the iron rungs. The small door to the pilothouse was still ajar.

He shouted with all the diminished energy he could muster. "Delaup! Get us out of here! Back us off the mud bank!"

Someone emerged from the pilothouse. *Delaup? The fool should be at the wheel, not running back here...no, it's Rutherford.* Micholson felt the great paddlewheels stir to ponderous life. The entire vessel trembled with the violent struggle between steam power and adhesive mud. Just as Rutherford reached him, a great sucking sound rent the air. With a shudder that nearly threw them both overboard, the *Eads* backed into the current.

Rutherford helped him to his feet. "Captain, that was a gallant thing you did—"

"Never mind that. Where is Delaup taking us?"

"Downstream, of course—"

"No. They'll be on top of us too quickly. Order him to swing us upriver."

"But captain—"

"Just do it, Mr. Rutherford!"

The executive officer scurried toward the pilothouse. A moment later, Micholson felt their rearward momentum slow as the gunboat's bow swung sluggishly to starboard, struggling against the powerful current. The double paddlewheel made such a maneuver less awkward than it otherwise would have been, but even so, the gunboat was more elephant than racehorse. The fog had begun burning off; he could see hints of distant green through the white haze.

He reached the pilothouse and pulled the door shut behind him. The crowded little room was already pervaded with the odor of nervous sweat. Delaup clutched the rim of the huge wooden wheel, peering intently through narrow slits for any signs of the approaching gunboats. "Captain, why did you order us upriver?"

"Those two gunboats have a full head of steam, and they're running with the current. They'll be on top of us in no time. I don't want to greet them with my unarmored stern."

"But captain," Rutherford said, "they have instructions to use only solid shot with half-charges, just like we do—"

"Their instructions didn't prevent their last salvo from nearly killing me and three of my crew. I will not leave my crew vulnerable, whether to 'friendly' fire or hateful fire."

Delaup watched a pool of water gather around Micholson's feet. "Jesus, Mary, and Joseph, you're soaked to the skin!" Not taking a hand off the wheel, he opened the hatch to the gundeck with a practiced kick. "Hey, you gunnies down there! Fetch some blankets and dry clothes for the captain! And have the cook bring up a bucket of hot coffee!"

"Mr. Delaup, you needn't fuss over me."

"Well, you won't be doing no one any good as a cold stiff corpse—" Delaup's eyes, staring through the thinning fog, suddenly widened. "Holy Mother! Here they come!"

Micholson moved immediately to one of the forward windows and pulled it halfway open. The approaching gunboats were abreast, about three hundred yards upriver. He could see only the tips of their smokestacks through the mist. *How can one gunboat appear to defeat two, with the opposing vessels being her near equals? The captains of the* Cairo *and* Mound City *won't turn tail and run from our unexpected aggressiveness; if they don't put up a convincing fight, the Confederates ashore will immediately know something is afoot.* He had only seconds to plan...

"Mr. Delaup, steer directly towards the vessel to starboard, as if we intend to hit her dead on. At the last possible second, sheer off and give her a glancing blow on her right quarter."

Delaup grinned. "A little bump and grind, *m'sieur*? I should be able to manage that." He spun the wheel to the right. The blunt-bowed *Eads* slowly complied, until the approaching *Cairo* filled her forward windows.

"Mr. Rutherford," Micholson said, "go below and instruct the forward gun crews to hold their fire until they are certain of striking that boat's forward armor shield. I don't want them to accidentally hole her."

Rutherford's eyes focused intently on the quickly approaching gunboats. "Yes, sir. I only pray they show us the same consideration."

"And direct the crew to lie flat on deck just before impact. I don't want to send Dr. Travis any broken skulls to mend."

The *Cairo* was now only fifty yards away. She turned hard to port to avoid the *Eads*, but Delaup matched her change for change. Micholson could now clearly see her three huge bow cannons. Just as he secured his armored window, the *Cairo*'s barrels belched flame and smoke. The roar of the cannon was obliterated by the deafening clang of her solid shot colliding with the *Eads*'s armor.

Micholson heard his gunners cheer. Their shield had held. Seconds later, they returned the fire. The *Eads* shuddered as though she were caught in the grip of an earthquake. He mentally complimented his gunners when all three shots perfectly struck the *Cairo*'s armor and rebounded high into the fog.

She's so close I could reach out and touch her—"Hard to port, Mr. Delaup!"

Micholson braced himself against the railing. Even so, the jolt of the collision nearly threw him off his feet. The sides of the ironclads scraped together with a sickening crunch. He recovered in time to see the *Cairo*'s starboard broadside pass, the tips of her guns only inches from his own. Were this an honest battle, his starboard gun crews would be firing with a ferocious will, hoping to pierce the enemy's vulnerable wooden sides at point-blank range, and the men on the *Cairo* would be doing the same. But the crews on both gunboats stifled their natural inclinations. The ironclads passed in relative silence. Only the grinding of their hulls and the screeching distension of tangled boat davits provided aural evidence of their clash.

Micholson threw open one of the starboard windows and leaned out of it. He craned his neck, trying to determine the *Cairo*'s heading. Would her captain take his rudely proffered suggestion, or would he turn back toward the battle? To his satisfaction and relief, the *Cairo* limped towards the near shore, pungent smoke pouring from her gunports.

Delaup watched their sister ironclad head towards the tree line, a quizzical look on his face. "Captain, you think maybe we really hurt her? All that smoke—maybe one of our shots went in through a gunport...?"

"No. Captain Bryant is good. He's very, very good. He must've had tar pots standing by in case he needed them. Marvelous effect. Remind me to compliment him, should we ever see him again."

"What about the *Mound City*?" Delaup asked. "We still need to deal with her."

They opened all the pilothouse windows wide and searched through the thinning fog. The *Mound City* was nowhere in sight. "She must've passed us when we veered off to ram the *Cairo*," Micholson said, peeling off his dripping coat and wrapping a blanket around his shoulders. "She's probably half a mile downriver by now, turning back around. With the current against her, she'll be slowed to a crawl. How long will it be until we have full steam?"

Delaup grabbed a voice pipe. "Mr. Oates, when will we have full steam?"

"Give us about another three minutes," the distant voice responded.

"Head us upriver another three minutes, then," Micholson told Delaup. "Make the tightest turn you can, and bring us back down at top speed. Commodore Foote told me the *Eads* is a good two knots faster than any of the City-class ironclads."

"True enough. And if they haven't scraped the muck off her bottom in a couple of months, we may be three or four knots quicker than the *Mound City*. With the river behind us and against them, I'd say we'll be running ten knots to their three."

"Good. That should keep matters short. Keep us well away from her, Mr. Delaup. I doubt our ramming trick would work so well twice."

The *Eads* began her southerly turn into the current. Massive gouts of black smoke belched from her twin stacks. Her rate of travel began increasing rapidly. Although most of the fog had burned off, it had been replaced by drifting clouds of powder smoke.

"Here she comes," Delaup said. The *Mound City* had completed her own turn and was lumbering slowly upriver, aiming to keep herself between the *Eads* and the seemingly stricken *Cairo.*

"Don't let her crowd you," Micholson said. "Hug the western shore if need be. At this rate, we'll have time to exchange only one broadside—"

The guns of the *Mound City* spoke first. Micholson could not help but admire the spectacle of that broadside, mushrooms of flame erupting in quick succession from bow to stern. Two shots raised plumes of water in front of the *Eads's* rapidly moving bow, but the other two struck home—unfused shells which shattered on impact. Fragments peppered the casemate and main deck.

Then it was the *Eads's* gunners' turn. They aimed high, as they had been instructed. The ironclad lurched violently to starboard as the port battery recoiled. Micholson followed the path of the flying iron. *What a pleasure it is to watch one's own shots fly,* he thought. *So distinct from the gut fear of observing incoming iron. The arc of the volley looks perfect—all four shots should pass harmlessly over her top deck...*

"No!" Micholson gasped. "Oh, no..."

One of the *Mound City's* tall smokestacks shuddered, tottered, then fell headlong into the river with a mighty splash. Swept away by the current, it chased its vanquisher with a vengeance, the only thing on the river capable of pursuing the *Eads.* The *Mound City,* her boiler fires robbed of half their draft, quickly lost headway and wavered in the current like a clubbed elephant seal.

Delaup clucked his tongue with mock regret. "*C'est la guerre,*" he said with a broad grin. "Such are the fortunes of war."

The Union corporal in charge of the mortar scow muscled his way between the boarding party and the bombardment mortar. He attempted to shield the huge, squat weapon like a mother bear protecting her prize cub. "This—this is piracy! I will not allow it!"

Micholson sighed. "I've already explained this, Corporal Wize. You have no choice in the matter. Our time table was unfortunately pushed forward. The *Molly Downings* is anchored here, next to your bombardment vessel, instead of downriver, where we were supposed to capture her later this afternoon."

The corporal looked bitterly unconvinced.

"We are rebels now," Micholson said. "The Stars and Bars fly from our flag post. I can't very well commandeer the freighter and yet leave your mortar boat untouched—it would look incredibly suspicious—"

"I don't *care* what it looks like! You will not burn this boat! This is U.S. Government property! Commodore Foote will hear of this! And General Grant, too!"

"Corporal, I daresay should you have the chance to tell either of those estimable gentlemen of this matter—and I sincerely hope you do—we will both be given commendations. As of right now, however, you and your men are our prisoners."

"*Prisoners?*"

"Prisoners or guests, whichever you would prefer. You and your men will be transferred to quarters aboard the *Molly Downings.*" The freighter's captain had surrendered with far less fuss, although surprised at the ironclad's early arrival. The side-wheel freighter sat low in the water, heavily burdened with a hold full of coal and loose iron armor plate stacked on her deck. A Confederate flag now flew from her mainmast.

The boarding party returned to the *Eads.* Micholson ordered Mr. Broadhurst to fire up the hot shot furnace. Once the furnace was roaring, the gunnery captain used special elongated tongs to place two thirty-two pound cannonballs into the blazing chamber. "Perhaps I should've been a baker," he said to his captain as the cannonballs began to glow red hot. After several minutes he carefully removed the glowing iron balls and, with the help of a gun crew, loaded them into two of the broadside cannons.

The two hot shots, fired at the negligible range of twenty yards, burst through the mortar boat's wooden shield in a shower of angry sparks. The small vessel soon blazed from end to end. Both the *Eads* and the *Molly Downings* moved downstream as quickly as their engines would push them. Most of the ironclad's wardroom boys and gunnery assistants gathered on the hurricane deck to watch the show. The fires grew so intense that branches of nearby trees ignited, startling a flock of egrets from their perches.

When the two vessels reached half a mile downstream, the fires spread to the mortar boat's magazine. The bomb shells exploded with a biblical fury, raising a pillar of fire that dwarfed the surrounding bluffs. The surface of the river for a quarter mile around was broken by a shower of wood and metal. A mushroom-shaped cloud of greenish-black smoke obscured the patch of water where the mortar scow had been anchored.

The lads on the hurricane deck cheered, favorably comparing the explosion with the best Fourth of July fireworks they had ever witnessed. "Mr. Rutherford!" Micholson called through the hatchway to the main deck. "Have someone clear those boys off the hurricane deck! We'll be rounding the bend any minute now, in range of Fort Pillow."

Delaup, fighting the tricky currents present at any bend in the great, ornery river, looked questioningly at his captain. "You think they need to get under cover, *m'sieur*? Surely, after we just blew up that mortar boat—"

"You seem like a betting man, Mr. Delaup."

"Indeed I am."

"Some gambles are necessary. Others are just damned foolish. I won't have those boys risking their lives merely for a better look at that fort."

As the *Eads* rounded the great curve in the river, trailed by the *Molly Downings*, the outline of Fort Pillow slowly hove into view. Micholson counted the batteries of long-muzzled, rifled cannons, mounted behind sturdy earthworks high in the bluffs and down at the river's edge. They held sufficient firepower to blast his gunboat from the water. The bright spring sun blazed high in the east, blinding his own gunners but providing perfect visibility for the rebels on the eastern shore. Should their ruse fail them, the subsequent battle would not go well for the *Eads*.

Now he counted down the yards which separated his gunboat from the closest batteries. *Five hundred. Four hundred. Three hundred...they may fire their first salvo any second now—*

A mass of men rushed to the fort's parapets. Micholson held his breath. The Confederates were close enough that he could see their faces. Young men, no different from the young men who manned his own vessel. They raised their rifles—

Micholson let his breath escape in an easy flow. The rebels waved rifles and hats high over their heads, cheering wildly as the *Eads* passed slowly below their silent cannons.

CHAPTER ELEVEN

A Murder of Crows at the Mouth of the Yazoo

Aboard the USS James B. Eads
*at the juncture of the Mississippi and Yazoo Rivers,
north of Vicksburg, Mississippi
April 22, 1862*

VICKSBURG CITIZEN GAZETTE
"All the News You Will Ever Need"

UNION IRONCLAD GUNBOAT *JAMES B. EADS* CAPTURED BY OUR BOYS!**

* Union Lt Cmdr August Micholson, Native Mississippian, Switches Allegiance, Pledges Loyalty to Confederacy
* Micholson and *Eads* Defeat USS *Cairo* and USS *Mound City*
* Newest Confederate Ironclad Sinks Union Mortar Boat, Captures Freighter
* CSS *Eads* Passes Fort Pillow to Cheers of Garrison
* *Eads* is Met by River Defense Fleet; Confederate Captains Exchange Toasts Aboard CSS *General Bragg*
* Mayor of Memphis Hosts Grand Banquet for *Eads*'s Officers; Ladies of Memphis Deliver Pies and Good Cheer to Crew
* Citizens of Helena Organize Parade and Band Concert When *Eads* Docks to Replenish Coal Stocks

In one of the most daring Exploits yet undertaken by our Soldiers and Sailors during this War Between States, Confederate

> forces captured and commandeered the mighty
> Union ironclad gunboat USS *James B. Eads*,
> adding immeasurable new strength to our
> River Defense Fleet, which was until now
> made up entirely of wooden Ramming vessels.
> The Union ironclad was holed by a Torpedo,
> an underwater explosive device, while
> engaging in patrols north of Fort Pillow.
> Union Sailors beached the stricken ironclad
> and left their vessel to seek assistance in
> affecting repairs. These Sailors were
> successfully engaged by a brave contingent
> of Arkansan Irregulars, who, although
> severely outnumbered, delayed the Federals
> long enough for the *Eads* to be captured...

Micholson crumpled up the newspaper and shoved it to a corner of his desk, unsure whether to feel triumphant or mortified to the bone.

So now all the world, save Commodore Foote, General Grant, and the crew of this gunboat, believe me to be a turncoat, he thought. *I suppose, were it required for the mission's success, I would be happy to be thought the Devil's gigolo.*

He stared out his cabin's open shutters at the banks of the Yazoo River, the profusion of greenery fading to black as the twilight descended into night. The *Eads* had anchored above Old River, a lake-like appendage of the Yazoo which was once its outlet to the Mississippi, and just below the narrow stream known as Steele's Bayou.

Dozens of conversations with the rebels of the past three days, and we've yet to uncover even a hint of the secret boat-yard's location. Every new contact with the locals posed the danger of their subterfuge becoming unraveled. The boat-yard was somewhere on this river, that he knew. Perhaps the most prudent course would be to simply press ahead until he stumbled upon it?

At least the mood of the crew had been ebullient. Some of the gunners and powder boys had taken up a bowling game on the gundeck, using a thirty-two pounder cannonball as their striker. And Jack Bainbridge, the boy he'd rescued from the Mississippi, had made a complete recovery from his near-drowning in the icy waters.

Yet everyone's mood had taken a turn towards the somber once they passed beyond the sandbar separating the Mississippi from the mouth of the Yazoo. Was it due to the coming end of the fairy tale-like portion of their mission, the accelerating approach of real combat? Or did the sudden cloud of universal foreboding reflect some aspect of the Yazoo River itself?

A knock on his door startled him. "Who is it?"

"It's Valery Delaup, *m'sieur.* I have some charts of the Yazoo with me. I was wondering if you cared to review them."

Micholson opened the door. The sky above the hurricane deck was marked with slashes of blood red cloud. "I'm pleased for the company. Do come in."

Delaup's eyes were caught by a blue glass decanter sitting atop Micholson's desk, glowing in the lamplight much like the indigo twilight that filled the skies above the Yazoo. His mouth eased into a broad grin.

"Am I to understand, Mr. Delaup, that you are a drinking man, as well as a gambling one?"

"Oh, yes, indeed. I am very catholic in my weaknesses."

"By all means, then, join me in a cup of brandy before we plunge into these charts of yours."

Delaup happily accepted the pewter cup that was handed him. "It would be unspeakably rude of me to refuse, *m'sieur.*"

Micholson filled Delaup's cup, then his own. "I hope you don't mind these pewter cups. My crystal ones were all shattered during our shoving match with the *Cairo.*"

"No matter. Brandy like this I would drink from a hole in the ground. To success, glory, and the acclaim of women!"

Micholson raised his cup. "To success, and safe return home."

Delaup spread the largest map on Micholson's cot. It was an old chart of the Yazoo, dated 1843, with more recent information penned in. "Tomorrow morning we will pass the Chickasaw Bluffs, and tomorrow afternoon Haines' Bluff, the most fortified place on Vicksburg's north flank. As these are both known to be defensive centers, it makes sense that in these spots our good friends have concentrated their torpedoes."

"So that any gunboat disabled by an underwater explosion can be quickly sunk by heavy cannon fire."

"Yes; you think like a rebel."

"What can we do about the torpedoes? We can't very well line the hurricane deck with sharpshooters and have them blaze away at the infernal devices. How would a Confederate boat make its way? Do you suggest we ask the garrisons ashore for their assistance?"

"That is an option, yes—although with every new contact with the enemy, we risk giving ourselves away. Some of the torpedoes are remotely detonated by onlookers on the banks. These, I believe, will cause us no trouble. Others, however, explode on contact with our hull."

"Is there any way to tell the difference between the two?"

Delaup grimaced. "Not until you bump into them, *m'sieur.*"

"What do you suggest?"

"We should send two teams of men in launches ahead of us. The rebels would not have permanently obstructed the Yazoo, for it is likely they will bring supplies for the boatyard up the river. And, in any case, someday soon those ironclad rams are going to want to come on down to the Mississippi."

"So the torpedoes must be removable?"

"Yes. The rebels must have a way to easily scoot them aside or disarm their firing caps. We'll probably need to confer with an officer ashore when we reach the first batch, but after that—"

A resounding thud cut Delaup off. Something had collided with the outside of the cabin. The first impact was followed quickly by another, then another. The collisions were accompanied by a frenzied screeching.

Micholson pulled Delaup to the floor. His heart raced. "My God! Can we be under attack?"

The thuds blended together into a continuous concussion, as though the ironclad were in the midst of a savage hail storm. "I—I don't think so," Delaup said. "I tain't never heard no gunfire that sounds like *that*. Only one way to find out—"

"Valery, don't!"

But Delaup had already cracked open the starboard shutter, trying to peer outside. Suddenly, part of the outside darkness burst through the narrow aperture.

" *What—?* "

A furious ball of feathers and talons bounded madly off the walls, upturning books and utensils, slashing maps and bed quilts. Protecting their faces, Micholson and Delaup tried to capture the creature. After a few futile tries, Micholson succeeded in throwing his greatcoat over the invader. The coat continued to thrash beneath Micholson's arms for half a minute. Then the movement ceased.

"Birds..." Delaup said.

"Yes." Micholson was breathing heavily. "What could be terrorizing them this way?" Cautiously, he unwrapped his coat. The large black bird was still, one wing nearly torn from its socket. "A crow. Dead."

The hammering against the gunboat's sides continued unabated. "*Mon Dieu,*" Delaup said. "There must be hundreds of them."

"There's no moon tonight. They can't see us. Just by being here, we're murdering hundreds of these poor creatures...Do we have any steam up?"

"There is probably some heat left in the boilers. Why?"

"I want us to re-anchor close in to the eastern shore. That's where they all seem to be coming from. If we're in near the trees, they can't pick up much speed before hitting us."

Delaup frowned. "Uh, I wouldn't advise that, *m'sieur.* Those overhanging trees are treacherous, and it's blacker than *ma grand tante*'s kettle out there. We could lose our stacks."

"Just be careful, Mr. Delaup." Micholson opened the hatch in the cabin floor that led to the rear gundeck. "Let's get to the pilothouse."

Delaup ruefully eyed the blue decanter on the floor, surrounded by a puddle of good brandy, then stepped onto the ladder after Micholson. The gundeck was in chaos, a tangle of twisted hammocks and half-dressed seamen in an uproar over their interrupted sleep.

"Captain, are we under attack?"

"What's out there, captain?"

Micholson stopped to answer them. "Something has frightened the birds on the eastern shore, making them all flee across the river. I'm going to move us closer in to the tree line, so they can't smash themselves against us. We should all be back asleep within the half hour, God willing."

He opened the door to the engine room and was gratified to see the burly chief engineer already inside. "Mr. Oates, good evening. I want us to move our anchorage. Do we have enough pressure left?"

Oates frowned. "There's barely enough heat left in the boilers to turn the wheel over. We may be able to crawl—"

"A crawl is all I ask for. Mr. Delaup will relay instructions from the pilothouse."

Leaving the grumbling engineer behind, Micholson and Delaup entered the forward gundeck, which was in every bit

125

the uproar the aft gundeck had been. The unnerving hail of birds against armor plate clanged even louder here. Micholson approached a seaman holding a lit lantern, wishing he had taken time to memorize the enlisted men's names. "Mister—?"

"Wilkerson, sir." The young man saluted. "I fight the starboard thirty-two pounders."

"Very good. Do you know the men who handle the anchors?"

"I do, sir."

"Have them raise them. We'll be moving closer in to shore."

Micholson and Delaup ascended to the pilothouse. The maddened screeching of birds filled the tiny octagonal room. Delaup groped in the thick darkness for the box of matches he kept under the pilot's chair. His hand landed on something soft and wet. It twittered.

"*Eegchh!*"

"Valery! What—"

"Nuh—nothing, *m'sieur.*" He retrieved the matches and lit a small lantern hanging from the wall. The light fell upon a tiny lump of feathers, quivering with its final, violent breaths. A sparrow, small enough to squeeze through one of the view slits. "What a foul, evil night this is," he muttered. "If I could hurry the sun, I would."

The gunboat lurched as the anchors were withdrawn from the muddy river bottom. Freed, the vessel began to drift slowly downstream.

"Give me all the steam you got, Mr. Oates," Delaup called into the voice pipe. "Either we get those wheels moving, or we drift all the way back to the Mississippi."

Slowly, as if unwillingly roused from a long sleep, the great twin wheels began to churn the silty, night-black waters. The gunboat's rearward momentum was gradually arrested, until the low black vessel hung suspended in the current. Then Delaup spun his many-spoked wheel to the right. The *Eads* turned her armored bow into the shower of birds, making a brief journey toward the eastern tree line. Then Delaup called on Oates to throw the paddle wheels into reverse. Micholson ordered the anchors to be released once more, and their chains clattered as the anchors pierced the river with resounding splashes.

The gunboat came to rest beneath gnarled overhanging branches of live oaks and sycamores. The maddened shrieks still sounded overhead, but the ironclad's sides were no longer buffeted by exploding flesh. "How long will they go like that?" Delaup asked. "What has possessed them so?"

Micholson wished he knew. The uneasiness he had felt ever since they entered this tributary river had been building steadily, like the beat of approaching dark wings.

A crash sounded from the hurricane deck, in front of the pilothouse. A heavy overhead branch had fallen. The branch slid down the sloping casemate into the water.

"What could've dislodged that branch?" Micholson asked, peering out into the darkness. "One of our boat davits?"

"I don't think so. The gunboat's been still for a bit. Wasn't no wind. Birds wouldn't be heavy enough to make that branch tumble—"

Micholson's lantern light glinted off a pair of eyes on the hurricane deck. Something low and large paced just outside the pilothouse. It emitted a thrumming, a constant, stealthy sound at the lower range of his hearing. *Purring?*

The thing sprung at the view slit. *It knows I'm here!* The collision shook the pilothouse. Micholson's lantern clattered to the floor. A heavy, reeking musk pervaded the air. *My face—it's seared, as though I'm standing before an open furnace!*

"*Mon Dieu!*" Delaup cried. "What in Hell was *that?* I thought the damned death-seeking birds were as bad as it could get tonight!"

Micholson felt his face. It throbbed with excess heat. *My eyebrows are singed. But that's impossible. Insane.* "Mr.

127

Delaup, go below and collect a party of Marines." He could hear it still, underlying everything: that terrible purring, like a deep rumbling in the earth. "That...*cat*—or whatever it is— it's still out there. Have them bring their rifles."

"Yes, captain." Delaup descended the ladder, leaving Micholson alone in the dim pilothouse. He experienced a brief flurry of terror. *What an infantile emotion*, he chided himself. *I'm protected by one and a quarter inches of iron, backed by sixteen inches of solid oak. That animal outside is merely a local variant of cougar or mountain lion. The heat on my face? Just a remnant of my fever, made acute again by this sudden stress.*

The hatch from the gundeck opened. "Back so soon, Mr. Delaup? You've brought some Marines—?"

But his visitor wasn't Valery Delaup. It was Nehemiah. "You mustn't have no Marines to kill that animal, Mister August," he said. "You must kill it yourself. Here. Take your pistol. The creature and the spirit within it have marked you. If you do not slay the animal yourself, you are doomed to die by your own hand."

More madness! "Nehemiah, with all respect, what *nonsense* are you spouting?"

His old friend pressed the pistol into his palm. "There is no time now to explain. Dear one, you must not let that possessed cat flee this vessel alive. Your face burns with the mark of the fire spirits. If the cat escapes into the forest, or if another man kills it before you can, I will be unable to save you. I spoke before about the river leading us towards evil, but that evil has arrived aboard this gunboat far more rapidly than I feared."

The thing on the hurricane deck snarled.

"*Go!*" Nehemiah pushed him toward the door with desperate strength that belied his years. "Go *now*, pursue it, and kill it! If you fail, all will be lost!"

August Micholson had trusted Nehemiah his entire life. Breaking that habit, even under circumstances which bent credulity to the snapping point, proved impossible. He opened the door to the hurricane deck and slipped outside, encumbered by lantern and pistol, heart pounding like the hailstorm of birds that had recently pounded the casemate.

It's just a mountain lion, he told himself, *despite whatever mumbo jumbo Nehemiah has convinced himself of. Nothing more supernatural than a wild animal, enraged by unexpected, unfamiliar surroundings.* But he would kill it before it could find a way inside and harm any members of his crew.

Even though its black coat makes it indistinguishable against the gunboat's deck, the lantern light will reveal it by reflecting from its eyes. The horrible purring had ceased. He swung his lantern, hoping to get lucky—

Those eyes!

He fired.

Missed!

The cat scurried away faster than anything its size should be able to move, almost quicker than the echo of the shot reached Micholson's ears. *That should bring the Marines running...*

Before he could get off a second shot, the panther slithered through an air shaft which also served as a sky light for the boiler deck. *It'll be after Oates and his men next!*

He had no time to wait for the Marines to catch up. He pounded down the steps to the gundeck, then raced past dozens of startled, half-dressed men to the ladder which descended to the boiler deck and engine room.

The panther had cornered Oates and the boy Micholson had rescued from drowning, Jack Bainbridge. They stood with their backs to a bulkhead. The overstuffed engineer had turned to a lump of sweating bread dough, ghastly white, biting his knuckles and whimpering. Jack looked as though he'd fallen into a trance. In sharp contrast to his companion, his cheeks and forehead glowed tomato red.

Micholson took careful aim this time. With the cat paying him no heed, he sighted on where he estimated its heart to be.

The shot deafened the shooter. The beast shrieked. Oates and Jack, freed from the creature's mesmerism, ran for the shelter of the boilers. The cat fell, then pulled itself upright again. It dragged itself to the firebox. Using an intelligence Micholson would never have suspected it possessed, it nudged the iron door open. Then, utilizing what seemed to be the dregs of its dying strength, it leaped into the firebox, burying itself in mounds of coals still glowing red.

A quartet of Marines led by the gunnery captain rushed into the room. "Captain," Broadhurst shouted, "where is the animal?"

"You're too late, Mr. Broadhurst," Micholson said. "I shot it through some vital organ, and it retreated into the firebox. If my bullet didn't finish it, those scorching coals certainly have done the job by now."

A pair of Marines approached the open firebox. One of them prodded the half-buried cat with the tip of his rifle's bayonet. It didn't move. "It's not breathing, Mr. Broadhurst," he said. "Shall I put another bullet into it, just to be sure?"

"Oh, I don't think that's necessary," Broadhurst said. "Enough noise. The crew's been riled up enough. Mr. Oates, do you have any tongs my men can use to extract that animal from your firebox, or shall I get my hot shot tongs? We'll heave it overboard."

"No—no need," Oates said, barely beginning to recover his composure. "Just cover it over with coals. Come the morning, the carcass should burn about as well as anything else we've ever shoved into a firebox."

Before any of the Marines could take a step toward the firebox, Jack Bainbridge grabbed a shovel and silently buried the cat with glowing coals.

"Mr. Bainbridge," Micholson said, hoping to break the pall which had fallen over everyone, "this makes twice in one week I have rescued you in some fashion. Make sure to repay my investment in you by growing into a fine seaman..."

Jack stared at him with empty eyes. Micholson noticed the boy's face had remained livid. "Mr. Oates, this lad appears to be in shock. Make certain he gets a good night's sleep, then report his status to me when he wakes. We may need to have Dr. Travis check him over in the morning."

"Yes, sir. And—and thank you for your marksmanship." Oates removed the shovel from Jack's hands; the boy had continued mutely piling coals atop the panther's body, even though he had already accomplished the carcass's complete burial.

"I suppose we can all get back to sleep now," Broadhurst said.

Micholson shook his hand. "I pray you are right, Mr. Broadhurst. Good night to you all."

He met Delaup on the aft gundeck. The pilot signaled for Micholson to follow him up the ladder to the hurricane deck. "Captain, there's something you need to see."

"Nothing more to do with animals, I hope?"

"Only the lack of them." He assisted Micholson through the hatch, onto the open deck. "Hear that?"

"I don't hear anything, save bullfrogs."

"That's just it. The birds are gone. They aren't flying madly to the far side of the river anymore."

"When did it stop?"

"As soon as you fired that second shot, maybe ten, twelve minutes ago. The birds, they just went quiet all of a sudden. The only loud noise since then was one of our boats falling into the river. Guess an overhanging branch must've snagged a davit, weakened the rigging."

"I imagine so. We'll retrieve it in the morning."

But his mind wasn't on a missing boat. It focused on what Nehemiah had said, trying to make sense of his old friend's cryptic words. "It's been a trying evening, Mr. Delaup. I'm afraid I no longer have the energy to review your charts. Let's plan to continue immediately after breakfast."

"Have a good sleep, sir."

Micholson knew that sleep would not be his to claim for many hours yet. He hadn't told Valery the truth, that he had more urgent matters to pursue than reviewing a chart. He needed to talk more with Nehemiah. Too much of the seeming nonsense his friend had related to him had been granted relevance, perhaps even believability, by the night's subsequent events. The birds' behavior. The dying panther's inexplicable attraction to a furnace filled with lit coals. The Bainbridge boy's deeply flushed face. Perhaps...perhaps Nehemiah himself was much more than he seemed, the simple, kindly servant he had always acted as...

Entering his cabin, he immediately saw the note laid out for him on his desk.

My Dearest August,

I know you are eager for an explanation from me of what I told you before, about the cat and the evil spirit inside it. I do not expect you to believe my revelations; at least not now. You may think I have gone senile with my years, or that the stresses of being aboard this gunboat have unhinged me. This is not the case, but I have decided my hope to conflate your mission with my own dread responsibility is both unwise and shamefully selfish. Now that you have slain the beast and placed yourself out of immediate danger, I am free to do what I realize I must. If I act quickly enough, I may be able to prevent a catastrophe which would leave no one untouched, not Northerner or Southerner, not White man or Negro.

Do not seek after me. You have brought me this far, most of the way I must go. I will travel the remainder of my journey alone. I have taken one of the vessel's small boats. I realize this is a crime, but I seek to prevent a crime far, far more heinous than theft. I hope you will find it in your generous heart, my son, to forgive me everything. Good fortune in slaying the demons you hunt; please wish me the same in slaying my own.

May all the Good Powers be with you,

Your Nehemiah

Micholson silently cursed. Should he have a party pursue his servant on the river, before Nehemiah could get too far? The men were exhausted, and he would likely be sending them on a fool's errand; a small boat wishing to stay undetected could easily remain hidden in this darkness, simply by taking cover in the foliage lining the river's banks. Besides, Nehemiah had asked for his trust. The man had shown him loyalty after loyalty since Micholson's earliest childhood; would it not be churlish of him to refuse to repay his friend in the same coin?

Hours passed before sleep visited him. And it came not alone, for the dream came, too...the nightmare of the *Virginia*'s rampage. Only this time, the rebel ironclad's casemate and deadly rifled cannons were wreathed with coronas of fire.

CHAPTER TWELVE

The Lunatic on the River

Aboard the USS James B. Eads *on the Yazoo River,
twenty miles southwest of Satartia, Mississippi,
April 23, 1862*

The crew spent hours the following morning scouring away the birds. They uncovered bedraggled corpses in every conceivable cranny—wedged between gun shutters and hull, inside small boats, fouling hammock berthing nooks. One large crow had managed to get itself caught in the iron grating covering the opening of one of the smokestacks. It dangled from a broken leg like a battered black flag.

It was nearly ten o'clock before the *Eads* got underway again. Her progress upstream was halting, slow enough a child ashore could have easily outwalked her. Sailors rowed launches ahead of the gunboat, sentries on constant lookout for suspended torpedoes. When these baneful devices were found, the sentries gently pushed them away from the path of the gunboat or, if the torpedoes were anchored to the river bottom, the sentries gingerly defused them. The *Molly Downings* steamed a hundred yards behind the gunboat and religiously kept to the latter's path through the dangerous waters. The few soldiers the two vessels encountered on the banks were friendly, respectfully eyeing the Stars and Bars and waving to the brave men in the launches, sometimes shouting bits of advice about the torpedoes.

The river appeared as flat and calm as a windless lake. Only the passage of stray twigs and logs downstream revealed the true strength of the current. "Compared to the Mississippi, this river is asleep," Micholson said from his post in the pilothouse. Each bend of the Yazoo had looked much like the last; they could unknowingly be steaming in circles, following an endless loop not noted on the charts.

"Old Yazoo is asleep, yes," Delaup replied, "but with one eye always open. Don't let this river lull you. In his own way, he's every bit as tricky as the Big One. The torpedoes don't worry me nearly so much as the snags." His experienced eyes scanned the river's surface for ripples and eddies, evidence of waterlogged, mud-trapped trees with sharp branches looming like harpoons beneath the murky surface.

Delaup called for the engineers to shift the paddlewheels into reverse as the men ahead paused to defuse a group of anchored torpedoes. "Seems funny, don't it, that we're spending so much time defusing those things, when we're carrying a whole arsenal of them down in our magazines?" He pried a stubborn remnant of breakfast hardtack out of his teeth. "Would've made more sense to just pluck any we need right out of the water. You think we'll end up using any of the infernal things?"

Micholson did not like to think about the spar torpedoes stored in their magazine. He would not have brought the weapons but for Commodore Foote's insistence. Once inside the rebel boatyard, he preferred settling the issue with guns, not skulking midnight sabotage. Yet who knew what might face them in that boatyard? "I can't say, Mr. Delaup. So much depends on how many of the rams have been made operational. One opponent, or two—I'll place my trust in our gunners. More than two rams? We'll have to wait and see."

Delaup signaled for the paddlewheels to revert to forward propulsion. "What is the word on young Bainbridge?"

"Dr. Travis tells me he's running a high fever, yet none of the symptoms which normally accompany a fever are present. Still, the boy remains disoriented, almost as much so as those birds which dashed themselves against our sides."

"Captain, you never did explain your great concern for the lives of those birds. *Molly Downings* stayed out in the middle of the stream. It didn't seem to bother her captain none."

"Captain Dodds is a river sailor, much like you. Birds have a much different meaning for a blue-sea sailor." Micholson paused. In his imagination, he was once more on the swaying deck of a square-rigged, four masted frigate, her sails unfurled in the salt air. "You can be at sea for months and never see a single bird. It gets to where you miss them terribly. And when you finally do see one flying overhead, it's like an angel, a messenger of land's proximity. It is extremely bad luck for a sailor to kill a bird, or allow one to come to harm."

"'Bad luck,' *m'sieur*? I believed you to be a rationalist of the strictest kind."

He thought again of the events of the previous night. "There's a bit of superstition in all of us. As perhaps there should be."

"You'll get no argument here. Me, I'm a good Catholic man, so I have my share, all right."

They steamed in silence for a while, the still air broken only by the sounds of oars slapping the brownish water and the occasional cry of an animal hidden in the tangled underbrush. Around eleven o'clock they approached the Confederate works at Chickasaw Bluff, a quartet of field pieces entrenched on high ground commanding the river. Micholson turned his spyglass on the guns overhead. Small cannons, twenty-four pounders; were they mounted at the water's edge, they'd pose little threat to the gunboat's armor. Mounted on the bluff, however, they could menace the ironclad's vulnerable upperworks during the coming run downriver, or sink the *Molly Downings*. He wondered what to do with the freighter once the enemy was roused.

Perhaps he should burn her, after taking her crew and passengers aboard the *Eads*. But could they fit another eighty men aboard the already cramped ironclad?

After passing Chickasaw Bluff, Micholson ordered a break for lunch. Before the launches could be turned around, sentries aboard the boats raised an alarm.

"What's that ruckus up ahead?" Delaup asked, fruitlessly trying to see around a bend in the river. "Did they find something?"

Micholson saw it first. "A small boat is drifting our way...and there's a man in it, lying on its floor."

He immediately thought of Nehemiah. Had his friend been hurt?

"Is he hailing us?"

"No," Micholson said, adjusting his spyglass. To his enormous relief, the prone figure wasn't Nehemiah. "He's not moving. The boat is nearly awash. It's overloaded with buckets of some kind, and bottles. How odd..."

The sentries in the launches guided the drifting boat to the *Eads*'s bow, where they secured it with a length of rope. By the time Micholson descended the ladder down the steep casemate face to the ironclad's broad bow, Dr. Travis had al-ready emerged from the gundeck and was examining the unconscious man. Pierce, the watch officer, stood behind him. He glowered at the prostrate figure, lying sodden and ragged in the bottom of the crowded boat. "Just lookit that arm on him! Some kinda circus freak, you think? I think we should throw this one back."

"That isn't your decision to make, Mr. Pierce," Micholson said as he stepped onto the bow. He realized with a shock of recognition that he knew this man. *Good Lord—it's Joseph Babbage, the scion of Adderwood Plantation. My onetime neighbor.* "What do you make of this, Dr. Travis? What's wrong with him?"

The physician took the unconscious man's pulse. "He's suffering from exposure; that much I'm certain of. He may have been in this boat two or three days. Perhaps longer, to judge by the quantity of fresh water his boat carries."

Micholson eyed the dozens of buckets and bottles that crowded the small boat. "He brought enough with him for a trip to the Azores."

"Yes. Strange, isn't it? Ample water, but no food. The only other indication of malady I find is that his stomach is distended. I'd like to bring him aboard and keep him under observation for a while."

"Doctor, I'm afraid there's a...complication. This man is known to me. A neighbor from childhood. He may well recognize me, also."

"Isn't your cover story valid enough? It's been in all the newspapers. I realize this gentleman most likely hasn't read those accounts, but if you were capable of making journalists credulous, why not this man? Besides, your personal connection might be useful in acquiring information about the boatyard, wouldn't it? Assuming he has any awareness of it."

Micholson considered the request. *We aren't a floating hospital. Yet leaving him to his fate on the river could bring suspicion down upon us, particularly with the soldiers manning the works at Chickasaw Bluffs. Being master of Adderwood, Babbage should have excellent knowledge of the Yazoo and any construction on its banks. Bringing him aboard seems worth the risks.* "I'll allow it, Doctor. But make sure that any interactions between this man and my crew are minimal."

Pierce scowled. "I advise against this, captain. I don't get no right good feelings about this man. He'll be trouble, I can virtually guarantee."

"I'm afraid I must side with Dr. Travis in this instance."

"Thank you, captain," the physician replied. He placed his hands beneath the unconscious man's armpits and looked to Pierce for assistance. "There'll be no need for this man to interact with anyone besides myself and my orderly, unless you choose to question him."

Micholson was about to order the recalcitrant Pierce to assist Dr. Travis when the derelict's eyes fluttered open. His bloated face was stricken with a mindless terror. He pulled away from Dr. Travis and weakly thrashed about on the floor of his boat, spilling much of his water. Then he lunged for the side and retched.

Once his uneven shoulders stopped heaving, he collapsed and lay bent over the gunwale, exhausted, barely breathing. But when Dr. Travis stepped into the boat, Babbage moved with astonishing speed. He grabbed one of the upright bottles and thrust it between his cracked lips, frantically ingesting the water. Only then did his bloodshot eyes begin to clear.

"Betrayed!" he gasped from a bile-ravaged throat. "I've been *betrayed!*"

Babbage proved beyond reasoning with. He displayed the strength of a madman. Two Marines were required to escort him to the infirmary. Dr. Travis advised that he be strapped down to the examining table, both for his own safety and that of those surrounding him.

"My water!" Babbage screamed. "Where is it? I must have it! *Give it to me!*"

"Dr. Travis thinks your body needs to recover before you drink again," Micholson said. "Otherwise, you risk rupturing your stomach. We have plenty of water aboard, don't you worry. You'll get some soon enough."

"You must...you must give it to me! You don't understand—I'll die without it. Horribly. And you'll all die, too, in a fiery holocaust!"

Again, this peculiar obsession with fire. The panther sought it out, and Babbage is terrified of it. "Please try to calm yourself. You're in very capable hands. I assure you, Dr. Travis will not let any harm come to you."

Babbage looked around the room, as though noticing his surroundings for the first time. "Where am I? Who are you? Why did you tie me to this table? This is outrageous! I own a thousand acres, and I'm a commissioned colonel!"

There would seem to be greater advantage in revealing myself than in dissimulating. "My name is Lieutenant Commander August Micholson. I am captain of this vessel. You are aboard the ironclad CSS *James B. Eads.* You are restrained for your own safety."

"The CSS *James B. Eads?* I've never heard of such an ironclad. Is this one of Louis Stoddard's new ironclad rams?"

Micholson's eyes narrowed. *Who is this Louis Stoddard? Could he be in command of the secret boatyard? I'll have to probe into this further.* "No, this isn't one of Stoddard's vessels, although we hope to rendezvous with the constructors of the new ironclad squadron and deliver a load of captured iron plates. Apparently, you haven't read the most recent newspapers. This ironclad was formerly part of the Federals' gunboat flotilla. We captured and commandeered her only four days ago, after she'd been damaged by a torpedo and beached. As I said, our plan is to deliver a load of iron plates to our comrades working on the additions to the River Defense Fleet. However, having originated in a different sector, my crew and I are unfamiliar with the boatyard's exact location. You would do us and our cause a great service if you could share any knowledge—"

"Wait..." Babbage's rheumy eyes focused on Micholson's face. "August Micholson...I've read about you. You commanded one of the Union warships which was sunk by the *Virginia.* How do you come to be in Confederate service? And—and I *knew* you at one time, did I not?"

Micholson nodded. "You are correct. You are Joseph Babbage, I believe? Of Adderwood Plantation?"

"Shamed though I am to admit it, being in such a wretched state...yes, I am he. We were...neighbors, were we not? Your family owned a small farm about two miles inland of Adderwood. Do they own it still?"

"When my parents passed, I sold the land, as I had become a commissioned officer in the Navy and could not care for it."

"An officer in the U.S. Navy...And you remained in Federal service after Sumter?"

"I did, to my regret."

"So how did you come to this state of affairs, commanding an ironclad commandeered by men of the South? Were you drummed out of the Navy following your former vessel's sinking by the *Virginia*?"

"There was to be an inquiry into my conduct during that engagement. Public condemnation of my leadership proved overwhelming. I feared a court martial, and so I deserted. I offered my services to the Confederate Navy and raised a naval battalion. Thanks to the Grace of God, my men and I were marching towards Fort Pillow to reinforce the garrison there when the *Eads* was damaged and beached, and she fell into our hands."

Babbage groaned and struggled against his restraints. "My stomach—it's *boiling*, I tell you! This is *torture*! When will you untie me? When can I have my water?"

"You can have your freedom and your water once you show me you have yourself under control. Prove it by answering some questions. You can begin by telling me what you were doing in that boat."

Babbage winced with pain. "Very well, Micholson. You leave me no choice, so I am at your service. You may think me a madman for what I am about to tell you. But I am not mad. I'm merely a man who tragically overreached himself, but who did so in the service of our glorious cause. Compared to the Northerners, we are a small people, deficient in manpower and manufacturing capacity. I sought to give us an equalizer. No, more than an equalizer. A weapon so terrible it would force Lincoln to sue for peace on our terms, so terrifying it would chase every last Yankee soldier from our lands. You might say my success in this venture has unmade me. Are you a well-read man?"

"Somewhat."

"You are familiar with Mary Wollstonecraft Shelley's work?"

"Passingly familiar."

"Then the notion of a 'Frankenstein's monster' will not seem foreign to you. For several generations, my family has retained the services of an African of specialized knowledge—" His eyes squeezed shut, and his voice evaporated. Perspiration dripped down the sides of his face. "I must—I *must* have some water immediately, or I fear I'll be...unable to finish this charming tale for you."

Micholson turned to one of the guards. "Get him a cup of water."

Babbage drank it in a single choking gulp. "As...as I was saying, my family owned a slave who, back in his homeland, had been especially conversant with the native Powers of that place. I refer to supernatural Powers."

"A witch doctor?"

"Yes...'witch doctor' is the colloquial term for what he was. As a child, I spent a good deal of time in the company of this slave—Old Daniel, we called him. I believe you may have met him, once."

Micholson recalled the inexplicably charged standoff he'd experienced as a child at Nehemiah's side in the woods between Adderwood and his family's farm, when he and Nehemiah had met Babbage and Babbage's slave. Nehemiah had stood between his young charge and the other Negro, as though he'd been protecting Micholson from a rattlesnake. The two Negroes had exchanged angry words in a language Micholson hadn't comprehended. Afterward, when he'd asked Nehemiah what the strange quarrel had been all about, his friend had refused to speak of it. He hadn't mentioned the incident ever again, not until this past week.

143

"To entertain me," Babbage said, "Old Daniel performed magic tricks...or everyone *assumed* they were tricks. But they were more than sleight-of-hand—they were echoes of an ancient power, power he'd wielded in Africa. He promised me he could replicate that power, that it would be mine to command, if only I would help him. He needed things, things from Africa—"

Good Lord, Micholson thought. *He must refer to that freighter captured off Ship Island which contained all manner of strange, dangerous flora and fauna.* "What kinds of things?"

"He needed to regain his connection with his birthplace. Oh, the unending lists he whispered into the ears of the slaves I was to send—the man was insatiable. Plants, trees, tons of earth, a whole menagerie of bizarre creatures...I spent a good deal of my family's fortune to be that monster's dry goods merchant. To ensure he would get what he needed, I hired two ships to sail through the blockade, each large enough to carry the whole package. One never returned, but the second made its way to Adderwood, perhaps ten days ago...I've lost track of time..."

"These things—what did your witch doctor do with them?"

Babbage suddenly appeared on the verge of tears. "He is so full of hate...the very picture of the Devil. Why couldn't I see that before? How did he hide it from me my whole life? You know, after my father died...I was a tiny child, I had no one else to turn to...Daniel was my only friend. He said he'd make me a king. Honored and dreaded, just like he had been, back in Africa. But he played me for a fool. My whole life, I've been nothing but that man's fool. And he hates all of us, every White man in existence, slave owner and abolitionist alike. He hates you, Micholson, and you, doctor, and your wives and daughters and mistresses...He wants to turn this whole Continent into a burning Hell for the White race, and he's started with *me*, with these infernal seeds he forced me to swallow, seeds like blazing *coals...*"

This isn't getting me anywhere. He's on verge of delirium again. "Mr. Babbage, tell me where the ironclad boatyard is, and I'll provide all the water you desire."

"I know where that pathetic boatyard is! But you'll never reach it, not alive! If you value your lives, your sanity, your souls, you must turn this boat around. *Immediately!* You must turn tail and head for the Mississippi—"

"Captain," Dr. Travis said, "this interview only seems to be agitating him, dangerously so. I must ask you to continue at another time."

"Dr. Travis, while I respect your medical judgment, my primary concern is for the safety of this vessel and her crew. This man is running from something, something which terrorizes him. Delusion or not, I must find out what that is." Micholson turned back to Babbage. "What are you fleeing? What are we steaming towards?"

Ensign Waddow, boyish face flush with excitement, stepped into the infirmary. "Captain, sir, excuse me, you're wanted in the pilothouse. We're about to pass the rebel fortifications at Haines' Bluff—"

Micholson's eyes, blazing with anger, darted toward the ensign. Babbage didn't miss the telling expression, nor the indiscretion which had prompted it. "'Rebel' fortifications, Micholson? What goes on here?"

"Nothing. The ensign misspoke—"

"No. No, I don't think he did." He looked around him with new eyes. "It's the ironclads—you're after my cousin's ironclad rams, aren't you?"

"You're confused, Mr. Babbage; you've been through an ordeal. I only asked the whereabouts of the boatyard so I could deliver my captured iron—"

"Don't *lie* to me, Micholson! I won't be lied to anymore! I may be gullible, but I'm no idiot. Your game is over. I demand and expect the treatment due a captured officer."

145

Ensign Waddow slunk out of sight. Micholson rubbed his temples. "Very well, Mr. Babbage, I won't lie to you anymore. However, your fate is now entwined with our own. What lies ahead of us?"

Babbage sneered. "Ah, wouldn't you like to know? What lies ahead? Only a fitting fate for a boat larded down with plebeian blackguards and spies."

Pierce made to strike the prisoner, but Micholson pushed him aside. "If you want so much as a drop of water, you'll both tell me where that boatyard is and what danger awaits upriver."

Babbage managed a ravaged smile. "I would sooner *combust*, sir, than betray my country. You won't find that boatyard. You'll steam right past it, into the yawing gates of Hell."

"Take Mr. Babbage to the brig."

"The brig?" Dr. Travis objected. "Look at him, captain. Prisoner or not, this man needs medical care—"

"Doctor, within a day's time, this surgery may be crowded with the wounded bodies of my own men. I won't have Mr. Babbage taking up one of your beds. You may offer him treatment in his cell, if you wish."

The guards took hold of Babbage and released him from the examination table. Before he could be dragged from the room, he twisted around to face Micholson once more. "To Hell with you, 'captain'! To blazing Hell!"

Micholson controlled an urge to heave Babbage into the Yazoo. "Give the wretch as much water as he requests," he told the guards.

Dr. Travis's mouth fell open. "*Captain—!* That, sir, is...ghastly. Should his stomach rupture—let it be on *your* conscience."

"Believe me, Doctor, should that occur, it will be the least of the things weighing on my conscience."

That night, Micholson felt himself caught in the grip of nightmare again. Yet this was a new dream, an alien dream, not the dream of the *Virginia*.

I'm Jack Bainbridge, he managed to tell himself, oddly certain that this was so. He tried forcing himself awake, but the dream held him fast. *I'm seeing everything out of the boy's eyes...I'm sweating in a bed in the infirmary, tossing as though my limbs are on fire...*

In the corner of the infirmary something flickered, like a candle sputtering to new life. Jack/Micholson saw that it was a tiny face, no larger than an ivory cameo. With each beat of his fevered heart, the glowing face pulsed larger in the darkness. It was the face of Jack's mother, a visage unseen for three years, not since she'd perished in the burning of her home.

Grief, loneliness, and yearning engulfed him. The glowing face's lips moved. *Missed you*, it said. Jack/Micholson heard the words, not with his ears, but in his mind. *I've missed you, Jack. We've been so lonely without you.*

A second face flared in the darkness, the face of Jack's father. *You abandoned us, boy.* This voice hissed, rather than cooed. *Worthless little pup! Fell asleep when you were supposed to be minding the stove. Then you left us to die in the fire you caused.*

Micholson heard himself speak with Jack's voice. "It—it was an *accident!* The fire was all around me—I was afraid. I wanted to save you—"

You wanted to save yourself, boy! Always you thought of yourself, never your family!

Jack/Micholson held his arms out to the image of his mother, imploring her to defend him. "No! Tell him that's not right! Tell him I was a good son! I loved you both!"

I know that, Jack. But your father won't listen. You have to show us, Jack. Show us what a good son you are.

"How? Tell me how!"

147

His mother's sad smile radiated love and pity. *You never truly mourned for us, son. You never sought absolution for your sins. Do you remember, from church, the ashes? Seek out the ashes, Jack. Then you can be with us. We can all be a family again.*

"Oh thank you, *thank you!*"

Jack/Micholson knew where to find ashes. His legs went wobbly when he pushed himself out of bed, but he forced himself to stand.

Don't do it, Jack! Micholson screamed in his thoughts. *Don't go with them! Don't do it!* Slowly, quietly, Jack Bainbridge followed the glowing shades of his parents to the engine room.

* * *

"*NO!*"

Micholson awoke amidst a bed made swampy by his own sweat.

No dream had ever been so terrible. Not the blood-soaked dreams of the *Northport*'s demise. Not even the dreams in which Elizabeth and Paul had both scornfully betrayed him.

"Jack...I've got to check on Jack..."

He pulled on his clothes, then glanced through his tiny window. The sky above the eastern tree line had just started turning gray.

No later than five A.M. I won't awaken any of the crew. Not yet; not on account of a nightmare. I'll see to Jack myself.

The boy wasn't in the infirmary. His blankets lay in a heap on the floor. Micholson's skin turned cold.

He shook his executive officer awake. "Mr. Rutherford. Please pardon this most untimely disturbance. But you must help me organize a search of the gunboat. Jack Bainbridge is missing."

Rutherford awakened four of the Marines. Micholson reserved the engine room for himself. The dream still fresh in his mind, he dreaded what he might find there.

Stepping through the doorway, he swung his lantern in a wide arc. "Jack? Are you here, Jack?"

No answer. The silent boilers dully gleamed, lying in the darkness like fat snakes awaiting some prey to stumble into their midst. The firebox beneath the boilers emitted not even the dimmest of glows, its coals having long ago surrendered their last reservoirs of heat.

Ashes...

He descended to the lowest deck, where the firebox lay. Expecting its iron doors to be cold, he grasped the handles. He drew his hands away, startled—he'd burned his fingers and palms. He pulled on one of the thick stoker's mitts and pulled the doors open, one at a time.

He shined his lantern inside. The ashes didn't look right. They were uneven, gullied. Like something had burrowed out of them. Or into them.

Could the cat have survived? Did it escape? No, that doesn't make any sense. It buried itself in the coals last night, and we spent much of today under steam. Surely its body was consumed.

Feeling sick, he used a shovel to probe the black sooty wastes on the floor of the furnace. His shovelhead met resistance. Sensing bile rising in his gullet, he cleared away the ashes.

His lantern revealed a human foot, sallow as melted wax.

CHAPTER THIRTEEN

The Fabulous Riverboat

*Aboard the USS James B. Eads and ashore in
Satartia, Mississippi, April 24, 1862*

I know what led to this, Micholson thought, looking
around the conference table at his convened officers. *But
how can I share my knowledge with them, and the source
of that knowledge, without being considered as much a
lunatic as Joseph Babbage is believed to be?*

"Dr. Travis," he said, "please share with us the results of
your autopsy."

Dr. Travis rose from his chair. "Gentlemen, let me
preface my comments by saying that this was a most
incomplete autopsy. Forensic medicine is not my specialty,
far from it. And I was further hampered by a lack of
specialized instruments and chemicals. Thus, I was unable
to discern whether Jack Bainbridge had been subjected to
any poisons prior to being deposited in the furnace.
Assuming he was, indeed, deposited there—"

"Of *course* he was deposited there!" Oates shouted.
"What do you think—he crawled in there *himself*?!"

"Please sit down, Mr. Oates." Micholson locked eyes
with his chief engineer. "I understand this has been
extremely upsetting for you. As it has for us all. But we have
to consider all the possibilities. Please continue, Doctor."

"Uh, yes. Thank you. In examining Jack's body, I did
not find any external evidence of foul play. There were no
contusions on his head or body, nor were there any
puncture wounds. So far as I am able to tell—again, I was
unable to consider the question of poisons—the cause of

death was suffocation, probably preceded by choking. His mouth and windpipe were clogged with ashes. As if he had ingested them."

"I'd say there's your evidence of foul play right there," Delaup said, looking around the table. "There's no man on this green earth gonna swallow a heap of ashes on his own." Murmurs of agreement sprang up.

"The boy had no enemies among the crew," Rutherford said. "Uh, did he?"

"Of all of us here, I probably knew Jack the longest," Broadhurst said. His voice, normally rich with good cheer, was a dull monotone. "He was part of my forty-two pounder cannon crew for the three weeks the *Eads* was working up, back in Cairo. Jack never had a bad word to say about anyone. Nobody so much as disliked him. His mates were all sorry to see him transfer to Engineering, as I was. But I signed the papers because he seemed eager for the change."

"We all know who committed this murder," Oates said. "Don't we? Why won't any of you come out and say it? It was that Confederate lunatic Dr. Travis brought aboard!"

"That's foolishness!" the physician said, his face reddening. "The captain had Babbage locked in the brig yesterday afternoon. He's still locked in the brig—check it yourself. Are you telling us this very ill man is some kind of escape artist?"

How can I convince them of the truth? Micholson asked himself. *Jack wasn't murdered, at least not by earthly forces. He died by his own hand, just as Nehemiah warned I would should I not slay the cat.* "Dr. Travis, four days ago I pulled Jack from the bottom of the Mississippi River. You barely managed to resuscitate him. During his last day of life, following the confrontation with that panther, several of us noticed him to be listless, uncommunicative, nearly catatonic. You've stated he suffered from a high fever. What was your judgment of his mental state? Could lingering effects from his near-drowning and the shock of nearly being mauled by a wild animal have produced some form of severe mental despondency or melancholia?"

"Actually, captain—"

Oates slammed his fist on the table. "I highly resent this line of inquiry! What you are suggesting is a smear on Jack's soul—suicide is against the laws of Christ and honor—"

"Mr. Oates!" Micholson shouted. "Be *silent*, sir! Your outbursts have disrupted this meeting too many times. You are not to utter another word until I request it from you."

Oates flushed a deep red, then reluctantly nodded his assent.

"As you were saying, Dr. Travis."

"Yes. What I was about to say was, Jack was in remarkably good spirits while he was under my care, at least until the panther attack. It was all I could do to make him rest—his greatest wish was to return to his duties in the engine room. He talked a good deal about wanting to be an engineer someday."

Micholson recalled his own brush with a watery demise. "Surviving violent death can bring on a temporary euphoria. I'm more interested in his general mental tendencies, which could have been exacerbated by his recent fevers and fugue. I understand he was an orphan. Mr. Oates, you became quite close to him. There was talk of you taking him on as a protégé. What had his mood been, since joining your staff? Did he—did he ever express feelings of guilt regarding his parents' deaths?"

Oates appeared to choose his words carefully. "He was an orphan, yes. His parents died in a fire, a conflagration he was rescued from. Like any survivor of such a tragedy, he could be somewhat...melancholy, at times. There were things...things he told me in strict confidence. He missed his parents. Is that so abnormal? But he was fine. Just fine, I say. A wonderful lad. Tell me this, if you can. If Jack—if the boy had determined to do violence to himself, why would he have selected the method the doctor's autopsy implies?

This gunboat is rife with guns. Why would he have chosen ashes?"

Because the shades of his parents demanded it of him, Micholson thought. *But I can't tell them that.*

"I...I cannot answer that, Mr. Oates."

Broadhurst raised his hand. "I'd like to ask Dr. Travis if he's through examining Jack's body."

The physician turned to the gunnery captain. "Yes, I've performed all the tests and examinations I'm capable of. Why?"

"I just wanted to know when and where we're going to bury the lad."

"Mr. Delaup," Micholson said, "once we get underway, keep your eye open for some dry, level ground that we can anchor near, and we'll assemble a burial party."

"Captain," Oates said, "if I may interject something—"

"Yes, Mr. Oates?"

"I am...somewhat familiar with the boy's preferences in this regard. He told me once—we were talking about the mission, and the subject of death came up—should he be killed, he wanted me to ensure he would be buried in a church cemetery. He doesn't have parents to bury him. The thought of being laid to rest in some anonymous field was too lonely and miserable a notion for him." Oates stared into Micholson's face, not with his typical disdain, but with pleading. "Please do this for him, captain. He was a good boy, a good sailor. It's his final wish."

"Thank you for telling us that, Mr. Oates. Jack was one of us. We will make every effort to ensure his wishes are followed." He turned to his navigator, who was already examining a chart of the Yazoo basin. "Mr. Delaup, where ahead of us might have a proper cemetery?"

"The nearest place that might," the pilot said, striking the chart with his forefinger, "is this little hamlet right here, just five miles ahead. Satartia."

Satartia's diminutive town cemetery was on a low rise overlooking the swollen river. Men from the gunnery and engineering crews gently laid the last clods of damp earth onto Jack Bainbridge's grave. *At least the lad will have an eternal view of a river,* Micholson thought. That notion was the only remotely comforting aspect he could salvage from this tragedy.

He turned to the handsome young woman standing next to him, their hostess at this somber affair. "Mrs. Schoenberg, thank you again. It is extremely gracious of you and your townsfolk to allow us to bury our comrade here. Especially considering your recent tragedy."

The black-clad woman took his hand. Her touch was strangely warm. He noticed her cheeks had remained flushed throughout the service, a display identical to that of the other women who had attended the burial. "Please, captain...no thanks are necessary. You only asked us to meet the minimal requirements of common decency. Providing a proper burial is the least we can do for our fighting men."

Micholson glanced down the hill to the charred ruins of the Baptist church in the center of town. *It must be so hard for these women to remain in Satartia,* he thought, *in the aftermath of such hideous tragedy. Do their husbands, off at various encampments, even know what has transpired here? Given the unreliability of the Confederate mail service, they most likely won't learn what happened to their fathers, sons, grandfathers, and in-laws until they return home someday. If they ever return home.*

The old men and underage boys had gathered to plan a home defense regiment, Mrs. Schoenberg had said. They met in the basement of their church, what should have been the safest location for miles around. Yet the fire that broke out above their heads, amidst the whale oil stored for the sanctuary's use, was no respecter of sacred places.

The young widow stared at the ruins of the church, her face unreadable. "Mrs. Schoenberg," Micholson said, "if my men and I can be of any service—"

"Captain Micholson, please call me Camilla." Her fair skin and green eyes presented him with a potent echo of his estranged Elizabeth. "I never cared for my married surname."

"Camilla, then. If you would like, my men could search the rubble for any holy objects that might have survived the fire. And—I regret there is no gentler way to say this—if there are bodies still remaining in the ruins, we could recover them and provide them with a proper burial, returning the favor you have done for us."

"Thank you, captain. That is a gallant and generous offer." Her voice was the softest sound he had heard in many months. "But unnecessary. The bodies of our lost loved ones have all been properly cared for. And the women and I have decided to leave the ruins as they are, holding all their holy treasures, as a memorial to our families."

"Of course. We'll continue on our way, then. We still have a few steaming hours left before dark."

"Why hurry on, captain? The day is nearly gone. You and your crew have just buried a friend. My neighbors and I, we so rarely get news from the wider world. Especially not from servicemen. All of our husbands are away in the Army. Any word we could hear of the war's progress would be precious to us. Let us make a supper for your officers. It would be an honor for us."

"Mrs. Schoenberg, no, we couldn't think of putting you to such trouble—"

Smiling, she looped her arm lightly around his own. Again he felt her heat. "It's Camilla, captain. And don't think of it as trouble. You would do us a great favor. Cooking only for ourselves, day after dull day, we're in danger of losing our skills of hospitality. There are very elaborate and unusual dining quarters aboard my late husband's steamer, docked next to your own vessel. I believe he'd be pleased to have you dine there. The *Germania* was the love of his life. Apart from me."

The breeze swung around, returning to him fragrances he had half-forgotten...citrus, rose, the subtle odor of a woman's skin moistened by the sun. He could think of no reason to refuse Camilla's invitation. The loss of a few hours steaming meant little; Satartia was as good a place as any on the river to anchor for the night. And he and his officers might glean some valuable information at the dinner table.

"We would be delighted to accept your invitation, Camilla. Simply name the hour."

Again she smiled, and he was transported across years and miles to the day when he and Elizabeth had first met. "I'm so happy you'll be joining us, captain. We'll see you and your men aboard the *Germania* at eight o'clock."

Micholson led his procession of crewmen to the gates of the small cemetery. He glanced at the uneven rows of graves. *The tombstones are all old. So weathered, I can barely read the names.* A tiny alarm sounded in the back of his mind. Pushing open the heavy iron gate, he realized what was disturbing him.

Jack Bainbridge's memorial is the only freshly dug grave in the entire place. There must be a second, larger cemetery somewhere. Perhaps this plot is an annex, with the main cemetery on the far side of the burned church?

He reminded himself to ask about it, later, at dinner.

Micholson could not help but be impressed. The *Germania's* long, narrow banquet table was resplendent, dressed in spotless linen tablecloths, adorned with graceful silver candelabra and sparkling crystal pitchers. Wotan, Thor, Frigga, and Odin thundered and soared above the guests' heads, their ancient Norse might captured in a fresco stretching the full length of the ceiling.

Delaup had dressed in the costume of a riverboat dandy, fringed in ruffles and silk, but his sour mien belied the gay frivolity of his clothing. "*M'sieur*," he whispered, "something about these ladies, it puts me off. Sure, they're all dressed in black, but it didn't seem to me they're mourning no one. The way they follow me with their eyes—hungry eyes, almost like they were a pack of dogs and I was a big, juicy piece of meat, roasting on a spit—"

"Why, Mr. Delaup, I'd think you'd relish such attentions." The levity in his voice was short-lived, and his face took on a serious cast. "But I know of what you speak. Things are far from right here. Have you noticed the fevered coloration of their faces? I'm reminded of Jack Bainbridge's face in the days before his death. I wish Dr. Travis were with us. I would appreciate his thoughts on this, but he decided to stay behind with Babbage when our prisoner took a decided turn for the worse."

"So you think this might be some kind of, uh, a sickness of some sort, and maybe Jack had it, too?"

"Possibly. Perhaps following this meal, I can contrive to have several of the women visit Dr. Travis in his infirmary. His expertise could prove invaluable, if indeed this is some new malady we're confronting."

Could the catastrophe Nehemiah predicted be some kind of tropical plague deliberately imported from Africa? It might explain the need for Babbage and his slave to procure two shiploads of plants and animals from that continent—perhaps they knew such flora and fauna would carry the disease here. That still doesn't explain Nehemiah's knowledge of the plot. But it could explain Jack's illness and death. The panther I killed could have come from Africa, bearing a plague which causes fevers and dementia. Jack could have fallen victim because his body had already been weakened by his near-drowning. Babbage must suffer from it, too. And these women—they could have proven especially susceptible due to their recent shared grief and a resulting neglect of their bodily needs. Satartia isn't that

*many miles downriver from Adderwood; creatures set free
at the plantation could have made their way here.*

Micholson accepted a glass of wine from one of his
hostesses and forced himself to smile. Her fingers left traces
of heat on the stem of the glass.

"Doesn't make no sense," Delaup whispered. "You'd
think they'd have all taken to their beds, eyes bleary with
weeping, but here they are, putting on a banquet for us river
rats...Well, at least our chief engineer seems to be enjoying
himself, if he's capable of taking pleasure in anything. Look
at him, will you? He's entranced by those mechanical men.
Probably scheming how to pilfer some of them metal
mannequins for spare parts for his boilers."

Oates couldn't take his eyes off the mannequins. Teams
of them waited stiffly on their tracks in the corners of the
room. Would he and the others be provided with a
demonstration of their workings? He was familiar with the
German genius for clockwork; as a boy, he had heard
stories from his grandfather about the wondrous clock
towers of Bavaria, where iron figurines clambered from
their nooks each hour to celebrate the passing of time.

The rich aromas of freshly baked hens, cornbread
muffins, and sweet, buttery sauces flowed into the dining
hall. Oates had had no appetite since the gruesome
discovery of the morning, yet these appealing fragrances
enticed his dormant hunger back to life. Camilla
Schoenberg emerged from the kitchen. No longer dressed
in mourning black, she stunned the eyes of all men present,
adorned in a gown of livid scarlet that amplified the red
tones of her auburn hair.

"Captain Micholson, officers of the *James B. Eads*,
welcome aboard the riverboat *Germania*. My late husband,
Johann, expended ten years of his life and most of his
personal fortune to ensure that this vessel would be the
most fabulous pleasure craft ever to travel American waters.

You do his memory great honor by dining here this evening. Let us all pray that this awful war be speedily ended with our victory, so that Johann's renown may spread throughout our new nation, as the *Germania* plies the rivers of a noble and free Confederacy."

Micholson led the officers in polite applause. Oates's ears perked up at the faint sound of steam cocks being opened, an odd noise to emerge from a kitchen. Mary, the young woman sitting next to him, noticed his attentiveness to the sound and smiled. "Mr. Engineer, you should be very interested in what happens next," she said.

All conversations around the table were interrupted by the clatter of metal wheels on metal tracks. Two pairs of mechanical waiters, dressed in the green velvet livery of Bavarian servants, emerged from the twin doors connecting the dining hall with the kitchen. Their outstretched tin arms carried silver trays laden with steaming tureens and platters. They stood ramrod straight, bolted to small wheeled platforms which advanced on narrow-gauge tracks. Oates noticed with great interest that they trailed behind them steam hoses, which pro-vided their forward momentum.

Oates's fellow officers responded like children, laughing or gaping with wide-eyed amazement. Oates stared intently at the advancing devices, wanting nothing more than to crack one open with a wrench and learn the workings of its interior mechanisms. He felt vaguely guilty to indulge in such fascination no more than five hours after he had laid Jack Bainbridge in the earth. Still, this was a most astounding and delightful display of mechanical ingenuity.

The tin waiters rolled to opposite sides of the long table, arriving at their serving stations nearly in unison. Then they bent forward in a series of precise movements, their rising arms synchronized with their bending torsos so as to keep the food trays constantly level. Oates marveled at the exactitude of their operation; a human waiter could have done no better job ensuring that the gravies arrived at the tableside unspilled.

Mary removed the tureens and platters from the trays and passed a basket of muffins to Oates. The mechanical waiters remained at their stations. *Hmmph...their designer made no provision for backward movement.* The mannequin's painted wooden face began dripping with condensation from the steaming tureens. Staring at that inhumanly still face, he realized whose face it reminded him of—Jack Bainbridge's sweating face, as the lad had tossed with fever. Oates felt his stomach roil. His new-found appetite evaporated.

"Is anything the matter?" Mary asked in dulcet tones. "Is the food disagreeable?"

"No. No, I'm fine. It's just...I'm not, uh, terribly hungry."

She stabbed one of the baked hens and lifted it onto her plate. "Really? I would think a big, strapping man like you, playing with your machines all day, would always have a healthy appetite. Oh, well—the less you eat, the more there'll be for the rest of us!" She slipped her strangely warm arm partway around Oates's ample midsection. "Now why don't you tell me just what it is that engineers do on a boat? I'm sure I'd find it simply *fascinating—*"

His queasiness worsening, Oates abruptly stood away from the table. "Please excuse me, ma'am—I'm feeling rather out of sorts. I—I need to seek some fresh air. Forgive me..."

He hurried to a door that led to the staterooms and, he hoped, to an open deck. The corridor between the rows of staterooms was lit only by the thin light of a quarter moon, peering in through intermittent windows. Searching for an exit to the outside deck, Oates tripped over a protrusion in the carpet.

He stumbled into a pair of hard, cold arms. Jerking back, he yelped with fright, then realized it was another of the mannequins. He had tripped over its track.

As his eyes slowly adjusted, he studied the figure, his queasiness temporarily forgotten. It was fashioned to be a woman dancer; its limbs were more finely articulated than those of the waiter mannequins. He noticed a key jutting from the small of its back. *At least some of its movements must be powered by clockwork, rather than steam.* He groped for the steam hose attached to the dancer's wheeled platform. It was cold and flaccid. He followed it to the wall, discovering the valve that, when turned, would release the steam to propel the dancer forward.

The steam pipe connected to the valve was hidden behind wall paneling. Yet even through this sheath of wood, Oates felt the heat of the trapped steam. He followed the pipe's hidden path simply by running his fingers along the surface of the paneling, sensing the heat with his fingertips. The pipe would lead him to the engine room.

What kind of powerplant would the *Germania* have? A sparkling new engine? Or an old workhorse salvaged from a wreck, held together with rags and a prayer? One could never tell with these boats; the magnificence of their accommodations was no gauge at all of the state of the engines.

Oates felt his way carefully from room to room, following the steam pipe. His nose told him something was amiss. *What can they be burning in their fire box? That certainly isn't the aroma of coal.* The scent he'd detected wasn't the aroma of burning pine or hardwood, either. If he didn't know better, he'd swear they had a second kitchen down below, with an imbecile cook who didn't know to keep the meat out of the fire.

He descended a dark staircase. The odor had strengthened, unpleasantly so. He felt waves of heat rising from the base of the stairs, then pushed open the door at the bottom. A lantern hung from the far wall, dimly illuminating a comfortably familiar tableau of boilers, pipes, and furnace.

Oates was grateful for the lamp; few activities were more dangerous—or stupid—than stumbling around an active engine room in the dark. The machinery looked immaculate. He read the brass plate mounted on a gleaming piston: *Haversham Ironworks, St. Louis, Missouri, 1860.* One of the better shops on the Mississippi.

Schoenberg paid good money for this setup. He'd probably be turning over in his grave if he knew what his wife is burning for fuel. What kind of garbage have those women stuffed in the firebox? Old cow carcasses?

He was utterly baffled. Satartia was surrounded by hundreds of acres of perfectly serviceable hardwoods. Burning anything else might leave a black scum in the firebox the labors of Hercules couldn't efface. *Didn't Schoenberg teach his wife anything about running a boat?*

A pair of furnace mitts hung on the wall near the lantern. He pulled them on. The flames trapped inside the brick and iron box hissed and roared, ravenous. Insatiable. The engineer grasped massive iron handles and slowly pulled the fire doors open. The sweat on his round face instantly evaporated in the blast of escaping heat. Shielding his eyes with his insulated forearm, he peered into the furnace.

Staring back at him were the blackened eye holes of a pile of skulls. Human skulls.

Blood ran down his forehead from the gash he'd suffered when he tripped on the stairs. The heavyset engineer thought his heart might burst as he ran headlong through the dark corridors. But he had to warn the others. *Good God—every bite of food they swallow could be laced with poisons!*

He smashed through the doors to the dining hall. "Stop eating! Stop *eating!*"

Every head in the room turned his way. Camilla Schoenberg rose from her seat and walked quickly to the rear of the dining hall. "These—these *witches,*" Oates gasped, "oh God, what they've done—"

Micholson stood from his chair. "Oates! What are you talking about, man? Your head—"

"Damn my head! They've stuffed their men and boys in the firebox! They're burning the corpses!"

Expressions of appalled disbelief appeared on the faces of the men. But then Rutherford's eyes widened with alarm. "Look out, Mr. Oates!"

Camilla, only a few feet away from the engineer, lifted a fire ax from its hooks on the wall and swung it. Oates stumbled backwards. He avoided the weapon's deadly arc. Yet he had not been her target. The heavy blade split open the main trunk line leading to the mechanical waiters—a thick hose pregnant with pulsing steam.

The frantic gas spasmed out of the vent in a scorching cloud. Its initial rush caught Camilla and Oates full in the face. The engineer saw white, then nothing. He no longer had anything that could be called eyes.

The steam embraced him with wildly kinetic passion, his worst nightmare, an embittered old lover he had tried desperately to escape. The nerves of his flesh screamed, then died. His ravaged body hit the floor like a sack of coal.

The last sounds his ears ever conveyed were the cries of the women as they swept past his boiled carcass. They screeched with delight, like children in a playground, joyfully overturning candelabra before rushing to immolate themselves in the blast of escaping steam.

* * *

M'Lundowi danced before the flames. He and his followers had built twenty-two massive bonfires on the now-abandoned grounds of Adderwood Plantation.

A powerful wind blew in from the south. The air filled with ashes, the ashes of sacrificed beasts, and those of Alakko, Alaltho's son.

163

M'Lundowi stared into the fires. They were different now. They stared back at him.

His blood sang a song of triumph and exultation. His pawns, his fellow Lundowans, prostrated themselves on the parched earth and hid their eyes.

The great fires walked.

CHAPTER FOURTEEN

The Charnel River

Aboard the USS James B. Eads,
*on the Yazoo River between Satartia, Yazoo City, and
Adderwood Plantation, Mississippi,
April 24–25, 1862*

Micholson had never felt such heat. Not even the sinking wreck of the *Northport*, with an arsenal's worth of black powder combusting, had burned as fiercely. Thirty yards from the *Germania*, dragging his horribly scalded executive officer along the pier that led to shore, he felt as though he were still in the heart of the inferno.

He desperately counted his men, struggling with their wounded fellows towards the Eads's gangplank. *Eighteen...how many were we? How many men did I take aboard that deathtrap?*

Delaup, shielding his face from bits of flaming debris, rushed back to assist with Rutherford. "Captain—thank God you got yourself out—"

"Who are we missing? Oates. Where is Oates—?"

Delaup took on more of Rutherford's weight. The executive officer, his face seared to unrecognizability, moaned through a lipless mouth. "Oates is dead, *m'sieur.*"

"Are you certain? We have to go back for him—"

Delaup grabbed hold of Micholson's shoulder. "Captain, I know what I saw. For a live Oates, I'd risk my life. But I'll not burn up in trying to rescue his corpse. And you won't, neither."

Micholson reluctantly acceded to Delaup's wisdom. Sailors poured forth from the *Eads*, running down the

165

gangplank to assist with the wounded officers. The wind, made drunken by the intense heat, swung about to the north, fanning the flames toward the gunboat and the *Molly Downings*. Bits of wooden gingerbread from the gaudy pleasure steamer caught fire and flew into the hot air, chasing the sailors and Micholson like sadistic sprites.

We need to get away from here, Micholson thought as he stepped aboard his own vessel. *We're too close. When the* Germania *'s boilers explode, the Molly Downings will go up in flames, and even this gunboat will be in peril, despite our armor.*

"Mr. Delaup, I need you to run to the boiler deck. See if we have enough reserve steam pressure to move us. We have to put distance between us and the *Germania*, as quickly as we can."

"Aye, captain." Delaup helped to rest Rutherford against a gun carriage, then sprinted to the ladder which led to the lower deck. Dr. Travis, in night trousers and an unbuttoned muslin shirt, directed wounded but ambulatory men toward his the infirmary and organized bearers for the more seriously injured. He spotted Micholson. "Captain! Good God in Heaven, what happened to these men? Was it some sort of trap?"

Micholson struggled for a reply that would make sense. "No, I don't believe so...I don't think the women ever saw through our ruse. They just—they went insane, Doctor. They killed themselves. With steam. And tried to take the lot of us with them. Rutherford took a blast of steam full in the face. Do what you can for him, Doctor—"

Delaup returned. "Excuse me, captain, Doctor. The men below say it'll be at least forty minutes before we'll have steam enough to move us..."

No power for forty minutes, Micholson thought. *By that time, we could be resting on the bottom of the Yazoo. The only option seems to be to put the* Germania *there first—*

Minutes later, the night's quiet, already disturbed by the incessant crackling of the burning riverboat, was shattered by the twin discharges of the Eads's aft cannons. A pair of thirty-two pound iron balls, fired at point-blank range, ripped into the Germania below her waterline. The echoes had barely subsided before a second set of projectiles crashed into the settling wreck.

The river rushed eagerly into the dying riverboat's hull, displacing the air in the steamer's machinery spaces with a series of piercing groans and crashes. Micholson expected that the sinking riverboat would be wreathed with a blanket of steam as the fires settled into the quenching waters. Perhaps it was a trick of his weary eyes, but the flames seemed to spread higher, avoiding the river's embrace like a water-wary cat.

The Germania sank five feet. Then, abruptly, her descent stopped. The infernos aboard her still threatened to explode her boilers at any moment. Micholson felt the small hairs on the back of his neck rise. "Mr. Delaup, what is the average depth of the Yazoo in springtime?"

Delaup skimmed through his book of charts. "It says here...for April, with an average snow-melt and decent rains, anywhere from twenty to, uh, eight feet."

"Damn..." Micholson stared at the now-stationary Germania, blazing like a devil's wedding cake, still close enough to pepper the *Eads* with a fusillade of fiery debris. A chunk of blazing gingerbread struck the pilothouse like a tiny meteor, startling Delaup into dropping his chart book.

Micholson gauged the narrow stretch of water between the burning wreck and the western shore. "Mr. Delaup, could you use the current to steer us downstream of the Germania?"

"It'll be a tight squeeze. I'd much rather do it with full engine power. Without it, the current might lay us flat alongside that pyre. But I'm willing to make a go of it."

Moments later, hard muscles worked cranks that dislodged the *Eads*'s anchors from the muddy river bottom. As soon as her anchors rose, the gunboat began drifting downstream. The river pushed the *Eads* closer to the giant

water torch that was the Germania. The crew slammed
every hatch on the gunboat's port side tightly shut.

"Captain, she's hardly more controllable than a barrel in
a waterfall," Delaup complained. With a sickening lurch,
the gunboat scraped against the side of the sunken
riverboat. Flames licked hungrily at the ironclad's armor,
blistering her paint. She clung to the blazing wreck for what
felt like an eternity. Then the current's pressure pushed her
free.

A hundred yards later, the ironclad was out of
immediate danger. The *Molly Downings* followed soon
after. Less cumbersome than the *Eads*, and with more
reserve power in her boilers, the freighter had an easier time
maneuvering around the flaming obstacle.

The more religious men aboard the two vessels prayed
the current would take them all the way south to the
Mississippi, away from the cursed Yazoo.

Yet the sound of anchors splashing into the river sunk
such feeble hopes.

The morning would bring worse horrors.

Delaup broke what had become an edgy silence in the
pilothouse. "Captain, Harold Pilger died this morning. Did
you get word?"

Micholson curtly nodded. "I was told, yes."

"So you've decided against turning back to Vicksburg, to
take the wounded to a hospital?"

"It is too risky." The words tasted like clay in his mouth.
"Vicksburg is an armed camp. Should we go, we might
never leave. Word of our ruse may have reached there by
now from those irregulars we fought in the Arkansas woods.
And we have no assurance that the doctors at Vicksburg are
any better prepared for treating severe burns than Dr.
Travis."

"Why not send the wounded back to Cairo on the
Molly Downings?"

"It wouldn't work. Believe me, I've considered it. The *Molly Downings* could never make it past the guns of Fort Pillow without either the *Eads* or other gunboats of the Flotilla to shield her. And sending away our coal boat would eventually leave us stranded."

Delaup's eyes flashed. "*Molly Downings* is a fast boat. She's got all that iron aboard—her crew could make barricades in an hour or two, I'm sure of it. And we've got plenty of spaces aboard where we could heap coal. Captain, listen, those wounded men deserve any chance we can give them—"

"Valery, please. Don't make this more difficult than it already is. I've made my decision." He turned back to the windows, his voice barely above a whisper. "If I start questioning myself, I'm lost."

Delaup, seeming to recognize the agony in Micholson's voice, remained silent a few moments. "We'll be coming up on Yazoo City within an hour or two," he said as they rounded a bend. "Any soldiers stationed there shouldn't have gotten wind yet of what we're up to. If they have a hospital, do you think—?"

"Yes, Mr. Delaup. If they have a hospital, we'll drop off our wounded there."

The Yazoo twisted like a tortured millipede. Although they had left the *Germania*'s smoking wreck many miles behind them, they had never escaped the pungent aroma of burning pine, which followed them no matter which way the wind blew.

Two bends further on, the gunboat's blunt prow struck the first of the floating corpses. Within moments, the bodies, bobbing on the river's surface like bags of waterlogged refuse, grew so numerous they were beyond counting.

"Oh, God," Delaup said. "It keeps getting worse. What region of Hell have we stumbled into?"

"I wish I could tell you," Micholson said.

"I—I used to pilot a snag boat. Used to clear rivers of barriers like giant rafts, formed from floating logs and debris. Those pile-ups could block a river for miles; a man could walk across the surface like it was a forest floor. This is just like that, only it's a raft of, of corpses..."

"Take hold of yourself, Mr. Delaup. I'm going out on deck. I need to see what types of injuries those people suffered."

Micholson found Gunnery Captain Broadhurst already standing on the bow deck.

"Do you think—do you think our boys could have done this?" Broadhurst asked.

"No. The nearest Federal troops are up in Tennessee."

"Cavalry—could it have been cavalry? A raid down into Mississippi, to disrupt spring plantings, maybe? But horsemen, they aren't monsters. They would've just chased the civilians away. They wouldn't have—they *couldn't* have done *this*—"

"Let's have a look at them, Mr. Broadhurst. I know it's a distasteful task, but pull one of them in with that grappling pole." Broadhurst knelt at the side of the bow and extended his boat-hook into the water. The first body he could reach was that of a little girl. Her white muslin dress was discolored by brownish stains, as though burned.

He hauled the body aboard. It lay on its face on the wet deck, its matted yellow hair belying the certainty that, days or hours before, a mother had lovingly combed this hair, teasing out all the tangles, brushing it until it shone like gold.

How quickly a person becomes a thing—when dead, Micholson thought. He turned the body over. His stomach rebelled, and he quickly averted his eyes. The burns were beyond grotesque. Silently apologizing to the unknown child, he took the grappling pole from Broadhurst and pushed the body back into the river.

The next body he hooked was that of a grown man. He didn't pull it onto the deck, rather turned face up in the river. The man's death mask, burned onto his features, told a story of leaping into the Yazoo with his dying strength, frantically seeking escape from the flames.

"Bring me Joseph Babbage," Micholson said with quiet fury. "Bring the prisoner here, to view his own deviltry."

A pair of Marines hauled Babbage in irons down to the bow.

"Leave us," Micholson said.

"But sir, this man is dangerous—"

"So am *I*, Sergeant. Never more so than now."

The Marines left Babbage alone with their commander.

Micholson grabbed the back of Babbage's neck and forced the prisoner to kneel on the deck at the water's edge. "Babbage, you may be pleased to know that I no longer consider you a lunatic. But you should be very concerned that I now consider you a *fiend*." He shoved the prisoner's face inches from the floating corpses which bounded off the ironclad's slowly progressing bow. "*Look* at it! Examine your work closely, monster! Is *this* what you intended? These aren't Federal soldiers and sailors floating face down in the river, Babbage. They're women and children—the women and children of your *own State!*

Babbage began laughing.

Micholson's grip on his neck tightened. "Do you find this a source of *humor?*"

He pulled Babbage's face back. The man continued laughing, but tears gushed from his eyes. "I...I could *introduce* you to these good people, Micholson, if that would please you. Turn them over. Show me their faces. Even given whatever horrible burns they suffered, I'm certain I would recognize each of them. They're the citizens of Yazoo City. My neighbors. I'm sure I've danced with many of these ladies, or at least had the opportunity to invite them to join me on the dance floor, and then been rebuffed. Oh, I wished many foul fates on those scornful women; I admit to that. But never *this*, oh, never, never *this*..."

"How do I stop this, Babbage? By all that is holy, you will tell me how to bring this horror to its end."

"I...I cannot."

Micholson dug his fingers into the space between Babbage's vertebrae and shoulder blade, ready to twist his head off. "That isn't a *request*, man! It is an *order!* Refuse, and I swear I will throttle you with my own hands and throw your miserable remains into the Yazoo with your victims!"

"You don't understand!" Babbage wailed. "I *cannot*—not because I refuse, but because there is no way to stop this! Daniel made that clear! The *Mikithi,* once unleashed, cannot be coaxed back into their bottles like some tribe of storybook genies. I doubt even he could manage to command them now, after they have tasted so much human flesh. They will kill and consume, as far as they can range, until there is nothing left to burn."

He stared up at Micholson with the eyes of a man irretrievably damned. "Kill me, Micholson. Please. You would do me an enormous kindness. Perhaps while my soul makes its journey from this earthly Hell to the subterranean one, I shall know only oblivion, blessed oblivion, even for only a few moments."

Micholson's fingers loosened around Babbage's collarbone. He let the prisoner slump to the deck. *I should never have vowed to slay him,* he thought. *Though I contest with fiends and monsters, I refuse to let myself become one of them.*

It must've been a pretty town, once, Micholson thought, *up there on its hill.*

Yazoo City was an inferno. He could feel the fierce heat through the layers of iron and oak that formed the pilothouse walls, even though Delaup had carefully hewn to the western edge of the river, as far from the blazing docks as he dared steer. He could barely make out through the thick smoke the remaining timbers of what had been a large building atop the main hill. Most likely it had been a church. He didn't trouble himself wondering whether its congregation had escaped safely. He had seen the parishioners an hour ago; their final prayers had not availed them.

"Do we keep on, captain?" Delaup asked. "Does it make any sense? Maybe—maybe whatever destroyed Yazoo City has also destroyed the boatyard?"

"Until we know that for certain, Mr. Delaup, we keep on." Though the acrid smoke seeping through the view slits threatened to blind him, he continued staring at the blazing ruins of Yazoo City, searching for any clue as to the nature of their unanticipated, deadly foe, this bringer of Apocalypse. "And we owe it to those poor souls we found in the river to learn how to stop this...this plague of madness and fire. We may be the only force on the river available and capable of doing so."

"You learned nothing from Babbage?"

"Nothing of use, no. He did not remain lucid for long."

"So we keep on?"

"We keep on. To Adderwood Plantation, the next stop on the river."

Micholson, Broadhurst, and Delaup stood in front of the pilothouse, beneath a blood-red sunset, and watched the majestic plantation on the eastern shore burn. Due to the barrier of the plantation's protective levee, only the tops of the compound's structures could be seen. Adderwood burned, but not in the same way Yazoo City had burned. The great brick columns, gables, and verandas of the mansion and its out buildings blazed fiercely, but they were not consumed.

This is no fire known to Man or Nature, Micholson thought. He trembled, staring at the multitude of faces wavering in the waves of ungodly heat. For this inferno, like the Hydra of myth, had an endless supply of heads. *A hundred and ten faces...* The faces of the lost sailors of the *Northport* stared at him from the flames, their features marred by bloody wounds, impaled by stake like splinters, or burned into twisted mockeries.

"What—what do you see, Mr. Broadhurst?"

The gunnery captain, now second in command, took a moment to reply. His voice, normally unshakable as granite, sounded close to breaking. "If I choose to believe my eyes, captain...I'd say it's the Devil himself out there. Just as Parson Jameson described him when I was a boy. Horns on his flaming head. Cloven hooves like a goat's. Horrible crooked teeth. And those *eyes*...Don't you see him, too?"

He's begging me to tell him I see what he does, so that I will vouch for his sanity. Yet I won't lie to the man. "No. I'm sorry, Broadhurst, I don't. And you, Valery? What do you see?"

The pilot's voice was low and brittle. "You know, my old grandmother, she was from the forests of northern France. Over there, they had nothing better to do than tell tales to scare the wits out of each other. When I was small, she used to tell me the nastiest stories...I don't think you want to hear it, *m'sieur.* And I for sure don't want to share it."

Micholson watched the crowd of men on the open deck below, common seamen now confronted with the inexplicable. Shouts arose:

"It's the Devil! Satan himself, I tell ye!"

"No, no, it's some fiendish rebel trick!"

"Was them corpses we steamed through a trick, as well? Believe your eyes, ye damned fool!"

A fight broke out. Fists and arms flailed before a pair of Broadhurst's Marines managed to break the combatants apart. *How long can discipline last,* Micholson asked himself, *in the face of this?*

Broadhurst pointed to a badly limping man, face swathed in bandages, who stumbled through a hatch onto the lower open deck. "Isn't that Rutherford down there? Who the hell let him out of the infirmary?"

Micholson watched the blinded man seem to stare at the eastern shore, then throw his arms across the bandages which covered his ruined eyes. "Yes. It's Rutherford. He can see it. No eyes to see, but he sees it, nonetheless."

The gunnery officer's mouth fell open as he watched Rutherford's terrified contortions. "Good Lord...I think...I think he can."

Not far from where Rutherford tottered, Quartermaster Pierce struck his own balding head repeatedly, as though he could jostle the blasphemous visions from his brain. His face grew livid with sudden fury. He turned sharply toward the pilothouse and pointed to where Micholson stood. "You monster!" he shouted, shaking his fist at the symbol of command. "How can you keep on steaming? You pushed right through the bodies, like they were mere flotsam— they're not, damn you! You desecrater! You're forcing us to steam into the Devil's own maw!"

"Captain...you're going to have to do something about Pierce," Broadhurst said, grimly. "He was Oates's friend, and he has followers. He can whip up something ugly among the crew if he's allowed to."

"I appreciate the warning, Mr. Broadhurst. But I'll place no man in the brig based on his reaction to that abomination across the river, nor on suspicion of potential future harm. I will, however, keep an eye on him."

The faces in the fire, the shimmering faces of his earlier crew, kept their eyes focused on Micholson. The faces of the *Northport* men were joined by those of Cyril Oates and Harold Pilger, men left dead on the *Germania* or who had died since. Their livid burns glowed like stigmata. The visage of Paul Legarde hovered above the others, a dark prince of accusation. And one other, a small, milky white face, features made soft and round by layers of baby fat— *Nicholas, my brother. Do you accuse me, too? Because I clung to life when death stole you away from our family?*

Rutherford's screaming grated against his spine like shrapnel. He felt a flood of relief when a Marine firmly guided the wounded man back to the infirmary. Hadn't his executive officer suffered enough? Weren't the horrors of ordinary war hellish enough, without—this?

An hour later, the door to Micholson's cabin slammed open. Pierce stood in the doorway, looking as disheveled and manic as the prisoner Babbage.

"What is the meaning of this intrusion, Mr. Pierce?" Micholson reached for one of his pistols, but Pierce already had a sidearm drawn and at the ready.

"You're to come down to the gun deck and talk with us, captain," Pierce said. He tossed Micholson the captain's shirt and coat from the back of a desk chair and gestured for him to put them on.

"You demand that I talk with you and whom else?"

"The majority of the crew of this gunboat. Get dressed."

Micholson allowed himself to be led to the rear gundeck below. It was packed with tense, sweating bodies. Not a majority of the crew; Pierce had lied. But enough men, about thirty strong, to show that Micholson was faced with a very serious, volatile confrontation. Most disturbingly, the three assistant engineers stood with this group, one of them guarding the door to the forward passages; Micholson knew the gunboat would not remain functional under his command for very long without the work of these men's hands.

Micholson locked eyes with his quartermaster. "Mr. Pierce, am I to take it that you are announcing a mutiny?"

"It's not a mutiny yet, captain." Micholson couldn't tell whether Pierce was threatening or pleading with him. "Not if you'll listen to reason. There's something out there, something unholy. Something we can't fight with carbines and cannons. If we keep blundering forward, as blind as poor Rutherford, we'll end up like those lost souls in the

river. Oates, Bainbridge, and Pilger were only the first."
Ugly murmurs of assent arose from the crowd of men
behind Pierce. "You must turn the gunboat around."
Pierce's face wavered between frantic determination and
something else. *Fear.* Micholson could smell the fear on
him. "If you won't turn her around...you'll be relieved of
your command. And we'll turn the *Eads* around for you."

Rifle butts battered the far side of the door. "We're
coming in, captain!" Broadhurst shouted. "And I pity any
man who stands in our way!"

"Not yet, Mr. Broadhurst!" Micholson said. "Let me
talk with these men first." He made eye contact with as
many of the sailors as would look him in the face. A
number of the enlisted men faltered, turning their gazes
quickly away. "Gentlemen," he said as calmly as he could
manage, trying to ignore the anger and sense of betrayal
raging within his chest. "We have been entrusted with a vital
mission. Earlier today, we were all sickened to the depths of
our souls by the sight of dead civilians floating down the
Yazoo. Imagine, if you dare, the same scene, multiplied tenfold, taking place on the Ohio River below Cincinnati. Or
on the Mississippi before St. Louis. If we flinch from our
duties now, we may doom our own mothers, wives, and
sisters to the kind of brutal treatment we so recently
witnessed.

"Each of you knows the penalty for mutiny—speedy
court-martial, followed by hanging. I refuse, however, to
stain my hands with the blood of my own men. Particularly
given the seemingly supernatural manifestations we have
seen across the river, which may make many fear that the
mercy of God has abandoned us. On the other hand,
neither will I have men serving alongside me unwillingly or
resentfully, for each such man is a hidden menace to his
fellows.

"I give you the following choices. You may continue to
serve in your present duties, so long as you do so whole-
heartedly, in which case your actions of this evening shall

not be reflected in your service record. Should you decide you are incapable of serving, you may transfer to the *Molly Downings*. There are skilled sailors and artillerymen aboard her who would be happy to take your places. I must remind you, however, that aboard the freighter you will run nearly the same risks as you would aboard this vessel, but with none of your present ability to strike back at the enemy.

"Your final option is to be put ashore. You may take adequate rations with you, but no weapons aside from your personal sidearm. You realize, of course, that we are several hundred miles from friendly territory. Also, the seemingly unholy terrors you seek to flee are far more likely to attack a few isolated men, lost in the woods, than a well-armed gunboat. The choice is yours."

The men packed behind Pierce stared into each other's faces, trying to read in their comrades' eyes what they should do. Pierce saw their solidarity begin to melt. "Men! Don't listen to him!" He grabbed several sets of wavering shoulders. "He's only trying to confuse you! Remember—he left Cyril Oates to burn aboard that steamer full of witches! He's the criminal who threw away the lives of nearly every man aboard the *Northport!* Do you want the same to happen to you?"

Each of his followers could hear the desperation in his voice, see the half-insane fear in his eyes. Several turned away, ashamed of the officer they had briefly thrown their lots in with.

Pierce, crowded in by his own followers, struggled to unsheathe his cutlass. But before he could manage to free his weapon, the boom of cannon fire reverberated through the room. Not one of the *Eads*'s own guns—too distant for that—but within two hundred yards, close enough to be felt in each man's skin.

Micholson took quick advantage of the distraction. He shoved Pierce to the ground, pushed his way through the confused sailors, and landed a solid blow on the startled face of the assistant engineer blocking the door. The sound of the man's nose breaking provided a weak echo of the mysterious cannon shot. Then he flung open the door.

Broadhurst, half a dozen Marines, and a goodly number of the gunnery crew invaded the rear gundeck. All of the would-be mutineers immediately dropped their weapons to the deck.

"Mr. Broadhurst, thank you for your timely intercession. Can you tell where that cannon fire came from?"

Broadhurst shook his head. "I'll send spotters out onto the hurricane deck to watch for a second discharge."

"Would you agree with my impression that the blast was too big to have issued from a standard Army field piece or mortar?"

"Maybe. Why? You think there could be a gunboat hunched down behind those trees on the western shore?"

"We are thinking alike, Mr. Broadhurst. Possibly our luck has begun to turn. We may have found our secret boatyard."

Broadhurst turned to the crowd, directing his words particularly to the would-be mutineers. "You hear that, you weak-kneed washer-women? The enemy is in range of our guns! Follow this captain, and you'll have your chance to catch the filthy murderers of women and children and make them pay for their crimes and sorcery! Are you going to crawl off into the woods like grubs, or will you fight?"

The previously demoralized and frightened men grabbed hold of the prospect of battle as though it were a lifeline. Their voices rang out, ragged at first, then in near unison:

"*FIGHT! FIGHT!*"

CHAPTER FIFTEEN

Into the Hidden Boatyard

Aboard the USS James B. Eads *on the Yazoo River adjacent to Adderwood Plantation, Mississippi, April 25–26, 1865*

Following a second shot from a concealed cannon on the western shore, whose fiery discharge was seen by spotters aboard the *Eads*, Micholson gave the order to approach a freighter anchored near the trees the missile had issued from. The vessel, secured by thick ropes tied to an oak jutting precariously over the water, appeared deserted. Five of her auxiliary boats were tied in a chain floating from her stern; they bobbed in the current like the tail of a kite.

"Her rigging," Micholson said, observing the freighter with a spy glass, "it's not an American pattern."

"Yes, you're right," Delaup said. "She's British. One of those small boats sports a Union Jack."

"Indeed. Commodore Foote's intelligence was accurate, then." He turned to Broadhurst. "Send a pair of men ashore. Let's see if these woods are as solid as they appear to be."

He watched the Marines land in their small boat and disappear into the forest. In a few minutes, he would know.

The Marines returned to the riverbank. The man on the left made the sign Micholson had prayed he would see—he crossed his arms above his head like the starred cross of the Confederate battle ensign.

The hidden boatyard was here. Now all they had to do was destroy it and emerge with lives and sanity intact.

A light drizzle had begun to blow in through the *Eads*'s open ports. Micholson convened a war council of his surviving officers. Looking around the table, he was surprised at how many faces were missing. He'd been forced to pull officers from both the *Molly Downings* and the sunken mortar scow, men he barely knew. Henry Dodds, captain of the *Molly Downings*, a serious-looking man of fifty-three, sat beside him. Micholson requested that Bud Wilson, the marine sergeant who had led the reconnaissance, begin his report.

"It's the boatyard, all right. They've got an incredible setup in there. The harbor must be a quarter mile across. My guess is, it was originally a swamp that they built a levee around and dug out. They've got the inlet blocked with some kind of barge, covered over with dirt and trees. Looks like there's a mechanism that makes it swing open like a trapdoor."

"How many ironclads are there?" Micholson asked.

"I was able to count five. Two of them are in dry dock. The other three are afloat."

Three of them already afloat! "Were you able to tell how many of the three are operational?"

"It was hard to tell. I only saw lights coming from one of them, the biggest. It had a heavy naval howitzer mounted on its top deck. That's where those shells have been coming from. We saw them fire it off. The other two boats looked dark."

Broadhurst leaned across the table. "Did the harbor have other defenses, apart from the ironclads?"

"Langley saw gun emplacements on either side of the inlet. But they weren't manned. The whole place looked deserted, except for that one big gunboat. Langley stayed behind to figure out how to operate that barge opener. As soon as he's got it working, he'll let us in."

All eyes turned toward Micholson. "Well, captain," Delaup said, "what is the plan? Do we go in with all guns blazing?"

Micholson felt the leaden weight of command settle on his chest. *All guns blazing*...the classic spirit of the fighting American Navy. John Paul Jones, battering HMS *Serapis* into surrender even as his own Bonhomme Richard was sinking. Edward Preble and Stephen Decatur, beating the Tripolian pirates at their own bloody game. Even his own reckless attack on the *Virginia*, that, too, had been carried out in the classic spirit, despite the harrowing outcome. Proof that stubborn courage and blind faith in one's own rightness didn't always carry the day.

"No, Mr. Delaup. We won't storm into the enemy's den half-blind. Despite Mr. Wilson's reconnaissance, I still don't have a complete picture of what we're facing—one opponent, or two, or three. Three operational rebel ironclads call for vastly different tactics than one. As of now, our veil of subterfuge remains our most potent weapon. Only a fool throws away his best weapon in the face of the enemy."

"So we enter the harbor under rebel colors, then?"

"Yes. Mr. Broadhurst, have a man in readiness to run Old Glory up the flagpole at my signal. Until I give that word, our guns remain silent. If luck is on our side, the enemy's own lips may provide all the information we need. Both about his squadron, and perhaps about that...phenomenon across the river."

Captain Dodds raised a hand. "Captain Micholson, should the *Molly Downings* follow the *Eads* into the harbor? She's a fast boat. I'm willing to bet she could serve as a credible ram in a pinch."

"No, there's no sense in putting your unarmed vessel in jeopardy. Your bows aren't reinforced for ramming. You could do yourself more damage than to the enemy. Also, should the *Eads* be disabled, your boat will provide our only way home. I appreciate your brave offer, Henry. But keep the *Molly Downings* outside the harbor with full steam in reserve, ready to run at top speed towards the Mississippi."

"Captain," Broadhurst asked, "what would you have me tell the men?"

"Tell them the time of waiting and uncertainty is over. Tell them to put the horrors across the river out of their minds." Micholson rose from the table. He felt strong, clear-headed; more solidly himself than he had in months. "You know what to say, Mr. Broadhurst. Tell them to prepare for the fight of their lives."

Johnny McComb bitterly missed Jack Bainbridge. Jack had been his partner and friend, a fellow neophyte among the long-toothed old tars of the gundeck. Now McComb had no one to help him drag the heavy tubs of water from the boiler hose to their places next to the great guns.

Sweating with exertion, doing his best to avoid the gunner's mates crisscrossing the dim gundeck with boxes of powder and stands of shot and shell, McComb lugged the tub into position beside the rightmost eight-inch cannon in the front of the casemate. *Four tubs down; seven to go.* Norm Hobart would take care of the two guns on the aft gundeck, thank God. He sat on the edge of the tub, resting a minute.

Suddenly his back was soaked. Someone had splashed him! He turned, ready to spit venom. It was Ray Manhasset, a junior gunner not much older than McComb. He had stripped to the waist and tied a red bandanna around his head, making him look like a pirate.

"Keep it moving, McComb!" Manhasset said. "You think you're tired now? Just wait until the fight starts. You've never been in one of these casemates when all the guns have been going off a while. The guns heat up like live coals, you work like a crazy mule, and the whole place fills up with smoke thick enough to slice. I worked one of the thirty-two pounders on the *St. Louis* during the fight at Fort Donelson. All the gunners do this a lot." He plunged his head into the tub, emerging seconds later with water streaming down his face and bare, hairless chest.

"Manhasset!" Tyler, a senior gunner, shouted. "You want to quit acting the fool and help me spread this sand?"

"Uh, sure, Mr. Tyler!" Manhasset flushed deeply, then humbly accepted the twenty-pound bag of coarse sand the senior man shoved into his arms. He tore open the bag and followed Tyler's lead, tossing fistfuls of sands onto the wooden floor, carefully ensuring complete coverage of the planking.

McComb watched, fascinated. He forgot his self-imposed ban on asking ignorant-sounding questions. "Ray! Why are you doing that?"

Manhasset looked at Tyler, then looked guiltily at the young deckhand. "It's, uh...it's so that we don't slip while we're working the guns..."

"Go ahead and tell him, Manhasset. The whole truth."

Manhasset remained tongue-tied. Tyler put down his bag of sand and turned to McComb. He patted the left side of the boy's chest. "You know the stuff that runs through here, son? The sand is to soak it up. On a smooth wooden deck, blood is as slippery as whale oil."

The *Eads* crept through the newly-opened inlet into the dark harbor. A large Confederate ensign, made damp and limp by the steady, light rain, hung conspicuously from her forward signaling mast. The only spots of illumination to compete with the dim were a few glows from the large ironclad anchored in the center of the harbor, and lamps aboard the *Eads* herself.

Judging from what he could see, Micholson was astounded by the sophistication of the boatyard's facilities.

The facility seemed to be as well-equipped as the most elaborate of northern shipyards. *What incredible effort the builders must have expended to erect this magnificent facility in a dismal, isolated swamp. Were we not at war, I would raise a toast to them.*

He turned his spyglass on the largest of the anchored ironclads. She was a stout-looking vessel, longer than the *Eads* but not as broad of beam. Only the front and rear walls of her tall gunhouse sloped; her port and starboard sides stood straight as the walls of a medieval fortress. She was pierced for ten guns: two fore, two aft, and three on each broadside, heavy cannons of a pattern Micholson had never seen before. A single, massive, squat smokestack crowned her casemate, dwarfing the conical pilothouse sitting in front of it.

She is much like the Virginia. Micholson winced at the thought of his old nemesis. He realized how great and monstrous she had become in his imagination: an iron-walled Angel of Death, invincible, unstoppable. *Balderdash! The invincible warship has yet to be made. Everything that floats has its weakness, its Achilles' heel. It's simply a matter of finding it. And this time, I bring iron of my own.*

And the other two ironclads? He scanned the inner rim of the harbor. He spotted one anchored alongside a pier jutting from the levee. She appeared only partially completed, her casemate fully timbered, but only half-armored. Her complement of guns sat next to an iron derrick atop the levee, waiting to be lifted through her still-open roof. He took a close look at these cannons, which appeared to be heavy breach-loaders of British make. *Possibly the new Armstrong sixty-eight or hundred pounders I've read of in the naval journals. Unmatchable as armor-piercing weapons. Or at least that is how they are advertised by their manufacturer.*

The third floating ironclad was anchored farther out in the harbor, away from the piers, suggesting that she was complete. Smaller than her slab-sided sister, with more delicate lines, she sported six heavy guns, and her casemate inclined on all four sides. Her single smokestack, tall and thin, towered gracefully over her fully armored gunhouse. She was the only ironclad Micholson had ever seen that he could call, even remotely, pleasing to the eye.

He spotted a flurry of activity on the deck of the larger ironclad. Her crew lowered one of her boats into the water, and four men climbed in. Their leader appeared to be an officer. *Good,* Micholson thought; *this will save me the trouble of contacting them.* Speaking through a voice pipe, he ordered the deckhands to drop anchor. Then he watched the small boat cross the hundred yards of harbor between their ironclad and his own.

"Mr. Broadhurst," Micholson called into the voice pipe, "have your men pull the bow guns in and close the gunport shutters. We're about to have visitors, and I'd rather they not see our preparations." He then pulled on his oilskin coat and descended from the pilothouse to the bow deck to greet the approaching Confederates.

He reached the edge of the deck just as the small boat pulled abreast. The visiting officer hastily stepped onto the ironclad's deck, pushing past his men tying their dingy to a mooring post. "Thank God you've come!" He grasped Micholson's hand with unseemly pressure. "It's so good to see a brother officer. I've been surrounded by Army types, as I'm sure you are, too. They hate serving on gunboats and threaten to jump ship at a moment's notice. It's been simply awful, these last two days—the world has lost its moorings and plunged into an abyss..."

He shut his eyes tightly. When he opened them again, he had managed to compose himself. "Sir. Please, forgive me." He stepped back from Micholson and smartly saluted. "Commander Louis Stoddard, at your service, sir."

Micholson returned the salute. "Captain August Micholson, of the gunboat *James B. Eads.*"

"Yes, I received word you were heading in my direction. When news was still freely available." The other three men climbed from the dingy and began examining the *Eads*'s armored shutters. "It's the first time they've ever been aboard a Federal gunboat," Stoddard explained. "My first time, too, of course. Congratulations on your capture and salvage of this vessel. A most impressive feat."

"Thank you, Commander. You give me too much credit. Quite a bit of luck was involved."

"Of course, of course. Luck always plays a part in great victories. We were all most gratified to hear of the solid whipping you gave your two pursuers. Let them consider it a foretaste of what is to come, once my squadron is fully operational. The Mississippi will no longer be a Union highway, I can promise them that! By the way, do you intend to operate in conjunction with my flotilla?"

Micholson wiped droplets of rain from his forehead. "That decision rests with Secretary of the Navy Mallory, does it not?"

"Yes, you're right, of course. But I'm sure he would give much credence to the opinions of local commanders. What a potent team we could make, you and I! And, I must admit, I'm rather short of experienced officers. I'm embarrassed to say so, but out of desperation, I actually offered a commission to my half-lunatic cousin—although I wasn't aware of his mental state at the time."

The rain worked its way down Micholson's collar. "Commander, why don't we continue this discussion in my cabin? Your men would be welcome in our wardroom, and I'm sure the cook could fix something for them."

Stoddard's eyes brightened. "Splendid! And it will give me a chance to see more of this captured boat of yours. She's a sister to the rest of their gunboats, isn't she?"

Micholson grasped the rungs of the ladder to the hurricane deck. "Yes, to most of them. Their *Benton* and *Essex* are built to a different plan, I hear."

Stoddard followed Micholson up the ladder, his men close behind. "Indeed? By the way, Captain Micholson, if you are interested, there are a number of English rifled cannons lying in the hold of the steamer outside the harbor. Breach-loaders, the latest Admiralty design. They were intended for one of the ironclads now in dry dock, but since your vessel is already afloat, and armed with such anachronistic weapons, I'd be willing to offer you a swap...assuming we will be blessed by some return of normalcy when the troubles across the river sort themselves out."

Troubles? Micholson noted how Stoddard had assiduously avoided any mention of the horror across the river. "These 'troubles,' Commander; what do you know about them? When did they first appear?"

Stoddard paused to look at the distant, unearthly flickering beyond the Yazoo. "Three days ago." All forced enthusiasm had left his voice. "Tuesday morning, we saw flames rising over Adderwood Plantation. Unnatural, demonic flames. Not long before, my cousin, Joseph Babbage, had babbled madly about some 'super weapon' he had under development, something beyond my comprehension. At first, I thought I might be witnessing it, until I remembered that no man would willingly burn down his own home."

He is a relation of Babbage's? "Did he explain to you the source of this weapon? Did he mention any counter-measures?"

Angry despair filled Stoddard's voice. "All he did was boast like some power-drunk lunatic. I wish I could answer your questions. But the only man who could is Joseph Babbage, and judging from the state of his home, he's most likely dead."

"I see." Micholson thought about the prisoner in the brig, located scant yards beneath their feet. *Could it be possible Babbage might reveal knowledge to his cousin he was unwilling to reveal to me? There's little risk in the likelihood he'll expose our ruse—I cannot allow Stoddard to return to his vessel under any circumstances.*

"My cabin is this way. What happened to your workmen? All the sheds ashore look deserted."

"Most had fled by Tuesday night. Into the woods...away from those things across the river. I suppose I've been lucky to hold onto my own crew; and most of them would be gone were it not for the rifles of a few hardy men. The crew of that freighter outside wanted to raise anchor and flee downriver. When I demonstrated to them I'd sink their damned boat before I let them take it, they ran into the woods with the rest of the cowardly vermin—"

"Get it *out of me!*" The anguished cry issued from the brig, two decks below their feet. "Get it OUT! OUT! IT'S BURNING MEEEE!"

"Good Lord!" Stoddard said. "I would almost swear that sounds like my cousin Joseph! Who do you have in there?"

Micholson halted. "A poor wretch we pulled from the river two days ago, driven mad by terrible things he had seen. Describe your cousin. Does he have a withered right arm?"

"By all that's holy, he *has!* I must speak with him, captain! I must make him reverse this horror he has unleashed!"

Micholson gestured for the party of Marines which had been shadowing their steps to join them. "Wilson and Richardson, please take these three visitors to the wardroom and give them some coffee." *Code for take them into secure custody.* "Falk and Simon, please bring the man, apparently Joseph Babbage, who is in our brig to me and Commander Stoddard in my cabin."

"He is in the brig?" Stoddard asked.

"Necessary for his own safety, I'm afraid. I would take you to see him there, but that tiny, dark room is no decent place for you to reunite with him."

They entered Micholson's cabin. "Commander Stoddard, would you care for some brandy? I recommend it, given the shock you will likely experience upon witnessing your cousin's current condition."

189

"You have brandy? *Real* brandy? How do you manage it?"

Micholson took two small glasses from the top of his bureau. "It came with the gunboat. The previous captain, undoubtedly in a great rush, left it behind. I take it you would appreciate a glass?"

"After what I've been through these past three days, I'll drink every drop you have."

"Cheers, then." They clinked glasses.

"I think you made a wise choice, Captain Micholson, in offering your services to your home State and the Confederacy. You saw firsthand how the Union's puny ships were mauled by the *Virginia*. Formidable as your old opponent is, I believe my *Arkansas* to be more than a match for her."

"How so?"

"English rolled armor plate is superior to anything either Confederate or Federal foundries can produce. My ram is shielded with English armor four inches thick, the same level of protection carried by the latest British ironclads. The *Virginia* is armed with Brooke rifles; acceptably good cannons, but not in the same class as my breach-loading hundred pounders. Were I ever to engage the *Virginia* or even the *Monitor*, I could drill holes through their armor as quickly as you can snap your fingers. And the *Arkansas* is far faster than the *Virginia*. My engines are the latest in high-pressure technology, straight from Leeds."

Micholson refilled Stoddard's glass. "If the *Arkansas* is fully operational, why haven't you taken her downriver to warn Yazoo City and Vicksburg of what has transpired at Adderwood?"

"You don't think I've wanted to? But I couldn't leave. Someone had to stay and guard the unfinished ironclads. To keep my crew from becoming unhinged, I've ordered them to fire off a few howitzer rounds at the 'living flames' each hour. The shells don't appear to have any effect, aside from adding to the damage to my cousin's house. But at least shooting them off gives my men something to do."

"How close are your other boats to completion?"

"The two currently in the stocks could be completed within a month, perhaps six weeks, assuming the workers all returned. It pains me that this all happened mere days before the *Vicksburg* could be made fully operational. She has all six guns aboard, as well as two-thirds of her armor, but we haven't been able to get her engines working properly. For the time being, she remains but a floating battery. I've released a few of my men to act as a skeleton crew for her. Would you be able to spare a few of your crewmen?"

"I'm afraid I can't—" A knock on the door interrupted him. "Yes?"

"It's Simon and Falk, sir. We have Mr. Babbage with us, as you instructed."

"Bring him in. And please remain with us."

The trio entered. Babbage, clutching his stomach and moaning, appeared to be a sodden jumble of rags and hair suspended between the two Marines.

"Joseph?" Stoddard half whispered. "Is it you?"

Babbage raised his head. His eyes had sunken into his face. His cheekbones stood out like sharp crags. "Who...?" His blackening gums had pulled away from his teeth, and his breath stank like the exhalation of an exhumed coffin. Stoddard took a lantern from Micholson's desk and shone it into Babbage's face. "Get...get that light out of my eyes. You're blinding me!"

"Joseph, it's your cousin," Stoddard said. "It's Louis."

"*Louis?*" Babbage blinked in the dim, yellowish light, trying to discern the face behind the lantern. "Oh, God, it *would* be you! I won't ask how you found me. Have you come to guffaw at the master of Adderwood, enslaved by the chief of his slaves? Laugh, then; laugh your pompous head off! I have no pride left."

Stoddard stood, disgust curling his upper lip. "I haven't come to laugh at you, Joseph. I only want information. Those—things—across the river. The creatures that surround your house. Did you have anything to do with them?"

Babbage's eyes narrowed with new alertness. "The *Mikithi?* Have you tried to chase them away with your mighty ironclads, cousin? Have you shot your mighty cannons at them, boasted to them they don't stand a chance against the latest British mechanical marvels?"

"*Mick-eethy?* That's what they are called? You admit you are fully aware what those things are?"

"Of COURSE I know what they are, you *idiot!* Without my money, my months of careful planning, they wouldn't *be* here! What did you think I was talking about when I met you aboard your ironclad? Did you assume I was spouting nonsense?"

"The thought did cross my mind, cousin."

"I hear the sneer in your voice, even now. You may sneer at *me*, cousin, but you can't so easily sneer at what I've done. I wasn't lying when I said I'd assembled the mightiest weapon on the continent. My one mistake was believing I could control it." His voice went soft. "I...I believed Daniel. How could he do this to me? I—I was almost a son to him. How could he hate me so?"

Micholson stepped forward. "Where is 'Daniel,' Mr. Babbage? His creatures have destroyed Yazoo City and slaughtered its people. Unless you help me stop him, you are complicit in every murder he commits."

"Where is Daniel? You might as well ask me where the wind is. He could have followed his *Mikithi* east, north or south. Or he may have remained at Adderwood. You know as much as I."

"You didn't mention 'west.' Are you saying they cannot cross the Yazoo? Does the river provide a barrier against them?"

"These are Lundowan gods, or demons; I'm not certain which. However, they seem to face the same limitations as a natural wildfire would. They cannot cross a river unaided. I suspect that the current light rain weakens them, at least somewhat. Daniel told me there are similar gods in our North American earth and waters, but he never learned how to talk with them, much less how to influence them. He needed his old, familiar tools. His old gods. And I—trusting Joseph, ambitious Joseph!—I provided them."

Stoddard grabbed his cousin by the collar. "You asinine *fool!* Do you realize what you've done? Yazoo City is destroyed! Vicksburg may be next! Good God—you may have signed the death warrant for the entire Confederacy!"

Babbage's eyes brimmed with tears. "Don't you think I *know* that, Louis? I'm the most miserable man alive. I love our country, every bit as much as you do!" He wiped his eyes. "But I'm not the biggest fool in this room. You're just as much a prisoner as I am. Only you don't know it yet. You think this Captain Micholson a staunch comrade, do you not? Well, I have news for you, Louis. He's come to destroy your precious ironclads."

CHAPTER SIXTEEN

Duel of Iron

Aboard the USS James B. Eads
*in an enclosed Confederate harbor and boatyard
to the northwest of Adderwood Plantation, Mississippi,
April 26, 1862*

An electric silence filled Micholson's cabin. The two Marines reached for their weapons. Stoddard stiffened. He turned to Micholson.

"Captain Micholson. On your sacred honor, is this true?"

Micholson had not wanted to play the game this way. But the *Arkansas* would be more vulnerable without her commander. The usefulness of his subterfuge had ended. "Yes. It's true."

"I take it, then, that I am your prisoner?"

"Regrettably, yes. I must request your pistol and your sword."

"Of course." Stoddard unbuckled his pistol belt and his sword with trembling hands. "Do take good care of these. The sword, especially. It is engraved with well-wishes from President Davis himself."

Micholson accepted the weapons. "They will be stored with my personal possessions. I will ensure that you receive them back at the appropriate time."

"Thank you." Stoddard stared at his cousin. Despite his haggard, decayed features, Babbage looked happier than Stoddard had ever seen him. "I trust, captain, that as a fellow officer, I will receive better treatment from you than my cousin has."

"My crew has treated Mr. Babbage admirably, commander. Whatever injuries he has suffered since coming aboard are entirely self-inflicted."

"Is this true, Joseph?"

Babbage assumed an expression of mock outrage. "What a base *lie*, cousin! They have tortured me horribly! Pulled teeth from my head! Scoured my flesh with hot pokers!" He grinned a black-gummed grin. "Actually, no. I have been treated reasonably well. These Federals will bear little responsibility for my coming death. But it will be a happy death, Louis. For I have lived to see you humiliated, as utterly as you and your kind ever humiliated me." He began to giggle, then laugh, wincing as he stretched his abused stomach, but laughing harder and harder nonetheless.

Stoddard's voice was listless. "Captain. Do me the favor of removing me from this abomination's presence. I pray I shall not have to share a cell with him."

"Very well. The Marines will escort you to separate quarters. Johnson, go tell Mr. Broadhurst to have his crews load and ready their weapons. I'll be speaking with them shortly. Perkins, accompany me and Commander Stoddard to the wardroom. Commander, you and your men will be quartered in a spare cabin. You should be secure and reasonably safe there." They exited the cabin, Babbage's laughter following them into the darkness. "Please make no attempt to signal your crew. It is a hazy night; I doubt they would see you. And Mr. Perkins would be forced to harm you."

"You have my word that I will try no such thing." Stoddard stared across the dark harbor at the unsuspecting *Arkansas* and the barely-manned *Vicksburg.* "How do you plan to do it, Micholson? Will you fire on my ironclads without warning?"

"I believe that would be the most logical way to proceed."

"The most logical, perhaps. But certainly not the most honorable. This sort of attack—I daresay, it is exceedingly un-American."

Micholson wheeled on Stoddard, his fists clenched. "And how 'honorable,' sir, was your plan to bombard women and infants in St. Louis and Cincinnati? I'll accept no such pious protestations from a man like yourself."

Stoddard's face hardened. "You insult me, sir. I have a proposal for you. Return me my weapons. You and I can settle this matter right here and now. The winner gains command of the harbor. The loser agrees to scuttle his vessel or vessels. Are you game, sir?"

A duel of champions? Micholson had dueled only once, as an eighteen year old midshipman, when a classmate had insulted Elizabeth's family. He had wounded the boy, and had nearly been evicted from the Naval Academy. "That is romantic nonsense. Dueling is as obsolete as your 'peculiar institution' will soon be."

"Very well. Fire your furtive, dishonorable shots, then. The *Arkansas*'s armor will hold. She and the *Vicksburg* will crush you like a rotten egg."

Micholson stared at the dim panorama of the harbor. This was his arena. The place of combat he had been granted by the grace of God to redeem his errors and perhaps save his Nation. The deck trembled slightly beneath his feet as heavy cannons were rolled into their loading positions. But his personal tremblings of recrimination were behind him.

"Who will crush who remains to be seen," he said.

Micholson could sense the difference in the men. They were a different crew now. For the first time since he had set foot aboard the *Eads*, they were *his* crew. He had fulfilled one half of his promise: he had brought them to the field of their glory. All faces, young and middle-aged, neophyte and veteran, looked to his with a single message—*Lead us! Let us be the sword you wield to cleave the enemy in two.*

"Who here mans our forward battery?" Micholson asked. Fifteen men, including Tyler, Manhasset, and McComb, raised their hands. "You are to be the vanguard of our attack. To you falls the duty of disabling and sinking our most powerful opponent, the *Arkansas*. Her armor is thicker than ours; her guns, possibly, more powerful. However, we claim two major advantages. The first is the benefit of surprise. Depending on how quickly you load, we may fire as many as two or three unanswered volleys. Equally as important, we have the boon of maneuverability. The *Eads* has a full head of steam. The *Arkansas* has, at most, a few pounds of reserve pressure in her boilers. It will be at least five to ten minutes before her crew can move her, and by then, God willing, we will have found her weakest point to concentrate our fire upon.

"It is of the utmost importance that you make every shot count. Aim carefully and deliberately. Load your guns with solid shot only. Do not be tempted to test your cannons against her armor, even though we will be fighting at close range. Aim first for the muzzles of her guns; each enemy cannon we disable leaves them one less to hole us with. When we are more distant from her and you have room to fully depress your guns, fire your bolts beneath her waterline. You may be lucky and strike bare wood. Hole her there and you send her to the bottom of the harbor."

He turned his attention to the remaining fifty members of the gun crews. "Men of the starboard and aft batteries, your tasks are equally as important. You have the responsibility of destroying the unfinished rams still in dry dock, as well as the *Vicksburg*, the partially-armored gunboat anchored between the *Arkansas* and the piers. Fire explosive shells at the boats in dry dock. They are yet plain wood and should burn nicely. Attack the *Vicksburg* with a mix of explosives and solid shot; load whichever you find wreaks the most destruction. She will be a 'live' target, for she has her guns and a small crew aboard, so do not treat her lightly. She has nearly as much power to hurt us as the *Arkansas* does.

"Do any of you have questions for me?"

"Sir?" Marine Sergeant Wilson raised his hand. "Will we go into battle under our own colors?"

Micholson smiled. "We most certainly will, Mr. Wilson. I thank you for the timely reminder. Our flag waits in the top drawer of the bureau in my cabin." He reached into his pocket. "I give you the key, sir. Will you do us all the honor of raising up Old Glory?"

Wilson beamed brightly as a bursting star shell. "Yes, indeed, sir!"

Cheers filled the gundeck, raucous and heartfelt. What better balm for the crew's spirits could there be? Micholson thought gratefully. Even a forced audience with the Devil himself cannot squelch the thrill in these men's souls at the thought of fighting our own colors again.

Micholson and Delaup bolted the pilothouse's iron shutters into place, leaving only narrow slits open for viewing. "Mr. Delaup, make sure to keep our nose pointed at the *Arkansas* at all times. I don't want to give her any shots at our weaker side armor. And as for the thirty-two pounders in our broadsides—I'd do as well to snap my fingers at her as fire those in her direction."

Delaup stared at his commander with open perturbation. "Now let me get this straight, *m'sieur*. You say you want me to slowly circle around her, looking for her weakest point, and you want me to point our bow at her at all times? Does this boat look like a crab to you?"

"Just do the best you can, Valery. If she's built anything like us, her weakest part is her stern. Take us there as soon as you can."

He peered out an aft view slit to watch the flag mast. Wilson had hurried aft two minutes ago. Then he saw it: a flurry of fluid movement, white and red stripes unfurling and ascending.

Micholson grasped the steam whistle cord and pulled.

"Run 'em out, boys!"

Heavy iron gunport shutters clattered open. The fifteen men of the forward battery struggled to roll their cannons out to firing position, heaving their shoulders against mammoth banded iron breaches. Some of the gunners wrapped aiming ropes around their fists and pulled the wooden gun carriages sideways until the muzzles of the cannons were pointing exactly where the master gunner directed. Tyler then took a final view down the sights of the three great guns before waving the aimers aside. "Stand away, boys! We're ready!"

The crews stood back ten feet from the guns, most with their hands clasped tightly over their ears. Only the three men given the honor of firing the first shots at the *Arkansas* stood by the iron breaches.

Two of the men jerked their lanyards, igniting their guns' firing charges. The humid air split with two monstrous explosions. Johnny McComb felt his eyes push back into their sockets. The port and center gunports were obscured by white, sulphurous smoke as violent recoil propelled the gun carriages backwards on small wooden wheels. Before his ears could fully register the twin explosions, they were stunned by a secondary crash, violent as a locomotive hitting the wall of a station. Through his yet unobscured gunport, he saw the two bolts bound like billiard balls off the *Arkansas*'s upright side.

"McComb!" Tyler barked. "What are you waiting for, boy? Fire your weapon!"

McComb crossed his fingers and pulled his lanyard. The blood in his head compressed with the incredibly loud discharge. He jumped back from the recoiling gun carriage, even though he had been careful to stand out of its way. His nostrils burned. His eyes watered. The smoke—he couldn't see anything...

The men behind him cheered. When the smoke blew away from his gunport, he saw why. The muzzle of one of the *Arkansas*'s fearsome cannons had been twisted into useless scrap.

McComb grinned broadly. That lucky shamrock he had chalked on the head of his forty-eight pound bolt had done the trick.

Micholson watched the partially armored *Vicksburg* take a merciless beating from the *Eads*'s starboard battery. The rebel ram was silhouetted by flames which had erupted from one of the incomplete vessels in dry dock. Shells exploded on the thinly manned ironclad's upperworks, scattering her freshly-painted boats and holing her smokestack. Solid bolts smashed against her armor or slammed into the water below her casemate, soaking the vessel with splashes thirty feet high.

When would the *Arkansas* begin hitting back? She was their main opponent, the deadliest of the serpents Stoddard had assembled.

A sudden, violent lurch threw Micholson and Delaup off their feet. A force even more powerful than the recoil of her own cannons had struck the *Eads*'s port casemate, rocking her starboard side deep into the murky harbor waters.

The guns of the *Arkansas* had provided their answer.

"Oh, God! Help me! Please help me!"

Fishing had been David Fife's greatest passion; he had slit open hundreds of them. He lay against his overturned cannon, holding a twenty pound shard of twisted iron armor against his lower torso. It had torn him open. Now the pressure of it against his belly was all that kept his innards in.

Had he time and inclination, Lawrence Broadhurst could count the stars through the jagged new opening in the port casemate. "Hodgson! Ackerman!" he cried. When they finished tying tourniquets around the limbs—or stumps—of wounded gunners, the two surgeon's assistants hurried to the gunnery captain's side. "Get Fife to surgery. Immediately!"

Ackerman began to pry the twisted iron from the wounded gunner's bleeding fists. Broadhurst pulled Hodgson aside. "Just put him someplace quiet and give him some whiskey," he said quietly. "He's done for."

They took the dying man away. Broadhurst judged that three of the four port side cannons were still useable. But nearly half their gunners were badly wounded or dead. The remainder gamely struggled to reload, swabbing sparks from the hot barrels before packing in fresh bags of powder. He'd have to pull replacements from the currently unengaged stern battery.

"Sweet Lord," he murmured to himself, "I pray those bastards don't hit us here again. The captain took a calculated risk, exposing our broadside to reach the rebel's stern, but what a calamity..." He began pulling a shattered wooden beam off one of the still workable cannons. His boot struck something slippery and yielding. He looked down, then immediately wished he hadn't.

Oh, God—the men from the stern battery mustn't see this. It would strip the fighting spirit right out of them. Nothing to do but pitch it overboard, Lord forgive me—

He tried lifting the nearly limbless torso but was only able to raise the slippery corpse to the level of the gunport. He lacked the leverage to force it through.

A young man stood against a bulkhead fifteen feet away, watching with dazed eyes. "You, there!" Broadhurst called to him. "Come help me!"

The sailor, no older than sixteen, remained glued to the wall. "I—I'm sorry, sir. I can't."

Broadhurst's arms threatened to give out. "Hurry up! I can't hold it here much longer. Are you hurt?"

"N-no, sir."

"Then get over here and help me pitch this out the gunport!"

"Please, sir." The boy's voice broke like splintering glass. "Don't make me. It's my brother."

* * *

M'Lundowi stood on the balcony of Adderwood Mansion and listened to the booming discharges of cannons across the river. He turned to his bound captive with a smile. "Do you see, N'Mehayah, my disgraced brother, why the cause of the white men is hopeless? Even now, faced with the prospect of annihilation by fire, still they insist on making war upon each other. You were a fool to think you could aid their cause, and a loutish traitor to try."

The *Mikithi* surrounding the mansion lit the night with a false, evilly flickering twilight. Nehemiah spoke slowly, painfully through lips swollen and split from the beating he had endured. "My brother, whom I still love, I do not seek to betray you. I strive to save you. Pride...your pride has always been your downfall, and the downfall of those of us who depended upon you. These foul gods you have unleashed here, in our new home—"

M'Lundowi spat. "This will never be my home! *Never!*"

"Have you not lived more than half your life here? Have you not witnessed babies grow to manhood here? How can you deny that this land has become your home?"

"This land? This land is a garbage heap, a charnel pit, and the grub men have made it so."

"*You* make it so. You have lowered yourself to the basest dregs among them." Nehemiah steeled himself for a further kick to the face. But his brother, although he raised his staff high for a crippling blow, stayed his hand. "You hesitate, M'Lundowi, because you know I speak the truth. The gods that parch the earth this house stands upon will not stop with consuming the evil white men. Nor will they stop with consuming the innocent white men, their wives, and their children. Your own people will die. They will die horribly—the old men stolen with you from Lundowa, their children, and their children's children. You were meant to be Lundowa's protector, not the destroyer of her seed. Here, in Adderwood, you struggled to a position of influence. The young man you conspired to raise, he could have grown into a leader of his kind. You could have taught him to be the instrument of our redemption. But instead, you malformed him into a tool of your vengeance. What a sad and needless waste, my brother!"

"You speak of Joseph Babbage?" M'Lundowi sneered. "A leader of his kind? You are worse than a fool, N'Mehayah—you are a willfully self-deluding fool. Babbage is the grub men's grub. Never have I worked with less promising clay. I thank the gods he was able to carry out the simple instructions I gave. I would much rather have worked through your young shapeling, the water warrior who throws his life away across the river. At least his heart is made of oak, not jelly."

"August Micholson will prove to be your undoing. He will find a way to turn back the evil you have unleashed. He is the faithful shepherd of those who serve under him, and he is a strong protector of his Nation. He is the man you should have been, Eldest Brother."

"You love him very much?"

"I do. I love him as I would have loved my own sons—as I love you, M'Lundowi."

"Then I will be the instrument of his demise. I tire of the easy slaughter of women and feeble-hearted workmen. I am the cunning man, the boar slayer, the master of the spirits! I wish to test myself and my gods against the white man's warriors—those men in their iron ships!"

"The river denies you, M'Lundowi. The *Mikithi,* mighty as they are, cannot cross it. It is their nature."

M'Lundowi's eyes bored into his brother's. "You say the *Mikithi* will not cross the waters? You underestimate me, traitor." He thumped his chest vigorously. "You boasted that August Micholson would find a way. *I* will find a way. As I always have. Have I not broken all shackles placed upon me? Did I not summon gods from lost Lundowa? No mere river shall deny me."

The ancient African stalked out of the mansion and hastened to the levee. He climbed that hill-like barrier, all that stood between Adderwood and inundation, and stared at the Yazoo River.

Half a mile to the north, adjacent to where the concealed battle raged, two steamboats rocked at anchor as ricochets and stray shells plunged into the frothy current around them. One, anchored near the center of the river, bustled with white men. But the other, tied fast against the far bank, appeared abandoned.

Could that vessel be made to ferry my gods across the river?

M'Lundowi began walking the levee toward a place opposite the dark freighter. He came across a small rowboat, half hidden in the reeds at the levee's edge, which had been used by his one-time master for journeys across the river. He wrapped the small craft's mooring rope around his fist and pulled the boat through the water as he walked. The nearing sounds of battle stirred his blood.

When he stood opposite the dark steamship, he could clearly see the ropes that tied its bow and stern to trees jutting from the bank. A long row of lifeboats dangled from its stern, pulled south by the current. He gauged the length of the ship, added to its string of lifeboats, against the width of the river. "Yes," he said, smiling. "Were I to loosen that vessel's far end from the trees, the river would push it out, and the line of boats would drift until they touch this shore.

The gods could then cross, leaping from one boat to the next as I might leap from stone to stone across a pond."

He pulled his boat another quarter mile north before he descended to the water's edge. The current would push him steadily southward as he crossed, and he did not wish to journey too close to the inhabited riverboat. He stepped into the small craft and used one of its oars to push himself out of the reeds. Once past these obstructions, he pulled hard at the oars, glorying in the new strength so recently granted him. In the sky to the southwest, shells that had careened off slanting armor burst against a backdrop of isolated stars and swiftly moving clouds, showering the trees with shrapnel.

Sharp eyes aboard the steamboat anchored in mid-stream spotted his progress. He barely heard the sailor's shouted challenge. "Hail the rowboat! Who goes there?" He ignored this and doubled his effort at the oars. "Identify yourself, or we'll be forced to shoot!" M'Lundowi offered no response. He winced slightly as he heard the sharp crack of a rifle's discharge, remembering all too well his first encounter with the white man's fire-sticks seventy years before. The bullet smacked into the water five yards in front of his boat. He wondered if the gifts of the gods had made him proof against the white man's deadly pellets. More rifles rang out. A bullet tore into the gunwale three feet from M'Lundowi's right oar, peppering him with splinters.

His blood sang with the thrill of danger. *Warriors! At last I contest with warriors!*

He reached the western shore, close by the abandoned freighter. He pulled his boat onto a mud flat and scurried over protruding roots to the vessel's stern. He stared up at the thick rope which tied the freighter's stern to a stout tree branch. My holy claw should prove sufficient to slice that rope. He climbed the oak's trunk and slid out onto the branch where the thick rope was knotted.

The rope had been toughened with an application of tar. His claw, dulled during his combat with the boar and its subsequent ritual slaughter, proved incapable of severing the fibers.

I will find a way!

Another branch jutted out a few feet above the one upon which M'Lundowi stood. He decided to test the strength the spirits had granted him. Bending his knees, he wrapped his arms around the branch above him, then nestled his shoulder snugly against the thick bark on its underside. Bracing himself, he began to push against the lower branch. The distance separating the two branches slowly increased, until his legs no longer bent. But the lower branch stubbornly refused to crack.

He straightened to his full height, then placed the undersides of his hands on the bottom of the branch above him. He pushed upward with all his augmented strength. The muscles in his back seized, but he refused to lessen the pressure. The lower branch groaned and began to split. Mustering the last reserves of his might, he heaved against the top branch. The branch on which he stood finally surrendered with a deafening crack.

M'Lundowi, the branch, and the rope plunged into the muddy shallows. The Yazoo's current now took command of the freighter's stern, which swept away from the shore in a great arc, carrying its tail of small boats into the river. They drifted toward the river's eastern bank. Toward where the *Mikithi,* having responded to M'Lundowi's mental call, waited.

The ancient African emerged from the river in time to see one of the towering flame gods ignite the first boat which touched shore, then leap like a drifting spark across the connecting rope to the second drifting craft.

As ever I shall, I have found a way!

* * *

Smoke doubled the night's impenetrability. The three ironclads circled the tight harbor like battered, blind pugilists, swinging wildly at each other in the darkness.

"The *Arkansas*'s beginning to move away, captain," Delaup said, struggling to make himself heard over the din.

"Keep on her, Mr. Delaup," Micholson shouted. "Follow her gun flashes, if you have to."

"I got my teeth clamped on her like she's my last meal. But we're really steaming blind, though. You don't worry about us running aground?"

"No. She'd strike bottom before we would. And then we'd have her at our mercy."

A cannonball fired from the *Vicksburg* ricocheted off the *Eads*'s casemate and smashed into the top edge of the pilothouse. The impact splintered a wooden panel and knocked both men to the floor. Broken bolts whizzed like bullets through the small room. Micholson clutched his right hip. Delaup's eyes widened with alarm. "Captain! Are you hurt?"

Micholson struggled to his feet, rubbing the place where the bolt had struck him. No blood seeped through the gray cloth of his uniform. "I—I'm all right, Mr. Delaup." He helped the pilot off his knees. "You'd better get your hands back on the wheel."

Delaup grabbed the spokes of the wheel, which had begun to spin of its own accord. He looked desperately for the dark shape of the *Arkansas*. A muzzle flash revealed their foe. Delaup spun his wheel hard right. "Captain? This is my first-ever gunboat battle. How do we know if we're winning?"

"If her gunfire becomes sporadic, or she begins to settle—" He smiled a tight, ironic smile. "Sometimes you don't know until it's all over, Mr. Delaup."

An orange flash pierced the clouds of smoke to their right. It was followed by a dull roar, then a series of splashes as debris hit the water. "What in hell was that?"

Micholson tried focusing his spyglass, even though it was virtually useless at night. "The *Vicksburg*, I believe."

"Our guns did *that?*"

"No. The explosion was too big. Stoddard said her crew was green, inexperienced. I suspect they double-loaded one of their cannons, and it burst." Micholson remembered the Confederate commander's boasts and smiled. "So much for his experimental English guns."

"Are we winning now?"

"Only God knows that. But we're doing better now than we were a minute ago." He lifted the hatch door and began to climb down to the gundeck. "I'll relay this news to the gun crews. It'll do their spirits good."

Johnny McComb's shoulders ached. His arms felt as leaden as the endless succession of fifty pound iron balls he lugged to the forward cannons. But he paid this no heed. All that mattered were the guns. The guns must fire. The quicker he moved his plodding legs—*why are they so damned rubbery?*—the faster the guns would roar.

Ray Manhasset yanked the lanyard on the center bow cannon, an eight inch smoothbore. It heaved against its restraining ropes, its muzzle crowned with flame and smoke. In the uneven lantern light, Manhasset's bare torso glistened with sweat. He plunged his head and shoulders into a nearby tub of water. The water streamed down his body as he grabbed his rammer pole. He stuffed the padded end of the pole into his gun's blisteringly hot muzzle, rubbing out the inside of the barrel to ensure no live sparks remained inside. Then he inserted his filthy index fingers in his mouth and whistled for one of the "powder monkeys," the young lads who toted thirty pound bags of black powder. Manhasset grabbed the bag and heaved it into the muzzle of his gun, the signal for McComb to haul his cumbersome iron cannonball to his friend's gun.

"Guess you'll be needing this now, huh?" McComb grunted as he struggled to lift the ball into the cannon's still hot muzzle. "Can you tell if you've been hitting her?"

Manhasset waited to reply until after Tyler fired the starboard cannon, ten feet to their right. "We been hitting her, all right. I hear my shots strike her armor. I just can't tell if they're doing any good." He rammed the cannonball snug against the bag of propulsive powder, then packed it all in tightly with thick wads of cotton. "This time, I don't want to hit her armor. I want to give 'er a good smashing below the waterline. Help us roll this forward, huh?"

Manhasset, McComb, and a burly gunner named Pine-wood put their shoulders against the massive breach and pushed. Once the cannon again poked through its port, Manhasset picked up a wooden wedge from the floor and handed it to Pinewood. While the older gunner held the wedge in place, Manhasset grabbed a heavy sledgehammer and swung.

"One!" He struck the thick end of the wedge.

"Two! *Three!*" He smashed it twice more, until it was fully inserted between the breach and carriage, lifting the breach and depressing the cannon's muzzle. The two men repeated the process with a second wedge, until their cannon was aimed low at the murky water lapping at the *Arkansas*'s armored stern.

Manhasset again took hold of the firing lanyard. McComb stepped back, wanting to be well away from the gun when it recoiled. Manhasset clapped Pinewood on the shoulder. "This one ought to send 'em to visit the catfish—"

He never pulled his lanyard. A giant fist pulverized the casemate. The front wall burst inward. Shards of iron flew inward, and the wood backing it exploded into splinters.

McComb opened his eyes. He was laid out on the floor, looking up at the ceiling. The stars shone through open latticework. *How long have I been out?* He picked himself off the floor. Everything had gone quiet, save for a constant, tinny ringing. There was a salty taste in his mouth.

The enemy's steel bolt had lodged in the deck floor, barely five feet from him. He stared at the projectile. It's like the head of a great big mole. Poking out from its burrow, real shy-like.

The men at the bow guns had been scattered like ten pins. Some, like McComb, were beginning to slowly pick themselves up. The center gunport was now twice the size it had been, a twisted, gaping wound. McComb limped over to the center gun. Despite the close and tremendous impact, it had remained in its carriage. Next to it, Pinewood lay crumpled atop Manhasset, slivers of wood protruding from his skin like the quills of a porcupine. *Ray's underneath him. Maybe Pinewood's body protected him? God, let it be that way, he's always been lucky...*

McComb sucked in his breath as he grasped Pinewood's shoulders. He had never touched a dead man before. "Give me a second, Ray—I'll get him off you—"

The struggling young gunner's mate thought he had lost his voice, because he couldn't hear himself. And he didn't hear his own shocked cry a second later. Ray Manhasset's luck had run out. His friend had no head.

"The bastards! The goddamned bastards! I'll kill them for you, Ray!" He yanked the lanyard with all his strength. The gun surged backward, wreathed in smoke, but remained eerily silent. Sound itself was in mourning. McComb had no idea when it would return. Nor did he care.

He grabbed Manhasset's rammer pole. It was broken in two. He stuffed the padded half in the gun's muzzle, furiously rubbing sparks from the inside of the barrel. *That powder boy—where in hell is he? Can't he see I need him?* He desperately waved his broken pole above his head. "Hey! Help me! Help me here!" He ran to the men lying on the deck. "C'mon, get up! I can't fire that gun by myself! Help me kill the bastards!" Enraged at his missing voice, he pushed his vocal cords harder with each shouted plea—

GET UP!

HELP ME!
WE HAVE TO KILL THEM!

Strong hands grasped him and turned him around. McComb stared at the face above him. It was the captain. His mouth was moving, forming words. But his eyes spoke more clearly. McComb listened to his eyes.

Your friend is dead. I know what it is to lose a friend. I've lost many. The emptiness you feel now will fill up in time. But the weariness will remain.

McComb tried to read the captain's lips. He seemed to be repeating words over and over.

"...Doctor...you go..."

McComb shook his head violently. "My place is at the guns!" Something trickled down the sides of his neck. The captain grabbed his hands and raised them to McComb's ears. The boy's fingers touched wetness. He looked at his hands. They were covered with red, as if he'd plucking overripe cherries.

"I don't care if I'm wounded! I can still fight!" He struggled to twist out of the captain's hands. But Micholson's grip held firm. The captain forced him to look at himself. For the first time, McComb noticed the splinters jutting from his own shirt. His feet had been sliding in his shoes. He'd assumed it was just sweat. His shoes were stained a dark wine color.

McComb's legs withered beneath him. The captain caught him before he could hit the deck, then lifted him into the arms of two physician's assistants. They carried him halfway across the gundeck, threading their way through broken timbers and shattered bodies, then stopped.

With great effort, McComb raised his head. His two helpers were listening to something, something that alarmed them. The captain heard it, as well.

Johnny McComb wished he could hear it, too. Then a sudden brightness, far more lurid than a cannon's fiery discharge, illuminated the gundeck, shocking his eyes into blindness, and his body finally surrendered to unconsciousness.

CHAPTER SEVENTEEN

Fire on Iron

Aboard the USS James B. Eads, *in an enclosed Confederate harbor and boatyard to the northwest of Adderwood Plantation, Mississippi, April 26, 1862*

That terrible light—I pray it's not what I fear...

The piercing shriek of the *Molly Downings*'s steam whistle echoed across the river and the harbor as Micholson raced back to the pilothouse. Captain Dodds must be trying to warn him of a new danger. Micholson climbed the ladder and pushed the pilothouse's hatch open. Whatever new danger approached, he would see it best from up here.

He found Delaup staring out the view slits. Transfixed.

"Mr. Delaup, do you know why Captain Dodds has sounded the alarm?"

Delaup's words trickled out as a dry gurgle. "Them. There's your answer, captain."

Micholson rushed to the view slits. The brightness was almost too much too bear. Fire giants exploded upward all around the rim of the harbor. Micholson had once witnessed a series of incendiary bombs ignited by a running stream of burning oil; this made that a fading ember by comparison. Within thirty seconds, the entire harbor was surrounded by a wall of living flame.

Their blind battle had brought both the *Eads* and the *Arkansas* dangerously close to the harbor's northern rim. A blazing giant extended a near-shapeless limb towards the gunboats, as if to test the reactions of these strange, unfamiliar water creatures.

Delaup stared out the view slits with mute horror. Micholson pulled him towards the wheel. "For God's sake, Valery, get us out of here! Steer us to the middle of the harbor!" The mass of flame drew closer. "Mr. Broadhurst!" he bellowed into a voice pipe. "Close the gunports! Get those iron shutters closed—"

Daggers of flame shot through the view slits. The sleeve of Micholson's coat ignited. "Christ in heaven!" He was thrown off balance as Delaup spun the wheel and the *Eads* lumbered away from the harbor's rim. Frantically, he tried ripping the coat off. He had known fire before. But no other conflagration had ever induced this visceral terror.

"Get it off me! *Get it off me!*"

"Captain, hold still! Stop thrashing so I can help you!"

Delaup tried unbuttoning Micholson's coat and vest, but the flames bit at his hands like a rabid wolf. He grabbed his bucket of drinking water, muttered a hasty prayer, and hurled its contents. Clouds of steam hissed from the captain's torso, filling the tiny room.

He shielded his face. "Captain! Are you all right?"

"I—I think so..." The air cleared. Micholson sat slumped on the floor, breathing heavily. His jacket and vest lay in burnt tatters on the deck. His face was whiter than his sweat-stained shirt, his eyes wide with shock. "Valery...God, I'm so sorry I panicked..."

A dozen of the nearest *Mikithi,* emboldened by their brother's probe, flung tendrils of flame at the slowly turning ironclads. The projections landed on the *Eads*'s casemate with an evil sizzle. The ironclad's port side became a live oven.

Micholson paled further as his men's screams echoed from below. "Oh God—they didn't get all the guns run in— the shutters were still open!"

"We're moving away, captain! Toward the center of the harbor! I don't know what kind of range those creatures have—"

As if in response, a second set of incandescent white fingers arced from the fire spirits. These fell just short of the ironclad's gunhouse. Three, however, landed on the *Eads*'s low wooden stern. Luckily for all aboard, this deck remained continually awash; the waterlogged planking's paint bubbled and cracked, but the deck failed to catch fire. Other livid plumes landed in the water around the *Eads*'s fleeing stern, creating boiling columns of steam that mixed with lingering clouds of cannon smoke.

Micholson steadied himself by holding onto Delaup's shoulder. "How the devil did those things cross the river?"

"I'll be blasted if I know...if we manage to pull our toasted hides out of this here damned place, maybe old Dodds can tell us."

Micholson's breathing finally settled into a normal cadence. "Valery...you saved my life. I want to thank you."

"Well, sure! What the hell else was I supposed to do? Maybe if I hadn't frozen up staring at those things, you wouldn't have gotten burned."

"Think nothing of that. I succumbed to the horror, too. Bring us to a full stop in the center of the harbor." He unbolted the small door which led to the hurricane deck. "I'm going out to assess our damage."

"How about assessing your *own* damage, captain? You could stand a visit to Doctor Travis."

"Later. Our entire tactical situation has changed. I can't see enough cooped up in here." He pushed the door open. It resisted him. The massive changes in temperature had warped its wood backing; it grated stubbornly against the deck. The night was unlike any he had ever seen. The stars were obliterated. *Is it merely the glare reflected off the clouds? Or do these beings have the power to extinguish the stars themselves?*

He forced the thought from his mind; there was no sense in making these creatures more formidable than they actually were. They had limitations. The fire that nearly consumed him had been quenched. The *Eads* had escaped their flaming tendrils, for now. And hadn't Babbage said they were tied to their native soil, the flora and fauna shipped from Africa? And that they were subject to most of the same physical laws which governed natural wildfires? The light drizzle continued falling. *Surely, if they are all-powerful, they would have stopped this rain.* Did the falling moisture affect them at all? Great tsunamis of flame, they dominated the harbor as an elephant would an anthill. Even an eighth of a mile away from them, he baked in the heat of a midday summer sun. Sweat evaporated from his skin as quickly as it trickled from his pores.

He stared at the harbor's inner rim. What had been nearly invisible five minutes before now stood starkly revealed. Squinting to shield his eyes from waves of heat, Micholson smiled grimly. What he and his crew had fought so hard to accomplish, the flame giants had executed in mere seconds. The two half-finished ironclads in dry dock would not see the coming dawn. Their skeletal timbers, barely discernible among the flames, provided fodder for the growing inferno. He watched with mixed emotions as fire raced along the main pier to engulf the gunboat docked at its edge.

"There goes the CSS *Texas.* Makes a nice bonfire, doesn't she, though?" Delaup said. They watched the half-completed ironclad die. Sharp pops and cracks assaulted their ears as moisture was brutally sucked from her timbers.

"It doesn't feel right, somehow," Micholson said. "Those creatures have robbed us of our victory."

"I wouldn't say that, *m'sieur.* I'd say they only finished something we got good and started."

Micholson walked the length of the hurricane deck, examining his vessel's scorched port side. He glanced quickly at the *Arkansas,* maintaining a position fifty yards distant.

"Captain, you think it's safe to be walking up here like this?"

"Not particularly. The *Arkansas*'s sharp-shooters could pick us off as easily, if they cared to." Neither gunboat had fired a shot since the fire giants had mysteriously appeared. "However, I'd say we've both been shocked into an undeclared truce."

Micholson paused above the spot where a Confederate projectile had broken through the port casemate armor. The hole was a gaping wound, some five feet in diameter. The two-inch-thick iron plating had been pulverized, smashed inward like so much cardboard. And the gunners behind that plating...Micholson tried not to think of what the shot had done to them. The two men walked to the stern, passing the tall, rounded—and wholly unarmored—paddlewheel housing. Micholson leaned over the rearmost railing to stare down at the stern deck, that section of the vessel that lolled in the water like a fat, happy duck. Also bare wood, but so wet, so slick with river scum, that the men drew lots to determine which of them had the sorry task of scraping it clean. Any other unarmored planking would have assuredly been consumed. "We've been lucky thus far," Micholson said. "Were we a few seconds slower escaping, our wheel house would be charcoal now, and we would be as helpless as the *Texas*."

The *Vicksburg*'s starboard broadside floated only thirty yards from the *Eads*'s stern—in perfect position to rake the Federal gunboat. Yet this did not worry Micholson, for the floating battery would do no more fighting this night. Orange flames flickered from her gunports. Five members of her skeleton crew raced about her hurricane deck, searching frantically for an undamaged boat in which to escape. Others, more fearful of blowing up with the powder magazine than drowning, dove into the water and swam towards the *Arkansas*.

And the *Arkansas* herself? Her upperworks looked as though a typhoon had swept through them. Boats were smashed into jagged timbers. Her smokestack was perforated like a cheese grater, which meant the draft to her boilers was cut, reducing her speed. Her casemate appeared intact; it was profusely dented, but Micholson's trained eye scanned the shadows for evidence of shot holes and found none. However, his tactics had borne fruit. His gunners had sheared off the outer muzzles of two of the five cannons he could see, rendering them useless. And the rebel ironclad sat lower in the water than she had an hour ago. The *Eads*'s submarine gunnery had done its work. He could imagine the scene on the *Arkansas*'s lower deck: men running frantically through rising water, grabbing hammocks, mattresses, spare planking, tables—anything to plug the holes with; swinging their hammers like possessed men, caulking the leaks with the shirts off their own sweating backs.

"She's settling," Delaup said.

"I know," Micholson answered. "We may be here to see her disappear beneath these murky waters. If we are unable to escape those flame creatures, we may be here a very, very long time."

He had ordered his Marines to swing the camouflaged barge shut once the *Eads* had entered the harbor. He had wanted to cut off any possibility of the rebel ironclads' escape. Now he had cause to regret this order. The crane that had maneuvered the barge was a smoldering heap of ashes. Guarding the door to the harbor, rising above the barge's false trees like a shimmering chimera, stood the demon of a hundred agonized faces, the accusatory embodiment of Micholson's sins and nightmares.

The harbor had become a deathtrap for the hundreds of sailors manning the *Eads* and the *Arkansas*, for hunters and hunted alike.

"When the day comes," Delaup said, "they will make the heat unbearable, won't they? I don't want to die in this place, captain."

"None of us do, Valery. None of us."

In contradiction to stories Micholson remembered from childhood, which specified that hobgoblins and other unnatural manifestations could not abide the touch of iron, the *Mikithi* ignored the *Eads*'s cannonballs. Firing an explosive shell produced hardly more of an effect. The shell detonated in the middle of what could be described as the targeted creature's "torso," and the flame giant's middle expanded spherically with the burst, like a swelling balloon of fire. The creature wavered between this new shape and its old one for several seconds, until it settled back into its accustomed form.

"I can't tell if we hurt it or helped it," Micholson said. "Mr. Broadhurst, what would you suggest we try next?"

Broadhurst gave his beard a thoughtful tug. "Well, captain, generally, there's two ways you can put out a campfire. You can douse it with water, if there's enough water around, and you have a way to lift it high enough. Or you can dump a shovelful of dirt on it, smother it that way."

"So you're suggesting—?"

"Instead of shooting at *it*, let's try shooting at the dirt it's *standin'* on."

This time, all three bow cannons were loaded with explosive shells. The casemate shook with a tremendous roar as the trio of guns fired in unison. The shells buried themselves in the earth. A fraction of a second later, twenty yards of the harbor's rim exploded in a shower of soil and debris forty feet high.

The creatures beneath the rain of dirt lost all semblance of organized form. They devolved into shapeless masses of flame, flickering and fading beneath the smothering avalanche. Micholson sensed their fury, their hate—these were the only meanings he could ascribe to the waves of searing energy that buffeted the *Eads*. For an instant he knew what it was like to be trapped in the earth's core, crushed by molten rock pressing in with the weight of the planet behind it.

He blinked rapidly, trying to force his vision back into focus. The flames giants had recovered and surged forward, reclaiming their recent positions on the ridge surrounding the harbor. Was there one fewer than there had been before? Micholson couldn't tell for certain. "Mr. Broadhurst, did you *feel* that? When we rained earth on them—that wave of revulsion—"

"I—I felt *something*, sir. What, I can't rightly say."

"We aren't beneath their notice anymore, like some insects or twigs to be consumed. They know we can hurt them, or at least disturb them. I'm not sure whether that plays to our advantage or disadvantage."

"How can you even bear to think about them, sir? Ascribe thoughts and impulses to them? I can hardly look at them without going mad. I wish to God I were as steady as you, captain."

Micholson couldn't suppress a wry smile. "Be careful what you wish for, Mr. Broadhurst. Have your men reload with solid shot, then fire into the water at the edge of the ridge. Let's see if a good soaking has a more permanent effect on them than falling earth did."

The crews reloaded their guns. Exhausted and battered as they were, they seemed grateful for the familiar, mechanical routine, scouring the insides of the hot barrels, lifting the heavy bags of powder and even heavier cannonballs.

Again the guns spoke. The trio of bolts slammed into the water and produced a soaring cascade, as if a mighty waterfall flowed to the skies. Micholson steeled himself for the ethereal feedback.

Take a bath, you misbegotten devils!

The night air erupted with steam. Galloping clouds hissed and wailed like a hundred drowning banshees. Micholson's mind and senses flooded with memories of the *Germania*—the furious touch of steam; the stench of burning flesh; his men's agonized screams...

He forced his eyes open. He wasn't on the *Germania*, and his men weren't being scalded to death. Many of them, however, were trapped in the eldritch horror that had invaded their senses; some bit the skin on their arms until blood dripped down their sleeves, trying to shock themselves back to the solid world. *How much more of this can we take?* Micholson pushed his way toward the open gunports. "The creatures—what has become of them?"

"They moved back, sir," Broadhurst said. "Away from the rim. They're hovering in those trees. Almost like they're afraid we'll hurt them again."

"Did we hurt them? How badly? Or did we merely annoy them?" Neither Broadhurst nor any of his gunners offered an answer. "Whatever we managed to accomplish, we're going to do it again. And again. Mr. Broadhurst, how much ammunition do we have left?"

"Let me think...we used up a lot of our solid shot. I'd say we've got, oh, maybe twenty-five, thirty bolts of different sizes left. Explosive shells we've got plenty of. Two hundred, at least."

"I see. We'd better conserve our solid shot, then, in case the *Arkansas* begins acting up. Tell your men to fire explosive shot into the ground at the creatures' 'feet,' just as they did a few moments ago. Have them repeat this every ten minutes. That should give us enough time to recover our wits and breath between shots, but it won't allow them to forget we can hurt them. I want them to be every bit as afraid of us as we are of them."

"Yes, sir! Anything else?"

"Gather as many of the officers as you can find. We'll meet in the wardroom in five minutes."

Micholson stared into the faces of his surviving officers. Some barely had strength enough to keep their eyes fully open; their eyelids fluttered at half mast, weighed down by exhaustion and temperatures soaring above a hundred and ten degrees. Yet they weren't the ones he worried about. It was the men with open, empty eyes, the ones with all emotion drained from their faces; these were the ones who concerned him. He had witnessed such blankness before. It had been epidemic on the bloody gundecks of the *Northport.* These men had signed on for war and battle; they had expected anxiety, fear, pain, the grisly sights of mutilation, and perhaps death. But they had not expected this.

Dr. Travis rose from his chair to speak. Micholson appreciated the effort it must have cost him. His white undershirt was smeared with other men's blood, spattered by particles of brains and other organs. His face was more deeply lined than any other at the table. But not blank. Micholson was immensely grateful for that.

"Captain Micholson, we cannot remain in this harbor. Those things surrounding us—they sap the will of the wounded to hang onto their lives. It's hard for me to explain; I'm not a priest...both those things eat away at their spirits. They're dying, even the men without mortal wounds, fading more quickly than I've ever seen. And who's to say it won't spread to the unwounded? Look at the faces around this table! Look at them!"

"I agree with you, Doctor," Micholson said. "To remain here is suicide. This is why I've brought you all together. I need your ideas—any ideas, no matter how farfetched—of how we can affect our escape."

A hollow silence settled over the room. Micholson feared silence more than anything. "Any idea! Speak up! Now is no time for shyness!"

Broadhurst cleared his throat. "The crane that moved that barge is gone. We might be able to chase off that fiery bastard that's standing where the crane was, but I don't know if we've got the engine strength to shove the barge out of the way."

"That barge swings on some kind of hinge," Phil Jackson, an engineer who'd transferred over from the *Molly*

Downings, said. "I'd want to know what that hinge is made of before I'd go butting against it. We don't have a lot of room in here to build up speed. And it's not like we're a ram. With our wide, flat prow, we might end up hurting ourselves more than we'd budge that barge."

Micholson looked back to Broadhurst. "Can we sink it and pass over it?"

"I'm sure we could sink it, captain," Broadhurst said.

"But that inlet's pretty shallow," Delaup said. "Not much more than twelve feet, I'd reckon. We couldn't pass over the barge, especially not with all those trees sticking out of it. Even if they are burnt. Sink that barge and we'd just be shoving the cork deeper in the bottle. No, our best bet would be butting it out of the way. And that's a sucker bet, especially since we'd be leaving our stern wide open to the *Arkansas* the whole while."

"The *Arkansas*..." An idea glimmered to life in Micholson's mind. "Thank you, Mr. Broadhurst, Mr. Delaup, all of you who offered your thoughts. You've been most helpful."

The gunnery captain looked confused. "How so?"

"I'll explain once I've paid Commander Stoddard a visit."

Perkins unlocked the door. Micholson entered the bare cabin; he carried Stoddard's sword and pistol. Perkins held up his lantern to illuminate the dark room. Stoddard squinted, his eyes struggling to adjust to the new light. "Who is it? Who's there?"

"It's Captain Micholson, commander. I have a proposal to offer you. One I believe will be of mutual benefit. Are you willing to listen?"

"What choice do I have, captain? I am in your power, am I not? But tell me, sir, and tell me truthfully, if truth is within your ability—why should I trust a word you say? Have you not shown yourself to be a liar, a sneak, and a scoundrel?"

"You should trust me, commander, because we are both boiling in the same cauldron. Think of us as two crustaceans. Hard shells on the outside, tender meat within. Separately, we can do little but float and die. Together, we not only have a chance of escaping the pot, but we may be able to put out the fire. You were correct when you said you have no choice but to listen. I, in turn, have no choice but to ask for your help."

Stoddard's eyes narrowed. "You *dare* ask my assistance? I'd sooner die than tell you the time of day."

"And your men aboard the *Arkansas*, commander? Would you condemn them to death, as well?"

"What are you talking about? It's *your* men you should be worrying about. I felt the blows this gunboat took. Your infirmary must be filled with dead and dying men. The *Arkansas*'s armor, however, was never pierced by your cannons; I witnessed the entire battle. My vessel is secure, my men safe. So long as their provisions hold out, they can remain in the center of this harbor indefinitely."

"Can they?" Micholson moved to the window. "Take a good look at your ironclad, commander. Wouldn't you say she's resting lower in the water than she should?"

Reluctantly, Stoddard peered out the window. "No. It's a trick of the light—"

"Don't fool yourself. She's holed below the waterline. She's been settling steadily for the last hour. I'm sure your men are making heroic efforts to save her, but without proper equipment, all they can do is forestall the inevitable. Where will your men swim to when the *Arkansas* sinks, commander? Here? We won't have room to hold them all. To shore? Those things would incinerate them in seconds."

The words came with difficulty, yet they came. "Very well, Micholson. Tell me this plan of yours."

"I am willing to return you to your vessel, providing that you agree to order your men to work in concert with us.

The mechanical device that once swung the barge away from the inlet is destroyed. Either of our vessels has firepower enough to sink the barge. Neither, however, is of such shallow draft that she can steam out above the wreckage. Only the *Arkansas* has an iron prow sharp enough to cut through the timbers of the sunken barge. This is the first task I request of you."

"Your logic fails you. Where is the need for us to work in concert? Your plan has the *Arkansas* performing all the essential work. Why can't my crew escape on their own? If you have figured out this route of escape, surely my officers will recognize the same opportunity."

Micholson sighed with barely concealed impatience. "Cutting through that wreckage won't be an easy affair. It may take four, five blows. Each time the *Arkansas* embeds her ram in the barge, she'll have to reverse her engines, wrench her prow back out of the tangled wreck. While she is doing that, those creatures won't be standing idly by. They'll turn your ironclad into an oven. Unless the *Eads* provides covering fire, putting up such a continuous shower of water that they'll be forced to keep their distance."

"Why should I believe you won't silence your guns and allow the creatures to attack me as soon as I've made a breach in the barge?"

"Because," Micholson slowly continued, "we'll still need you. During the second phase of my plan, you'll be required to cover *our* backs. I told you we have a chance to put out the fire, didn't I? In my forward storage hold, Commander Stoddard, I may have the means to send these entities back to whatever blazing hell they sprang from."

Delaup stared out the pilothouse windows, watching the *Arkansas* slowly steam into position. "How far do you trust this Commander Stoddard?"

Micholson waited tensely for the cannonade to begin. "About as far as he trusts me, I imagine. Do you recall Ben

Franklin's words during the signing of the Declaration of Independence?"

"Um, let's see, now. 'We must all hang together...'"

"'—or we will surely hang separately.' Yes. A declaration of *inter*dependence. Stoddard and I are tightrope walkers, without a net, each hanging onto a shared balance pole for dear life. If either of us lets go, we both fall."

Delaup lit one of his short cigars. The glow seemed to float in the dark room, anticipating the cannon fire waiting to erupt. "We've been lucky so far, *m'sieur*. Most of the fleet we came to ruin is ashes, now. Maybe, if luck sticks with us, ol' *Arkansas* will take a dive in some deep part of the Yazoo, eh?"

"Only after we do what must be done. Not one second before."

The *Arkansas*'s bow cannons flashed. The *Eads*'s gunners seconded this with impressive fire of their own. Five shells tore through the thin hull of the barge, exploding inside and blowing out the square obstruction's bottom.

"She's sinking like Atlantis!" Delaup said. The enormous pull of sucking water snapped the iron hinges holding the barge to the northern bank of the inlet. Tons of earth and trees began to slip off the slanting deck into the murky water.

The spirit that had been guarding the barge scurried to the tops of the trees like a gigantic flaming rat. As its perch began sliding toward the rising waters, the *Mikithi* tried frantically to bridge the growing distance between its own fiery mass and the nearest dry vegetation. It shot tendril after tendril, which streaked the early morning sky like comets. Each fell just short, landing in mud with an agonized sizzle. Its furious terror crackled through the air—Micholson could feel it. *Let it bombard me with all the purloined emotions it wishes,* he thought. *It will be worth it to see the damned thing suffer and die, as my men have suffered and died.*

The barge hit bottom. The blackened tops of two trees still stood above the waters. The creature, now a white-hot, compact ball, retained its sanctuary in the highest branches, barely five feet above the water. Micholson grabbed the voice pipe to the forward gundeck. "Open fire at those tree tops!" he snarled. The shells hit the trees like sledgehammers, scattering the charred fragments over much of the Yazoo's breadth.

The river exploded in a burst of red-tinged steam. Micholson felt his body come apart—his limbs melted, his face atomized, and nothingness sucked him in. *So this is death...*

Then, as quickly as it had begun, it was over, and the gloomy pilothouse surrounded him. Delaup was sprawled on the floor next to him. His body spasmed. His eyes turned back into his head.

"Valery!" Micholson struck him hard across the face, twice, three times. "Damn it, man! The creature will *not* suck you down with it!"

Delaup uttered a sharp cry. His eyelids blinked rapidly. "Captain—?"

"Yes, I'm here."

"Oh, Blessed Virgin...that felt like...like I was drowning and being blown up at the same time. The demon. Did it—?"

A belated cheering rose from the decks below. "There's your answer. That particular walking inferno shan't trouble us again."

"Sweet Mary and Jesus," Delaup muttered softly as he stumbled back to his station at the wheel. "Will we have to go through that every time we kill one of those things?"

Micholson chose not to answer. Instead, he spoke into the main deck voice pipe. "Mr. Broadhurst? Have the men soak themselves thoroughly from their buckets. Are the hose extensions fitted to the boiler tubes?"

The hoses were designed to put out fires or repel enemy boarders with scalding water. "They are, sir."

"Have a crew wet down as much of the gunboat's exterior as they can. This drizzle hasn't done more than make us slightly damp. Make certain they take extra care with our stern—that's naked wood back there."

"Captain," Delaup interrupted. "You'll want to watch this."

Micholson moved to the front windows. The *Arkansas* lurched forward, heading straight for the gap. Just as it appeared she would pass through into the river, she shuddered to a sudden halt. Micholson heard the muffled sound of the underwater crash. The water beneath the *Arkansas*'s tail churned furiously as her propellers were driven in full reverse. Her first efforts to extricate herself got her nowhere. On both necks of land surrounding the trapped ironclad, towering *Mikithi* surged forward.

"Now!" Micholson shouted into his voice tube. "Don't let them get close!"

The *Eads*'s first volley threw up a cascade of water along the northern peninsula. The flame giants reared back and retreated with stunning swiftness.

"Quick, Mr. Delaup! Swing us around!"

The pilot spun the wheel and barked orders into his own tube leading to the engine room. The *Eads*'s two paddlewheels were thrown into opposition, and the clumsy gunboat turned with surprising alacrity, bringing her starboard battery to bear on the southern spit of land. Her broadside cannons boomed, sending their own missiles plunging into the water near the *Arkansas*'s straining casemate, raising a series of plumes higher than the trapped ironclad's tall smokestack.

What if she is too deeply embedded? Micholson thought. *We can't protect her forever. If she remains stuck in the breach, she'll be a worse impediment than the barge ever was—*

The air rent with sounds of bursting timber as the *Arkansas* wrenched herself free. Her iron ram had proved itself an effective axe. The rebel vessel backed away until she was abreast with the *Eads*. Then her engineers threw her engines into forward gear again.

This time the impact sounded like breaking bones. Once more, the *Arkansas* struggled to disengage herself. The enormous torque of her propellers pulled her stern one way, then the other. *What if she tears off her ram with all those gyrations? Then she'd have no more power of cutting through that barge than I do.*

Plunging sheets of fire landed on the *Arkansas*'s casemate. "Mr. Broadhurst," Micholson shouted into the voice tube, "why aren't your gunners keeping those devils at a distance?"

"We're trying, sir," the voice echoed back. "But they've changed tactics. They're hanging back now, hiding behind trees where our splashes can't reach them. But they're still close enough to lob those gouts of flame."

Micholson watched with consternation as a falling fireball set the *Arkansas*'s auxiliary boats and signaling masts aflame. *How can I expect Stoddard to live up to his end of our bargain if we can't live up to ours?* "Mr. Broadhurst! Have your men run their cannons inside and close the gunports tight!"

"Why, sir? They may be able—"

"Just do it! We're getting out of here! Now!"

"Now how're we gonna do *that?*" Delaup said. "You have some way of making this iron elephant fly?"

"We're going to give the *Arkansas* a little shove. Tell the engineers to give you maximum steam pressure, then aim our bow straight for the rebel's stern. Hit her flush on, or we're liable to sink ourselves, and her with us!"

"So she is the chisel and we're the hammer?"

"Exactly. Go!"

The *Eads* backed her way to mid-harbor. Her huge water wheels stilled momentarily as her engines shifted from reverse to full forward throttle. Then the paddlewheels began churning black water again, and the six hundred ton mass of oak and iron launched itself at its target.

Micholson grabbed the voice tube. "Broadhurst! Order the men to lie flat on deck!"

The *Mikithi* emerged from behind their cover of vegetation and rained fresh plumes of fire on the *Arkansas*'s upperworks. The *Eads* steadily picked up momentum. A low speed wave formed off her bows. The *Arkansas* loomed larger and larger. Micholson wedged his shoulders against the pilothouse wall.

The impact shattered every undamaged piece of Wedgwood China in the officers' mess hall. It sent a wounded seaman flying off an operating table, raising unholy curses from Dr. Travis. It slammed six unwary men into casemate walls and knocked them senseless. Hundred pound chunks of sodden wood landed in the middle of the Yazoo. The *Arkansas*'s iron prow carved through the remainder of the barge like a spear through wet paper. The force of the blow knocked the southern half of the sunken barrier part-way into the river, where it was sucked away by the powerful current. The sudden vacuum wrenched the *Arkansas* around and pulled her broadside into the river. The *Eads* followed immediately after, engulfed in a canopy of vengeful flame.

Micholson rose to his feet, his heart surging. "We're out, Valery! We've escaped!"

Delaup's struggled to control the gunboat in the violently unsettled current. The *Eads* twirled like a toy boat in an eddy before he could gain her head again. Only then did he realize what they had done. "Jesus, Mary and Joseph and all the rest of the gang! We made it!"

The boiling cauldron was behind them. But the joy in Micholson's breast was short-lived; their job remained undone. *It would be so easy to escape down the river now. Haven't my men earned a rest from the danger, the horror?* He sighed, knowing what his next order must be.

"Steer us toward Adderwood Plantation, Mr. Delaup. When we reach it, plant us hard against the levee."

The drizzle had stopped with the rising of the sun. It seemed a bad omen. But Micholson didn't have time to dwell on this. He had a levee to smash.

"My men and I have things well in hand," Wilson said respectfully. "You don't need to remain with us, captain." The corporal assisted a group of Marines struggling to transfer a torpedo, big as an upright piano, from the *Eads*'s stern to the grassy slope of the Adderwood levee. Five more remained to be dragged up from the hold.

"I'll remain with you until the job is complete, Mr. Wilson." Micholson uncoiled the fuse wire that would allow all six torpedoes to be fired at once, then tied the wire to the torpedo's powder detonator. "I've decided to blow up this levee, at additional risk to all your lives. So I'll share that risk, sir, if you don't mind."

He could see the scorched upperworks of the *Arkansas* quite clearly now. She had anchored in the middle of the Yazoo. The muzzles of her broadside cannons flashed. The roar of their discharge shook the earth beneath his feet. The shots smacked into the river, raising water spouts higher than the *Eads*'s smokestacks. "It's unnerving, isn't it," he said to Wilson, "to have those guns firing in our direction, and the shots landing so nearby?"

Wilson skimmed river water from his forehead. "It'd be much more unnerving if they weren't. Those things—" he nodded towards the land side of the levee "—they'd be on us in a second if it weren't for the *Arkansas*. I just hope they don't make any 'slip-ups.' You think we can trust Stoddard?"

"I'm betting my life on it." *And all of yours*, he thought; but he didn't say it. They sank their boots into the mud surrounding the *Eads*'s stern while helping to lift another torpedo onto the levee. "Stoddard is a loyal Mississippian. He knows this is our only chance to put an end to these creatures; on this shore, at least. And, if what Babbage said is true, that the creatures require a physical connection to their native soil in order to remain incarnated here, perhaps our actions here may dispel them from both shores."

The heat at their backs grew fiercer—if one of the *Mikithi* struck now, when he and his men carried hundreds of pounds of black powder, their lives would end in an eyeblink. But then cannon fire erupted again from the *Arkansas*, and cascades of water fell on the men and the far side of the levee. The ominous heat retreated.

The sun continued its ascent above the tree line. Upriver, where the hidden boatyard had been, a pillar of ash-colored smoke rose a mile into the hazy air. The Marines and Micholson unloaded the sixth and final torpedo from the *Eads*'s stern. They manhandled it into position and Micholson attached it to the detonation wires. He glanced up at Wilson, intending to compliment him and his men on a job well done. Rather than the relief he expected to see, however, he saw a look of stunned horror on Wilson's face.

"The *Arkansas*! She's running! She's abandoning us!"

Smoke poured from the Confederate's stack as she moved downstream. When she came abreast of the *Eads*, the *Arkansas*'s broadside cannons flared red. The blows rocked the Union gunboat against the levee.

The heat at the men's backs grew suddenly intense. Above the rim of the levee, flames blotted out the sun. An inhuman face, maddened with hatred and a lust to destroy, towered above them.

Wilson froze. Micholson grabbed him and heaved him down the levee into the river. "Dive! Dive!" he screamed to the men. "Get yourselves into the Yazoo!"

Some dove. Some half ran, half slid. Others, made clumsy by terror, tumbled feet over head. A flaming limb reached for them all, blocking the sky. Micholson dove.

The river engulfed him like a protecting womb. The water, clogged with silt, blocked his sight like a liquid blindfold. *How long can I stay under? Will that creature incinerate my head as soon as I emerge for air?*

After sixty seconds he had no choice. He kicked towards the distended light. His face broke the surface. Grateful as his lungs were for air, his eyes, confronted by the awful results of Stoddard's perfidy, craved renewed blindness. The demon hadn't been reaching for the men—it had reached for the *Eads*.

Micholson choked on a cry of rage. The entire stern of his gunboat was ablaze!

CHAPTER EIGHTEEN

Drowned Plantation, Abandoned Gunboat

Aboard the USS James B. Eads *on the flooded grounds of Adderwood Plantation, Mississippi, April 26, 1862*

The *Mikithi* exulted on the scorched levee as the water beast blazed. Inside the water beast, like bees in a melting hive, the dreaming animals screamed.

Yet the fire spirits did not have long to savor their apparent victory. Six torpedoes lay between the flame giants and the now burning ironclad. The first device, loaded with a hundred and twenty pounds of black powder, ignited at the *Mikithi's* touch. Almost instantly, the other five exploded in a massive chain reaction.

The levee ruptured like the cone of an erupting volcano. Huge chunks of damp earth were thrown to every point on the compass. The creature that set off the torpedoes was hurled into the river. Its death in a mushroom cloud of steam seared into four hundred human minds.

The Yazoo immediately surged through the breach. Its irresistible pressure undermined the intact portions of the levee from all sides, making the breach larger and larger, pouring into the lowlands which surrounded Adderwood Mansion, heading for the tall mounds of Lundowan earth and the suddenly immobile *Mikithi.*

The death of the fire giant battered his senses, but Micholson did not allow himself to succumb to paralysis. If he lost consciousness and let go of the *Eads*'s broken steering chain, he knew he would never awaken again.

The distended Yazoo cupped him and his gunboat in a frothy palm, tugging at the ironclad's anchors, pushing Micholson and the *Eads* through the breach and out of the river's main channel. All around him, the ravenous river erased the work of decades—land which had been made dry by the back-breaking labor of hundreds of slaves was immersed once more, walls of brick and plaster tumbled, and animals swam through the broken doors of barns lifted from their foundations.

Two of the *Mikithi* escaped the onrushing flood by climbing to the top of Adderwood Mansion, the highest point for miles around. But the other fire giants who had remained on the plantation grounds seemed frozen by the same horror which they had so recently inspired in men. The invading Yazoo surged against their lower extremities, and Lundowa's most terrible gods began to die.

The world dissolved from Micholson's senses. His body was rent inside out. Quivering organs exploded like super-heated balloons of blood; his limbs were stretched a thousand miles in four opposite directions, still connected to his brain by throbbing cords of screaming gristle.

The acrid stench of burning resins from the *Eads*'s blazing stern drew him back to the physical world. His mouth was filled with warm saltiness. He had bitten his lower lip nearly through.

He still clung to the steering chain. He choked on mouthfuls of silty water. His crippled ironclad, completely in the river's control, headed on a collision course straight for Adderwood Mansion.

One thought blazed through his mind—
Was it enough? Have we beaten them?

* * *

The torpedoes' explosions had hurled M'Lundowi to the floor of the balcony of Adderwood Mansion. Waves of pain smashed into him as the onrushing flood banished one god after another; the death throes of his *Mikithi* felt like a half-molten iron poker being thrust through his skull.

The screams of his underlings reached his slowly recovering ears from the grounds below.

"Flee! Flee! We are undone!"

"We will drown in the flood!"

M'Lundowi pulled himself from the floor and forced himself to look upon Micholson's work. N'Mehayah's pup had created an elemental horror nearly the equal of any M'Lundowi himself had ever called forth. Thousands of tons of furious Yazoo River rushed through the breach, carrying acres of topsoil, broken wagons and plows, drowned cattle, and massive chunks of broken levee.

M'Lundowi stared at the onrushing wall of water and his fleeing attendants. "Come back, you spineless fools!" he screamed. "We must save the sacred soils! All is not yet lost!" But the men now feared the river's anger more than they feared that of their terrible master.

Only Alaltho and the bound Nehemiah remained at his side as the flood waters surged up the steps of the mansion's porches. "Alaltho, my comrade! We must secure some of the sacred soils in containers that will resist the water!"

Alaltho backed away from the man who had been his guide and guardian. "I will serve you no more, fallen one," he said through lips pinched with unending grief. "I go to join my son's ashes in the waters below."

He leaped out a window and disappeared into the rising flood.

M'Lundowi cursed with frustration, then raced down the steps towards the mansion's ground floor. Grand rooms once filled with European finery now overflowed with gray-black soil. He ran toward the pantry. *Pots made of copper metal—if I can save even a few dozens of pounds of earth from the Motherland, it will be enough to summon fresh* Mikithi.—

When he opened the door to the pantry, a wall of water flooded into the dining room and hit him like a battering ram. He was hurled to the floor, buffeted by an armada of floating pots and pans. The dining room's stained glass windows exploded outward as the internal surge of thick brown water hit them.

"*Micholson!*" M'Lundowi screamed. "You may think you have destroyed my work of half a lifetime, but I will ensure you will die a lingering, humiliating death!"

He retreated up the stairs, only to find his captive brother smiling at him. "Grin while you can, my traitorous brother," M'Lundowi said. "This continent of soulless grub men shall still be cleansed by fire, no matter my temporary setback. Do you forget that some of the fire spirits lingered in that place called Yazoo City, and others continue to stalk the opposite bank of this river?"

"Without you to guide them and enflame their passions, the gods of the fires shall tire of this alien place and shall return to their origin place."

"And why do you assume I shall not be present to lead them on future rampages?"

"August Micholson shall see to it."

M'Lundowi swept a pair of wizened seeds, each as big as a walnut, from the top of the chest of drawers which had once held Joseph Babbage's silk undergarments. He brandished the seeds beneath Nehemiah's face. "Know you what these are, you disgrace to our shared blood?"

"I do," Nehemiah said grimly.

"These were the agency of my dispatch of the fool Babbage. And they shall be my agency of revenge against your precious Micholson—these, and the young fire spirit which dwells safely within the machinery of his own damned iron boat!"

* * *

Micholson clung with desperate strength to the *Eads*'s broken steering chain. He saw with horror that two of the Marines who had positioned the torpedoes on the now vanished levee bobbed helplessly in the raging current between the *Eads* and Adderwood Mansion. Even if they avoided drowning, their own gunboat was poised to soon crush them against the great house's brick walls.

"Perkins! Wilson!" he screamed. "Don't try to swim against the current! Swim out of it! *Perkins!*"

Wilson managed to swim to the gunboat's far side. But Perkins clung to a floating barrel and spun like a chunk of driftwood. The *Eads*'s blunt bow pinned him against one of the mansion's white columns.

"Perkins!"

The gunboat's momentum and massive weight smashed her bow and forward deck through the mansion's front wall, burying the vessel up to the front of her casemate in the flooded wreckage of Adderwood Mansion. The impact created a giant wave which overtopped the three story house. It dislodged two of the *Mikithi* from their precarious sanctuary, knocking them to dissolution in the rising water and immediate banishment. The current sheered the *Eads* sharply to starboard, resulting in a second collision with the great house. Portions of the mansion's front facade and second and third story balconies collapsed onto the ironclad's starboard casemate and hurricane deck. Yet this additional violence did the *Eads* a favor—the resultant waves and slosh quenched the fires which had reduced her twin paddlewheels to charred, ruined timber.

Micholson pulled himself along the steering chain until he was five feet from the smoking ruins of the stern deck, then swam to the *Eads*'s port side. What he saw there was enough to make him momentarily forget the heartbreak of seeing his vessel crippled.

"Wilson! You're still alive!"

The corporal clung to the wreckage of a lifeboat which dangled from the ironclad's side. He smiled a lopsided grin at Micholson. "You, too, captain, I see. Thanks for tossing me off that levee. Those fire things sure are ghastly when they die, huh?"

"No creature dies easily, Wilson. Certainly not us."

A gunnery crew heard their shouts and pulled them aboard through a gunport. Broadhurst ran to meet them.

"Wilson's marines—did they make it?" Micholson asked.

"Three of them are aboard. The other three...no. We'd thought you two were goners, as well."

"Do any fires still burn on the gunboat?"

"The Yazoo did us the favor of quenching the big one on the stern, but not before we lost most of our wheel power. We're as much of a floating battery now as the *Vicksburg* was, captain. Without major repairs in a dockyard, we aren't going anywhere."

They passed groups of gunners, still disoriented from the *Arkansas*'s most recent attack, the deaths of the *Mikithi*, and the collision with the mansion. The less-hurt tended to their more grievously wounded comrades, digging splinters and shell fragments from flesh with pocket knives, wrapping torn limbs in the cleanest bandages they could find. The men's eyes widened as they saw the trio approach.

"It's the captain! And Wilson! They made it back!"

The gunners raised a series of ragged cheers as the three men passed. Bandaged hands reached out to touch Micholson's dripping, torn coat.

"You showed 'em, captain!" The speaker, his face a purplish bruise, grinned; half his teeth had been knocked out. "You showed them flaming bastards they can't fuck with the U.S. Navy!"

This bit of bravado, answered with further cheers, was repeated endlessly up and down the gundeck. Micholson was embarrassed; Wilson and Broadhurst just laughed.

The rear section of the gunboat proved to be no laughing matter. The three men stood in the paddle wheel chamber, blinking in the glare of unexpected sunlight. Hunks of steaming charcoal fell from smoking rafters, bouncing off broken wheel blades and shattering into sodden ash. Dust-filled shafts of daylight streamed through blackened holes as big as lifeboats.

"We have no choice, I see," Micholson said bitterly. "Mr. Broadhurst, order the men to ready themselves for transfer to the *Molly Downings*. Despite the dangers of the passage back north, the freighter will have to make the journey alone, at least until the fleet can be summoned to cover her run past Fort Pillow."

"Can't we have the *Molly Downings* take the *Eads* under tow?" Broadhurst asked.

"No. The *Molly Downings*'s only protection is her speed and maneuverability. I won't sacrifice those slim advantages and endanger hundreds of lives just to salvage a half-burned gunboat. Uncle Sam can build another; but he can't restore life to the dead."

The *Molly Downings* anchored near where the levee had once stood; had she attempted to anchor closer to the stricken ironclad, the force of the Yazoo's new second current would likely have pushed her miles inland, depositing her like drifting debris against some far rise or trapping her amidst an island of partially submerged pine trees.

Broadhurst and Wilson organized the freighter's auxiliary boats into a transport chain that stretched from the *Eads*'s port side to the *Molly Downings*'s stern. Moving the wounded proved to be the most arduous task. Dr. Travis prepped the more grievously injured with extra injections of morphine and swallows of whiskey, hoping to ease the agony of torn limbs and torsos being manhandled from rocking boat to rocking boat. Even so, the flooded remains of Adderwood Plantation echoed with the cries of brave men overwhelmed by bodily agonies.

Micholson stood in one of the middle boats. He accepted, carried, and passed along human bundles until his shoulders and back pleaded for relief, then carried on.

Captain Dodds of the *Molly Downings* sounded his signal whistle, a mournful warning shriek that sent shivers down Micholson's spine. Soon dire word came back to him along the chain of boats—"The *Arkansas*! She's coming back!"

"Double your efforts, men!" Micholson shouted. "Get every wounded man aboard the *Molly Downings* without a second's delay! Abandon all personal possessions—every man who can swim should do so, leaving the boat chain to those who cannot!"

Two rowboats closer to the *Molly Downings*, a stoker named Herbert Madison misjudged his balance as he tried to assist a one legged sailor into his boat. "Oh, Jesus—I'm losing hold!" The two men both tumbled into the inlet when the boat upended.

The blood drained from Micholson's face. "A line! Throw them a line!"

Delaup, who stood in the next boat over, leaped into the water. A strong swimmer, he pulled the wounded man from beneath the surface first, then performed the same service for Madison. Then he and Micholson assisted the last of the wounded men across the boat chain. The shock of a cannon blast again distended the surface of the Yazoo. A shell landed in the water just twenty yards short of the *Molly Downings*, raising a splash as high as her smoke stacks.

Micholson turned away from the freighter and ran towards the stricken *Eads*, jumping from boat to boat.

"Captain!" Delaup called after him. "Aren't you going in the wrong direction? We've got to get the hell out of here—"

"Dodds and his boat will never escape the *Arkansas*'s guns unless I can distract her!" Micholson called back, not breaking stride.

"How can you do that?"

"The *Eads*'s cannons are still loaded and run out, ready to fire! Stoddard must've come back to see what happened to the flame creatures, and in hopes of finishing us off. If I fire the *Eads*'s guns, he'll think the crew is still aboard her. His pride will compel him to close with the gunboat and try to sink her. If God is with us, it'll give all of you time to use your greater speed to escape!"

"But—but what about *you?*"

"Forget me, Mr. Delaup! Save the men! Get back to the freighter and tell Dodds to run upriver until I can decoy Stoddard into the inlet! I grew up in this territory—I can make my way back to friendly lines!"

Delaup began running toward the gunboat, leaping boats just as Micholson had. "I ain't leaving you behind, captain! No way in hell!"

"Valery, I order you to cross to the *Molly Downings*! Now! *Go!*"

Delaup refused to turn back. Micholson grabbed an ax from the deck and severed the rope holding the last boat in the chain to the *Eads*'s capstan. He saw Captain Dodds standing in front of the *Molly Downings*'s pilothouse, watching the *Arkansas*'s lumbering approach upriver. "Dodds! Get my men out of here! Immediately! Have your crew pull the small boats back whether Mr. Delaup likes it or not. Then run upriver until I draw the *Arkansas* out of the main channel!"

Dodds signaled that he understood. Seconds later, Micholson heard the welcome sounds of the freighter's anchors being raised, and white smoke puffed from her twin smoke stacks as her side-wheels began maneuvering her backwards into the main channel. He ignored Delaup's impassioned and profane objections as he quickly stepped through one of the *Eads*'s middle gunports.

Empty now except for the corpses of the valiant dead, the gunboat felt somehow alive, a seething presence which surrounded him, as though he had crawled into the belly of a dying leviathan. *Is there any chance at all she'll survive the pounding she'll soon receive? How bizarre, that I should willingly, even happily, call destruction down upon my vessel. But far better my vessel than my men.* He stood by one of the loaded cannons, waiting for the *Arkansas* to lumber into view, the firing lanyard wrapped around his fist. The cannon's breach was caked with blood.

Peering anxiously through the gunport, he saw the leading edge of the *Arkansas*'s casemate out on the river. One of her bow cannons flashed; she pursued the fleeing *Molly Downings.* Micholson yanked furiously on the firing lanyard. The gun roared. The wounded ironclad bucked like a branded stallion; the recoil battered the partially demolished house the vessel leaned against, and more pieces of Adderwood Mansion fell, clattering against the *Eads*'s casemate and hurricane deck. He watched his shot smack into the river several dozen yards short of the rebel ram—the *Eads* sat at a precarious angle, and aiming the guns was impossible for one man in any case.

He ran to the next prepped and fused cannon. *Turn, you bastard! I'm the enemy! Turn and face me!* He pulled the lanyard before the *Arkansas* could pass from view. This shot proved more fortuitous—it also landed in the river, but much closer to the *Arkansas,* and Micholson watched the rebel ram shudder as the bolt struck her below her waterline.

The enemy ironclad slowed, then began to turn east, toward the *Eads. Yes! I'm pulling her in! After giving the gunboat a good pounding, Stoddard will undoubtedly send a boarding party to demand our surrender. All of which will consume time, precious time.* He thought of his friends and comrades aboard the *Molly Downings. They'll make it. They're in God's hands now. May He have mercy on men who have striven so hard for so long.*

The *Arkansas* steamed slowly through the inlet, her powerful bow cannons facing the *Eads* head on. *He's choosing to not waste his shots; he'll wait until he's virtually on top of me to fire.* He thought of another way to delay his foe and give his men more time to escape. *We still have enough powder and explosive shell in our magazine to blow this gunboat to Kingdom Come. If I can just lay a powder trail long enough to let me jump overboard, I can leave one final surprise for Stoddard. I won't let that brigand salvage even a scrap of useful iron from my ship!*

Just as Micholson turned to head below, the *Arkansas*'s twin bow cannons thundered. This first salvo hammered the gunboat's casemate armor square on, deafening him and hurling him against a bulkhead. A trickle of blood slid down the side of his face. He gathered his wits and propelled himself down steep steps to the forward hold, lit by a single dim battle lantern.

Another bolt smashed into the *Eads*'s casemate. Micholson could tell from the sound of splitting timbers that this latest shot had pierced the unarmored, wooden portion of her gunhouse, then ricocheted between the unmanned cannons, multiplying the havoc already rampant on the gundeck tenfold. *Thank the Lord there are no live gunners left up there. Bless this boat's builders—she's a sturdy old tub. If only she'll remain afloat long enough for me to do what I must...*

He grabbed a thirty pound bag of powder, then used a bayonet from a discarded rifle to stab a hole in the bag's bottom. He began laying a trail of black powder from the stacks of racked shells to the stairs. *I'll use that lantern to ignite the powder, then pray my legs have strength and luck enough to outrace both the explosion and Stoddard's gunners—*

The *Eads* lurched under a tremendous hail of iron. The beams supporting the forward hurricane deck collapsed, raining colossal timbers onto the gundeck and blocking egress from the hold's stairs.

Something struck Micholson from behind. A directed blow, aimed at his head—he felt his senses flee, dribbling out of him like blood from a burst bruise. Too late, he realized he hadn't been alone on the doomed ironclad.

He struck the floor and tasted black powder. His last sensation before darkness pulled him under was that of fingers forcing his mouth open and shoving something down his throat, something hard and vile...

CHAPTER NINETEEN

The Smelting Fire

Aboard the USS James B. Eads
on the flooded grounds of
Adderwood Plantation, Mississippi,
April 27, 1862

His stomach burned. Something tickled his nose. Tiny legs scurried across his skin.

Micholson's eyes snapped open. He immediately clawed at his face. His sudden motion dislodged most of the flies, but a few of the more persistent insects remained, incessantly exploring the crevices of his pockmarked skin.

He sat up, breathed deeply, then gagged. The air stank of rotting flesh. He nearly doubled over from stabs of pain in his guts; yet he had suffered no wound there.

He realized he wasn't in the forward hold anymore, where he'd been ambushed and knocked unconscious. *Someone has moved me...I'm on the boiler deck.* Sunlight streamed onto the boiler deck through a multitude of fissures in the gundeck above and shot holes drilled through the casemate. *Where is the* Arkansas*? Where are Stoddard's men? Did they take me for one of the dead?*

He pulled himself painfully to his feet, then climbed a partially shattered set of steps to the gundeck, where he could look out through the ports. All but two of the broadside cannons had been dismounted, and the bow guns were partially buried by the ruins of Adderwood Mansion. Micholson did not spot the *Arkansas* anywhere, neither inside the inlet and lake which covered the plantation grounds, nor out on the Yazoo proper.

—Stoddard has left this place. His own vessel was too damaged, too much in danger of sinking, for him to risk remaining to salvage this gunboat.—

Micholson reeled with confusion. The thoughts, which could have been his, had not risen from his own volition; nor had they been "spoken" with what he recognized as his own mental voice. *That voice in my head...were it not impossible, I would swear it was the voice of Paul Legarde.*

He stumbled over something. He looked down. The shapeless mound at his feet, black with flecks of fluttering silver that reflected the fading sunlight...writhed. A gunner's corpse, covered entirely with ravenous flies.

"Oh, God. The fallen men. We never had the chance to inter them in the river..."

Retreating with involuntary revulsion, his foot brushed against something else, which skittered across the floor. He looked down again. Between his boot and a pair of dead men lay a piece of broken planking. It had writing on it. Micholson knelt to read the words.

As you are now, so once were we.
As we are now, soon you shall be.

The ink appeared blotchy, congealed, like drops of black wax. He dabbed the letters with his fingertips, trying to determine how recently they had been written. Startled, he drew his hand away. The letters had been formed from the charred, crushed bodies of flies.

Below him, beneath the broken, holed gundeck, a set of boilers throbbed into life. The heat buried within his stomach answered this beckoning with a kinetic surge of its own.

"Who is there?" he cried. "Who toys with me? Are you Daniel, sorcerer who was owned by Joseph Babbage?"

—Good guess, August. Not on the mark, but clever.—

"Paul?" He felt both foolish and afraid as he gathered his breath and called the name again. "Paul Legarde! Ghost or demon, show yourself!"

No sound answered his call, save the unending buzzing of flies.

He descended once more to the boiler deck. He walked the precarious planks between the long, black boilers and the fireboxes beneath them, encased in their conical iron shields, which formed the bases of the gunboat's smoke stacks. The boiler deck and the fireroom were empty, save for scattered piles of coal abandoned around the bases of the fireboxes.

A muffled roar erupted from Firebox 7; an orange glow burst through the seams of the brick and iron furnace. Micholson pulled on a pair of fireman's mitts, which reached beyond his elbows. Steeling himself against the anticipated heat, he grasped the handles on the cast-iron furnace doors and pulled them open.

He quickly backed away from the wave of heat which emerged. Cautiously, he peered into the flames. They looked ordinary enough, no different from the thousands of coal fires he had witnessed during his naval career.

"What did I expect to find?" he muttered to himself, wiping sweat from his forehead. "Paul's severed head, grinning at me from the fire like some out-of-season jack o' lantern?"

Micholson closed the furnace and discarded the fire mitts. "Where is your next trick, magician?" he called into the dark emptiness of the boiler deck. In response, a high-pitched whistling issued from the boiler suspended above the inexplicably active firebox. The whistling gradually lost its discordance and took on the order and rhythm of a tune; one Micholson easily recognized.

"'Woodman, Spare That Tree'...my whole life, I've only known one man to whistle that song."

A lone figure walked onto the boiler deck from the charred timbers of the rear gundeck and the paddlewheel housing. "Hello, August. I thought you might recognize that song."

Micholson's breath caught in his throat at the sight of Paul Legarde. His old friend looked and dressed just as he had the morning of the *Virginia*'s attack. "I've seen many illusions these past several days," Micholson said. "Malevolent shadow shows made from fire and ash. Prove to me you aren't one of them."

"But of course," the figure said. He picked up a stray twenty-four pounder cannon ball and tossed it toward Micholson's feet. The ball rolled across the deck, coming to a stop between the commander's boots. "Lean down. Touch it. It's solid, and quite heavy. Could an illusion pick up that cannon ball? Could a phantasm made of fire and ash roll it across the floor?"

The mannerisms, the slightly superior, mocking tone of voice—they were strikingly identical to those of the living Paul Legarde. "Why are you here?"

"To beg an indulgence of you, old friend. Not merely for myself; I actually represent the wishes of many, many men. Cyril Oates; James Rutherford; Jack Bainbridge; Johnny McComb; more men than I can name from the *Northport*. You won't let us go, August. You won't let us fully depart this world for the next—your memories are so potent, they trap us in a cruel limbo between earth and heaven. We request only that you allow us to pass on to our final reward."

Every word tore into Micholson's soul like bits of bursting shrapnel. "And what...must I do to allow this?"

"As you led us in life, so must you lead us beyond life. We cannot cross the wastes of limbo and pass through that glowing portal unless you precede us. You must sunder your ties to this earthly existence, willingly surrender your flesh, and ascend to the world which awaits."

Micholson almost laughed at the absurd finality of the figure's instruction. "You would have me kill myself?"

"It is the only way, August. We laid our lives down for you. Now we ask merely even payment." He held out a pistol. The weapon, a Colt Navy revolver, gleamed in the soft light of the dying afternoon. "Take this. It will make the work quick and easy, far easier than the final earthly fates we were burdened with."

Micholson accepted the revolver. Its metal blazed hot enough to nearly scorch his fingers. Now he did laugh, aiming the laughter at the broken rafters. "You play your hand too unguardedly, sorcerer! I know too much for such tricks and lies to shove me into death's embrace! I'm quite familiar with your creatures' voracious appetite for suicide. I saw it play out on the decks of the *Germania*. I won't join those poor women in their rush to self-destruction."

"Are you so certain of that?" the figure asked darkly. "There are reasons aplenty for you to end your wretched existence, aside from mere guilt." Tiny tongues of flame erupted through what appeared to be the pores of Paul Legarde's skin. "We are brothers beneath the skin, do you realize that? Oh, I know it's something we told each other many times when we were boys; sentimental nonsense, it was then. But now, it's far truer. Do you sense the ravenous heat within your guts, August?"

Micholson gasped as his stomach seemed to consume itself.

"Do you recall the 'madman' you plucked from the river, Joseph Babbage?" the figure continued. "Do you remember the gallons upon gallons of water he frantically gulped down, seeking to forestall the terrible birth of something that dwelled inside him? He carried a seed in his belly. The seed of a foetal *Mikithi*. The same type of seed which my master forced you to swallow yesterday. Do you like the notion of serving as a human incubator for a *Mikithi*, August? You may flee from me. You may flee this vessel, flee this drowned plantation, return to your home. But you cannot escape what is inside you. Eventually, it will claw and burn its way out. And in your last terrible seconds, you will curse yourself for not ending your existence when you were first given the chance."

"I'll be the judge of what I can escape and what I can withstand. Babbage still lived when last I saw him; he may remain alive yet." Micholson leveled the revolver at the figure's flickering chest. "You seem to be much more solid than your brethren, monster. Which would make you more vulnerable to a bullet. Why should I use this weapon on myself, when I can more efficaciously use it on you?"

The creature rubbed its flaming beard and smiled. "That would be a tragic error, 'old friend.' Before you impetuously pull that trigger, let me show you something."

The figure lifted his hands to his face and rubbed away the visage of Paul Legarde. The face beneath the vanished mask was darker, older, suffused with the strain of having its muscles worked against their will. It was the face of Nehemiah.

"You see," Nehemiah's lips said, unwillingly, in Paul Legarde's voice, "in order to converse with you physically and offer you the mercy of that pistol, I've required the use of a material form to undergird the face of Paul Legarde. My master graciously offered me this rather worn out body to use; he thought it would make for a lovely bit of irony. Nehemiah, isn't it, or N'Mehayah? The traitor to his own blood? He's still alive, you know. The bullets within that pistol are beneath my contempt. But they can most assuredly kill this elderly worm beneath my chosen face."

The sight of his oldest, dearest friend shook Micholson to his core, but he managed to keep his aim steady. "How do I know he remains alive? He could be a corpse already, dangling like a puppet from your strings. I'm willing to bet this revolver contains enough destructive force to make his body a much less usable puppet...unless you can prove to me he still lives. Allow him to speak. Free his mind, too—if you try to act as his ventriloquist, I will know it."

"You demand much, for a little fleshling with the seed of a *Mikithi* sprouting within your innards..."

Micholson rubbed the revolver's trigger with his forefinger. "You must need that body, creature, or you would not have possessed it. Do as I say, or I will destroy it."

"Very well...hear the voice of your friend and know despair."

Nehemiah's jaw jerked from side to side as he regained control of his facial muscles; then his mouth sagged open with exhaustion. "Aug...August...it steals substance and energy from your memories...pull your memories back and you will help free me—"

*—*Enough from you, you elderly bit of gristle!*— * The visage of Paul Legarde flowed upward from the creature's neck to smother and encase Nehemiah's face again. The figure cast its mockingly familiar gaze upon Micholson. "I trust you now believe your friend still lives?"

"I do. And I will find a way to break your hold on him, monster."

"Hah! Why should you bother? This base fleshling's thoughts are an open tome to me. He isn't worth your loyalty, August. He did not only betray his own family, you know. He betrayed your family, too, when you were just a lad. He let your brother Nicholas, your precious younger brother, die of fever when he could have saved his life. But why hear it from me when N'Mehayah can tell the tale of his cowardice far more effectively himself?"

Nehemiah's face surfaced like a battered reef emerging from a receding sea. "That guilt, that shame...I have lived years with both, and I will not deny either, my son..."

"This—this is true, then?"

"I failed Nicholas...I failed to act. I had the learning, the knowledge to possibly save him, but I feared to use it."

"Why, man? *Why?* You loved Nicholas every bit as much as I did."

"I was afraid...terrified that, should I ever use the knowledge of the spirits I had retained, I would be damned. I feared plummeting down the same dark, evil path as my brother had before me. I had seen how he had been tempted, and how he had succumbed, how his pride had swollen into arrogance and ultimately into a lust for vengeance upon all who lived. By the time I steeled myself to use my knowledge, it was too late...Nicholas had slipped through my fingers, leaving me only you."

Micholson was seven years old again, feeling half of himself being hacked away as his brother descended farther and farther into the angry embrace of his fever. He was nine years old again, raging against an intolerable void. He was a young man of twenty-one, graduating from officers school and knowing his pride was doused by loneliness and loss, wondering for the thousandth time how his life would have differed had Nicholas survived to remain his constant companion.

Tears dribbled down his cheeks, only to be swiftly evaporated by the heat the creature exuded as it approached. "You vile creature," he said, unsteadily backing away, "you want to drown me in my own bitter memories...you want me to hate Nehemiah as I have so often hated myself. But I can't hate you, Nehemiah; I can't hate one who has been a second father to me..."

Nehemiah's eyes flashed with renewed strength. He held off the *Mikithi*'s struggle to submerge him. "I will not lose you, August, as I lost your brother! You must pull back what is yours—I will show you how—"

—You will show him NOTHING, gristle!—

Nehemiah disappeared, but the *Mikithi* did not act quickly enough. The elderly man had mentally tugged an invasive presence within Micholson's mind, alerting him to its presence. Micholson sensed the other, its aura like the stench of burning dung. It had reached into the chaos of his soul and gathered loose and swirling strands of his remembered life into a braided rope. It pulled this rope from him, tugging the essence of his memories and fears through a scorched tunnel.

Micholson pulled back. He felt maddeningly weak at first, but the barely detectable voice of Nehemiah cheered him on, and Micholson gathered strength from the faces of his shipmates, Valery and Broadhurst and Wilson, as he imagined them reaching safety behind the iron walls of Commodore Foote's gunboats. He tugged with renewed vigor, and he felt the creature respond with the fury of a cornered animal.

"What are you doing, insect?" it howled. "Are you so certain you wish to regain the puerile thoughts I have stolen from you? She was a good tussle under the sheets, you know...Elizabeth, your sweet, faithless wife..."

Micholson's mind flooded with the sickening images he had suppressed for months—his wife's pale white arms clasped around Paul's neck, his friend's lips and tongue playing upon her skin, nibbling her shoulders, her breasts, his engorged maleness sliding slowly inside her...

Repulsed, Micholson almost let go of the searing rope within his mind. But before it slipped from his mental fingers, he lunged for the image of his shame and fury, the source of so much heartbreak, and clung to it. *It is mine—I will not surrender it—I drink my own poison, creature, and swallow it whole!*

The rope he wrapped around his forearms grew hotter and hotter, until he feared his skin would combust. He clenched his eyes shut in an effort to block out the pain...

When he opened them, he was on the deck of the *Northport*, in Hampton Roads. Black smoke drifted above the Elizabeth River—the enemy's river, which led to Norfolk, where the *Virginia* was being built.

He removed his spy glass from its case. His fingers shook as he adjusted the focus. A barn roof floated down the river, smoke belching from its fat smokestack. "She's coming out!" he cried, his voice strangled with emotion. "At last, she's coming out to fight!" Thirty feet above his head, high upon a signaling mast, an excited young seaman struck the alarm bell with all his strength. Men raced to their stations; every sailor in the squadron had waited months for this moment.

"Captain Micholson, what is our battle plan?" Lieutenant Paul Legarde did not often address Micholson in such formal terms, particularly when they stood alone, as they did now. But their relationship had changed, irrevocably, and they both knew it.

"Our forward pivot gun is one of the most powerful in the fleet. I plan to steam straight for that sluggish monstrosity and give her a good taste of it."

"Don't you think that, as the squadron's senior officer, Captain Marston of the *Roanoke* would want us to follow him and support his ship's attack? We have no idea how powerful that rebel is. A lone attack would be foolhardy—"

"Lieutenant Legarde, we are here to deny the use of this bay to the rebels. The enemy steams forth to challenge our blockade. I command the fastest ship in the squadron, armed with one of its most powerful weapons. I would be derelict in my duty if I failed to bring my vessel to battle in the shortest time possible. Go below and tell the engineers to raise full steam."

The color drained from Legarde's face. "Aye, sir."

The smudge of smoke grew gradually closer, slow as the movement of the sun through the cloudless sky. The sails of the Federal squadron hung like wet rags on the arms of scarecrows. "The air is dead," Micholson told himself. "The *Congress*, *Cumberland*, and *St. Lawrence* are trapped at anchor. The *Minnesota* has run aground. Three quarters of our squadron is useless. It's up to the *Roanoke* and us."

He felt the mechanical vibrations beneath his feet grow more rapid and intense. The *Northport* picked up speed. Soon the *Virginia* was little more than half a mile distant, creeping towards the fleet like a tortoise with a burning log impaled in its leathery back.

"Captain, she's in range of our eleven incher," gunner's mate Keanston said. He stood, tense but proud, alongside the reassuring black bulk of the pivot gun, the firing lanyard waiting in his hand.

"Fire when you are ready, Mr. Keanston. Pray whatever carapace she's covered with is no match for that gun."

The quiet, windless morning was shattered by the vicious discharge. An enormous iron ball soared toward the *Virginia*. It struck the side of her greased casemate, squarely, then bounded into the air like a scalded goose, leaving only the echoing *clang* of its impact as proof it had struck home.

"That was our most powerful weapon," Paul Legarde said. "And we might as well have skipped a stone at her. I recommend we fall back on the massed guns of the squadron. Multiple broadsides concentrated on her might give that monster pause—"

"You aren't in command, are you, Lieutenant Legarde? Give her as many as it takes, Mr. Keanston. As many as it takes."

Events took on a helter-skelter pace. The pivot gun fired again and again, its only effect being to spew noxious fumes across the *Northport's* upper deck. As the two warships drew closer to each other, the cannons of the *Northport's* port broadside battery added their eruptions to the growing din. They were soon answered by five of the *Virginia's* guns. Explosive shells crashed into the *Northport's* high wooden sides, shattering walls of oak into deadly splinters. Growing fires ate the sloop-of-war's timbers.

Micholson felt the skin of his hands blister. *I'm not here, not on the deck of the* Northport—*the creature is assaulting me with my most dire memories, forcing me to relive my worst day...*

He heard himself give the desperate order that doomed his ship. "Ram her! Bring us about at full speed and ram her amidships!" The *Northport's* prow, traveling at eleven knots, crashed into the *Virginia's* midsection. He was thrown against the deck, his ears riven by the clamor of shattering wood. The Union ship's slim bowsprit cracked like a twig against the *Virginia's* armored side. His ship pitched forward like an ox stumbling off a cliff. He watched in horror as the *Northport*'s foremast cracked in two, its greater half plummeting onto the slanting decks of both warships, creating a web of tangled rigging and broken spars which bound the enemies together.

The *Northport* righted herself sluggishly, indicating that she was taking on water. The *Virginia* backed away, dragging the *Northport*'s broken masts with her. The sloop shook like a palsied old woman as a fresh salvo from the *Virginia*'s cannons tore into her already battered side.

Rivulets of blood ran down the slanting deck, pooling around the soles of his boots. Shaking with impotent rage, he fired his pistol at the *Virginia*'s impenetrable side. "Damn you!" he screamed at the black ironclad, his face twisted with hideous grief. "Damn you to hell, you monster! Where is your pity? Can't you see we're done for? You've killed everything I ever loved!"

He fired again and again. The black monster before him changed shape, turning from an ironclad ram into a man—the mirror image of August Micholson, but an August Micholson no colleague or friend would recognize. This was the Micholson he knew from his darkest nightmares, the Micholson who had killed hundreds of men with a fatal mistake, the Micholson who sacrificed his crew in a vain effort to regain his lost manhood. Its mouth twisted in a leer of self-aggrandizement; its hands twitched with a lust for glory and vengeance. Its heart was an abyss, void of compassion for its comrades' agony, seeking only to blot out the source of its hatred and shame.

Micholson was sickened by the image which confronted him at the far end of the burning rope. Every cell in his body shouted for him to let go, to finally be rid of this nightmare *doppelganger*. But he did not. Against every impulse, he pulled harder on the strands of his memories, yanking his mirror image closer.

I cannot run from you. I cannot loan you out to monsters, and thus hope to be rid of you.

I cannot diminish you by flailing my guilty soul with you.

I cannot destroy you. You are part of what I have been, of what I am.

He wrapped his arms around the burning mirror. His hair and clothing ignited. The nerves running within his arms and chest screamed as his skin blistered and blackened. Yet the agony of his flesh receded the more tightly he squeezed, as he accepted the fire at last, and welcomed the inferno.

I forgive you.

I forgive myself.

Micholson opened his eyes. He was back on the boiler deck of the *Eads*. The demon in front of him uttered a choked cry. It fell face forward onto the deck and twitched within the shadows of the boilers. Paul Legarde's visage and form melted away, until only fire in the rough shape of a man remained.

The flames blazing in the furnaces beneath the boilers died down. *I don't know whether it is vanquished, or merely stunned. Water—water is the only substance which can banish these creatures. The boilers—they haven't had time to build up too much steam pressure. The water will be near scalding, but not yet turned to steam—*

The creature lunged for his leg.

"Forgive me, Nehemiah," Micholson said. "This will hurt." He aimed the still warm pistol at the boilers and fired all six shots, holing them in six places. Streams of scalding water poured through the punctures, inundating the prone fire spirit.

It screamed.

Micholson waited until its flickering flames disappeared beneath clouds of steam and its unearthly screams turned human. Then he dragged Nehemiah's body from the scalding shower, ignoring the fresh agonies every droplet of water caused. He threw the old man over his shoulder and pulled both of them up broken steps to the shattered gundeck.

M'Lundowi blocked his path.

"I curse you, adopted son of excrement." The ancient sorcerer spat forth phrases in a harsh, guttural language Micholson had heard only once before, as a child, when he and Nehemiah had confronted Babbage and M'Lundowi in the woods outside Adderwood.

"August," Nehemiah gasped, "don't—don't let him finish that incantation—"

Micholson charged. Nehemiah's limp body crashed into M'Lundowi, shunting aside the menacing claw he had brandished. Micholson's momentum carried the three of them toward the place he had intended to go all along—the great hole in the *Eads*'s side where the *Vicksburg*'s point-blank cannon fire had torn away the iron and oak of her casemate wall. Clinging tightly to the two old men, he propelled the three of them off the crippled gunboat's deck, into the Yazoo's newest channel.

The black water exploded with steam. Tumbling through the depths, Micholson experienced again the mental rending of his limbs, the implosion of his heart, the burning away of his blood that heralded the death of a *Mikithi*. Repeated exposure to this ordeal had partially inured him to its worst effects. Yet, as he dragged his two companions to the surface with a series of forceful kicks, one central agony remained—the burning within his guts grew more intense with each passing second.

"Fool!" M'Lundowi sputtered as soon as his head broke the river's surface. "Your...pathetic effort...came too late. No-thing...nothing can now halt the flowering of the *Mikithi* within you, nor within my hated brother. Your only choices? Suffer immolation...or drown yourselves, knowing your self-destruction will serve only to drive the remaining fire spirits to new extremes of bloodlust!"

"Or I can drown *you*, monster!" Micholson grabbed the top of M'Lundowi's bald skull and forced his head back beneath the water.

"August, *no!*" Nehemiah cried. "You must not kill him!"

Micholson fought to keep M'Lundowi's bucking body below the surface. "Why not? Because he is your *brother?* I'll not let him curse this land with more vile, murderous demon-spawn, no matter what may happen to us!"

"Spare his life! Not because he is my brother, but because his spirit is too strong! Extinguish his body, and his spirit will arise elsewhere, in some other form, some place we would never find him, and his evil would begin anew!"

Micholson reluctantly allowed M'Lundowi to fill his lungs with air; the sorcerer's violent choking provided small satisfaction. "What would you have me do with him, then? Can he be tortured into reversing his spells, into banishing his fire creatures back to Africa?"

"No. His will is too strong. And he has doomed us with his incantation; both of us hold the seed of the *Mikithi* inside us, and we would lose our lives in fire long before we could begin to bend his will. Besides, any such effort would be futile, my son. The magicks he has unleashed are far, far too powerful to be reversed or even contained. They can only be rechanneled, repurposed so that their outcomes are less violent and murderous, although perhaps no less dire."

"Such a thing is possible? Do you have the knowledge, the skill?"

"I do. But I cannot accomplish such an awesome task alone. Both you and my brother must add your sacrifice. Because he is in your power, my brother's sacrifice can be made unwillingly. Yours, however, must be made willingly. It will entail horrors of the flesh and of the spirit. I will endure those horrors alongside you, my dear one; never again will you find yourself alone. Are you willing?"

Micholson grimly smiled. "What horrors of the flesh or the spirit have I *not* endured these past few months? Are you certain the fire giants' rampages will be stopped?"

"The *Mikithi* will be banished. The magicks that brought them here and that keep them here shall be rechanneled."

"Into a less deadly form?"

"Less deadly, yes. But we must hurry, or we shall be unable to do anything but burn."

He could tell Nehemiah left much unsaid. Yet the raging, intensifying heat within his guts seconded his oldest friend's call for haste. "What do I need to do?"

"Take us back to the furnaces aboard your vessel. There I shall instruct you."

Micholson heaved the choking, coughing M'Lundowi onto the *Eads*'s low deck, then assisted Nehemiah out of the river. Only now did he see what terrible damage the shower of scalding boiler water had done to his friend; he was amazed Nehemiah was able to speak at all, much less intelligibly.

"Do not be concerned for me, my son," Nehemiah said as Micholson helped him step inside the battered casemate. "My time is done. I shall not need this old body much longer, and in my remaining moments I will put it to excellent use. Your time, however, is just beginning...with the help of our gracious God and His ministering Powers, I shall ensure that this will be so."

They made their way toward the boiler deck. M'Lundowi, still retaining a portion of his purloined strength, struggled in Micholson's grip. "I cannot contend with both you and this thing you've inserted in my guts," Micholson said. "So eat iron, you bastard." He smashed M'Lundowi's face against the breach of a dismounted cannon. "This should make sure you can't utter any more spells." He aimed the sorcerer's mouth at the cannon's butt end and was satisfied to hear several teeth clatter to the deck.

Micholson dragged M'Lundowi down the broken steps. The three of them stood before the furnaces. "Open the one in the middle," Nehemiah said. Micholson found a pair of furnace mitts and pulled the iron doors open. The coals with-in smoldered.

Nehemiah began to chant. The language was the same M'Lundowi had cursed him with a few moments earlier, but Micholson found the words less sharp and guttural, more melodic. He waited for the burning which now consumed all of his lower body cavity to subside. Nothing changed.

"What is supposed to be happening?" he asked when Nehemiah fell silent.

"Nothing. Not yet. I have not yet called upon the power of the infant *Mikithi* inside me. You banished the other, the one who took on the face of Paul Legarde. But this less-than-a-child remains within me, and it will provide the spark for the fire we need."

"'Fire?' I thought we were done with fires...?"

"Fire comes in many forms. Please remember the story of Moses and the Burning Bush. God spoke to him through the fire. So fire can be revelation, and revelation is also fire, fire of the soul."

He kissed Micholson lightly on the forehead. "I make one last demand upon you, dear one, before we part. Redeem my brother. He is not irretrievably lost to corruption and evil. Within him dwells the neglected seed of a once-good man, a man of great knowledge and valor. Redeem him, August. I could not. You are the only one who can."

"But *how*...?"

"All will become clear to you very shortly." Wincing with pain from every inch of his ravaged body, Nehemiah crawled onto the still hot coals. "Once the fire is renewed, you must grasp M'Lundowi's right arm with your own right arm and plunge both into the flames, which will flare for only a few seconds. You will become a cage for him, the only cage in the known world which can contain him. Yet you will not be merely his prison. I offer you the gift of a new brother; a brother to replace the one my fears helped take from you. Do you trust me?"

"I...I trust you, yes."

"All is well, then. May you come to love M'Lundowi as I love him, and as I have always loved you."

Nehemiah smiled and closed his eyes. He chanted again in the language of lost Lundowa, and a great tremor shook his body. His voice cracked as his throat dried out and withered, but he managed to complete his incantation. His nostrils flared; he gasped, opening his mouth wide, and what dribbled out was not saliva, but liquid fire.

Smoke curled from his pores. His skin erupted. The coals surrounding him glowed bright red, then began blazing. The sudden inferno incinerated Nehemiah's form.

Whatever sufferings lie ahead, let none befall my crew, and may they remain safe...

Micholson grabbed M'Lundowi's right arm and thrust it and his own fist and forearm into the fire.

CHAPTER TWENTY

Dark Reunion

*Stephen Decatur Naval Hospital, Cairo, Illinois,
June 4, 1862*

Joseph Babbage could not recall ever having enjoyed a meal more. Sitting up in his convalescent bed, he chewed vigorously on a hunk of hard bread, then wolfed down the hospital's thin stew. Just six weeks ago, he would have hurled such culinary abominations across the room. Yet now, after such a prolonged absence from solid food, this humble meal tasted more delicious than any banquet he had ever been served at Adderwood.

He was amazed at how his luck had turned for the better. When the *Molly Downings* had run past the strangely silent guns at Fort Pillow and arrived here in Cairo, he had expected to be tried as a war criminal—assuming the thing in his guts would give him time to face the tribunal. Yet the widespread "hysteria" into which Daniel's magicks had seemingly metastasized had thus far provided Babbage with ample co-ver. This hospital, and Cairo as a whole, had been inundated with sufferers of a psychic contagion which spread, beginning five weeks ago, from some origin point within the heart of Mississippi throughout the South and the border States. Many of the incapacitated men had come from General Butler's army, whose soldiers had just begun the occupation of New Orleans when the bizarre phenomenon struck Louisiana. The flood of physically and mentally wounded produced chaos and confusion; doctors here had assumed Babbage was among the *Eads*'s injured sailors, a misunderstanding he had made no effort to correct. Most fortunate of all, his primary accuser, the one man who could credibly make a case against him, was missing in action, presumed dead.

Due to the overcrowding, Babbage, apparently suffering either from some subtropical malady or a form of the "hysteria," had been placed in a bed cobbled together in the building's basement. He shared the space with a motley collection of cleaning supplies, broken furniture awaiting repair, and, at the far corner of the room, a coal furnace, which emitted a steady hissing.

These shabby surroundings failed to lower his spirits, however. Victoria would soon pay him one of her twice-daily visits, and her presence cleansed even a dung pit of its stench. He was due to be discharged any day now; the thing Daniel had inserted into his guts had either died or gone permanently quiescent. Victoria had not yet given him a firm indication of how she would respond to his hinted-at entreaties to marriage, but he felt fully confident of his abilities to make her recognize the advantages of such a liaison. The damned war seemed to be breathing its final gasps, according to the newspapers she had provided. It did not appear likely to end on terms advantageous to the South, nor for its plantation economy. But there was more than one way to skin a cat—he would hire a hundred Irishmen, if need be, to repair his levees, drain his land, and restore the fields of Adderwood to full productivity; the world still required cotton, and that demand would provide him with all the credit he'd need. No reason existed why he should not soon return to his pre-war status as a wealthy and distinguished gentleman.

Footsteps sounded on the stairs. He hurriedly wiped his mouth and picked stray shreds of beef from between his front teeth, then straightened his sheets and blanket as best he could. The door opened. The visitor wasn't his nurse, as he'd expected. Rather, it was that hulking gunnery captain from the *Eads*—Broadhurst.

"To what do I owe the 'pleasure' of this surprise visit?" Babbage asked.

"It's no pleasure for me, either, you scoundrel," Broadhurst said, towering over Babbage's bed. "I came here to visit my wounded men, including many who will bear the scars of your creatures' touch for the rest of their lives. The doctors, assuming you were one of mine, told me you are to be discharged soon."

"They spoke truly. As soon as it is practicable, I shall bid these Northern climes *adieu* and return home. My health has greatly improved. I anticipate my financial situation shall follow the same trajectory, quite soon."

"And so that's it for you, you figure? You cause the deaths of thousands and the suffering and disfigurement of hundreds more, and you think you can just waltz out of here as though you had clean hands?"

"I honestly don't see why not." Babbage smiled. Under these circumstances, toying with this brute seemed good sport. "Before we disembarked in Cairo, you admitted yourself how difficult it would be to make a case against me based purely on hearsay evidence. After all, the man to whom I supposedly gave my 'confession' of sorcery and witchcraft and whatnot is no longer among your number, is he?"

Broadhurst's face darkened. "Aye, he is not. And it is a mark against Divine Justice that such a man as August Micholson is likely crushed beneath the timbers of his sunken gunboat, while a specimen like yourself lies comfortable in bed."

"I happen not to be a believer in Justice myself, either of the divine or the manmade sort. I think it an overrated commodity."

"It is important to me. And to my men, both living and dead." Broadhurst brought his face close to Babbage's; the latter could smell liquor on the gunnery captain's breath. "So let me tell you something, Mister 'Master of

Adderwood.' If legal or military justice will not lay a hand on you, there are other forms of justice that shall."

"Am I to consider that a threat, you oaf?" He was in no immediate danger; the shower room was right next door, and orderlies there would sound an alarm and intervene if he cried out. "Know you this—my home will be guarded like a fortress. Should my guards see you or any other crew members from that misbegotten gunboat lurking about, you shall have more holes in you than were drilled through the *Eads*'s hull, and the dogs will feast on what remains."

Broadhurst's fists tightened, but he shoved them into the pockets of his greatcoat. "You make your plans, then, scoundrel, and I'll make mine." He turned to leave. "Oh. One more thing. I saw your cousin earlier today. Stoddard."

"You saw Louis? Where?"

"In a column of prisoners from the mass capitulation at Vicksburg, being marched to one of those temporary camps the Army built north of here. He recognized me first, called out to me as I stood on the side of the road. I walked with him a good long while. He told me his ironclad had gone aground on the sandbar separating the mouth of the Yazoo from the Mississippi. In the midst of trying to free her, he and his men were laid low by the hysteria, what he called the 'mind invasion.' The poor devil claims he now shares his skull with the personalities of two of his slaves. Since those days on the sandbar, he's been unable to sleep for more than twenty minutes at a time because of the nightmares that pair inflict upon him. Twenty-seven of his men killed themselves those first three days. Another quarter of his crew fell into strange trances, becoming unable to do so much as feed themselves. Stoddard led the remainder into Vicksburg, but they found no aid there. The hysteria had preceded them. The city was an anarchy, even its military garrisons. No semblance of order was restored until Admiral Farragut's fleet arrived, fresh from the surrender of New Orleans.

"Stoddard seemed eager to tell me these things, even though they were a long litany of disaster for him. He wanted to unburden himself. He no longer believes in the cause he fought for. He feels himself punished; punished and chastened, and hanging onto his sanity by the rope's frayed end. I pitied him. Although he and I were fierce opponents on the battlefield, and he laid many of my men low, still I wished him God's speed. The man has a soul. Unlike his malformed cousin."

"Did you think to dishearten me with that report?" Babbage shouted at Broadhurst's departing back. "Did you think telling me my cousin has two niggers rattling around in his head would break me, or disturb me in the least? You *idiot!* I *hate* Louis Stoddard! I hate every preening, medal-worshipping poltroon on this planet! All you've done is to increase my happiness a hundredfold! It doesn't perturb me to know Vicksburg has capitulated—the whole Confederacy can fold like a damp paper sack for all I care! The only cause I stand for is my own!"

"May you choke on that cause, then," Broadhurst said, climbing the steps to the main level without looking back. "Oh, pardon me, miss. I was just visiting with one of 'my men.' Good evening."

A young woman, dressed in muslin with a white apron, descended the stairs carrying a bundle of fresh linens. Her pretty, somewhat plump features were shadowed with weariness and worry. "Mr. Babbage, who was that man? His tone of voice...if he hadn't described himself as one of your comrades, I would fear he wished to do you harm."

"Miss Victoria!" Babbage cried, breaking into the most charming smile he could muster. "My angel! I've looked forward to your visit all day. How I missed you this morning! Please disregard that disreputable person. He is beneath my concern. And haven't I begged you to call me 'Joseph'? There is no need for formality between us."

She began to undo Babbage's old linens from the corners of his bed. "I'm sorry, Mr. Babb—uh, Joseph. It's just that, if any of the doctors were to hear me call you by your Christian name—"

Babbage grasped her left hand with his own. "Really, Victoria," he said, clumsily gesturing at the otherwise deserted room with his withered right arm. "Who but us is here to listen?"

Flustered, Victoria pulled her hand from Babbage's gentle grip. Perhaps hoping to cover her spreading blush, she pointed to the meal table. "I see you've eaten all your food! That's very good! And your water jug—it's still half full."

"Yes. My delusions have subsided, thanks mainly to your care."

Her lower lip quivered into a frown. "I...I wish..."

"You wish what, my dear? Simply tell me, and if it is within my power, I will make it so."

"I wish my sister Anne could say the same. That her delusions have subsided. That she's been granted peace."

"Your sister—am I to understand that she is among the victims of the mass hysteria?"

Victoria nodded, and her eyes filled with tears. "She and I grew up here in Cairo, but when she married, she followed her husband Oliver to his farm in Arkansas. He—he was killed at Fort Henry. She kept the farm going with their slaves and some hired hands. I hadn't received a letter or any communication from her in nearly three months, when just last night she appeared at my doorstep, babbling like—like some madwoman."

"There, there..."

"She begged me to help her—"

"She wants you to drive the voices from her head? What does she mistake you for—one of the papists' exorcists?"

"No, no, that isn't what she asked for, not at all. She says she has a husband out there somewhere. Not Oliver. A...a Negro husband. That's what the voice in her head tells her. She says she needs to find him, and she wants me to help her. He...this is confusing—he resides in two parts, you see. His spirit, or his soul, resides in the head of some white man, most probably his owner or one of the overseers on the plantation where he served prior to—to the transmigration, as Anne calls it. The Negress who lives in Anne's head—Missy—she and her husband were split up three years before the war, when she was bought by Oliver, Anne's husband, to serve as Anne's helpmate. The husband's body—Missy's husband, I mean—didn't I tell you this was confusing?—it's most likely still on the plantation, but in a state of grace, like Missy's body."

"A 'state of grace'—?"

"Alive, healthy, but with a mind like a newborn child's. No memories, no ability to talk or reason or do much more than feed itself in the most basic way. Anne has had to care for Missy's body like a nurse cares for an invalid. I saw this myself last night—she brought Missy's body with her. She couldn't leave it back in Arkansas, not with it being so helpless; nor would the voice in her head allow it. I'm the only family she has. Anne is terrified that the war has made it impossible to find Missy's husband. All Missy can tell her is that the plantation where she lived when she and her husband were separated, Cedar Grove, was in Mississippi, not far from Vicksburg—"

"Cedar Grove? I *know* the place! Yes! It's not more than fifty miles from my own home of Adderwood!"

"Then—then you might know people...people who might be able to help?"

"Do I know people? Hah! I daresay I know the faces and names of everyone who lives within a hundred mile radius of Adderwood, and half the population of Vicksburg, besides!" He grasped her hand, causing her to lay the pile of linens on his lap. "Miss Victoria, if I may be so bold...I would like to offer you and your sister my aid. I shall soon be discharged. At that time, I would consider it an honor to make my initial and primary piece of business assisting you in gathering together your—*ahem*—'extended family.'"

Victoria's eyes grew wide with wonder. "You—you would do that, for me?"

"But of *course*, my dear! Have you not nursed me back to health, both in body and spirit? Have you not given meaning and joy to my shadowed days with the pure light of your presence? Such a small boon as you ask, why, it is the *least* of the ways in which I could repay you!"

"Oh, Mr. Babbage!" She knelt down and kissed him on the cheek. "This—this is a miracle, surely! I—I can hardly wait to tell Anne our amazing good fortune! We will have to start making preparations immediately. I'll apply for a leave of absence from my position, then find a boarder to take up my apartment. I'll need to pull my savings out of the bank—"

Babbage waved this last comment off. "Never mind that. I will fully cover the costs of your and your sister's journeys, as I intend to accompany you until your quest is successfully completed." Various setbacks had left him somewhat short of ready cash, but the countryside of western Mississippi was densely seeded with individuals who owed him money. At least a few of his debtors had made out quite handsomely from running cotton through the blockade.

She flung her arms around his neck. "You are God's own angel, sent to serve as my savior!" Her display of gratitude sent the linens tumbling to the floor. "Oh! The beddings! I'd completely forgotten! How clumsy of me...here, let me do what I originally came to do—"

"Oh, pish-posh on that! I'm certainly capable of making up my own bed, thanks to your healing touch. Your shift is nearly over, is it not? Do not let me delay you—hasten yourself to your sister, and tell her the good news. We will speak again on the morrow."

"Thank you, Mr. Babbage! Thank you so much!"

She virtually flew up the stairs, her feet hardly touching the wooden steps. Babbage nearly floated out of bed himself as he stripped the old linens from the mattress. What an evening! What a triumph! Victoria was the only woman since his own dear mother to have ever looked upon his withered arm with anything less than revulsion. What a pearl beyond price to discover in a place such as this!

She could hardly refuse his proposal now. They would be married. He would invite the entire town of Vicksburg and all survivors from Satartia and Yazoo City to the reception, so they could see with their own hateful eyes how wrong their foul predictions about him had been. He and Victoria would have children! Adderwood would have an heir!

He finished making his bed. Then he settled back into it, eager to enjoy dreams of the bliss to come.

* * *

*—He is asleep now.— *

"Do you know this for certain? I wouldn't want him to try to flee."

*—The spirit that resides within his stomach tells me so, from the midst of its dreaming rest. I am certain. Are YOU certain you wish to do that which you intend?— *

"It is...regrettable. But necessary. I cannot take the chance that someone else with your knowledge, or even Babbage himself, might learn how to awaken that *Mikithi* and set it loose."

*—I do not object to the elimination of Joseph Babbage. I DO object, however, to your throwing away such a mighty asset as the fire spirit. I—we could find such a tool useful, in months to come. Would it not be better to keep Babbage at our side as a lackey, maintaining the fire spirit in its slumber until such time as we—as you decide how best to make use of it?— *

"I have already made my decision. The spirit that sleeps within him is too willful, too dangerous. How can you not recognize the certainty with which I know this? I know it in my own flesh...the flesh, muscle, and bone of my right arm.

A thousand times a day, the flames whisper to me, entreat me, beg me to take off the glove, to expose them to the air they crave. Only the hide of your African boar, stitched into this long, brown glove, stifles their flickering. And I'll keep those flames stifled—until such times as they are of use to me."

*—What's you plan—will it require awakening him?— *

"It will. I cannot do to him what needs to be done while he lies in his bed. This building is filled with hundreds of wounded men, including many of my own. I would do nothing to endanger them."

*—Then you must grant me temporary control of your voice.— *

"Why?"

*—Do you want him to cry out as soon as he sees us? I know a chant that will reduce his voice to a gurgling whisper.— *

"Teach it to me."

*—There is not time. Your lips are still too clumsy and ill-learned to say the words properly. You must give me control of your voice, only for a moment.— *

"Very well. But make any attempt to betray me..."

*—How could such an effort be successful, even if I would wish to try? You are a cage of iron, oh most august of commanders. We are in accord. Events will proceed as you desire.— *

August Micholson descended the steps to the basement where Joseph Babbage slept. The room was almost entirely dark, illuminated through the narrow, high windows only by the weak light of a half-moon. For the first time Micholson could remember, Babbage looked like a man at peace. He experienced a twinge of remorse, but quickly submerged it. That man did not grant such peace to his neighbors in Satartia or Yazoo City; nor have the results of his machinations allowed tranquility for the tens of thousands who now find their minds invaded by other consciousnesses, or their accustomed bodies lost. Yet his mission tonight was not one of vengeance. It was to ensure that the men, women, and children he'd seen floating face down in the Yazoo had not died in vain.

How to surrender his vocal cords? It proved simpler than Micholson had expected—he simply pictured himself speaking in M'Lundowi's voice, allowed his jaw to go slack, and within seconds, the chant began. The voice which emerged from his lips was pitched low as a bullfrog's croak, half an octave lower than his normal speaking voice. He was amazed and bemused that his tongue could produce such sounds, and with such practiced fluidity.

Babbage stirred slightly, then coughed. Micholson waited until the chant was finished, then touched the sleeper's shoulder.

Babbage opened his eyes. "Wha...who's there?" His voice was a ragged whisper, barely audible above the sounds of the coal furnace and the ticking pipes of the shower room next door.

"Good evening, Master Joseph," Micholson's lips said.

Babbage shrieked, but the sound was like a kitten's mewling. He stared up at Micholson's shadowed face, his eyes widening with horror and disbelief. "Mi—*Micholson?* How—how did you find me? That voice—do you...do you have D-Daniel with you?"

"In a manner of speaking, yes...he does."

Babbage's breath caught in his throat. "Micholson's face...but Daniel's *voice!* How? Am I awake? Is this some nightmare?"

"You are awake. Do not call me by that slave name; it insults me greatly. As for how I found you, that is simple. Once the essence of a spirit I have conjured is inside you, I will always know where you go."

Babbage began to shake uncontrollably. "What—what do you want of me?"

"My...partner...he wishes you to surrender that which I once gifted you with. Unfortunately for you, that surrender shall entail what a poet of your race once termed 'a pound of flesh...'"

Enough! Micholson mentally thundered. *I will not allow you to make this any more brutal than it needs be. I reclaim my voice.*

—We shall see if you can still credibly claim your mantle of moral superiority once this night is over.— *

"Indeed, we shall see," Micholson said. "Get out of bed," he said to Babbage. "Make no attempt to cry out; no one will hear you but me."

"Is this—is this about the seed that Daniel—I mean, M'Lundowi—forced me to swallow?"

"Yes. The counter-spell Nehemiah cast with my assistance did not affect you. By the time we banished virtually all of the *Mikithi* from this continent, you were hundreds of miles away from Adderwood, aboard the *Molly Downings*, and shielded from the incantation's power by the waters of the Mississippi. The counter-spell's strength attenuated with distance. Thus, you and I came to be the only men in the Americas who still house the essence of the fire spirits. For the safety of my country, I must ensure that their corrupting, ruinous influence is blotted out, or held in check by the strength of my own right arm."

Babbage stared at the crude glove which covered Micholson's right hand and forearm. "Let me help you!" he gasped. "Whatever you want to do, I can help. I have money, influence. I know people. Important people, hundreds of them, in the U.S., the Confederacy, even in England! Think of what I have been able to accomplish! M'Lundowi would never have touched a single clod of dirt from Africa without my organizational skill!"

"There is only one way in which you can help me, now." Micholson pointed to the door next to the coal furnace. "Come. We must go to the shower room."

"The showers—?"

Micholson grasped Babbage's stunted arm with his gloved hand and directed him toward the door. "Yes. We will need copious water."

"Wa...water. Oh. I see. I see! What you intend—you'll extract the *Mikithi* from me, won't you? With a spell? And then you'll destroy it with water from the showers! Isn't that it? You'll free me from it—won't you?"

Micholson said nothing.

"Why won't you answer me?" He stared into Micholson's eyes, desperately searching for evidence of another. "Daniel! For the love of God! I was almost a son to you! Don't let him do anything horrible to me!"

The coal furnace hissed. Micholson continued his relentless advance toward the shower room. "In another place, perhaps," he said, "you would have been like a son to him. In another time, another world. That is the world I hope to help build. But in this place, in this time, I still must fight a war, against those who would sow chaos and division. It is a long war, and a hard one. M'Lundowi asks that I tell you...he is sorry things could not have been different between you."

—Why do you lie in my name?—

"I do what I think is best," Micholson said.

He pushed Babbage through the door which led into the back of the shower room. As soon as the door swung shut behind them, they were enveloped in complete darkness. Babbage tried to break away, to escape through the opposite door, which led to a workshop and storage rooms. He slipped on the damp, slick tiles. Micholson retrieved him with his left arm and held him fast. Babbage's terrified screams emerged sounding as muffled as though his face were wrapped in layers of bandages.

Micholson pulled the long glove from his right hand and forearm using his teeth. Suddenly, the shower room was no longer dark. Prickles of flame ignited all along the ravaged, scar-puckered skin of Micholson's right arm and hand, rapidly coalescing into fiery thorns. The tile walls reflected the dazzling lights, surrounding the two figures with a tableau of meteor showers and glowing stars.

Micholson cast Babbage to the floor beneath one of the shower heads. Then he pressed his blackened, blazing right hand against Babbage's stomach.

"Burn," he said.

The light in the shower room suddenly intensified a thousand fold.

Micholson averted his eyes. He pulled back on his long glove and counted to thirty. Then he turned on every shower in the room, until he stood surrounded by steam and darkness.

ABOUT THE AUTHOR

Andrew Fox was born in Miami Beach in 1964. He lived for many years in New Orleans before he and his family relocated to Northern Virginia. His other books include *Fat White Vampire Blues* (2003), *Bride of the Fat White Vampire* (2004), *The Good Humor Man, or, Calorie 3501* (2009), and two upcoming novels, *The Bad Luck Spirits' Social Aid and Pleasure Club* and *Fat White Vampire Otaku.* He has won the Lord Ruthven Award for Best Vampire Novel and the Moment Magazine Award for Best Short Fiction and has been nominated for the Prometheus Award. Visit his website at www.fantasticalandrewfox.com

Courtesy of your friends at

MonstraCity Press

here is an advance preview of

Book 2
of
"Midnight's Inferno:
the August Micholson Chronicles"

the opening scenes of

Hellfire and Damnation

*Watch for it in trade paperback
and all your favorite ebook formats come*

August, 2014!

CHAPTER ONE

Mistaken for a Traitor

Western Navy Headquarters, Cairo Naval Station
Cairo, Illinois, June 8, 1862

— When are you going to read the letter, Micholson? Are you afraid?—

The question—a bold taunt, dripping with undisguised disdain—echoed in U.S. Navy Lieutenant Commander August Micholson's skull as he stood on muddy Commercial Avenue. He had just exited the Cairo Post Office, where he had found the letter waiting for him in his rented box.

The taunting voice was not his own, although it originated inside his own head. It was the voice of his worst enemy. It was the voice of the person most intimate to him in all the world; closer to him than the sailors who had served under his command, than his deceased brother or parents, more intimate with him even than his wife, Elizabeth, had ever been. For it was the voice of M'Lundowi, the African man of the spirits whose soul dwelled within Micholson's mind—the ruthless, vengeful sorcerer for whom August Micholson had been forced to become a living cage.

The letter, postmarked Washington, DC, sat in his inner coat pocket, perched against his heart like an unknown fruit, succulent in appearance but potentially laced with deadly poison. Micholson had recognized the handwriting. The envelope had been addressed to him by his father-in-law, Edward Briarly. Briarly dwelled in Petersburg, Virginia, in rebel territory. Micholson was aware his father-in-law, an influential landowner, maintained a network of friends and acquaintances in Washington; undoubtedly, he had prevailed upon one of them to mail the letter, which would have risked confiscation had it been mailed to him, a Union naval officer, from Petersburg.

*—Are you going to read it, Micholson? Or are you too afraid of what it may reveal about your wife, your precious Elizabeth?— *

He's always tearing at me, Micholson thought, probing me for weakness, seeking some way to take over this body we share...*"That's not the case," Micholson murmured angrily under his breath. "The letter will wait until after my conference with Flag Officer Foote. It's vital that I inform Commodore Foote of the results of my mission, that the Confederate boat yard on the Yazoo and the five ironclads being built there were all destroyed. Reading the letter now would distract me."

*—If meeting with this leader of yours is a matter of such urgency, why have you waited five days since your arrival in Cairo?— *

"You know the answer to that without asking, you fiend," Micholson whispered, struggling to keep his voice low. He turned away from the street when a man passing by, having noticed his lips silently forming words, looked at him strangely. "We murdered Joseph Babbage at the naval hospital only four nights ago. I could not risk having my reappearance in Cairo after my presumed loss in action be associated with Babbage's death by burning."

*—So are you experiencing what you white men call "moral qualms" about the killing you performed?— *

"The killing we performed. No; I do not regret my— our—actions. We are in the midst of a war. War means killing. Babbage, by conspiring with you to unleash the fire spirits, the Mikithi, against the civilian populations of all the States, both loyal and rebellious, had made himself a war criminal of the most heinous sort. Of more crucial import, he carried within him, thanks to your machinations, the seed of an infant *Mikithi*—"

—As do you, Micholson. As do you.—

"True. Babbage and I had that much in common—we were both impregnated with the fetus of an African fire god, thanks to your wicked ministrations, and both intractably tied to you. But Babbage was a dangerously weak, unstable man. His *Mikithi* seed had gone dormant, due to the powerful spell cast by my now departed man servant and friend, Nehemiah—"

—My treacherous, traitorous younger brother, N'Mehayah, may his name and memory be forever cursed...—

"Do not cast aspersions. You, monster, are not worthy to kiss your brother's shoes. Nehemiah was one of the finest men I have ever known, of any race. He was a champion of all men, whether their ancestry be African, European, or savage Indian. Unlike you, a serpent, an enemy to all mankind—"

—Not all mankind, Micholson. Only to those men who waged war on my people, to those who placed chains on their wrists and cast them into ignominious bondage at the far side of the ocean sea, and to those who have grown rich and powerful from the fruits of their stolen labor. But we were speaking of Babbage. You were justifying yourself to me, explaining why burning him to a cinder was a virtuous act, in complete alignment with your oft-touted morality. Do continue.—

"Babbage was a weak man, incapable of mastering his whims and passions. Had that *Mikithi* seed ever fully awakened within him, it would have swiftly enslaved him to its own destructive lusts. All the good of Nehemiah's saving enchantment would have been undone. At least one fire spirit, virtually unstoppable, would have ravaged these bountiful lands, reducing men and all their works to ashes and smoke. I could not allow that to happen. Babbage had to die, so that the infant *Mikithi* within him could be destroyed while it still slept."

—And you, oh wise, virtuous and unyielding judge, you who also hold the seed of a Mikithi *within you, you are unlike the weak reed Babbage? You are strong enough to hold the god inside you at bay, for as long as you shall live?— *

"I am as strong as I need to be," Micholson said.

*—And what do you plan to tell Commodore Foote? Will you reveal to him everything? Even those matters which conflict with his Christian beliefs? Will you tell him that, far from there being only one God with one Son and a Holy Ghost, the earth teems with gods and spirits undreamt of by him?— *

"I will tell Andrew Foote what he needs to know as the commanding officer of the Western Flotilla of the United States Navy. I will tell him everything, to the limits of what is comprehendible to him. I will not bedevil him with accounts of matters he will not believe, and which will only cause him to doubt my sanity."

*—So you plan to dissemble, then, my virtuous Micholson? Ahh, what a pass we have come to, my good and upright officer. At best, you will withhold portions of the truth from your commander. At worst, you will bend his ear with lies. Have you not associated me with the Prince of Lies, oh virtuous one, many, many times? Have you not condemned me for my willingness to manipulate my fellow men, to invent tales, to deceive? This shift is most interesting to me, dear one. I welcome your newfound maturity. Perhaps the notion of our working towards mutual ends is not so far-fetched, my brother of the skull...?— *

"I am nothing like you, M'Lundowi," Micholson scowled under his breath. "*Nothing.* And I never shall be. Now, we shall go see Flag Officer Foote, and I will resume my place among the captains of the Western Flotilla."

—And all will be as it once was, before you ever ventured upon the Yazoo River? Before you lost your

vessel, before my accursed brother merged the souls of the African captives with those of their white enslavers? Before you were ensnared into becoming my living prison?— *

"It will be as near to my former situation as I can make it, you devil. Now stop yammering inside my head, or you will endanger us both."

Micholson crossed Commercial Avenue, then Halliday Avenue, heading for the docks and wharves which lined the Ohio River. The Cairo Naval Station, which served as Western Navy headquarters, was a motley collection of wharf boats and barges, connected by a maze of wooden gangplanks and walkways suspended a few feet above the river. The Naval Station sat near the southeastern tip of Cairo, less than half a mile from where the Ohio River poured its waters into those of the Mississippi, one of America's great river junctions.

Before climbing the gangplank which ascended to the deck of the *Maria Denning*, the Cairo Naval Station's receiving boat, Micholson paused to view and admire the ironclad gunboats of the Western Flotilla. The looming "Pook's Turtles," as they were known (named for their designer), each nearly two hundred feet in length and sixty feet across the beam, their iron-plated casemates pierced for thirteen cannons, twin smoke stacks towering above their paddlewheel housings, sat anchored in the Ohio River, each one a black island, a floating fortress. The early summer heat manifested itself in shimmering waves of hot air which rose from the sun-broiled iron plates of the gunboats' casemates; Micholson knew the interiors of the ironclads must feel like cooking pots over an open flame. Their crews had erected awnings on their vessels' hurricane decks, atop the gunhouses, between the armored pilothouses near the bow and the tall stacks near the stern; every man who could find the slightest reason or excuse to avoid duties below decks sought relief from the heat below the awnings, praying for breezes off the river.

Micholson saw the *Cairo*, the *St. Louis*, the *Carondolet*, the *Essex*, the *Louisville*, and the *Pittsburg*; identifying the nearly identical vessels by the differing patterns of colored stripes painted on their stacks. The mighty *Benton*, the Western Flotilla's flagboat, needed no such visual aid to stand out from her squadron mates; having been converted from a gargantuan snag boat, she was a third bigger than any of them and carried a third more artillery. He wished he would see his former vessel, the *James B. Eads*, anchored peacefully among her fellow ironclads, stilled both by the drowsy summer heat and the cessation of offensive operations on the western rivers. But he knew her to be a partially burned wreck, her casemate holed like a sieve by the rifled cannons of the *Arkansas*; she was presently abandoned on the flooded grounds of Adderwood Plantation adjacent to the Yazoo River in central Mississippi, her battered prow lodged against the southernmost wall of the plantation's manor house, the very home inside which M'Lundowi had physically and mentally twisted the child Joseph Babbage to serve his foul plans of vengeance.

Micholson hoped his own appearance would strike Commodore Foote as more acceptable and in accordance with Navy regulations than that of his derelict, abandoned ironclad. Earlier that morning, he had retrieved a spare uniform he'd kept in a storage locker at the St. Charles Hotel. After so many weeks of wearing what had amounted to rags, it felt strange to be wearing an intact, fresh uniform, one not shredded and burned by a combination of battle against foes both earthly and unearthly, his forced merging with the infant *Mikithi*, and his rough three hundred mile trek up the east bank of the Mississippi River to Cairo. Running his fingers down his dark blue wool overcoat, double breasted with its two parallel columns of eight gold buttons, flexing his toes inside a pair of fresh boots, their leather still stiff with lack of wear, he could almost make himself believe that the bizarre events of the past two months had never happened. But when he glanced down at the doubled bars and twin gold stars sewn to his coat's cuffs, he experienced a sudden premonition that those insignia of his rank would soon be stripped from him.

That's just nerves, he told himself. How could Commodore Foote even consider demoting him? He had lost the *Eads,* that much was true. But hadn't Commodore Foote implied that he, his men, and his gunboat were all expendable, weighed against the danger of a fleet of Confederate ironclads laying waste to Northern cities arrayed upon the banks of the Mississippi and Ohio Rivers? Hadn't Micholson accomplished all that Foote had ordered, and far more? The Confederate fleet was a collection of shattered, blackened planks floating on the Yazoo River and rusting iron plates sitting on that river's bottom, thanks to a combination of his crew's martial valor and the feral, fiery destructiveness of the *Mikithi.*

Of even greater significance, due to the spell Nehemiah had cast with Micholson's assistance to banish the *Mikithi* back to their spirit realm, the entire Confederate war effort along the Mississippi River basin had collapsed. Rear Admiral Farragut might have succeeded in capturing New Orleans even without the supernatural intervention, Micholson thought; but Vicksburg, the Gibraltar of the Mississippi, might have withstood a siege lasting months, if not years. However, when he had passed through Vicksburg less than a month ago, it had been a shattered fortress— shattered, not by force of Union arms, but by what residents and Federal sailors alike referred to as the madness plague, the mass delusion (not a delusion, Micholson knew, but the hard, unbearable truth) that the souls of enslaved Negroes had been siphoned out of their mortal bodies and dropped into the skulls of the white citizens who had formerly considered them chattel.

Micholson ended his musings. He did not want to delay his reunion with his commander any longer. Yes, he might need to withhold parts of the truth from Commodore

Foote. But he would endeavor to keep such evasions to a minimum.

He ascended the gangplank to the main deck of the *Maria Denning* and strode through the doors which led to the receiving boat's anteroom. He saw a young face he immediately recognized: Cadet Sumner, sitting at the reception desk. Back in early April—what seemed an eternity ago—Sumner had been the youth who'd introduced Micholson to the Cairo Naval Station and had ushered him in to his first meeting with Flag Officer Foote. "Hello, Sumner!" Micholson said with enthusiasm, glad to see a familiar face. "Marvelous to see you again, lad! You're looking well!"

Sumner did not return his greeting. The boy's mouth fell agape. *Is it my appearance?* Micholson thought. Had his experiences of the past two months aged him even more than he'd believed? His mind flooded with memories of earlier such encounters, times when strangers had flinched at his off-putting combination of fire-red hair and pale skin pocked with childhood smallpox scars. Or had the boy been startled by something else? Had M'Lundowi twisted Micholson's countenance into a grotesque sneer without Micholson being aware of it, part of his unending campaign to bedevil his host?

Then a more relevant explanation for Sumner's discomfiture occurred to him. *Of course—there's no mystery to it. The boy thinks I'm dead. My men reported me as lost.* "I imagine that you did not expect to ever see me again," Micholson said. "My crew must have claimed upon their rescue that I'd been lost along with the *Eads*; that I had sacrificed myself to abet their escape. I did indeed expect to die that day. But kind Providence decreed that I should continue breathing. I have only just now arrived back in Cairo. My passage through rebel-held territory was greatly assisted by the chaos induced by the madness plague, of which you are undoubtedly aware. No one paid any mind to a lone straggler, not even one wearing the shreds of a Union officer's uniform. Please inform Flag Officer Foote of my arrival. I have much to report."

Cadet Sumner's stunned lips at last formed words. "Fla... Flag Officer Foote?"

"Yes, of course, Flag Officer Foote. He gave me my last set of orders directly, back in April. I'm sure he has heard much of our exploits and successes from my men since their return, but I need to debrief him myself, as well as declare that I am once more available for fresh assignment."

"But—but—but Flag Officer Foote—he's, uh..."

"He's *what*, Cadet?"

"He's..." Sumner's lips froze for a few seconds, and his eyes widened as he seemed to frantically consider his best course of action. "Suh-sir, I'm sorry, sir, but could you, uh, could you remain right there, just for a moment? I—I'll need to check with Commodore Davis, sir. I'll need to see if Commodore Davis can speak with you."

"Commodore *Davis*...? But what of Commodore Foote?"

But Cadet Sumner had already darted through the anteroom's rear doors to the offices beyond by the time Micholson had mouthed his question.

Two minutes later, a pair of naval police entered the anteroom through the door which Cadet Sumner had left by. Micholson noticed they had both unholstered their Colt revolvers.

*—This does not bode well, Micholson,— *M'Lundowi intoned inside his head.

"Be *quiet*," Micholson whispered fiercely.

"Come with us, please, sir," the senior of the two security officers said.

"Of course," Micholson replied, taking care to keep his voice even and agreeable. "Is there any problem?"

"Only if you wish to cause one," the man said. "We hope you do not."

They escorted him back to the stateroom where Micholson remembered having been interviewed by Flag

Officer Foote in early April, prior to his being given his secret assignment. Andrew Foote no longer occupied the stateroom; all of his belongings, such as the model of the old frigate *Constitution* which Micholson remembered, were gone. In Foote's former chair sat a senior officer whom Micholson had never before met.

Micholson saluted. Oddly, the senior officer did not answer his salute. He looked pained at the very sight of Micholson. He slowly rose from his seat. "I am Commodore Charles Henry Davis," he said slowly, not offering his hand in greeting.

"I was expecting to meet with Flag Officer Foote, sir," Micholson said. "Has the Flag Officer been reassigned?"

"Flag Officer Foote is dead," Davis stated, watching Micholson's face for his reaction.

"Dead—?" The word hit the bottom of Micholson's stomach like a stone being dropped into an empty well...

* * *

Be on the lookout for the next installment in the adventures of Lieutenant Commander August Micholson

Hellfire and Damnation

in

August of 2014!

www.ingramcontent.com/pod-product-compliance
Lightning Source LLC
Chambersburg PA
CBHW070835280626
47161CB00015B/664